The
EMPIRE
of
SHADOWS

Also by Richard E. Crabbe

Suspension

The
EMPIRE
of
SHADOWS

RICHARD E. CRABBE

THOMAS DUNNE BOOKS

St. Martin's Minotaur ⚏ New York

THOMAS DUNNE BOOKS.
An imprint of St. Martin's Press.

www.minotaurbooks.com

Title page photo by James Sinclair

Library of Congress Cataloging-in-Publication Data

Crabbe, Richard.
    The empire of shadows / Richard E. Crabbe.—1st ed.
       p. cm.
    ISBN 0-312-20614-3
    1. Adirondack Mountains (N.Y.)—Fiction.   2. Family recreation—Fiction.   3. Wilderness areas—Fiction.   4. Mountain resorts—Fiction.   5. Mohawk Indians—Fiction.   6. Serial murders—Fiction.   I. Title.

PS3553.R18E47 2003
813'.6—dc21   2003046937

First Edition: November 2003

10   9   8   7   6   5   4   3   2   1

For Wallace and Shirley Crabbe

For their love
of the written word

For their love
of the Adirondacks

This is the forest Primeval. The murmuring
    pines and the hemlocks,
Bearded with moss, and in garments green,
    indistinct in the twilight,
Stand like druids of eld.

The
EMPIRE
of
SHADOWS

One

For brick and mortar breed filth and crime,
And a pulse of evil that throbs and beats;
And men are withered before their prime,
By the curse paved in with lanes and streets.

—GEORGE WASHINGTON SEARS,
"OCTOBER" (FROM *FOREST RUNES*)

No man knows the season of his passing. His grandfather used to say that, one of the many things the old man was in the habit of repeating. Tupper figured it was pretty true for the bastard he was standing over. He hesitated, standing alone in the dark, mesmerized by the gaudy brilliance of the welling blood. It held him spellbound. A single shaft of light from a nearby street lamp seemed to jab an accusing finger at the still form with its apron of red. Blood still oozed from the hole in the man's chest, turning to black where it escaped the defining light. Tupper noticed how an occasional bubble would surface from the wound, the last breath escaping the deflated lungs in tiny blisters of crimson. He loved the color, revered it in his way. That the pale human body could contain something so jewel-like was always a wonder to him.

He mumbled the prayer he'd learned so long ago, an age it seemed. It was fitting even for an enemy that he say the words. He felt his grandfather's spirit beside him as he did so, and an approving echo seemed to whisper through the darkened construction site. He knew it was good, and he let the old man's spirit wash through him. But there was something else. Tupper tensed as a chill, humid breath of air stroked his neck. In a slow crouch, he scanned the dark around him. He thought he sensed a presence, something beyond the benign sense of his grandfather, long past. Though he saw and heard nothing, it was a reminder of his peril. It wouldn't do to be seen here. He'd stayed too long already, stunned as he'd been by the death at his feet. Death could do that, stun and disorient the living. It shocked the very roots of life's assumptions, the next breath taken for granted. It was like that when he killed. It always was. The world slowed for things like this. Time stretched. It was the *Hodianok'doo Hed'iohe*'s way of showing him the weight and importance of life. He said the prayer again.

"*Hodianok'doo Hed'iohe* must be thanked. The spirit of the dead as well, Jim, for the power it gives you."

Of course, his grandfather hadn't been referring to human prey. It was the spirits of the deer and bear, the fox and coyote he sought to appease. Still, Tupper liked to think the old prayers worked for him in their way, even for this—perhaps especially for this.

The body let out a low moan, startling him in the silence of the deserted construction site. He cast a wary eye at the maze of cast iron and brick. Great piles of wood, bags of concrete, and stacked iron girders were cast in confusing shadows and light by the brilliant new electric lamps out on the street. Nothing moved. He looked back down at the body. The eyelids flickered.

"Sonofabitch!" Tupper growled, staring curiously at the man. Jim bent low over the body, his hand dipping into the pool of blood as he steadied himself. His other hand went to the neck, feeling for a pulse. It was barely detectable, nothing more than a birdlike flutter in the veins. He pressed the chest, feeling for life. A small fountain of frothy blood was his only reward. There wasn't much reaction, just a momentary stiffening. Jim Tupper watched unblinking as the body relaxed. There was nothing in his eyes, no passion, no fear or exultation. If there was anything definable, it was satisfaction, hardened and glazed over like a frozen lake, black beneath the ice.

Tupper stood, putting a small roll of greenbacks in his pocket as he did. The man wouldn't need it, he reasoned and the cops would only pocket it once they found the body anyway. He grunted at the prostrate form at his feet.

"Bastard had it coming," he mumbled as if arguing with himself. The man had been his foreman and a nearly constant source of annoyance, riding him day after day like some bowlegged, beer-bellied jockey. The Mick had taken a dislike to him from the day he started working the job. He never understood why. Tupper knew it was because he was an Indian; but knowing and understanding were different things.

Tupper had made the mistake of staying after work, drinking with the man in hopes of finding some common ground. At first it had gone well, but the Mick quickly turned into an ugly drunk, angry at the world and especially him. Things had gotten out of control, and when the Mick tried to brain him with a huge wrench, Jim gave him a knife in the chest for his trouble. He hadn't wanted to do it but it couldn't be taken back. He hadn't hated the man, but he wasn't about to let him crack his skull with that wrench either.

Tupper guessed the man had taken his silence for timidity, but that wasn't it at all. He'd simply needed the work. Life in the city cost more than he'd ever imagined. It was hard to keep fed and sheltered, let alone put anything by against his dreams.

He hadn't come to the city to fail, and he was not about to let that bastard drive him off the job, as he'd done with others he didn't like. Tupper had always figured the winds would change and blow him a different fortune. It was only a matter of time and patience. It had become the foreman's season, so it seemed, though the man never saw the change in the weather.

Tupper turned to leave, slipping silent as a falling leaf past the hulking form of a steam derrick. Despite his care he nearly tripped over a small pile of steel braces hidden in its shadow. The site was dangerous in the dark. An unwary step could be painful at best, even fatal. Not much different than the Adirondacks at night. Jim was used to the dark. More than once he'd stalked the woods after wounded deer. He knew how to set a foot in rough terrain. Still, there was danger for any man foolish enough to ignore it. City or forest, it was much the same that way. Only the dangers differed.

A minute later he slipped through the gate in the surrounding board fence and into the glare of a streetlight. It glowed with an unnatural brilliance, casting the nearly deserted street in violent shades of black and white. Tupper hated the things, hated electricity. It was outside the natural order, a work of man, purely. They had a cold, hard light, so bright at their core that it hurt to look at them. Not at all like the gaslights they were replacing. He shielded his eyes as he would against the angry ball of the sun, not seeing the cop in the glare.

"Ho there, bucko!" a voice boomed from just feet away. "What the hell're *you* up to, eh?"

Brass buttons shone like stars in the incandescent glow. Tupper froze, a jacked deer caught in the hunter's light. Though he'd looked out on the street through the gap in the gate and listened for approaching footsteps, the cop had somehow appeared without him knowing it. He must have been just standing there, silently, out of his line of sight, perhaps leaning against the fence. He realized all in an instant that his hands were red, and blood was smeared in a crimson swath across his pants. The cop realized it too.

He must have, for he stopped asking questions and started swinging. Tupper ducked under the nightstick, feeling the blackened hickory rustle his hair as it passed. He could have fought, could have gutted the cop easily, but something about the light, the infernal unnatural light, and the way it gleamed from inside those buttons, made him turn and run.

Tupper could run. Since he was a boy he could run like a deer. He'd made a game of it when he was young, stalking and chasing deer through the heavy, dark forests of the Adirondacks, dashing after them as they bounded through thickets, over logs, up mountains, until he could hear their crashing no longer. He knew he was fast, faster than any electric-buttoned cop. He had full confidence in his abilities, so he ran with a smile on his lips.

By the time the cop got his gun out, Tupper was a shadow flitting between the street lamps.

"Jesus H. Christ!" the cop cursed in amazement. "Fastest sonofabitch I ever saw!" He trotted after, his heavy shoes clumping on the granite sidewalk. As he ran he pulled out the deadliest weapon in his arsenal.

Jim heard the cop's whistle behind. It carried with a shrill, warbling echo through the city's canyons. Tupper's heart sank at the sound. He'd used whistles for hounding deer or other critters. He'd called to the other men on a drive, keeping them on track in the dense woods, driving true toward the lakes, where the game could be cornered and slaughtered at will.

Tupper bounded ahead at the sound, knowing what it meant for him if he allowed himself to be driven. He thought of himself as a deer, herded by answering whistles and heading for the gaps in the hounding warbles. Nightsticks clacked on sidewalks. Leather-soled feet clumped on flagstones. Twice Tupper saw the looming shadows of cops cast by street lamps, but was able to round a corner or duck into a blackened doorway.

First from his right, then from somewhere to the north, then again from behind the whistles sounded. The occasional pedestrian gaped or stood back, afraid to interfere. He heard a man he'd passed shouting to the converging cops behind. "This way! West on Twenty-fifth."

He ran like the wind itself, trusting his speed and skill instinctively, no different from the deer in his way. This was one they'd never catch though. But, like a deer he ran from the whistles and the hounds in blue suits and glowing buttons. They were not hounds after all, he reasoned. They were big, slow city dogs, used to taking a horsecar to go around the corner.

He grinned with a wolfish determination as the whistles started to fade behind. He continued west, past the brothels and bars of Satan's Circus in the west Twenties, where pianos tinkled through the night and laughter was mixed with curses in equal measure. He'd put just a little more distance between them before he slowed, then he'd double back north, circling behind and out of the box they thought they had him in.

The el was up ahead on the next block, the tracks a looming horizontal scar. They were another thing to hate about this blighted city. The smoke of the engines, the noise and clatter and crowds and ugliness and perpetual gloom beneath the overhead tracks were evils out of all proportion to the good of getting someplace faster. He took them only when absolutely necessary. He'd take one now, he decided, if he saw one coming. But as he neared Seventh Avenue it was plain there'd be no train. The tracks were silent, not a surprise at 3 A.M.

Tupper rounded the corner of Twenty-eighth, figuring to head north under the deeper night of the el. He'd lose those fading whistles easily within a few blocks. He wasn't even winded yet, still springing ahead with each stride, widening the gap with confidence. He was passing a darkened doorway when something shot out in his path, too quick to avoid. Tupper's feet caught. He went down hard on the big stone pavers, his momentum throwing him forward, rolling him into the manure-clogged gutter.

"Gotcha!" he heard above him as he tried to understand what had happened. He looked up in time to see the club coming down. One of those goddamned electric street lights seemed to explode in his head, blotting out the world. He was blinded, dazzled, dizzy with its brilliance, then the light vanished, leaving only stars and welcoming darkness.

Ella Durant paced the soft wool carpet of her room in the Fifth Avenue Hotel. The whistling of the police had broken her fragile sleep. Even now she could hear, from somewhere off to the west, the blast of a single whistle. She gave no thought to their cause. There was too much on her mind to give anyone else's troubles even passing attention.

It annoyed her that she couldn't seem to get back to sleep, and that as soon as her eyes were pried open by the sounds down on the street her troubles came rushing back. So she paced, going over yet again the things she had set in motion. A soft breeze stirred the curtains of her open window. She stopped her pacing for a second to glance down at Madison Square Park. The leafy little oasis billowed beneath her.

"Damn my brother," she breathed in the darkness. "Let him keep his stupid trees." But what was hers was hers, or at least should have been, and she was not about to let William keep her from it, not if she had to cut all the trees in the Adirondacks.

She was done with writing letters, done with appealing to her brother, *her brother,* for what was rightfully hers. It was the lawyer's job now. The time for begging was done. Her mother had sided with

William, as Ella had expected. There was no money in siding with *her,* after all. It was William who controlled it all, since their father died. It was William who paid Mother's bills for her and kept her in luxurious ignorance of what he'd done. Millions. *Millions!*

She was sure her father's estate was worth at least two million. She knew her father had gotten well over $235,000 for the land around Prospect Park alone, and that was back in '69. And there had been many more holdings, the railroad, and all those acres in the Adirondacks, nearly six-hundred-thousand of them, and houses, steamboats, and a long list of other things. And what had William sent her? What had he thought his sister's share to be? Not even twenty-five thousand.

It was the yacht that had done it. Even now the great steam yacht was being built in a Philadelphia shipyard. When she'd heard that she'd been more furious than ever. The thing was supposed to cost two hundred thousand! The nerve! She should keep her mouth shut, take a beggarly one percent of the estate and go quietly away while William sails the world with Huntington, or Morgan, or the Prince of Wales. Well that was *not* going to happen, not if she had anything to say in the matter.

Van Duzer would see to it now. The old Dutchman with the shocking, white muttonchop sideburns had told her he'd set her brother on his ear in two shakes. She believed him. He was a crafty and well-connected old codger—if her friends were to be relied upon—and he traveled in rarified company. As a very old and respected name in New York life, and for the last thirty years at the New York Bar, he knew what strings to pull and pockets to line. The law, strictly speaking was only part of it.

"We can make life difficult for your brother, Miss Durant—if you like," he'd told her. "Very difficult indeed. I'll need my head though, a clear rein to see to the things that need seeing to. You are willing to trust me in these matters implicitly, correct?" he'd said to her in a tone that allowed for no disagreement.

"I'll need to perhaps employ some, shall we say—unorthodox methods, if we are to be successful. I want your full agreement on that," he'd insisted from under bushy eyebrows, his piercing eyes boring into her.

"I'll need to fight fire with fire to break him to your case, and once I set a course, I'll brook no second-guessing."

"Do what you have to, Mister Van Duzer," Ella had said. "My brother has earned it and more."

"Good. I'm glad to hear you say that, Miss Durant. Your brother is well defended, legally speaking, and can tie us up in court for years if he likes, while he hides assets like a squirrel hiding nuts. Even if we win that way, I'll guarantee it will be a hollow victory," Van Duzer said, his fingers steepled under his bright red nose.

Ella had sighed in his office that afternoon, sighed, then took a deep breath and said again, "Do what you must, Mister Van Duzer," her fists clenched at her sides. "My brother has forfeited the right to civil action, though we'll need that, too, I'm sure. But, by God, if the methods you employ are less than orthodox, well it's nothing more than what William has done to me."

"The wheels will be set in motion this very day, Miss Durant."

That's what Van Duzer had said as they parted. His fleshy, dark-spotted hand had held hers in a firm but very soft grip, a lawyer's grip, like blades of steel in a velvet pillow. A chill had run through her then, but she had choked it down and simply said, "Thank you, sir. I place my future in your hands."

But that wasn't all she'd placed in his hands, not by a long shot. And though she had walked from Van Duzer's office with a grim set to her mouth, she could only think, *"He's still my brother."*

So Ella Durant paced her hotel room floor while whistles sounded in the night, and heavy-shoed cops did whatever it was they were doing. It was nothing to her.

Two

And lungs are smothered and shoulders bowed,
In the poisonous reek of mill and mine,
And death stalks in on the struggling crowd,
But he shuns the shadow of fir and pine.

GEORGE WASHINGTON SEARS, "OCTOBER"

"Little Benny" Corrigan was a hard case. He'd been in the basement interrogation room of the Third Precinct station house for almost eighteen hours and he still didn't show much sign of cracking. He sat shackled to a chair in the center of the room. Both ankles were chained to the chair. The chair was bolted to the floor. Benny wasn't going anywhere.

"Who's to say there's no honor among thieves, eh, Benny? I admire you for that, I really do. That's one reason why we haven't been as hard on you as we might. But Benny, you gotta know my patience is running thin. You have to make up your mind that we're going to get what we want and you're the one's gonna give it to us."

Captain Braddock had been working long hours for weeks and, though he was happy to have the chance to break Corrigan and bag his accomplices, he needed to do it fast. He was leaving town this evening, going on vacation. He'd arranged for a two-week leave and wanted to wrap Corrigan in a neat little bow before he left. It would be good to leave with a victory to his credit, something left on the plus side of the ledger.

With the calls growing louder for yet another round of police investigations, it was just good policy to be seen the hero, especially when not around to defend yourself. Serious though those concerns were, Tom didn't dwell on them. The truth was that Braddock's head was already on vacation, already dreaming of fresh air, fishing, and long, lazy mornings abed with Mary. Tom heaved a sigh.

Benny looked up at the captain of the Third. "You take me for an addle-cove? Never been a snitch. Ain't about to start now," he mumbled. Braddock exchanged a glance with the two detectives behind Benny's chair. Benny claimed he'd been working alone when he'd been caught cracking a safe in the office of an import-export business on Pearl Street. Tom hadn't believed that, though Benny didn't let anything slip until now. It was the first crack in his story, and Braddock would stick a wedge in that crack and hammer away till Benny broke.

Tom Braddock could have cracked prisoners quicker if he did things like some of the other captains. There were those who were notorious for the number of prisoners injured "resisting arrest," beaten by other prisoners, or found hung in their cells. It wasn't that Braddock was a soft touch. In fact, he had one of the best records for cracking prisoners of anyone except Inspector Byrnes, the chief of the Detective Bureau.

Like Byrnes, Tom Braddock preferred the third degree. He and his team would sweat a man like Benny for days if necessary, depriving him of sleep or rest, or even food and water. Taking turns, they'd turn a prisoner's story inside out, picking at the smallest inconsistencies, till even a man with nothing to tell wished he had. Tom had learned the intricacies of the technique from Byrnes himself, who was the acknowledged master. Braddock wasn't far behind.

" 'Fat Charlie' Logan and Lonnie Burke, right? I know they were the ones, Benny. Lonnie on the lookout and Charlie with you to jackscrew the safe."

Benny squinted up with eyes so bloodshot they looked like red roadmaps. At around six-one and two twenty-five, Thomas Braddock could look quite menacing. But it wasn't Braddock's size, or even his formidable reputation as a fighter among the Rabbits, Divers, and Hackums in the precinct, it was his absolute refusal to give up. It was a trait even more widely respected than Braddock's physical power.

Still, "Little Benny" had a reputation to uphold. He knew that Braddock wouldn't do him any permanent damage. He wasn't too sure about the other two detectives, though, but for his own self-respect he figured he could push this a bit further. "Don't know no Logans nor Burkes. I work alone, see. Told ya. Been tellin' ya fer—"

A loud crash, like furniture breaking, somewhere above their heads cut Benny's words short. Heavy feet stamped and shouts could be heard echoing down the stairs, though they were on the other side of the building. For a moment the four of them were frozen, each looking at the ceiling as if it might fall on their heads.

Braddock turned back to Benny, seeming to put the ruckus out of his mind. He knew the safecracker was weakening. He didn't want to quit on him now, and he knew there were plenty of officers on duty and in reserve who could see to whatever was going on.

"Don't know 'Fat Charlie'? I got three fellas say you were drinking with him in . . ." Another crash interrupted Braddock, followed by a shot and more pounding and yelling.

"Watch him!" Braddock told his men. He turned and strode out of the room and down the hall, his shoes echoing. "Stay right there, Benny," he called back. "We're not done yet, you and I."

Braddock bounded up the stairs and along another short hallway. He burst into the main booking room as shouts of, "Let him go!," "Drop the nightstick," and "Shoot the bastard" tumbled over one another through the open door. To his left a long, heavy bench was overturned and splintered. To his right an officer lay face down in a widening pool of blood on the worn, white marble floor. Before him two more officers stood shouting, the fear in their voices so palpable it was like the nervous barking of dogs.

They were dangerous dogs despite their fear. Two pistols were pointed at the other men in the room. The pistols were shaking and waving in an impotent attempt at making the danger go away. The danger had a human form out of all proportion to most things human. The form had a name that Tom knew well.

Moishe "Tiny" Rothstein was an immense Polish Jew, maybe the biggest man in the city, if you didn't count Chang the giant Mongol in

Barnum's show. At nearly seven feet tall and somewhere around four hundred pounds, "Tiny" was a frightening presence. More frightening still was what Tiny was doing. With two massive, handcuffed hands he had a fourth officer hanging in front of him, a kicking, gurgling blue shield.

Like a marionette, he dangled and danced in front of the giant. The officer's face was nearly as blue as his uniform. A long black nightstick was tucked hard under his chin. Though he pulled with whitened fingers and kicked like a mule, nothing seemed to make an impact on Rothstein. The giant just gritted his teeth and frowned in concentration. Braddock could see in an instant that the man was about to lose consciousness.

"Tiny!" Braddock shouted in a voice that cut through the chaos and had the two officers gaping back over their shoulders at him. Tom walked past them with no more hesitation than if he were walking into a bar. "Put your guns away, gentlemen." He said without looking at the two officers. He held out a signaling hand, palm down. It made the waving pistols vanish, if somewhat uneasily.

"Braddock!" Tiny said in his odd, high-pitched voice. "Tom, the hawse they took, took hawse, my hawse, you know—black—hawse with whitish thing?" he said, so agitated he was swinging the officer around with each word.

"Tiny, be good enough to put my man down, would you?" Tom said in as reasonable and restrained a voice as he could manage. The officer went slack. Braddock continued in a reassuring tone, "Don't worry. Nobody's going to shoot you. I won't let them." The officer was let slip to the floor where he lay as motionless as a pile of laundry.

"Thank you, Tiny," Tom said, stepping close with an outstretched hand. "The nightstick?"

The stout, lacquered club looked like a toy in the two huge paws that handed it over.

"There's a good lad," Braddock said with a reassuring pat on his shoulder. "Now, don't be giving us any more trouble, eh?" he added, peering at the giant's darting eyes. "You'll have me to deal with if you do."

Tiny seemed to flinch at that, but rallied enough to protest. "But hawse? What they do wit her? My hawse. Tiny need it for wagon—you know wagon? And they was bad to Tiny, Tom. Bad. When they bad Tiny don't like it. Get mad. Tiny not bad to them. Told them I hurt them if they was bad to me, told them an' told them, Tom. Hurt them some more if they're bad again."

In Tiny's case this was no idle threat. People Tiny decided to hurt usually stayed hurt for a long time, sometimes forever. His career as an enforcer and bare-knuckle prize fighter was littered with those he had hurt. "Tiny" Rothstein, "The Giant Jew," was far too clumsy to be a professional boxer, but he was as close to unstoppable as any human could be, once the rules of the professional ring were put aside— except for Braddock.

Braddock and Tiny had had their own set-to many years before in a brawl in the Five Points. The thorough beating Tiny had taken had created an indelible respect for the man who'd bested him and shown him kindness afterwards.

"Now listen, Tiny. You have to let my guys take you in, alright?"

Tiny nodded, looking glum, but resigned to whatever Tom asked of him.

"I'll have a little talk with them. They won't hurt you and they won't be mean to you," Tom said with a warning glance over his shoulder at the two officers, who'd now been joined by a half-dozen others, drawn by the ruckus. "And I'll see what I can do about that horse of yours. You have my word on it," Braddock added.

The pile of laundry at their feet began to groan and move. Braddock was glad to see it. Tiny looked down at the officer with a curious cock of his head, as if he'd just seen him. Bending down, he grabbed the man by the back of the neck with one shackled hand and hauled him to his feet.

"OK, Tom," he said in an absent sort of way as he brushed dirt from the wobbling man. "Tiny not mad now. Not mad. No I'm not. You good friend, Tom. Take care of Tiny's hawse like you say. Trust you, Tiny does."

"Good. Now go with these men and I'll be down a little later to sort things out, right?" Tom said, guiding Tiny toward the officers with a hand on one shoulder.

"Now listen, boys. No rough stuff. Don't hurt Tiny, and he'll be good," Braddock with a sideways glance at the giant. As they took him, Tom said in a low voice to one of the officers, "Put a second set of cuffs on him, Jimmy. He can break out of just one, if he has a mind to." Turning to the other men who were bent over the downed officer, he ordered, "Get Farley to the hospital, boys. He isn't shot is he?" The one named Jimmy answered, "Nah. Just hit his head, Captain."

Braddock looked hard at Jimmy. "You fire that shot?"

The officer gulped once, then nodded and started to explain, but Braddock cut him short. "Hit anything?" he asked.

"No sir."

"I'm docking you two days, Jimmy," Braddock growled. The man started to protest, but Tom cut him short again. "Two things, Jimmy. First, never fire your *fucking* weapon in the station house! Second, if you fire your *fucking* weapon in the station house you *fucking* well better hit what you're aiming at!"

Braddock turned and started back toward the interrogation room. As he walked past the bright, red smear of blood on the white marble floor he mumbled, "That'll leave a stain."

Braddock stumped back down into the basement, checking his watch as he did. "Goddamnit!" he said under his breath. He'd hoped to break Corrigan long before this. The idea of going off on vacation and leaving the little safecracker for someone else grated on him. One thing Braddock hated worse than anything was a job left unfinished.

"So, Benny, where were we?" Tom said as he reentered the interrogation room.

"What was that upstairs?" The other detectives asked almost in unison.

"Nothing," Tom said, shrugging. "Tiny Rothstein don't like being arrested much, that's all."

"Rothstein! Don't I know it," one said.

Braddock turned to Corrigan, leaned over and put both hands on the arms of his chair, his face on a level with Benny's. "Benny, I'm getting tired of this shit. Now, you know and I know that you're gonna give us Fat Charlie and Lonnie. Why not do it and get it the fuck over with, make it easier on all of us?"

"Don't know no Fat Lonnie," Corrigan mumbled.

Braddock's knuckles went white.

"Don't know them, huh?" Tom said.

"Are ye deaf as well as stupid? No!" Little Benny knew right off he shouldn't have said it like that, but he was just as tired as Braddock, maybe more, and he wasn't thinking straight. He looked away, not wanting to meet Braddock's glare.

"Stupid is it?" With a groan and a loud crack, Benny's chair was wrenched from the floor, the bolts ripping away. Braddock let out a grunting shout, lifting Benny, chair and all, and throwing him against the brick wall of the basement.

Little Benny screamed like he'd been set on fire. The tough oak chair splintered under the impact. Benny went down in a heap, still handcuffed to the arms. The other detectives stood gaping, almost as surprised as Corrigan.

"*Stupid? Stupid,* Benny?" Tom bent and grabbed the leg of the chair. With a heave he broke the leg off. "I'm gonna break your god-damn kneecaps. How's that for stupid?" He raised the heavy oak leg high overhead.

"No! No! I'll tell you where Fat Charlie is, Lonnie, too!" Little Benny screamed. "They got the boodle, too, and from lots of other jobs. You'll get it all, I swear!" Benny's eyes were almost all white. His fingers scrabbled at the arms of the chair, straining at his cuffs.

"Start talkin', Benny," Tom said, whacking Corrigan's leg for emphasis, but not hard enough to do any permanent damage. "I got ten minutes."

Tom whistled as he left the stationhouse. Corrigan had given up his partners. Tom's men would round up Fat Charlie and Lonnie Burke in short order. Rothstein was safe in a cell, his horse eating police department oats. Tom's officers would live to fight another day, and the blood on the marble floor had been swabbed up before it soaked in. Tom strode away with a grin on his face. He didn't look back.

Jim Tupper was swimming. He was deep under water, and the light from the world above filtered down through the shifting currents in kaleidoscopic beams of light. He stroked for the surface, holding his breath till his lungs burned. His head broke through the liquid ceiling as if it was going through a wall of glass. Consciousness shattered.

The reek of horse shit was so strong it was like a slap in the face. That there should be shit in the lake was such a shock he couldn't convince himself of the truth of it. He shook his head and cleared his eyes. There seemed to be a huge pile of it, mountainous and steaming, just inches from his face. He moved and bits of gravel dug into his cheek, but when he tried to brush them away his arms wouldn't respond. They were locked behind his back and, despite his best effort, they wouldn't budge.

From somewhere behind him he heard a footstep. A large black shoe descended into the pile of manure before him.

"Looks like he's coming to, Blackjack," a voice said above him. Tupper's eyes followed the blue-clad leg up as far as his neck would bend. A nightstick twirled in a big, dark hand, and a bushy mustache under a massive nose came into view. The rest of the cop's face was a black mask under the shade of his cap. A street lamp behind outlined his immense form in stark contrasts of shadow and light.

"On your feet," said a voice from the blackened face. Jim Tupper remembered where he was.

Jim pulled his knees up and rolled over using his head as a pivot. It took three tries, but he finally managed it while the cops watched and laughed. "Tough with no hands, eh? Get used to it. You'll be spendin' plenty o' time in cuffs, Injun, for what you done," one of them said.

Tupper rose slowly to his knees. Blood trickled down his forehead and into his eyes in a stinging, blinding cascade. He shook his head, blinking out the blood, sending a spray left and right. It fell in red-black drops on the smooth cobbles.

"Shit!" the cop to his right shouted, stomping his feet in the manure-clogged gutter. "Blood on me spankin' new pants!" A tremendous blow caught Tupper in the right shoulder, sending him crashing to the street. With no hands free to break his fall, his head hit hard. He didn't get up.

Tupper woke some time later to the insistent pounding in his skull. BOOM, BOOM, BOOM, BOOM. It felt like a nightstick coming down over and over, and for an instant he imagined it was. But when he opened one eye, sticky with drying blood, what he saw was the rough wool of a blanket, and beyond that, bars. He let the image seep into his pounding head like a sponge under a dripping faucet.

Slowly it came back, the blood and the whistles and the cops and clubs. He was in a jail somewhere. How long he'd been there was harder to say. His head put that question off. There was nothing to be done about that. What needed his attention was what he was going to do. But even that had to take a back seat to the pounding, which seemed to drown out both sight and thought itself.

Tupper slipped away again to the sound of the drumming. He was in the council house, the central fire casting gigantic, distorted shadows of the dancers on the walls. They shuffled and stomped to the sound of the drums. The old songs were being sung and the prayers repeated. The code of the prophet, Handsome Lake, was being celebrated. It held the people to the old ways, when the Six Nations ruled for a month's travel in any direction. Smoke from the council fire wrapped the congregation in bonds of sacred smoke. The drumming was good.

It was morning when Tupper woke again, though in the damp basement cell there was no daylight. The smell of overcooked coffee gave him his only clue to time. There was no pounding this time, just a distant drum, as of a signal calling him to the council fire. It didn't hurt, not even when he sat up. A grim smile slithered across his lips. There was magic in his dreams. It had lifted the hammer from his temples and restored balance to the world. "You better be off that cot in ten seconds, Injun, or it's another whack you'll be getting," an approaching voice boomed. "Get up! We're goin' for a ride, ye bloody bastard."

Ten minutes later Tupper was in the back of a Black Maria. His only view of the world was through a small, barred window in the rear door. He saw enough, though, to know he was somewhere on the West Side, heading south. Over the next half hour or so the wagon stopped at two precinct houses. Each time more prisoners got on, some cuffed, some not. The back was nearly full after the second stop, and Tupper heard one of the cops say, "It's one more stop, then straight on to the Tombs, Harry."

Tupper had heard of that place. It was a place he didn't want to go. Once inside, he didn't give himself much of a chance of coming out again, ever. Murderers were treated harshly in the Tombs, very harshly indeed, from what little he'd heard.

Like an animal in a trap, he was willing to chew off his own leg for freedom. He figured he'd do it now, if that was the only way. But, as a hunter he knew that patience must always outweigh fury. Banging his head against the walls of the wagon would gain him nothing. Time enough for fury when he saw the opportunity, if it ever came.

The back of the wagon was tight and hot. The August sun slowly turned the cramped space into an oven. Tupper and the five other prisoners glistened with sweat, and small pools of it started to form on the floor around their feet as they leaked and dripped. The other prisoners were trying to keep their distance, though the cramped space didn't allow it. At least now, with his hands cuffed in front, he could run his fingers through his long black hair.

He was caked with dried blood. It was on his pants, hands, face, and hair. He was dirty and damp from his roll in the gutter and the smell of manure clung to him like a guilty conscience. He could only imagine what the others in this black box thought of him. They probably figured he was an escaped lunatic, gone on a spree of baby-killing. He smiled at the thought. The man across from him looked away.

That man, of all of them, didn't appear to belong there. His foppish scarlet necktie, only slightly askew, and his straw boater gave the thin, serious face an innocent look. Tupper rocked and bumped with the wagon, trying to figure what a neat, unassuming haberdasher—for that's the image that immediately came to mind—was doing in this rocking-oven-ride to the Tombs.

Jim guessed he had to be some sort of confidence man, forger, or an embezzler, maybe. Whatever he'd done, though, soon took a backseat to how he looked. He was sweating even more heavily than the rest. Little waterfalls were rushing out from under his straw hat, down his face, and into his paper collar. He was deathly pale, and getting paler with every rock and jolt of the wagon. He loosened the tie from around his green-tinted neck with a shaking hand. He shifted and craned toward the tiny rear window, sucking air like a landed fish.

"You gonna be all right there, Mister Boater?" one of the others asked.

"Mister Boater" said nothing, but nodded and gave them a pitiful smile. Then the wagon stopped.

One of the cops got down to go into a station house, leaving the other on guard. They hadn't sat there for more than a minute when it happened. "Mister Boater" had turned so pale and green he looked like death itself, and Tupper could see his Adam's apple bobbing like he was trying to swallow something whole.

Without warning the man erupted. There was no other word for it. Tupper had never seen the like of it in his life. "Mister Boater" convulsed, throwing his head back so hard his straw hat flew across the wagon, then he jackknifed forward, a monstrous stream of vomit spewing from his mouth with the force of a fire hose.

In an instant nearly everyone in the wagon was hosed down. Successive convulsions blasted the hot men with half-digested food in a soupy broth of steaming bile. The other men cursed and shouted at the top of their lungs. One of the others, who now wore a vomit shirt, doubled over and let loose on the shoes of the men to his left and right.

"What the bloody hell's goin' on back there?" the driver shouted. All he got back were shouts, cursing, and an insistent pounding on the front wall of the wagon. The cop must have smelled the cause of the ruckus then. "Goddamn you fuckin' drunks!" he shouted. "Make you bastards wish you never done that."

The back door was thrown open, blinding Tupper in the bright morning sun. "OUT!" the cop shouted with a menacing wave of his daystick. "Out, and be smart about it."

Tupper was on his feet and stepping over "Mister Boater's" feet before the words were out of the cop's mouth, but so were the rest. It didn't take much really, a shove from behind, a slip on the vomit carpet and Tupper was launched out the door.

It was all in slow motion for Tupper. The falling face-first, the impact with the surprised cop, the crash to the pavement, the sound the cop's head made when it hit the belgian blocks, were all distinct and vivid events spliced into an uncontrollable whole. The thing he remembered with crystal clarity was the way the cop's eyes rolled back in his head, leaving almost nothing but white. From there things started moving fast, very fast in fact.

The cop was out. Waiting for him to come to or for the other cop to come out of the station house was not an option. A quick search for the keys to his cuffs paid off. His hands were free a fumbling instant later. The cop's gun and wallet were his a moment after that. He threw the keys to one of the other men, then walked away.

He wanted to run, wanted to put all the distance he could between him and the cops, but in broad daylight, with witnesses on every sidewalk, walking was the safer course. Tupper made his head control the animal instincts of his feet, forcing his legs to slow until he felt like he was hardly moving at all. It seemed to work though, because he saw people on the street point, not at him but at the others who were running like scared rabbits.

Tupper turned two corners and ducked down an alley in quick succession. He could hear the whistles already. Still, he did not run. He crossed Canal Street, dodging the wall of freight wagons that always seemed to clog that roadway. Heading north on Thompson, he saw a half-loaded wagon rumbling away from a loft building. Tupper was on the back and hidden among the boxes within a minute. Peering out between the crates, he watched as the cobblestones marched away behind. No one followed.

Jim Tupper had stayed under the cover all day. The wagon he'd hidden in had headed for the North River docks. He'd kept his head down, particularly when the driver stopped after a few blocks to get lunch in a steamy little shack on Varick Street.

Tupper kept a wary eye for cops, peeking out from between the crates. He saw only one patrolman a couple of blocks off and no sign of a chase. When the driver finished lunch and the wagon had rattled to within a couple of blocks of the waterfront, Jim hopped down.

He ducked into a vacant doorway set deep in the side of an old prewar warehouse. He stood for anxious minutes, watching the street, his hand on the butt of the pistol. He was there for some time taking stock of his situation. The first thing that occurred to him was the need to change his appearance. His clothes were filthy and blood-smeared. His face and head were a mess of dried blood and manure. His hair, he decided, had to be cut.

Tupper hated the idea. His hair was his pride. Every man in his family had worn their hair long for as long as he could remember. To cut it was to deny his heritage and admit defeat. He thought at first that he'd just buy a hat, but he finally admitted to himself that a hat was not enough. His hair was sure to be a red flag to the cops, once his description got circulated. It had to go.

While Tupper tried to figure how to take care of his clothes and hair he noticed a pack of boys about twelve to fifteen years of age. There were five of them. Tupper watched as they approached. Their clothes were mostly ragged, but some articles had recently been stolen, he guessed. There was a new shirt with sleeves that didn't reach the wrist, a pair of expensive, pinstriped pants so long they were tied up at the bottom with string, and a bowler hat on one of the older ones, perched on a head two sizes too big.

Most had shoes of one sort or another, but two had no shoes at all. One limped on a twisted foot. None had weapons he could see, but knives or short lengths of pipe were easy enough to hide. As he watched he noted the eyes.

They had the eyes of hunters, roving and scanning for an easy mark, an unattended wagon, an open doorway, or a rival gang. Still, they laughed among themselves as boys will, but with a hard and brutal edge to their fun.

Tupper pulled out the cop's wallet, checking its contents. The gang was almost by when he looked up. Two of them were watching him with focused, dark eyes. Tupper knew the risk he was taking when he called to them.

"You boys like to make a couple of dollars?" The leader of the gang, a compact kid with hard blue eyes in a pockmarked face stopped and looked him over. He looked up and down the street, then sidled over. The other boys fanned out to either side like well-trained troops on a flanking maneuver.

"What kind'a man're you? Look like an Injun or somesuch," the boy said, punctuated by a spit of tobacco juice.

"I am Mohawk, an *Ongwe´onwe*," Tupper said. The leader of the gang seemed to accept this, as if coming upon one of the *Ongwe´onwe* here in the bowels of the city was an everyday sort of thing. He shrugged and commenced to negotiate, doing the talking for the group as naturally as any clan chief. Tupper kept his back to the wall and the rest of the boys in sight. Within two minutes he had handed over two silver dollars, a day's wage for a skilled worker. Tupper followed two of the boys with one hand in his pocket.

They walked away from the riverfront for about two blocks or so, then ducked down an alley at the back of a ramshackle row of ancient buildings that sagged and leaned on decaying wooden bones. The alley was choked with garbage, junk, and the stench of more emptied chamber pots than the rain could wash away.

A huge gray rat almost as big as a cat gnawed at the decayed leg of a pig. It stood its ground as they passed, baring yellow teeth. Neither of the boys spoke, and Jim said nothing to them. He cast an occasional eye behind as they slipped through a gloomy succession of connecting alleys and courtyards till even Tupper's excellent sense of direction was slightly muddled.

They came at last to a grand old door in a red brick wall. Oaken lions' heads, now gray with weather, adorned each side just below where a large window might have been. The glass had been boarded over with crudely cut pine. Deeply carved panels, one with a crest of some kind were in the center of the door and though aged, seemed solid as a tree trunk. It was something salvaged from a fire or stolen long ago from a carpenter's shop or construction site.

Three raps on the old wood produced a long wait. The boy was about to knock again when there came a creaking and groaning of wood from within and the sound of bolts being drawn. The door opened just enough for the gaping muzzle of a shotgun to poke through.

"Put it up, Ma. It's me," the larger of the two boys said. The shotgun didn't waver. Tupper saw a shadowed face over the shotgun.

"What's this then? 'Oose that with ya?"

" 'e needs to get cleaned up, Ma."

"So tell 'im to go to a bathhouse. This ain't no bloody hotel."

The boy looked at Tupper with a dark squint and a cock of his head.

"Don't think he can—'e's the one what escaped," the boy added. All illusions Tupper had of anonymity vanished. All the more urgent to change his appearance, if every urchin in the neighborhood knew he'd escaped.

"Man can pay. Gave us a dollar just to bring 'im 'ere."

The shotgun wavered. "Show it to me, boy," the woman said with gravelly interest in her voice.

The boy held out the money for her to see. There was a moment's hesitation, a wavering of the shotgun.

"I can pay more, ma'am," Tupper said evenly in his best and most cultivated white man accents. He reached for his wallet. The shotgun came to bear on his chest like the needle on a compass.

"You don't want to be doin' nothin' foolish, Mister," the woman said, sounding more like a growling dog than anything human. Jim took his hand out slowly.

"Just getting my wallet, is all. Relax," he said, trying to sound like the prospect of being cut in half by the shotgun hadn't tied his guts in a knot.

"I says when it's time to relax, Mister. What you done? You do the job on somebody? That it? Looks like it from the looks of you. You some kind o' Indian or somethin'?"

Tupper looked steadily through the crack in the door, doing his best to look sincere.

"Haven't killed anybody. But the cops don't see it that way. The cops're wrong," Jim said. "I'm Iroquois. Mohawk tribe, if you got to know," he added. He told her his proposition before she had a chance to say anything more. The woman listened and slowly the shotgun lowered.

When at last the shotgun was put up and the grand old door opened on protesting hinges, Tupper was amazed by what he saw. The woman, as mountainous a mass of female flesh as he'd ever seen, filled the hallway from wall to wall, actually from box to box. The hallway was stacked high with boxes and packing crates of every description, leaving only a narrow passage between.

The woman, who said her name was Bess, had stopped pointing her shotgun at Jim, though she still gripped it in one bloated, freckled hand. It was a wicked, sawed-off affair, with the stock cut down so it fit the hand like an enormous pistol. She let the hammers down carefully, muzzle pointed at the floor.

"This way," she muttered, maneuvering her bulk between the boxes.

Bess disappeared back into the blackness of the house, or whatever it was. He heard the boys bolt the door behind. There was so much packed into the place it was hard to say if it had been a house or not. The only light filtered in through a pair of tightly louvered windows in front, which left most of the place as black as pitch. One room they passed seemed to have nothing but furniture in it, seemingly stacked at random all the way to the ceiling—chairs, dressers, chests, steamer trunks, desks, armoires, vanities, commodes, china cabinets, and sideboards in every condition teetered in the gloom. They passed hogsheads stuffed with cavalry sabers, carbines, muskets, and bayonets, and bales of clothes and boxes of liniment, laudanum, and baking soda. Bess lumbered to the front stairs, saying, "Watch the third step. It's iffy."

The staircase groaned under her weight. Tupper could feel the banister wobble under his hand. The third step had a hole in it big enough to put a foot through. Even on the rickety stairs items were stacked in a crazy kind of order. Tupper said nothing and asked nothing. Bess was probably fencing or warehousing for a gang. Maybe the gang was the bunch of kids, although he doubted that this was all theirs. He didn't know and he didn't care, so long as Bess stuck to her end of the bargain.

"In here," Bess said over her massive, rounded shoulder. She led him into a bedroom, at least that's what Tupper figured it for, because it had a bed and a bit less clutter than the other rooms.

"Washbasin's over there," Bess said, pointing to an alcove off to the right. "God, you stink," she said as he passed by her. "No offense, mind."

"Don't mind it," Jim said. "It's the damn truth."

"I'll find you some clothes, but let me see your money first," Bess said stoutly, holding out one big hand. Tupper handed her a five-dollar gold piece.

"This much now, the rest later if you've got things that'll fit me," Jim said. Bess hesitated, hefting the shotgun for a moment. She looked him up and down.

"Got plenty to fit you, Mister," she said, rumbling off into the gloom as Tupper watched her broad back disappear. The house vibrated.

Tupper stripped down, wincing at the collection of bruises and scrapes he'd accumulated. He took the pistol out of his waistband and put it on the washstand close to hand. He sponged himself off, washing away the blood and dirt and horseshit. The lavender soap Bess had by the basin smelled better than anything he could remember. He started to feel human as he washed his hair.

The floor shook as Bess returned, a bundle of clothes in her arms and a large pair of scissors balanced on top. Finding Jim naked didn't seem to faze her in the least. He followed her lead and didn't make any attempt at modesty.

"These oughta do," she said, throwing the pile on the bed. She stood there for a moment, hands on hips, looking him over with a studied gaze. "You don't clean up half bad fer a savage," she allowed, her eyes lingering on his cock. "Wouldn't care for a bit o' sport would ya? Used to be a sportin' gal back a few years. Catered to the gentlemen who liked their ladies large," she said with a grin that showed a broken tooth. "I'm a bit thinner now though," she said, her tone one of apology.

Tupper stood before her feeling suddenly embarrassed. He turned away and forced what he hoped looked like a reluctant grin, saying, "Thank you, *gako´go,*" calling her a gluttonous beast, but making it sound like a compliment, "but my time's run out in this city. I must go; the sooner the better."

Bess shrugged. "Better cut your hair and get on out then," she said, picking up the scissors. Tupper thought she might have a mind to stab him for rejecting her, but she handed them over without a word.

He cut his hair short, letting it fall to the floor in shining black clumps. With each cut he felt diminished. His hair was his most visible link to his heritage, a tattered flag worn with the pride of a last warrior. A true warrior, Tupper reminded himself, did what was necessary.

The gluttonous beast watched from the doorway, more out of caution he might steal something than for any interest in him, he figured. He took his time, cutting until there wasn't more than a finger's breadth left. A different man stared back at him from the mirror. Tupper scowled at the reflection. He dressed, putting on everything she'd brought and finding that Bess had a pretty good eye for size, with the exception of the pants, which were a tad too short.

"Wouldn't recognize you," Bess observed. "Got the rest of me money?"

Jim paid her as agreed. They were going back down the stairs when Jim asked, "Got ammunition for a thirty-two Smith & Wesson?"

Bess didn't miss a step. "You got money, I got cartridges. How many?"

"Box of fifty. How much?"

"Two bucks." Bess rumbled with a curious look, but in a sudden burst of charity said, "But, for you, a buck. Been on the wrong side of the cops meself," she said in a tone that was almost sympathetic, "which ain't quite the same as bein' on the wrong side o' the law, if you get my meanin'."

She led him to a front room where a china cabinet was stacked with boxes of cartridges in every caliber from .22 to .45-75. They settled up on a box of .32s, which he stuffed in his pants pocket. They were about to go when Tupper spotted a large wooden ammunition box on the floor filled with knives and bayonets. He bent and pulled out a medium-size belt knife with a five-inch blade. As he did, something else caught his eye and he dug it out and held it up to the light.

It was a handmade weapon with a blade, a spike actually, made from a bayonet. It had been cut down and fitted with a bone handle, banded and capped with brass. The spike, maybe eight inches of blued steel, was perfect for hiding in a boot. There were two of them, relics of some soldier's handiwork.

"Two dollars gets you both, the knife and the bayonet I mean," Bess said before he had a chance to ask. Tupper handed it over without a word. He didn't have much cash left. "You ain't takin' much chances, are ya, Mister?" Bess commented over her shoulder as they walked towards the back door. Tupper had looped the knife onto his belt, but still fingered the needlelike point of the spike as he followed her. "No I ain't, Bess," he said in the dark.

Three

*The stage is the worst form of traveling you can possibly imagine,
unfit for anyone to ride in. I have heard that invalids sometimes
die on their way to the Adirondacks; now I know why.*

—VERPLANCK COLVIN

A steam whistle shrieked against the vaulted glass ceiling of the Grand Central train shed. The tortured water writhed and sputtered as it screamed from the boiler of an idling engine. Tom Braddock watched as the cloud of steam drifted up toward the roof. Slowly it shifted and shrank, cut here and there by unseen currents of air eddying uneasily. Change was never easy, Braddock thought as he listened to the mournful echoes of the whistle. He glanced at Mike, aloof and slouching against a nearby railing. Not all change was for the better either.

Mary watched him from the corner of her eye. A cloud passed across her face. It was gone nearly as quickly as it appeared, but a crease in her brow seemed somehow deeper, a care line carved with a chisel of frowns. It wouldn't smooth away any more, this last year had seen to that.

"Where is that porter?" she said, craning back in the direction of Forty-second Street. Tom shrugged.

"Got time." He mumbled. Mike said nothing. Even Rebecca seemed to keep her distance, letting her brother be for once. The girl flitted about Mary's feet, a bundle of gingham energy. She'd been talking about this trip for weeks, asking most every day how much longer it was till they'd leave. The questions had been unending.

"Where will we sleep on the train? Does the man who drives the train sleep, too? Will we see deers, do you think, Mommy? Can I go fishing with Daddy? How much longer till we leave, Mommy? I'd like to pet a deer, a baby deer. Do you think I could do that, pet a baby deer? I would like that so, so much. We won't see any bears when we go there, will we? Bears are bad, except baby bears, they're cute. I'm scared of bears. We won't see them, right? When are we leaving, huh Mommy, when?" Rebecca had pestered and pouted, but it never bothered Mary. The girl was hers, a perfect jewel of a girl, all honey curls and wide eyed enthusiasm.

She danced at Mary's feet humming a tune of her own making. She skipped and swayed and twirled to the music in her head, all the while painting graceful little arcs and parabolas with her arms and hands, her fingers just so. She seemed to have been born with music in her. It filled her up so much it would spill out and be wasted if she didn't dance it away. Where or when didn't matter. It could be A. T. Stewart's Department Store or on a crowded el. When the music called she would dance. Everyone said she'd be a dancer someday, but everyone was wrong. She was a dancer already.

Mary had always been grateful for Rebecca, but never more so than the last few months. She pushed back the darkness and the worry that Mike seemed to manufacture with grinding repetition as he grew older. Rebecca didn't know that, didn't see herself as some sort of angel, driving away her brother's teenage demons. She was just being Rebecca and that was enough.

Even Mike, standing like a growling thunderhead, had to grin at his sister's antics. The glimmer of a smile lifted the sullen corner of his mouth when he thought Tom wasn't looking. He lowered his head, though, when Mary noticed, hiding behind the brim of his cap. It brought an exasperated sigh from Mary, and she was about to say something when Tom grunted, "There he is."

The porter was finally coming. He pushed a cart piled high with their trunks, his head barely visible above. The cart and its load sailed across the terminal like an ocean liner, breasting the waves of people rushing about the station. A pug-nosed face peered over the trunks, its dull eyes looking straight ahead despite the crowd of people who seemed all on fire to dash across his path. A shock of red hair dangled from under a round brimmed cap, pushed back on his head at a jaunty angle.

"Found ye then, I did." The porter lilted. "Such a boilin' mess I never did see. Everybody rushin' like ants whot got their hill stomped."

Tom shrugged. He'd seen about every kind of crowd New York could muster. They rarely made an impression on him one way or another, unless it was a riot. "Not unusual for a Friday night in August, I guess," he said, turning toward their train. "Well, let's go then. C'mere, my little ginger snap," he said, holding his arms out to Rebecca. She stopped her dancing and charged at Tom, jumping into his arms with a whoop.

"Chu, chu, chu, chu—whooo, whooo!" she cried, doing her best train imitation. Tom hoisted her up so she sat in the crook of his arm. "Wha'dya say we go on vacation, eh?"

"Yeah!" Rebecca yelled in his ear. Tom winced, grinning all the while. "Right!" he said, shaking his head. "Off we go!"

Later, after their trunks had been stowed in the baggage car and the porter had shuffled off in search of another tip, the four of them settled into their compartment. It was cramped but elegant, with oversprung seats in claret velour. They were "bouncy," Rebecca exclaimed with delight, springing up and down almost nonstop. Tom pulled his watch from his vest pocket and flipped open the case. "Best settle down, 'Becca. We'll start moving soon," he said. Just then a shadow darkened the door of their compartment.

"Uncle Chowder!" Rebecca shouted. With a running leap she jumped into his arms.

"Came to see ya off, especially you!" he said, giving Rebecca a big hug.

Everyone smiled except Tom. Though Chowder Kelly was as close a friend as Tom had, he knew him well enough to know that seeing them off on vacation was not why he'd come. Tom watched as Chowder made a fuss over Rebecca, kissed and squeezed his wife more lustily than was proper, and slapped Mike on the shoulder. A wary eye cast in Tom's direction was all that was needed. Mary caught it and gave Tom a dark frown as he stood.

"I'll just see Chowder to the platform. Back in two shakes." When they were out of earshot, he scowled at Chowder and said, "So what's so goddamn important, aside from groping my wife's bum, you bastard."

Chowder grinned. "And a lovely bum it is, too."

"Go fuck yourself," Tom said with something between a grin and a scowl. "What's going on?"

"Murderer escaped from a Black Maria a couple hours ago. Busted a guard's head. Got clean away."

"What'd he do?"

"Stuck a knife in a construction foreman. Caught him last night."

Tom started to question Chowder, asking what he knew about the man, where he came from, who he worked with, where he lived, whether he was married or had any other family in the city, where he drank, banked, and whored. He stopped himself after some minutes.

"What the . . ." he said, stopping himself in midsentence. "I'm on vacation, Chowder. You're a big, grown-up lad. You handle this. You weren't thinking I'd stay and help, were you? If you were, forget it!"

"Well, I was kinda . . ." Chowder started to say, then got serious as he watched the conductors swing their arms and pull up the steps to the cars.

"Listen, Tom, this is a big one. That foreman was a Tammany man, kept an eye on the construction trades for the big bosses at the Wigwam. The chief's fumin' an' every damn captain in town's got their boys on the jump. You goin' off on a trip now, well it don't look so good."

The train jerked and bumped as the engine pulled up the slack in the couplings. It rumbled to life, wheels squealing.

"Byrnes ain't looking for me, is he?"

"Not yet," Chowder allowed.

"I'm leaving," Tom said. He knew the truth of what Chowder was telling him, but he'd put off far too many trips already, given far too many late nights to the job instead of to Mary. A part of him hated to go, hated leaving in the middle of a crisis. For an instant he hesitated, letting the thrill of a good case lure him, but only for an instant. He could picture Mary's face when he tried to explain.

"Have fun catching the bad guys," he said with a tone that almost sounded like regret.

"O' course, Tommy. 'Course. Just figured you'd want to know, is all," Chowder said, seeing how things were. "Get your ideas, see if we're thinking along the same lines. You know. Always a help to kick the ideas about."

Tom grunted as Chowder stepped off onto the platform. "You're gonna have to kick 'em about with someone else, pal. I'm off to the north woods, where the likes o' you dare not tread. I'm gonna do my best to forget we ever had this little chat. Catch some fish, or whatever they do up there." He gave Chowder a wave. "Good luck. See you in a couple o' weeks."

Mike lounged, his cap pulled down over his eyes in studied boredom when Tom got back to the compartment. Windows in the next train over started to slide by, sometimes showing brief frozen images of riders napping, porters stowing bags, a woman in a large pink hat, a child's face pressing the glass. They began to dance away as their train picked up speed. Mary didn't ask about Chowder. It was enough that Tom had come back and not run off on police business as he had so many times before.

They burst from the monstrous train shed into the early evening sun. The orange ball cast long yellow heat waves through the compartment. Mary struggled with a window, at last getting the catches to release. She threw up the sash, with Tom's help, letting in a refreshing, warm blast of air into their little furnace.

The sun hovered over the roofs of the distant mansions on Fifth Avenue, setting mansard roofs, turrets, and cornices gleaming. To the east, the river glistened here and there through the canyons between the buildings. The city slid by, the grubby factories belching smoke, steaming breweries, rendering plants, row houses all trooped past their windows, growing more sparse and shabby the further they went. Uptown, the naked streets, many still unpaved, were laid out neat and square. Tall new brownstones stood like teeth in the barren jaws of the city.

Not far was desolation, treeless, shanty-littered no-man's lands where squatters grubbed for what the city cast off. The park was a green mirage in the distance. Tom watched it all pass, amazed as always at the wealth and the squalor of the place.

Mike studied his feet. Rebecca's nose bounced against the glass.

"It's good to get away from this place at least once in a while," Tom said as he watched ragged people picking through an uptown dump. That was particularly true in the summer months, when disease often swept through the tenements in merciless and arbitrary waves. In a real hot spell the only people left were those with nowhere else to go. Undertakers were plentiful in the summer though. It was their busy season.

"Place isn't healthy," he said to the window.

"Be good to get some fresh air," Mary said. Though she stared out the windows, too, she didn't seem to see.

"They have baby deer where we're going," Rebecca said to Tom. "There's no deer here anymore. Mommy said. No deer for-ages and ages." She shook her curls and pushed out her lower lip in mock mourning. "They all went to the Ron-dacks, I guess."

Tom smiled. "Sort of like us, right, 'Becca? Just like us."

The train rolled north through the evening. The orange sun kissed the tops of the trees before sinking into New Jersey. After a while, stops were made. As they got up into the Hudson Valley, the stations became veiled in night. They often didn't know exactly what stop it was, only that it was not theirs. They were going to the end of the line.

Dinner was eaten to the rhythmic rumble and clack of the rails. Beds were unfolded. Sleep came on as the land passed by. Not everyone slept soundly. Albany arrived at 6:30 A.M. They transferred to the Delaware-and-Hudson line for the trip to Saratoga.

Mary wasn't sure what time it was when the car rumbled to life. It was another two and a half hours till they had to switch trains again at Saratoga. Mary dozed on and off, not so much sleeping as doing a groggy imitation of it. Listening to Tom snore hadn't done anything for her rest in the hot, cramped compartment. She looked at Mike's sleeping form, thinking for the hundredth time that if this trip could help set things right there was no amount of sleep she wouldn't forsake.

The transfer to the Adirondack line at Saratoga was weary and tedious. A handful of shuffling, sleepy passengers boarded the short train for the sixty-three-mile trip to North Creek, although some were probably bound for other stops in between. North Creek was the last stop. The mountainous cost of carving a rail line through the Adirondacks and the economic reverses of seventy-six had put an end to the line. Still, it shortened the trip from Saratoga to hours, where in the past it had taken days.

Beyond North Creek there was nothing but endless miles of forests, mountains, and bad roads. The closest thing to paving was the spots that were "corduroyed" with logs laid crossways in the wet patches. Mary was bleary-eyed and blinking in the early morning sun. Tom carried Rebecca. She hung limp and sweaty-faced in his arms, her damp forehead resting on his shoulder. No amount of prodding could wake her. Mike brought up the rear.

Nobody slept but Rebecca on the ride north from Saratoga. She had curled up in a corner of their seat, her head on the pillow that she had insisted Mary bring for her. Tom, who had a window seat, tried to doze but found his eyes drawn to the world outside. A cool breeze blew in through the window. It was cool enough so that Mary asked him to shut it for fear Rebecca would catch a chill. He left it open an inch, enjoying the fragrant air after the heat of the city.

In the distance, they could see the smoke from the mills at Glens Falls, where the growth of centuries was sawed, chipped, pulped, and otherwise shaped to fit the hand of man. The smells grew sweeter north of there, and the towns smaller. At a little place called Riverside, a narrow suspension bridge swung across the rolling waters, looking as out of place as a Bowery B'hoy at a Sunday sermon.

The Hudson swept close by the tracks, and when they stopped the river's whispering voice could be heard. The water spoke its own language, laughing and roaring at stones in its way. When again they began to roll, the rumble and clack that had lulled them through the night seemed an annoyance as Tom strained to hear the voice of the Hudson.

At last, North Creek chugged into view. All Tom could see of it was maybe a dozen houses and stores strung along a dirt road close by the tracks. The station was small and ordinary, with a raised platform and a freight warehouse at the far end. A couple of porters pushed luggage carts forward as the train came to a smoking stop. They leaned on their handles, eyeing the passengers as they descended. One of the men said something to the other that made them both laugh. They slapped their thighs at their private joke.

"I think those men are laughing at us," Rebecca said, frowning at them.

A slow hurricane of activity blew people and luggage about the platform. A couple of shays, a buckboard, and a plain, faded-red farm wagon took away the locals. The rest waited. The stage to the Prospect House wouldn't be in for another two hours.

It was close to 1 P.M. when all the passengers were finally loaded. Mary and Rebecca managed to grab a cramped seat inside, but Tom and Mike, in deference to the other ladies of the group, had to scale their way up the side of the stage to the bench seats on the roof. There were nineteen passengers all told. Nine men and one woman perched on top.

"Everybody up?" the driver called as the horses stamped and chewed their bits. When all were safely seated, luggage stowed and tied in the separate baggage wagon behind, he clambered up and gripped the reins. He was joined by another, riding "shotgun."

"Five miles to North River, folks. Stop there for lunch. Pretty good road hereabouts, so you can sit back and enjoy the ride."

Breakfast was good, the road less so. About an hour later they were off again. The road from North River began to climb only about a mile outside of town, getting steeper and rockier as they went. Everyone on top clung to their seats as the tall stage lurched and bucked. In places the road was corduroyed. The big coach stuttered across these, setting teeth on edge and turning knuckles white on handrails. Mike hung on in silence.

After a time, the slope became so steep that the coach slowed to a crawl. The six horses strained, leaning forward, stomping the slope as harness leather creaked. Finally they came to a halt. The driver set his brake and turned to the passengers on top.

"Gotta lighten the load," he said with a jerk of his head over the side. Tom and Mike got down with the other men.

"Great vacation," Mike said, making sure it was loud enough for Tom to hear. They were the first words Mike had uttered in hours.

It was a long uphill climb following the coach. Even when the driver finally had to tell everyone to get off except Rebecca and two small boys, the stage went no faster than a slow walk. Tom, Mike, and especially Mary trudged and stumbled. Rebecca all the while kept up a game of peeking out the coach windows, calling to Mary or Tom when she thought they weren't looking. Mary did her best to keep up her spirits. She stopped for a moment at last, turning to look back.

"Isn't this gorgeous?" she said, waving a hand at the view of the mountains. "The river looks like a ribbon of silver from up here." She brushed some loose strands of raven hair that had come loose about her flushed face. Tom gave her a secret grin, blessing her for trying to lighten the mood. He put his arm around her waist as he stood by her side, not caring if it wasn't proper.

"Sure is pretty," he said. He thought to say more, something about how wonderful she looked with her face flushed and her hair flying loose, or maybe about how he was glad he hadn't let Chowder shanghai him into not coming, but the moment passed. They turned to follow the coach.

It wasn't all that far to the top of the slope, a mile or so. Still, it took over an hour to make it. When the road leveled out, the women, and finally the men climbed back aboard. The driver passed a couple of canteens of cool water. Tom and Mike were rocked into a fitful doze, jolted now and again by boulders in their path.

Hours went by. After a time, they started to see signs of lumbering, with ugly tangles of cuttings scattered about and rutted tracks back into the woods. Some were old and weed-choked, others fairly new. "Comin' to Indian Lake soon," the driver threw over his shoulder. "Stop at the Arctic for a little refreshment. Old Jackson sets a pretty good table. Get you set up proper for the ride on ta Blue."

"Sounds good," one of the men behind said. "This seat's got a lot harder the last hour."

"How much more after that?" Tom asked.

"*More?* Ya mean miles or time? One's pretty sure, t'other ain't. Been wet up here. Rained up ta Blue last night. Roads get iffy."

For a moment Tom considered this. He finally settled for "Uh-huh," as if all was crystal clear.

"It would appear that time is a decidedly relative thing in this part of the world," a dapper gentleman in a black top hat mumbled from the back seat. Tom folded his arms, letting his chin fall back on his chest. If this was a vacation, then by god he was determined to treat it like one.

The Arctic Hotel, or the Cedar River House as the place was called, depending on who was doing the talking, was about a mile on the other side of town, though "town" was a generous word for the scattering of houses and the couple of stores that comprised Indian lake. A dog, and two locals whose feet were propped on a porch railing, seemed to be the only inhabitants. The three of them watched the coach full of fancy-dress flatlanders pass as if it were a parade. Mike said something under his breath that Tom didn't catch.

The coach was barged across the narrow Cedar River about a mile outside of town. "Just another coupla three hours ta Blue, folks. Got a bit o' rough road here 'n' there but h'ain't lost a fare yet." A yell from the driver set the coach off again. Soon the rattle of the wheels and the jingle of harness lulled Tom back into a doze. Mike slumped in his seat, and in a few miles was leaning on Tom's shoulder. Tom stole a look at him through a half-open eye. He let the boy get comfortable.

Tom woke with a start, disoriented by the sudden jolt to wakefulness. The forest clung close to the road. The trees overhung it in spots. They were passing under a towering white pine that stood sentinel by the road, a grand and powerful presence, its head in the clouds, roots gripping the earth in a gnarled embrace. Feathery-needled branches reached far out over the narrow dirt track. Tom could have reached up and touched them. But it wasn't the tree that drew his attention.

His eyes were drawn to the forest. It was thick with fallen trees under a lush blanket of moss and fern. Spruce, too young for cutting, grew close under the overhanging shade of tall hemlocks. Silver birch struggled. It was cool, green, and fragrant. Tom saw the eyes first, but once he did the rest of the fox seemed to materialize as if pulled from a magician's hat. It stared, unblinking, muzzle slightly open. Tom could see white points of teeth. The eyes held him, man and animal locked in recognition.

"Mike!" Tom said, elbowing the boy out of his doze.

"Wha?" Mike grunted.

"Look, a fox!"

"Huh?"

"There." Tom pointed, but it was gone. Vanished. A single fern swayed. Mike craned but saw nothing, nor did anyone else on the coach. They were all set to looking and pointing. Mike grumbled, annoyed at the interruption but even more so at his father making a fool of himself.

"Probably a stump," Mike mumbled.

"Fox ain't easy ta spot," the driver said over his shoulder. "That was a pretty one."

"Might get a touch wet," the coachman observed a while later with a nod toward the west. They'd cleared the forest near a large marsh that the driver had called "Thirty-four Flow." With an unobstructed view they could see a mountain of cloud was rolling down on them. "Off a ways ta Raquette. Mayhaps ten mile or so," he added with an appraising squint. "Comin' on fast. Might jest make it dry-shod." He flicked the reins hard, calling, "Get-up now!" to the team, setting them into a rolling canter. Everyone held on as the coach stuttered from gully to rock as they raced the storm. The horses sensed the coming weather. With widened eyes and flared nostrils they pulled together. Distant thunder rumbled.

The first drops were falling as the coach stopped before the Prospect House. Guests on the veranda watched with curiosity and amusement as the coach emptied, the passengers dashing for cover. Coachmen and porters unloaded bags and steamer trunks, hurrying them up the stairs to the porch. In minutes the coach was emptied, leaving only the steaming horses, heads held low and muscles twitching in the growing downpour.

The Prospect House was nothing short of magnificent. It stood poised at the edge of the lake, tall and commanding. The forest around the hotel had been cut back into broad, undulating lawns that surrounded it like a great moat keeping the wilderness at bay. The thunderheads had piled up behind, casting the world in a weird half-light, as if seen from under water. The lake was choppy. Whitecaps danced to the gusting breath of the storm.

The Prospect House glowed in the odd light, its tiered verandas standing out in delicate relief. It was as though it had been transplanted here intact, uprooted whole from Saratoga or Newport and levitated to this spot fifty miles within the forest. Like some marvelous confection, a wedding cake or a marzipan castle, it seemed to exist in sparkling suspension, awaiting the time when the patient forest would reclaim its own.

"That was fun!" Rebecca cried, dancing from one foot to the other in the shelter of the wide veranda.

"Yup. Just made it, 'Becca," Tom agreed, stomping a bit of mud off his boot. "So, what do you think?" he asked her, waving a hand at the hotel.

"Oh, it's a very big house, Daddy. Is it all mine? Can I play in it?" she asked, hopping more than ever.

"Sure it's yours, but just for a couple of weeks, okay?" he said as they marched into the lobby.

They were registered quickly by a polite, liveried clerk behind the long, polished walnut front desk. Tom signed in and the clerk fetched his keys, handing him a folded telegram as well.

"This came for you earlier this morning, Mister Braddock," he said. Tom looked at it as if it might bite. Though he had known that there was telegraph service to the hotel, he had hoped never to actually get a telegram. A telegram on vacation was like a rabid dog, best avoided till you were out of the neighborhood. Tom opened it and read quickly.

"What is it?" Mary asked. She was familiar with inconvenient telegrams.

Tom heaved a sigh and frowned. "Note from the chief," Tom said with a downcast look. He let Mary wait while he read it all. "Oh no! Says I should . . ." Tom hesitated, ". . . forget about the job and concentrate on my family, especially you, my beautiful wife," he said with a mischievous twinkle in his eye. Mary grabbed his arm and pinched it for all she was worth.

"Ow!"

"Serves you right for fooling me," Mary said as she straightened her skirts. "I hate when you do that. For once I agree with the old walrus, though." Tom put his arm around Mary's waist as they started to follow a bellman to their rooms.

He hadn't told her everything that was in the telegram. What would be the point? Byrnes's rumblings about important cases and new police investigations were nothing for Mary to be concerned with. Tom knew how huge a rationalization that was. He also knew where his priorities lay, or should lie at least. There had been no orders in the chief's words, nothing more than concern, and Tom wasn't about to alter his plans for that.

"Now, is that any way to speak about the chief of the New York Detective Bureau, one of the most respected men of law enforcement in the nation?" Tom asked with mock seriousness.

He knew very well how hard Byrnes had been leaning on him and the pressure it had put on the entire family. Though, as a precinct captain Tom no longer reported directly to Byrnes, he still worked closely with the legendary chief detective.

They had developed a strong bond working on the East River Bridge conspiracy a few years before. The deft way Braddock had managed to handle his troubles with the corrupt Captain Coffin had earned Byrnes's respect. But with that respect came expectation. Tom knew he was ignoring Byrnes's concerns at his peril. He put it out of his mind as best he could though, determined to be on vacation, no matter the cost.

"Byrnes will tell you what he wants when it suits him," Mary said. Tom nodded. It was almost as if she'd read the telegram herself.

In short order they were settled into their rooms, with Mike and

Rebecca sharing one and Tom and Mary the other. They had a door between them and shared a spacious porch one floor above the main veranda. The rain was hammering the glass of their windows like nails falling from a molten steel sky. The far side of the lake was a gray-green mass of forested mountain, all detail sponged away by the slanting rain.

"We want to go exploring," Rebecca said before the bellman had even closed the door behind him. It was clear that Mike was a reluctant part of that "we," but he seemed willing enough, if it got him away from his parents. They left with Mary's warning to Mike to look out for his sister.

"Hmm," Tom muttered after Rebecca slammed the door. "How long you figure they'll take?"

Mary picked up on his tone. "Oh, an hour at least, I'd imagine. It's a very big hotel," she said with a raised eyebrow. A tug at her hair, letting it cascade over her shoulders was all the invitation Tom needed.

"And I thought you might be too tired," he said playfully as he took her in his arms, feeling the answering press from thigh and breast and hips.

"I'm exhausted," she sighed, nuzzling his neck. "Hardly a wink on the train and seven hours on that horrible stage. If I don't lie down I'm going to fall down." Tom bent, sweeping her up in his arms, though he was every bit as tired. "Let me help you, Missus Braddock."

The bed was a cloud, the sheets crisp, cool, and billowing. In a few languid minutes their naked flesh was streaked with liquid light from the rain-running windows. The storm, unnoticed, grumbled and flashed and drove at the glass. In a short time, though, it was spent and passed on rumbling gray feet off into the east. Slashes of blue slowly rent the reluctant clouds, sending brush strokes of light to color lake and forest. The world outside their windows emerged sparkling and renewed. Tom and Mary drifted off to sleep.

It was more than an hour later when a slamming door jolted Tom out of his nap. Mary didn't stir, not even when a rhythmic thumping announced that Rebecca was jumping on her bed in the next room. She giggled and laughed and Tom could hear Mike's deeper voice laughing with her. It was good to hear him laugh. Tom couldn't remember when he'd heard it last. He lay there listening, soaking up the sounds of play while Mary snored lightly beside him.

Pleasant images of laughter past started to flicker against Tom's closed eyelids, Rebecca in her bath, Mike and him flying kites in Prospect Park four or five years ago, the surf at Coney Island and the face Rebecca had made when she got her first mouthful of salt water. The images blended and flowed, merging into a dream when 'Becca bounded into the room.

"They have magic lamps, Daddy! Magic! They go on when you turn the secret switch!" she cried as she took a running leap onto the bed. Then, in a conspiratorial whisper she said, "I know how."

The Prospect House was unique in a lot of ways, but first among those was that it had electric lights in every room. It was the first hotel in the world to boast of it. Thomas Edison designed the system and the generator, a contraption that was dubbed "Long-waisted Maryann," because of its unusual design featuring two long poles a bit more than four feet high, tightly wrapped with wire.

Its boiler, which produced the steam to power the generator, would burn about a quarter of a cord of wood each evening to produce light for the hotel. It cost only six or seven cents a night to light the place. In New York or Boston it would have been a marvel, here in the wilderness it was magic.

"That's amazing!" Tom said to Rebecca with hug. "Can you show me how?" Tom knew about the lights. It was one of the things that had attracted him to the place. Rebecca was on the move before the words were out of his mouth.

"This is how, Daddy," she said, running to the ceramic, insulated switch on the wall. "You turn it like this." Her small hand grasped the black switch, twisting it with a loud click. Tom and Mary looked at the ceiling fixture, expecting the little glass bulb to glow, but nothing happened. Rebecca and Mike started laughing and 'Becca finally managed to say "Fooled ya! It's not turned on yet, not till supper time."

"Okay, you win," Tom said, throwing his hands up. "Now, out of here while your mother and me get dressed. I want a full tour before supper. I expect you two to know the place up, down, and sideways by now."

"Oh, we do, Daddy. Do you know they have a two-story outhouse and a bowling alley and a pharmacy and steam heat and—"

"And a billiard room," Mike broke in, "a shooting gallery and a boathouse, all sorts of things."

"All right. All right. Get going you two. We'll be ready in a couple of minutes." Mike and Rebecca closed the adjoining door behind them while Mary said, "This might just be worth the trip after all."

Four

*He added whole townships to his inherited holdings; he built the first
artistic camps the woods had ever seen, and opened the Raquette Lake region
by facilities of transportation unknown before. From 1885 to 1900
he enjoyed an unrivaled regency of prominence and popularity.*

—ALFRED DONALDSON

The sky above Raquette Lake was menacing and gray. Angry thunderheads, black-bottomed, crowned in dirty white, were rolling in like the
devil's own blanket. The waters of the lake shifted and slapped at
the shore. The lake was empty, save for the steamboat *Killoquah,* alone
and still glistening white and brassy in a last shaft of sun far out on the
roiled water.

Durant watched it, a small smoking chip of white, as it steamed for
the carry to Forked Lake. He watched as the gray sky overtook it,
shrinking the last of the blue water until it disappeared and the lake
was conquered by cloud. The *Killoquah,* too, turned from white to a
ghostly gray, as if somehow it no longer plied the choppy waters but
had slipped into the past, a memory steaming only in dreams of what
might have been. William West Durant shivered, shaking off the sudden gloom. Such thoughts were not for him. He was an optimist.

Durant turned from the window as the first drops began to fall.
They plopped in a sporadic tattoo, as the storm tested the ground with
a tentative toe. A few seconds more and the rain jumped in with both
feet, streaking the world outside Durant's window in little rivers of silver. The surface of the lake seemed to leap up and the choppy outlines
of the waves were lost in the froth of droplets beyond count.

Durant dropped the letter he had been holding onto the top of his desk. Ella just didn't understand, he thought, shaking his head with a troubled frown. She had no idea, no notion at all of how business was conducted. He was the master of the estate now, he and he alone. Father had wanted it that way, knowing that Ella was in no way capable of running their vast holdings. She was a writer and an artist, a dilettante more accurately, dabbling in the arts for lack of anything else to do.

She had no head for numbers. He doubted she could even balance her own accounts. All she knew was that their father had left them money and she wanted more of it. And that lawyer of hers; a bloodsucker of the first order, by the sound of it.

He'd have to find out about Van Duzer, have his lawyers give him a report or something. The man was demanding far too much, even for a lawyer. William considered his letter, which came in the same post as Ella's. There was something about it, something beyond the usual lawyer's language. He couldn't put his finger on exactly what it was, what combination of threatened legal and financial ruin had made that impression, only that when he'd put it down it was with an overwhelming feeling of dread.

Thunder boomed across the lake and Durant looked out at the broad, empty sheet of water. It must be the storm, he thought, the sudden gloom and the downpour. It was enough to bring any man down a bit.

He looked at the old photograph on his desk. Father, Ella, Mother, and he were lounging on the porch of the original main lodge at Pine Knot. He was standing by one of the wide windows Father had insisted on, talking to Ella who sat inside. Father, his beard white by then, was sitting on the porch, Mother on the stairs. Ray Stoddard had taken it back in '77. It had been Ella's idea, an effort to pull the family together in an illusion of close domestic life. She supposed that having the photograph done would make it so.

They had rarely seen their father during the years he'd worked on the Union Pacific. He'd sent them off to Europe, to school and tour and hobnob, and it was only through his letters that they knew him at all. So Ella had tried to build bridges in any way she could. The photo

was one of her attempts. It was a good thought, a worthy attempt, but it was an artist's effort after all, a dreamer's conjuring of a loving family.

William admired her dreamer's soul, but as always Ella let it rule her practical side. Father and Stoddard had ended up using the picture to promote Raquette Lake for development. They knew that a view of a relaxed family, enjoying the civilized comforts of a rustic camp in the woods would speak volumes. That was one thing William liked about Stoddard, he was an artist, but he'd always had a sound head for promotion and business. William looked out over the lake again.

He couldn't see the far shore now, veiled in slanting rain. The downpour hammered on his roof with an insistent roar. "I can't let you win," he said to the smiling face in the photograph. "Sorry, Ella, but I simply can't."

Durant walked out the screen door onto the porch of what he called "The Cottage," built just the year before. The door slammed behind him on squeaking springs. He stood, hands in his pockets, staring out over the troubled sheet of water. Hundreds of thousands of acres of forest, lakes, and mountains surrounded him. It was a wilderness, not so much different than when the Iroquois hunted there.

There were some hotels now, and his little fleet of steamers ranged the lakes carrying sports and excursionists, but these were only scratches on the surface of an otherwise pristine natural setting. Such things were necessary. The sort of men he wanted to sell to, the Huntingtons and Vanderbilts of the world wanted their wilderness in civilized doses, easily enjoyed from the comforts of a sheltering porch.

His father, Thomas C. Durant, had come to love the Adirondacks somewhat late in life. William recalled how excited he'd been after returning from his first surveying trip.

"It's spectacular, Willie! Unspoiled forest as far as the eye can see, lakes and rivers jumping with trout. And lumber! Trees without end, William. Can't cut them fast enough. And when our railway is done, we can haul the logs out and the tourists in."

As with any grand plan, there were those who did not agree, those who'd gotten in the way. Most had welcomed the Durant family's investments in the area, but enemies were made nonetheless. William

wondered about that, wondered if somehow those enemies had resurfaced.

Ella had known something of it, though she'd paid little real attention to anything financial or legal years ago. Could she have remembered those troubles, told Van Duzer of them? It was possible, though unlikely.

William considered the idea, considered how it might help Van Duzer and Ella. After a while he dismissed it. It had all been perfectly legal after all, and, unpleasant as it had been, it was in the past, buried. What any of it could have to do with Ella's getting her share he could not fathom. Father had kept it very quiet. Father had always known how to keep things quiet.

His father was a great man. His mother had told him. It had been clear to him at an early age that his family enjoyed a special status. The family of the president of the Union Pacific deserved no less. He, Mother, and Ella cruised through the upper channels of European society, had been received by royalty, and became accustomed to the very best that a cultured upbringing had to offer. There were the homes in New York and Saratoga and North Creek and Raquette Lake, the private railway cars, the servants, all of which had come as a birthright. But somehow, none of that truly symbolized his father's wealth and status, at least not for him. For him it was always the golden spike.

Ella had actually held it once, out in Utah when they held the ceremony. His father posed with the spike, a ceremonial hammer held as if he'd driven spikes himself. She'd been sixteen then, and Father had let her hold it afterwards.

"It was hot and heavy, Willie," she'd told him. "The sun had warmed it up so it almost burnt my hand." William had always imagined what that golden spike must have felt like, hot from the forge of the sun. The man who could drive that spike was more impressive, more important than any number of houses or private Pullman cars could ever make him. Thomas C. Durant had earned his golden moment. William was determined to earn his.

At first, after his father had pushed through the deal with the New York legislature securing the rights to build the Adirondack Railroad, it was hard to see any golden moments in his future. The Adirondacks seemed a dreary backwater compared to the great cities of Europe or even New York. It was fit only for lumbermen, failing farmers, and the occasional sport, so he'd thought. It hardly seemed a place to leave his stamp on life. William settled into a chair on the porch, watching the rain cascade in sheets off the roof. He hadn't thought much of the Adirondacks then. Compared to building the Union Pacific, it was entirely less glamorous.

He remembered the first time he'd seen this place. "Camp Pine Knot," his father had called it. It wasn't much more than one rather crude one-story main cabin and a couple of tented platforms that served as kitchen and dining rooms. The exteriors were rough-hewn timber with the bark still on. The outhouses were sided in sheets of bark, as was part of the main lodge. He laughed aloud at the pouring rain, remembering how Mother and Ella had almost refused to stay, even for one night.

"It's horrible, Daddy!" Ella had cried, stamping a high-laced boot on the old porch. "I won't stay here. I won't! You and Willie may like it, but it's not for Mother or me!" she'd said, looking to their mother for support. "Mother, you tell Daddy. I'd rather stay in that horrible Merwin House, back on Blue Mountain than this—place."

She had been convinced at last. Father could be very convincing. But, in truth, it hadn't been Father's doing entirely. The place itself had cast its spell. William had seen it many times since. As certain as the moon and tide, those who came were taken in. The effect was nearly always the same, but the causes were infinitely different. The green cathedrals of the forest, the blue-green vistas from the mountaintops, the cry of the loon warbling across the lake, these things could charm beyond all understanding.

Ella had fallen under the spell for a time, though she was loath to admit it. The parlors and drawing rooms of London or New York held her in sway now. But, for William the spell had never faded. Though he loved the luxuries and varieties of the city, he found himself drawn ever more often to this single remote place in the world. He was tied to it in ways he understood all too well and others he understood not at all.

Five

Now faith is the substance of things hoped for,
the evidence of things not seen.

—HEBREWS 11:1

The Albany night boat was bustling with activity. Tupper had spent over an hour watching it from a safe distance, noting the steady stream of passengers, stevedores, and deckhands filing on and off. He watched for patterns and opportunities. He'd changed his location more than once for a better view, or to avoid undue attention from the occasional cop. There did seem to be more of them out this evening, not that he was any judge of police presence on the North River piers. Cops or no cops, he didn't want to be noticed.

Getting on that steamer without notice was a puzzle, prepared though he was. He had no intention of buying a ticket and having some clerk recall his face, or get his name on a passenger list, even if it was a false name. He had to get passage with no one knowing.

"Patience and cunning are the tools of the hunter," his grandfather had told him more than once when he was a boy learning to hunt. They were more important than a gun, though Tupper's hand never strayed far from his. A bullet was just an exclamation point, a conclusion and a reward for cunning patience. A bullet could be a failure too.

"A hunter shoots when the choice is *his*. Anything less is the way of the butcher and a waste of lead." His grandfather had been a very wise man.

Tupper saw his chance as he knew he would. He ambled across West Street, hands in pockets, eyes darting from under the brim of his hat. Without pausing he grabbed a large bag of rice from the pile of provisions the stevedores had been loading. Throwing it over his shoulder, he marched slowly up the rear gangplank. He reached the deck of the big triple-decked steamer and turned toward a rear gangway where he'd seen others go before.

"Hold up there!" a voice bellowed behind him. Tupper pretended not to hear, hoping the man was talking to somebody else. "You. Hold up! The rice goes straight to the blasted galley, goddamn it. How many times I got to tell you idiots?" Tupper stopped and looked at the man from the shadow of his hat, holding the sack close to his face.

"You deaf?" the fellow shouted. He looked like a foreman and carried a manifest in one hand and a pencil in the other. "Get going," he shouted, waving the pencil toward the midships area. Tupper grunted in reply and walked in that direction. He figured he'd take the first door into the interior of the ship. Beyond that he planned on trusting his instincts.

Across West Street, opposite the dock, a man emerged from the shadow of a low front porch of a chandler's shop. He'd been there almost as long as Tupper had been waiting, concealed by barrels and piles of cordage. He dodged across West Street, avoiding wagons with an athlete's grace, all the while keeping focused on the deck of the steamer. He waited by the gangplank, leaning against bales of cotton, watching everyone who went on and off. His arms were crossed and he picked his teeth in a leisurely way, but his eyes were bright and darting. He knew there were only two ways Tupper was likely to leave New York, the Albany night boat and the train from Grand Central. Another man was watching there, though the train was the less likely of the two. He congratulated himself on guessing right about the boat. As the last of the luggage, ship's stores, and freight were loaded, he felt for his ticket. He grinned and walked up the gangplank.

As luck would have it, a deckhand popped out of a door just in front of Tupper.

"That the way to the galley?" Tupper asked without showing much of his face.

"Two doors on the left."

Jim found his way and after a bit of searching dropped his sack with a pile of others in a storeroom off to one side. He asked a distracted cook where he could find a water closet and was directed to the "head," as the cook called it. He closed the door behind him and latched it tight. Ten minutes later Jim peered out while a couple of waiters passed up the corridor. When it was clear he slipped out and made his way up through the ship to the main saloon. As he did he heard the massive walking-beam engine start to shudder and throb to life.

The main saloon was spacious and well appointed, with rich Belgian carpets, carved and gilded woodwork, large crystal and brass chandeliers, and a number of comfortable upholstered chairs scattered around the room. A balcony ringed the two-deck-high space allowing access to staterooms around the sides of the ship. There were a few gamblers at the tables in the center of the room trying their luck early at faro, roulette, or poker. No one noticed him as he picked a copy of the *Tribune* from the news rack and settled into an overstuffed, high-backed chair deep in one corner.

It was a very different Jim Tupper who spread his *Tribune* out in front of his face. The work clothes were gone, stuffed into a small carpetbag at his feet. He was dressed like a gentleman, or as close to it as he could come from Bess's inventory. Deep claret pants, pleated at the waist, a paisley vest in matching burgundy and black over a ruffled, white shirt with a high celluloid collar, and a floppy bow tie completed his transformation. A trim bowler covered the stubble of hair on his bruised and wounded head, shading his eyes just enough for safety.

He felt like a peacock, and about as unnatural as an *ongwe´onwe* could feel in the clothes of the *honio´o,* but he fit in well with the other passengers. The baggy work clothes had covered his fine duds as neat as bark on a cedar. Tupper relaxed in his chair, feeling more confident with each passing minute.

He was smirking behind his paper, hardly noticing the headline about the murder of the night before and the dramatic capture of the wild Indian suspect. The evening editions hadn't made it to the ship yet, or there would surely be a story about the escape as well. He had signaled a waiter for a drink when he saw the cop.

The light from the chandeliers made his double row of brass buttons shine like searchlights. An electric jolt shot through Tupper, nearly sending him to his feet in panic. His heart jumped in his chest, as if it would burst out and run off on its own. The waiter stepped up to take his order just then and blocked the cop from view. Tupper ordered a whiskey, and when the waiter turned the cop was gone.

It had happened so fast, Tupper almost doubted he'd seen the man at all. It was with a grateful hand that he took his tumbler of whiskey a few minutes later. He wanted to down it in one gulp but forced himself to sip as he felt the ship start to rock. The engine rumbled louder and Tupper could clearly hear the river's protest as the immense side wheels thrashed the stinking Hudson.

Tupper was exhausted and the chair was deep and soft. He ached from his beating and his nerves were fried from the constant vigilance of the last day. The whiskey warmed him into a drowsy stupor. He stretched his legs out before him, easing deeper into the chair. He didn't notice how his pants rode up, exposing the bone handle of the bayonet at the top of his boot. As the sun set over the palisades, Tupper's eyelids drooped and his chin fell on his chest.

Despite the noise of the boat and the chatter of voices in the parlor, within an hour he was about as unconscious as a man can be. It was some time later when the man from the dock slid into place behind Tupper's chair. He listened to him snore while watching the rest of the parlor. Leaning against a fancy, fluted column, he hid behind a newspaper and watched. After a while, once the crowd had dwindled, he folded his paper, then as he appeared about to walk off, he dropped it beside the chair. When he bent to pick it up, he slid the bayonet out of Tupper's boot and inside the folded paper. Tupper snored undisturbed.

Six

It was the largest and by far the most luxurious hotel in the woods, and its erection in that remote spot, thirty miles from a railway, was a stupendous and remarkable achievement.

—ALFRED DONALDSON

The elevator operator closed the gate and moved the large brass lever at his right hand to the down arrow. The steam elevator sank fast and Rebecca smiled and clapped. This was about the sixth time she'd ridden the elevator this afternoon, but the novelty hadn't come near to wearing off yet. With a deft flick of his lever, the big box, which had its own electric light, came to a billowy halt. It bounced twice, settling at last on a level with the floor. The operator winked at Rebecca as he opened the gate to the parlor level of the Prospect House.

"It stopped raining! It stopped raining," Rebecca cried, looking out at the dying sun sparkling off the lake. The last of the storm was just a gray smudge over the mountaintops. "We can see it now, right Mommy? We can see the deers?"

"I don't know, 'Becca, might be the only deer you'll see today are on the walls," Tom said, pointing to the mounted heads in the hotel office.

"No, Dad. She's right," Mike said, supporting his sister, a rarity to be sure. "They told us before that they have a deer in a pen down by the lake, a white deer."

"A white deer?" Mary said.

"Down by the lake? In a pen?" Tom said with a grin. "Lead on Michael. This we have to see."

Walking out on the wide verandah that the hotel termed a "piazza," they had a spectacular view of Blue Mountain Lake and the mountains that hemmed it in for miles around. Blue Mountain shouldered everything else aside. Rising almost from the water's edge, it thrust its massive scar-faced head over two thousand feet above the lake. Forest covered everything except the tiny town.

The other hotels, Merwin's and Holland's, which nestled against the mountain's feet, were visible, set amidst broad areas of cleared land spotted with stumps. A large windmill stood close by the shoreline, the only scar on the sparkling blue and green landscape. The air was fresh and cooled just a touch by the storm.

Balsam and spruce scented the breeze, and it seemed to Tom that he breathed deeper there. He didn't know if that could really be, but it seemed that way. He supposed it was the years of breathing city air—coal smoke, manure, garbage, fish markets, abattoirs, breweries, stockyards, and fat-rendering plants—that had constricted his lungs. It was not the kind of air a man wanted to drink deep, especially not in summer, when the smell of death could crawl through the streets like a fog in some quarters.

Mary must have been thinking the same. She sighed. "Isn't that wonderful? I love the smell of the pines." Rebecca, less impressed with the country air, pointed, and pulled at Mary's hand.

"It's down there. The man in the elevator told us. It's in the pen by the windmill." A fence surrounded the windmill creating a corral maybe a hundred feet across. The earth within, bare, black and muddy was studded with small boulders. Not much grew there except tufts of struggling weeds, cropped close. There was no deer in sight.

"They said it was out here," Mike said, scanning the pen with a frown.

"Maybe it's around the other side," Mary suggested, hoping Rebecca wouldn't be disappointed. She could be a handful when she got in a mood. Just then a small steamboat rounded a point of land off to the west. It was creamy white with a gay, stripped fringe of canvas awning hanging from its flat roof. Two small boats were stowed upside down on either side of its tall, black funnel, which rose from the center of the single-decked craft. A group of passengers lined the rails. With a puff of steam, a whistle tooted twice, the sound echoing off the mountains in fading multiplication. It was at once a friendly, human sort of sound, but profoundly out of place as well.

It left Tom with an odd feeling as the whistle was absorbed by the forest. It was a fleeting thought, pushed out of his head by the appearance of the white deer. Like a ghost, it materialized from behind the windmill and charged from one end of the enclosure to the other, wide-eyed and agitated.

"See! See! I told you there was a white deer!" Rebecca cried in triumph.

"The whistle must have spooked him," Tom said as he watched the deer bound about the pen in the mud. "Damned if I ever saw a white deer before," he said with a raised eyebrow. He'd seen too much fakery at the freak shows on the Bowery and Coney Island to take much of anything at face value.

It was a buck, about four years old judging by his antlers. He was a creamy, yellowish white, though his legs and belly were black with mud.

"I want to pet him. Can I pet him, Mommy?"

"I'm not sure, sweetheart," Mary said. "Is it safe with him being so agitated?" she said, turning to Tom, who shrugged and shook his head.

"Make him come to us, Daddy," Rebecca pleaded, as if Tom had magical power to command white deer.

The burden of her innocence, her trust that he or Mary could bend the world to their will was still hers to bestow. Tom looked around and saw a bucket of oats outside the pen, placed there for the tourists. It took a couple of minutes of calling and coaxing for the deer to settle down and show some interest. Rebecca cooed to the deer, which finally stood quite still, studying them with large, brown eyes and twitching ears. It drew closer, until its muzzle was inches from their outstretched hands.

Rebecca stopped her cooing. The animal was a good foot taller than her and was intimidating despite the fence. Rebecca's hand pulled back, spilling some feed. Mike kept his out though, and the buck nuzzled it, nibbling the offering. Mike's success encouraged Rebecca. She pushed her hand out for the buck to feed. "His tongue is so wet," she laughed. "I'm all slobbery." She beamed as the white buck ate like a contented housecat.

Mike offered up another handful as the steamer neared the Prospect House dock. Tom noticed the name *Utowana* on the bow and wondered if it meant anything, or was just someone's idea of a quaint Indian name. He watched it dock. His eye was caught by the boats resting on the steamer's low, flat roof. They were elegant little craft, high and knife-edged at bow and stern, curving out wide and low in the middle. They weren't canoes, at least not like any he'd seen. They actually looked more like little yachts or sailing boats, though they had no sails he could see.

The *Utowana* cut her engines and bumped to a halt while a deckhand jumped out and tied off to cleats at the bow and stern. The captain gave a final toot of his steam whistle.

"Ow!" Mike yelled. "Damn, he bit me!"

Tom looked back to see Mike holding a bloody hand. Rebecca stared at the blood, which had started dripping on the bare ground in bright little splatters. The buck was going mad again, running about the enclosure. Rebecca's lip started to tremble as tears welled in her eyes.

"Let me see that, Mike," Tom said, pulling out a handkerchief. Mike held out a hand that was so bloody it was hard to tell where the wound was. Rebecca turned and clutched Mary's waist, burying her head in her skirts. Her tears fell almost as fast as Mike's blood, and she started to sob.

"Here," Mike pointed. "Got my thumb pretty good."

Tom took a quick look at the wound. It was deep, but Mike made no complaint. Tom watched his face from the corner of his eye.

"He get ya?" a voice asked over Rebecca's crying. Tom turned to see a man ambling up behind them. The ankle-length boots, woolen trousers with leather suspenders, flannel shirt, and sweat-stained green felt hat marked him as a local as much as the sound of the mountains in his voice.

"He all right?" the man asked with a nod toward Mike's hand.

"I suppose," Tom said.

"I've seen worse," Mike volunteered. "Saw a horse take two fingers off a kid on Delancey Street once. Ain't as bad as that." Mike held the hand with whitened fingers as the kerchief turned red.

"Don't know what's got into that buck," the local said. "Been caught since he was a fawn. Never know'd anything but this here pen or the barn." He hooked his thumbs behind his suspenders and watched as the buck started to settle down. "Funny thing is," he finally went on, "the longer he's been here the ornrier he gets."

"You'd think he'd be tame by now," Tom ventured. "What with all the hand-feeding and petting he probably gets."

"You'd think," the man agreed. "Most times he's gentle as a kitten, but then there's times . . ." He looked out over the lake and the forested mountains beyond. "Some things just don't tame I guess. Name's Busher, by the way. Chauncey's my given name. I do some guidin' here." He shrugged a shoulder in the direction of the hotel. Tom stuck out a bloody hand. Busher took it with no visible concern.

"Braddock, Tom Braddock. This is my wife Mary, my boy Mike, and the little one's Rebecca. There a doctor at the hotel, Chauncey? I think my boy should get this looked at." Tom could see that Mike was a little pale.

"Sure is. Go down to the pharmacy on the first floor, west end of the building," he said, pointing back at the hotel. "Ask for Doc Whelen. He'll fix yer boy up in two shakes."

"Thanks, Chauncey," Tom said, turning toward the hotel.

"Sure thing, Mister Braddock," Busher replied, then doffed his hat to Mary. "Pleased to meet you, ma'am. And don't you worry," he patted Rebecca's head as she went by. "Your brother'll be all right, Missy," he said with a warm smile. "Don't you cry neither. This here's your vacation."

It was some hours later when Tom stopped in the hotel bar. The doctor had done an efficient job with Mike's hand, though it required a couple of stitches. Mary had taken him and 'Becca up to their rooms to rest, but Tom felt the need for a beer.

There was a group of men leaning against the polished mahogany when Tom entered the bar, One was holding court while the others listened in rapt attention.

"Not a sound from his paddle," the man said, a prosperous-looking sport with an expanding middle. "Just feet away, and I couldn't hear so much as a swish. Took us in amongst the lily pads where he said the deer come down to drink."

Tom ordered a stout and asked the bartender who it was doing the storytelling.

"Chittendon's his name. Lawyer from Vermont, I think," the bartender said. Tom sipped his beer and listened.

"Heard a little splash by the shore and Sabattis told me to uncover the jacklight. Sure enough, there was the most splendid buck you ever laid eyes on, caught in the light. I fired, but I regret to say I was a bit off the mark, for he bounded off. So I said to Mitchell how I was sorry to lose such a noble animal.

" 'We can't lose what we never had,' says he, 'but we'll have him before daylight. He's hit hard and will not run far.' Needless to say, I was skeptical, but Mitchell said, 'He did not snort or whistle, as unwounded deer always do when startled, and one of his forelegs appears to be crippled, by the sound of it.' "

"He could tell that from the sound of a running deer—at night?" one of the men in his audience said with a decided note of skepticism. A couple of the others shook their heads.

"Oh, I was as skeptical as you gentlemen, I assure you," Chittendon said. "But Sabattis showed me the blood, though he had to practically put it under my nose for me to see. He saw it plainly though, and actually said it was as bloody as a butcher's shop, though I swear to you that in the dark I could not make it out amongst the leaves, not even with the jacklight right on it."

Chittendon took a sip of his brandy. " 'I'm going for him,' Sabattis said, *'stay with the boat and wait for my shot. Then you fire a pistol, which will give me my bearings.'* Then, off he went into the forest, the lantern in one hand and the gun in the other.

"I can tell you, gentlemen, it seemed like hours that I waited there by that boat, and I suppose it was hours, though I didn't check my watch. Then, up on the mountainside, I heard a faint report. I signaled back with my revolver and waited again until I heard something thrashing down the hill."

"You mean to say this Sabattis fellow tracked a wounded deer through the forest at night, ran it down and killed it?" Tom said. "And then he dragged it out of the forest single-handed?"

"Indeed, sir," Chittendon said. "But I can assure you it was as I say. Told me he held the lamp in one hand and shot it with the rifle in the other. Tracked the animal over a mile, following the blood," Chittendon said, shaking his head in disbelief. "I tell you, gentlemen, if you have an opportunity to hunt with Mitchell Sabattis, take it. The best damn guide I ever had, and a truly uncanny man in the forest. Good cook as well, I might add."

Tom shook hands with Chittendon and thanked him for the story before he put his empty glass on the bar. "Quite a tale," he said as he left.

The band was quite good. They had set up on the wide verandah of the Prospect House once dinner was finished in the main dining room. Tom and Mary could hear them from the far side of the lake. After dinner they had boarded the *Utowana* for a night cruise. The steamer was gaily lit, glowing in a halo of reflected light from the still water. The boat had boarded over thirty guests. Ripples of laughter mixed with the distant strains of a waltz. The Prospect House burned with electric brilliance, casting its own rippling reflection across the lake and throwing up a starlike glow against the vault of the blue-black sky.

"I hope this was the right thing—for Mike, I mean," Mary said as she and Tom leaned against the port rail.

"Had my doubts," Tom admitted. "He did seem better once we got here, at least until that damn buck bit him."

"I think it bothered 'Becca more than him," Mary said.

Tom nodded. Rebecca had always been the sensitive one. "Yeah, he took it pretty well, especially when he saw that girl in the pharmacy."

"Pretty little thing," Mary ventured. "They had eyes for each other right away." She was a maid apparently and her long blonde hair, tied back in a bun, had framed a fresh face, with startling green eyes over a pouting mouth. She had been there when they went to find the doctor. The chemistry had been instant.

"Probably why he didn't want to come with us tonight. I bet he's on the prowl," Tom said with a faint grin.

"So long as he's got 'Becca with him, he can prowl all he likes. But I'll bite his whole hand off if I find out different." Mary said this with a smile, but it didn't conceal the hard edge to her words. Tom grunted, listening as the distant band launched into a polka.

"Don't trust him yet do you?" he asked, putting a hand on Mary's as they rested on the railing. "Not that I do either, really," he hurried on before she had a chance to answer. "Suppose we have to give him some rope though. We try to keep him on too short a lead and we'll lose him. He's got too much spirit to stand that for long, even if he deserves it."

Mike was not theirs. He was the son of Terence Bucklin, a man whose murder had started Tom on the Brooklyn Bridge conspiracy case six years before. Tom had grown close to the boy then, a wild but promising ten-year-old who ran with a pack of boys in his Lower East Side neighborhood. When his grandmother, his last living relative, came down with consumption, Tom asked if he could adopt Mike. That was before he and Mary had married. They made it official after the wedding. They had taken Mike into their lives in eighty-four and moved to Brooklyn Heights late that same year. Yet, despite the separation, Mike's ties to his old friends remained as strong as harness leather.

The gang became more daring as the boys got older; it got larger, too, including boys from other streets in the old neighborhood, according to reports Tom got from the local cops. With both he and Mary working the hours they did, it was close to impossible to stop Mike from running with them. The fact that Mary was a madam who ran two respectable houses in the West Twenty's didn't help. It was only natural for Mike to feel that the usual rules didn't apply to him.

Tom had hoped that so long as Mike did well in school the gap between him and the gang was bound to widen. Mike's grades put him near the top of his class, but they didn't do much to break his old ties.

The pull of the gang and the old neighborhood around Norfolk, Suffolk, and Rivington Streets was too strong, the temptations too great.

They'd been his family, Mouse, Smokes, and the others, and they were on to bigger things, so big that Smokes boasted that he had to start paying the great Monk Eastman a percentage of everything they got.

Tom got the telegram early on a Sunday morning. Mike had been out all night, something he never did before. Tom had sent his own telegrams to all the station houses on the Lower East Side during the night, alerting them to keep an eye out for the boy.

The telegram was not good news. There had been a break-in at a warehouse, a watchman was bludgeoned and a fire set to cover the crime, the building badly burned. Mike and Mouse, whose real name was Moses Schein, were caught driving a wagon loaded with the stolen goods. Tom had been boiling when he got the telegram.

"There's only one way I can help you, Mike," Tom told him. "You have to give up the rest of them. Mouse isn't talking now, but if he does and he spills it before you do—well, I can't help you. You understand?" Tom remembered pacing Mike's cell in the Fourth precinct; three steps, turn, three steps, turn, three steps.

"Who hit the watchman, who set the fire, who was on watch, who was fencing the stuff—everything, and no bullshit." Mike sat silent as a stone. "I already talked to the prosecutor," Tom told him. He knew the system and the players well enough to know what would get Mike off. "You do this and you're out. No record, no jail, nothing."

Mike had taken some convincing. Not even the threat of what might happen if the watchman died could budge him at first. It took two more days to get him to bend. They were bad days for all of them.

Mike gave up the names at last. Tom knew it was an agony for him, a cutting away of a piece of himself. No matter what he or Mary might think of Mike's old gang from the Suffolk Street tenements, they had been like brothers, a street family with bonds fanning out like the tendons in the back of his hand. The cutting of those tendons had been done with a dull instrument, a tool of coercion and fear. An ax cuts more than a scalpel, even in the deftest of hands. Their own bonds were left hanging by a thread.

"He's a good boy, Tom, a good young man I should say," Mary said. "I don't believe for a second he had anything to do with what happened to that night watchman."

"No," Tom said. "I don't believe that's in him."

Mary watched his face from the corner of her eye. They both had their doubts.

The trout had been superb, the venison steaks done to perfection, with just a touch of natural "gaminess" to remind the diners they weren't at Delmonico's William and his cousin, Frederick Durant, sat down to a late supper once the main dining hall had emptied and only a few guests still lingered over coffee and desserts.

"You're going to have to keep her happy somehow, Will," Frederick said, his fork poised over a last morsel of trout. "Even if this Van Duzer fellow can't break down the walls you say you've erected, he can certainly make life inconvenient, expensive, too."

William grunted. He had plenty of money for now, though, God knows, he was spending it fast enough between his projects up here and the new yacht. He considered for a moment what it might take to make his sister go away. He quickly concluded that either the bulk of his plans or the yacht would have to go. The truth was he wasn't willing to give up either, not for Ella.

"Van Duzer can end up costing you more in lawyer's fees than it would take to pay Ella off," Frederick went on. He looked at his cousin as he cut into a last bit of venison. He wondered if William was even listening. "It's your money," he finally said with a shrug. "Your sister, too."

William looked across the table at his cousin. Fred owned the Prospect House and everything in it. He had built the place from lumber cut and milled on the spot, carving this fabulous place from the grip of the forest. He'd built a camp for himself way over on Forked Lake that he called The Cedars, a rival of the finest camps in the Adirondacks. He was the heir to a fortune of his father's making, a prosperous sugar business in New York, and was a wealthy man by any measure.

Between them they could turn this part of the world into the finest resort area in the East. The Adirondacks were protected now, at least on paper. The state legislature had seen to that with the Adirondack Preserve act of '85. It was the largest park in the country, bigger than Yellowstone and Yosemite combined, and far closer to the money capitals of the East. If they were smart, he and Frederick and perhaps a small circle of investors would turn these forests into a fortune the likes of which had rarely been seen. His sister's clamoring for her "share" of the estate was a trifling matter against such plans.

"Morgan will be up in a couple of weeks," William said after washing his venison down with an excellent burgundy.

"The nose himself?" Fred asked, surprise painting his usually placid features. Morgan's outsized strawberry nose was as huge as his reputation in business, and, if rumors were true, with the women as well. William enjoyed the moment, letting his handsome cousin dangle for a few seconds.

"In person," William confirmed with a smug smile. "He's coming to look at the site on Mohegan Lake. He'll be staying at Pine Knot of course, and I'll be showing him the hunting lodges on Sumner and Shedd, too," Will said. "Of course, the lodges are nothing compared to Pine Knot, but mainly I wanted to show him the sites and let him envision the possibilities."

"Hmph!" Fred grunted. "You get Morgan for a client, it'll open up a world of possibilities, Will. You know the kind of friends he has? Of course you do. What the hell am I saying?"

His cousin was excited and Will was loving it. Morgan's interest would be good for both of them. Just his presence in the Adirondacks would give the region a caché beyond anything they could have done on their own. Will took another sip of wine.

"Collis helped," Will said in as offhanded a manner as he could.

"Huntington's a good man. Your father thought very highly of him," Fred said.

William nodded. "He's been a help and a fair man to deal with; loves the Adirondacks, too. He sees the future of this country. May be selling him a camp as well," Will said, as if the deal was already done.

A waiter arrived and cleared the table, taking their orders for coffee and ice cream before scurrying back to the kitchen. William watched him go.

"You've managed to get good people in here, Fred. Must've been a problem." There hadn't been enough people living in the vicinity to provide even half the staffing needs, not if every man, woman, and child had been put to work.

"Had to bring people in from all over. Some even from New York, but mostly from Glens Falls and Saratoga."

"Hiram! Over here!" he called as Hiram Duryea strode into the dining hall. Duryea craned to see where the hail had come from. It was a big room. "Come, join us," Frederick said, waving him into a chair. "We were just about to have coffee."

Hiram Duryea was a prosperous man who owned a hugely successful starch business. In his late-middle years, he still had all the robust vigor of a much younger man. He'd been brevetted a brigadier general for distinguished conduct at the battle of Gains's Mill and still wore an air of command as naturally as some men wore a hat. He loved the Adirondacks, too, and had built a camp about six years before on a point about a half mile up the lake from the hotel.

"Evening, gentlemen," he said, with a smile that took in both Will and Fred. "Not interrupting anything, am I?" he asked, hesitating just enough to be polite. He may have noticed the fleeting frown that passed across William's aristocratic features.

" 'Course not, old man!" Will assured him. "By all means, join us." He shot Fred a quick glance as the general sat. There'd be no more talk of Morgan and Huntington this night.

She had been off duty for some hours now, but she hadn't gone back to the maid's quarters like the rest. Instead, she had done a little detective work. She found out enough to keep her interested too.

Letitia Burman—"Lettie," as everyone called her—knew what his name was, and what his father was, too. It was only prudent to check on these things after all. Mike was a beautiful boy, as handsome in a slightly dangerous sort of way as any she'd seen this summer. But handsome wasn't enough. There were plenty of handsome loggers and river drivers to choose from back in Warrensburg. They were fine if she was lonely enough, but she had yet to find one of them who could rub two dimes together.

So, she'd done her homework. New York City police captains could do very well, from what she heard, as good as a doctor or lawyer if the precinct was fat. That's just what she wanted, too, had come all the way to the middle of nowhere to find. Not that her motives were purely mercenary. She'd have to love the man she picked, not any police captain's son would do.

Lettie walked almost the entire hotel without luck. Maybe he was back in his room, she thought. That bite on his thumb looked nasty, though Mike had done his best to look rakish for her through the pain. Maybe if she didn't find him she'd think of some pretext to knock on his door. She dismissed the idea almost as soon as it came. If she wanted to keep her job there were proprieties she'd have to observe. This had to be a chance encounter, if she could arrange it. The rumble of bowling balls on maple drew her. The bowling alley was the only place she had yet to check.

Mike rolled another ball with his left hand. The last one had bounced into the gutter as 'Becca laughed and clapped. It was the first time she was beating her big brother at anything. She was enjoying every minute. Lettie watched from the corner near the door.

He really was beautiful, she thought. She took him in from ankles to ears, lingering on the best parts in between. Little butterflies swirled and fluttered in her middle. She almost lost her nerve, but she forced herself to stay. She watched as Mike rolled his ball at the pins with a frown of concentration. The ball stayed in the alley this time and toppled seven. The pin boy scrambled to clear them and set up for the next frame.

"Not bad for an injured man," Mike heard from behind him. He turned to see the girl from the pharmacy watching him with a mischievous smile on her face. He stood stunned for a split second while his brain somehow ceased to function. He'd had almost the same reaction in the pharmacy, a sudden suspension of all rational thought. It didn't last long.

"I," he said, pausing for an eternal second as his brain shifted gears, "I'm not much of a bowler, even with my good hand." He held up his bandaged thumb like it was something she needed to see. He gritted his teeth through a ridiculous grin, knowing how incredibly stupid that sounded. Still, she smiled back as if they had some secret understanding.

"I'm Lettie," she said, extending a white hand. Mike took it. It was small in his fist, soft on the back, but rough on the thumb and fingers, a working hand. He looked into Lettie's blue eyes, marveling at their light as if he'd never seen their like before.

"I'm Mike," he replied at last. "I'm Mike. We're staying here, at the hotel," he went on, knowing with instant horror how obvious and stupid and unsophisticated and bumptious he was, and how he could never hope that a dazzling gem of a girl like this could ever see past it and to the real boy who clutched her hand in his sweaty palm. Lettie just giggled. She loved what she could do to a boy, especially the beautiful ones.

Tired?" Tom asked Mary as she stifled a yawn.

"That nap this afternoon wasn't long enough by half," Mary said, her words slow and cottony. Tom put a strong hand around her waist, pulled her close enough to breathe in the scent of her.

"We can sleep late," he said. Mary grunted, doubting every syllable. "You think our little darling will let us?"

Tom shook his head, but said, "Miracles could happen. Maybe the mountain air will put her out." The *Utowana* bumped into the dock and the thrumming of the steam engine suddenly ceased. The silence of the wilderness filled the void, as if its weight alone had stopped the engine. Tom and Mary filed off with the rest of the guests ambling up the slope toward the glowing hotel, now silent after the band had packed up.

"What're the odds those two are back in their room?" Tom asked with an appraising twist of his mouth and one raised eyebrow as he looked at his pocket watch.

"Sixty-forty against," Mary said. " 'Becca can run circles around Mike if she gets going. I wouldn't bet against her."

They had just entered the main hall when Tom said, "Care for a port before bed?"

"Ooh. That sounds nice. I hope it's not too late," she said, looking about at the few guests still in the place. "Lead on, Captain."

The dining hall was empty, except for a group of three men at a far table and a young couple seated near a window. The couple leaned close across their table, drinking each other in as they spoke in intimate whispers. Tom noticed how Mary looked at them. "I remember when you used to look at me like that," Mary said after they'd ordered. Tom couldn't quite tell if she was serious, or if it was just one of her teasing provocations.

"I look at you like that all the time, Missus Braddock," he said with mock seriousness. "You just don't notice," which was quite true. There wasn't a day that went by that Tom didn't appreciate Mary's looks. But Mary, for all her dark beauty, didn't see herself as beautiful, and never truly had. She knew that men seemed to think her so, but she didn't believe it, not really.

"I notice more than you imagine, Tommy," Mary said more seriously than Tom was expecting. "I notice how you come home so tired you fall asleep in that old chair of yours. Not that I'm any better," Mary said, holding her hand up when she saw Tom about to protest. "We're an old married couple," she said with a tone that was a mix of warmth and remembrance, but of longing, too, and perhaps just a little fear.

"I suppose we are," Tom said. "And what of it? What else are we supposed to be? We are old; well, not old really," he said, because he didn't see himself and Mary as old. "And we are married," he went on. "Funny. I used to dream about what this would be like, being married to the same woman for years and years."

"It hasn't been that long," Mary said. "You make it sound like forever." Though she frowned as she said this, Tom could see the play in her eyes.

"No. Not forever at all. Not nearly long enough." Tom nodded toward the other couple. "Those two, they'll find out if they're lucky."

"But it's not luck," Mary said. "It's work in a way, I mean staying together when there are a million things that could pull people apart if they let them. We've managed to make it. I mean, your job could have separated us a dozen times if we'd let it. My . . ." Mary lowered her voice ". . . houses, what with the payoffs, and politics, and problems with the girls; any of that might have separated someone else. And Mike . . ."

Tom sighed. "Yeah, Mike. He's put enough strain on us for any three kids." Tom made an effort to brighten the mood, though, and smiled, saying, "Then there's 'Becca."

Mary smiled too and reached across the table for Tom's hand. "An angel," she said, but it wasn't just an endearing phrase. "She's everything I ever imagined. Even Mike loves her."

Tom smiled. "Yeah, I suppose he does. No. I know he does. He's a good kid. He just needs to get over this rough spot." Tom knew how trivial he was making Mike's troubles sound. He'd seen the night watchman, seen the burned warehouse. But he still had faith.

Mary nodded. "He'll come out stronger," she said. "This trip . . ."

"Yeah, A couple of weeks away is just what he needed, us, too, for that matter."

"We'll have to work on him," Mary added. "Well, not work exactly. Just pay attention really, time and attention."

"The boy needs to know he's loved," Tom said. "You get right down to it, and that was what hanging with that gang was all about. They'd been like family long before we ever came along. Things like that you don't give up easy."

"No," Mary said. "You don't. I suppose that's what old married couples do," Mary said. "Not give up."

Tom smiled. "And we haven't, have we?" He squeezed her hand. "You know . . ." Tom searched for the right words, and looked over at the spooning couple before he found them. "We may be an old married couple like you say, but I would never change that. I am precisely where I want to be. Precisely," he said with an urgency that drew them even closer.

The corners of Mary's wide mouth turned up and her dark eyes flashed. "From time to time Tommy, you *do* say the right thing." Her eyes flickered from him for an instant as her foot stroked his leg under the table. "They're watching us," she murmured with an imperceptible nod toward the other couple. "I hope they're jealous."

They sat nursing their drinks for some time, talking softly of things they had done and things they had yet to do.

"I want to spend some time with Mike," Tom said. "Just the two of us. Thinking maybe we'd go fishing."

Mary nodded. "It'd be good for both of you," she agreed.

"I'll see about getting us set up with a guide, maybe that Busher fellow."

Mary smiled in a playful sort of way. "What is it about men and catching fish?" she asked, not really expecting an answer.

"Ah, my dear," Tom said with the voice of an old sage. "This is a question women have pondered for thousands of years. It is one of the mysteries of manhood, a closely guarded secret known only to the male of the species and passed down from father to son."

Mary laughed. "In other words, you don't know."

"It is unknowable," he answered.

They were laughing when Tom felt someone looking at them. Turning to his right he noticed that the three gentlemen from the far table had gotten up and were strolling toward the door. One of them seemed familiar to him. He was about to say something, when the man asked, "Do I know you, sir? You seem familiar to me in some way, but I can't place you. Have we conducted some business or other, or was it perhaps from the service I recall your face?"

Tom looked at him hard but nothing came. "I was with the eightieth New York," he said. "Served all over. Could have—wait!" Tom said, pointing a finger at the man. "Hold on. You're General Duryea."

"At your service, sir. And you are?"

"Thomas Braddock. *Sergeant* Braddock," Tom said with unusual emphasis. "Currently Captain of the Third precinct, New York City Police. And this is my wife, Mary," he said as he rose to shake Duryea's hand. There was a look of shock on the general's face, as if Tom had just produced a rabbit from his hat.

"I never thought to see you in the living world again, Sergeant," Duryea said, his eyes in a squint as if they might be deceiving him. He shook Tom's hand hard, pumping it with vigor as his wonder turned to delight. "My friends," he said, turning to William and Frederick. "I'd like you to meet a dead man."

Seven

Civilization is pushing its way even toward this wild region.
When that time shall have arrived where shall we go
to find the woods, the wild things, the old forests?

—S. H. HAMMOND

Tupper dozed as the train rumbled northward. The trip up the Hudson had gone well. Nobody except the waiter had taken notice of him. He'd got a bit of dinner on the boat, as much as he could afford. His pockets were stuffed with buttered rolls when he left the table, not knowing how long it might be till he could afford to fill his stomach again. Tupper nodded off thinking of breakfasts he'd had the winter before when he was logging near Long Lake. Stacks of wheat cakes, bushels of eggs, corn bread, fried hams, blackened steaks, and rivers of coffee had his stomach growling.

Tupper slipped into a dream. He was in the longhouse of his old village. He saw the council fire but it was just ashes. All was in silence. He kicked at the ash and watched as a gray cloud rose. The ashes spread as he watched. Snaky gray tendrils groped in the longhouse. They seemed to almost have life and will, fanning out, blotting the contours of the lodge.

He stood speechless. He looked down and saw he was a boy, as he had been when he last saw the council fire burning. The cloud towered above him. It billowed in the darkened rafters and writhed in the corners devouring the place. He feared to move. The cloud would know. It would know, and come for him. But to stand still was to give up.

He turned to run but found himself falling. He fell and fell, landing on his back, staring up at the ashen cloud as it reached for him. He held out his hands to ward it off, but it did no good. It touched him on his legs and arms and chest. A deathly chill spread like ice on a pond.

Tupper woke with a gasp. He looked about him. People were staring. He put his head down again and tilted his hat over his face. He knew he should have slipped into a freight car. Tupper looked at his boots, stretched out before him. It wouldn't be the first time he'd walked the Adirondacks. By his reckoning, it would be thirty-five or forty miles to where he was headed. If he stuck to the woods by day and the road after dark he could cover that in a day and a half. He took a deep breath. The prospect of a long walk sent a warm rush through him, though the horror of his dream still lingered.

"The dream world is for men to use and learn from, Jim," his grandfather had told him once when he'd been troubled by a nightmare. "Nothing in it can hurt you. The real monsters walk on two legs in the sun." Tupper grinned to himself at the memory. He wondered what his grandfather might think of him now.

Tupper put that thought aside. He considered the things he'd need. A couple of buttered rolls were not going to see him through to where he was going. A good rubberized canvas tarp, a pack basket, some salt pork, a frying pan, and fishing line were added to his mental checklist. The trick was getting them without being remembered. Tupper closed his eyes once more, certain that something would come to him. Something always did.

Hours passed. North Creek had arrived and now was far behind. Tupper had walked off the train and out of town without looking back. The man from the North River docks got off the car behind, blending with the small crowd of tourists. He was different now. His clothes had changed and he looked like a local. Though he watched Jim go out of the corner of an eye, he made no move to follow. He waited for the stage with the others.

Tupper had been walking all through the afternoon and the dying of the day. The fancy clothes were gone. A sturdy pair of canvas pants and a plaid flannel shirt had replaced them. He was still disturbed at finding his bayonet missing.

He'd discovered it when he'd changed on the boat early that morning. He was still angry and couldn't imagine how he'd lost it. The only thing he could think was that it had fallen out of his boot somewhere between Fat Bess's and the docks. He'd liked the weapon and especially the bone handle. It had been made by a man who knew his knives, though it wasn't made for cutting.

Jim promised himself he'd fashion one just like it when he had the opportunity, and thought about how he'd make it as he walked north. All he carried was his small satchel. He'd stuck to the woods until he was beyond North River, though the going was rough and his progress slow.

Once dusk had settled on the forest he came back to the road. It had been empty as far as he could see. He made good time, though he had to watch his footing on the rocky, rutted ground. Glancing at the moon he guessed it was somewhere after eleven. Tupper loved the moon, always had.

Soi'ka gaa'kwa, was the moon in the tongue of the Iroquois. Unlike the sun, it demanded nothing. He could gaze upon it and not lose his sight. It would not burn the skin nor wring the water out of him as its sister the sun would in the summer. The moon was there for him to touch, to enjoy at his ease as he would a lover. Though it wasn't his totem, it was always a source of power for him, a heavenly guide and secret strength. The night was Tupper's friend.

He walked stumbling little, though the blackness was almost complete. His stomach was empty. One last roll, flaking and hard, bounced in his pocket. He saved it for the time when his energy flagged. But for now his legs were strong and his lungs bottomless. He would walk like this for hours before food was necessary. He'd learned long ago how to put hunger aside, to dig deep into the reserves his grandfather had taught him were his.

"An *ongwe'onwe* can walk the sun into the earth," he used to say. The old man had proven it many times, taking him on hunts for days at a time with hardly anything to sustain them but boiled corn bread. "A man hunts better on an empty stomach," the old man said.

Tupper did not walk alone. There was the moon to guide and the spirit of his grandfather for council, but other things were with him too. The voice of the wind in the forest reminded him of his dream on the train. More than once he stopped, hand on the butt of his pistol, listening. In those times the forest seemed to mock him, whispering that his senses were dulled by his time in the city of the white men. He somehow felt it was so, and walked in caution.

Only once did he see anyone on the road. It was a man in a carriage with a lantern swinging from a pole to light the way. He'd seen the light from far off and hid himself in the forest as the shay passed. Tupper couldn't make out the man's features, but a chill went through him when the driver turned his face toward him, as if sensing his presence. Jim stood a long time watching the bobbing lantern fade before following.

The sky in the west was showing the barest shade of charcoal gray when Indian Lake drew near. Tupper didn't need to see the town. He could smell it. Even before the dawn the rich spice of wood smoke flowed over the land. He was instantly hungry. Jim had left North Creek with none of the things he needed, deciding to find what he could on the way, rather than risk being remembered in the little town.

"If you don't want to be tracked, then don't walk in the mud," the familiar voice counseled. The smell of wood smoke grew stronger, so strong in fact that Tupper wondered at it. He came to a dirt track leading off to his right. It was not much more than a converging shadow. The smoke seemed to be coming from that direction, so he veered off the main road and followed the track into the woods as the first gray ghosts of the day appeared between the trees. As he walked the smell of smoke grew stronger.

"*Odia 'gweot,*" he grunted, speaking the old word for "smoke." Tupper liked to think in the old language, even though few spoke it now. It came more naturally here after lying dormant in the city.

A mist of smoke lurked in the hollows as if it oozed up from the earth. He stayed well clear of those places but still kept on for a little way, hoping to find a cabin perhaps and an opportunity to take some of the things he needed. He walked like a bobcat on a scent, pausing now and again to sniff the wind and test the dark with narrowed eyes.

He found the pistol in his hand but put it back in his pocket and reached into his boot for a more silent weapon before remembering it was gone.

Tupper turned a bend in the road. In the darkness it looked like a dead end but it wasn't. The road opened before him, the trees receding on either hand, scattered like a defeated army in full retreat. Before him a vast clearing spread into the distance.

In the wooly, gray halflight an army of stumps stood in a barren wasteland. Branches lay about in tangled confusion, reaching like gnarled and withered fingers. The mist of smoke was thicker here, flowing about the decaying stumps. Tupper shivered as he stood rooted before the field. Far off on the other side, maybe half a mile or more, there were spots of red glowing within high black piles that he knew to be the bodies of trees. From those piles the smoke oozed spreading across the land. "Charcoal burners!"

For a long time Tupper stood brooding. The fallen forest, the stumps, the sickly gray cloud of the slowly roasting logs held him in a morbid spell. This was what *honio'o* did, spoiling and burning till nothing was safe, not fin nor fur, bark nor rock itself. The forest would be made to yield, skinned like a beaver, the carcass left to rot.

This had been Six Nation land, the hunting ground of the Mohawk, the keepers of the eastern door to the Iroquois longhouse. This land had been theirs for as long as the elders had memory. *Hodianok'doo Hediohe* had given it into their care long before the time of Hiawatha, and the trust had been passed from one generation to the next, unbroken.

Now, in the span of just a few generations, their land was plundered. The beaver were first, trapped almost to extinction for the fancy hats of the English and French. Their land had been whittled away by trade or treaty or theft. Once the *honio'o* had it, the trees were next, then the iron from the ground and the game from the forests. Gone were the wolf, the moose, and the mountain lion, *never* to return. Streams and rivers ran brown with mud from logging and river drives. Even the fish were fewer now.

To those who knew it not, the Adirondacks were pristine. To those few of his race who still walked these woods, it was a bitter husk of what had been. That there was still hope for what remained seemed little consolation. Tupper felt these things more than thought them. They smoldered in his wilderness-wired brain with the sickly scent of singed hair and hide. It was as if some part of him had been burned away, he felt, as he squinted through dampened eyes over the wasteland before him. The low fog of the smoldering logs lapped at his feet as though he smoldered too.

An hour later Tupper was leaving Indian Lake. The hamlet had yielded what he needed with no more than the flutter of a sleeping eyelash. A clothesline, an open tool shed, a quiet barn, and an unlocked smokehouse were plundered. He had enough to keep him going if he had to take to the woods. He could disappear, drop below the surface of the green sea around him, and not come up for weeks.

That wasn't what he wanted, though. His notion about earning enough to buy himself a place had grown. It had driven him to the city to earn more than he ever could in the Adirondacks. But he had been cast back, a fish too foreign and too far from its native pond. Maybe he was meant to stay, and in the staying find his own path. If the long arm of the police did not reach him, he would find that way. That his might be the way of pain did not concern him.

Eight

O'er all there hung a shadow and a fear,
A sense of mystery the spirit daunted.

—THOMAS HOOD

"Oh, it's you," Bess said, peering out over the barrels of her shotgun through the half-open door.

"Yeah, it's me. Put up that damn thing an' let me in," Chowder said.

Bess huffed. "Let me in is it? Not so much as a 'by your leave'?"

The door opened and Chowder heard another door slam at the front of the house. "Not disturbing anything, am I, Bessie? Not that I give a shit, mind."

Bess looked around. "Nah. Just one o' the boys. They like ta be scarce when cops're 'round."

Chowder nodded. "Bright young lads they are. Enterprising too," Chowder said as he stepped into the cluttered hallway. He looked around in the gloom. "Jesus, Bess them boys've been busy. They empty out a shop or something?"

Bess laughed, a low, rumbling deep in her chest. "Nah. Just a rash o' poor, unfortunate souls sellin' the last o' their worldly goods for a crust o' bread."

Chowder grinned. "Sure it was now."

There had been a series of fires in the area over the last few months, talk of things going out the back doors while the firemen fought over their hydrants. So far nobody had been killed, but it was only a matter of time before that would happen. Chowder wasn't particularly opposed to plunder, but arson and people getting themselves burnt up, well that was a touchier thing.

"I'd advise you to lighten your inventory, Bess. Who knows where some o' them poor folk got this stuff." He looked at her like a schoolteacher would an undisciplined student.

"You'd be wise to clear it out before my boys come round."

"Oh, for Christ's sake! You see how much I got 'ere? Take me a month o' Sundays ta move it all. You get yer cut, what d'you care how it comes to ya."

Chowder frowned as he craned to look into the room that opened on the hallway. It was stacked to the ceiling.

"I like my cut, Bessie. Trouble is, your boys've been a bit too ambitious. Just lighten the load is all I'm sayin'. Hey, if I wasn't a friend, would I be tellin' you this? No! You'd find my lads breakin' down that old door o' yours an' haulin' your fat ass off to the Tombs! So be a good lass an' tidy up a bit, eh?"

Bess coughed and brought up a wad of thick phlegm, spitting it on the floor at Chowder's feet. She wiped her mouth on her sleeve and turned a bloodshot eye on Chowder. "Not in the best o' health at the moment," she said. "Give me a few days; a week, maybe."

"Sure, Bess. Sure. No sense ruining your health. An' tell them lads o' yours not ta play with matches, eh?"

Bess gave Chowder a disgusted frown and a shrug of a shoulder. "So what brings ya here, Chowder? Yer lookin' for that Injun ain't ya, the one's in the papers. C'mon in then," she said, turning to rumble down the hall. "What'll ya have, a shot or a beer?"

Chowder had hoped to get Bess's aid in finding the escaped Indian, have her send her gang of boys to comb the streets. He'd used them like that many a time before and was always pleased at how quickly they could come back with information. Her gang paid tribute to the Whyos and fenced for them, too. As a result, Fat Bess had a network of gang contacts that spread over the West Side, from Greenwich Street to the waterfront, and from the Battery to Canal Street.

"I'll have a beer if you don't mind, Bessie," Chowder said as he followed her broad back. In spots she had to turn sideways to fit between the crates and boxes, piles of clothes, bags of rice, and a thousand other things. The old building shook as she went, and dust sifted down from the floor above.

Chowder wondered when the place would simply collapse. The house had been a substantial residence, once upon a time. Chowder could recall when it was still respectable. But as the well-to-do moved uptown, the place had been sold to a speculator, and rented to prostitutes who could afford to pay the highest rents in the city.

The place had become a dive, catering to out-of-town merchants and the dock trade. Bess had gotten her start there and had never left. She owned the house now and used its cavernous interior as a warehouse for stolen merchandise. It was a profitable business, relatively risk-free if she paid the cops on time—which she did, and the gangs, which she made doubly sure of.

"Hear anything about this escaped fella? Busted out of a Black Maria with a bunch of others. Name's Tupper," Chowder said to her back. They went into the kitchen, which was surprisingly neat and clean, though great sacks of produce were stacked in one corner.

"What's so interestin' about 'im? Not the first one to escape, I reckon. What'd 'e do?"

"Gutted a foreman on a site up around Madison Square. Trouble is, this foreman was a Tammany boy, you know, keepin' tabs on who gets the jobs, pays their share, that sort o' thing. Got the bosses in an uproar, so they go to the chief, the chief goes to the captains, an' before you know it we're all runnin' about like ducks in a Chinaman's basement, bouncin' off the walls for fear o' the hatchet."

He wiped his forehead with his sleeve. It was stifling in the kitchen. Bess kept the windows nailed shut for security. She handed Chowder a bottle of beer. He flipped the porcelain stopper off and took a long pull.

"Thanks."

"Sure. No idea where this Injun is?" Bess said, not looking at Chowder but listening intently. She popped open a beer and took a long gulp, setting her chins quivering.

"Nothing yet. He's probably still in the city. No reports of him at any of the terminals or docks," Chowder said, leaning against a hutch filled with expensive china.

"What's 'e worth to ya?" Bess said, wiping her mouth with the back of her hand.

Chowder gave her a long look. "Kinda depends on who's asking," he said. "If it's you, then we can make all sorts of arrangements. For example, I might be able to keep the captain o' your precinct from getting too curious about your inventory situation. Or maybe I could talk to a friend or two in the Wigwam and convince them to sell you that warehouse you've been wantin' on Broome Street."

Bess's eyes narrowed. "You could, eh?"

"Can't promise for sure, but yeah, I can get that done, I think," Chowder said.

"Deal," Bess said, sticking out the neck of her beer bottle. Chowder clinked his bottle against hers with a curious frown. "So, whadaya know?"

Bess told Chowder how the Indian had found his way to her the day before, and how he'd changed his appearance and left within an hour. "Paid me for it proper, too," Bess said.

Chowder was writing it all down. "Bought a knife, a bayonet, you said, some clothes and ammunition for his pistol? Must be the pistol he stole from the patrolman."

"I guess. I didn't see it. He was real polite for a savage."

Chowder chuckled. "Yeah, except when he gutted that foreman. What kind of bayonet did he buy? I don't get what he'd need a bayonet for."

"I got another," Bess said, pushing off from her rest against a table. "C'mon." They squeezed their way through the jumbled hall and into a front room that she apparently reserved for weapons and ammunition.

"Jesus, Bess! You got a fuckin' arsenal here."

She just shrugged and reached into a barrel, pulling out a long blade with a bone handle.

"Hmm. I've seen stuff like this. During the war. Damned wicked weapon," he said, fingering the sharp spike. "And you say he bought one o' these?"

"Yup. Still got his clothes, too."

Chowder nearly jumped. "No shit? Lead on, darlin'." He followed her to the stairs, letting her go up first. He found himself on eye level with her tremendous ass as it shifted and trembled up the darkened stairway. "Don't tell me," Chowder said. "Third step, right?" Bess just giggled, rumbled was more like it.

As Chowder went up he thought about the first time he'd seen Fat Bess. He'd arrested her in one of the periodic crackdowns. Her madam hadn't been keeping up with her payments. Bess had been in mid-hump, on her hands and knees with a Brooklyn alderman, when Chowder burst into her room.

Even at sixteen she'd gone well over two hundred. She did have a pretty face back then and a total lack of shame. He remembered how she shook her immense ass at him once the alderman jumped off and asked him if he'd like seconds. In all the years since, the vision of that vast, rounded expanse of white flesh had never left him. And now it seemed to float before him as he clumped up the darkened stairs, a white moon in the benighted house.

Another hall went back to front through the second floor. There wasn't quite as much swag clogging this one, but it was cluttered by any standard. Chowder looked in each of the rooms as they went by. They were much like the ones below, jammed to the ceiling with dark masses of things beyond counting.

They worked their way toward the back of the house, a window at the end of the hallway casting the only light. At the doorway to the third room, a bedroom by the look of it, they stopped. On the floor was a pile of clothes. Even from the doorway Chowder could see they were filthy and stained with dried blood. Long black hair lay in clumps on the floor and on the bureau near a large bowl and pitcher.

"Haven't had a chance ta clean up," Bess said. "Was kinda thinkin' one o' you boys might pop by. I know how you like to keep yer evidence fresh and all."

Chowder stood for a moment taking this in. Bess pointed to the pile with her shotgun, which she hadn't put down for a moment. Even when drinking her beer, she'd tucked it into the broad, leather belt she wore about her middle. Chowder bent to examine the clothes.

"Oh shit, they stink!" he said, pulling his hand back before touching them. He pulled out his daystick and poked through the pile. "Looks like his stuff, from the description I have," he said. Looking at the pile of hair, he added, "And that'd be about the right length hair, too."

"You say he didn't tell you where he was going?" he asked, turning to look at Bess.

"Sorry. Just said he was a Mohawk or somethin' and how 'e had to get outa town."

A short while later they went back down the groaning stairs, Bess leading. Chowder carried the clothes and hair in a sack to bring back to the detective bureau.

"When am I gonna hear 'bout that warehouse?" Bess asked over her shoulder. "Sure as hell I need a good place to move all this shit. Goddamn house is about to fall down, I got so much in here." As she said this, one of the steps groaned louder than usual and wood splintered with a shriek. What happened next was so fast Chowder didn't really know what happened until it was over.

Bess's foot had gone through one of the treads, pitching her forward. Her leg, massive though it was, snapped like kindling. Bess's scream was cut short, though, obliterated by the roar of her shotgun as she crashed down the stairs.

Chowder, who had reached out to try to catch her from falling, was splattered and at first didn't understand why he was wet. It was so dark in the stairway it was hard to see the blood.

Bess lay face down on the stairs, motionless, her leg at an impossible angle. A huge, red hole gaped where her shoulder met her neck. Chowder scrambled down to her, but all he could do was watch as blood fountained from her neck and spilled down the broken stairs.

It was some hours later before Fat Bess's body was carried out of the house. Two men from the coroner's and three roundsmen finally worked her free. She lay on a steel table in the morgue at Bellevue. The lights hanging from the ceiling made her pasty flesh appear almost translucent, except where the blood had pooled down her front.

"Here, I want you to see this," the coroner said. Chowder wasn't all that anxious to get a closer look. Fat Bess was not an appealing sight. He leaned closer anyway.

"Been tellin' Bess for years she'd end up this way if she wasn't careful," Chowder said with a shake of his head. "Merciful quick though. Always supposed it'd come from one o' the Whyos, or somesuch, not at her own hand."

The coroner looked at Chowder and said, "Not her, man. It's no mystery how *she* died.

"But I want you to take a look at that skull over there on the shelf," the doctor said, pointing to a yellowed, dusty skull. When Chowder picked it up the doctor said, "See the hole in that one? See how it's round and broken at the edges, cracks radiating from the wound?"

"Uh-huh," Chowder agreed, paying more attention to the skull than the doctor.

"Notice, too, how on the inside there are pieces of bone broken away? That is the sort of wound consistent with a bullet."

"No argument there, boyo," Chowder said as he swirled a finger around inside the skull. "What's this got to do with Bess?"

"Nothing, detective. I'm onto something else entirely. Just stay with me on this," the doctor said like a weary headmaster. "The bullet basically blows the bone back into the brain, carrying shards from the edges of the wound away as well."

"Now take a look at this." He pointed to the body of a man lying on a table a few feet away. "Harbor police fished him out this morning," the coroner said. "Been in the water about a day, day and a half." He pulled back a sheet to reveal the pasty white body, which had huge, deep, diagonal slashes from torso to mid-thigh.

"Whoa," Chowder exclaimed. "Looks like somebody tried to cut him in half!"

"Not what killed him. That was after he went in the water. Propeller, I think. Probably got run over while he was floating."

"Plenty of screw steamers on the river," Chowder said. "Makes sense. Never seen cuts like that before. Why are you so sure it wasn't this that killed him?"

"No water in the lungs. This man was dead before he hit the water. What's interesting is that he's got a hole in his head, but it's not like that one at all," the coroner said, pointing to the skull in Chowder's hands.

"That's something you don't pick up swimming," Chowder mumbled. He put the skull down and turned back toward the body. The coroner had peeled the skin back from a wound in the man's head and swabbed it clean so the bone showed. "You can really see the difference," he went on.

"The edges are smoother," Chowder noted. "The hole has a kind of regular angle to it, like a triangle. What did this?"

"Right. Slower impact," The doctor said, ignoring the question. "Sometimes a bullet will carry away whole sections of bone, shattering the skull like a china bowl. None of that here."

"So, you've convinced me then, Doc. It wasn't a bullet; but I'm still not following you. Who is this man?" The coroner didn't answer him at first. Instead, he said, "This may sound odd, Detective, but I've actually seen wounds like this before."

Chowder raised an eyebrow. "Really?" he said.

"Yes. And I'm guessing you did, too, though not from the same perspective exactly."

"Still not followin', Doc. I've never seen any sort of wound like this 'ere. Unless—maybe . . ." A light came on behind Chowder's eyes. "The goddamn war! A bayonet wound. For the love o' Mike!" Chowder said, scratching his head.

He remembered Bess telling him about selling the bayonet to Tupper, but couldn't imagine how that could be connected to the body in front of him. "That would be my guess, detective. A long, pointed steel spike, roughly triangular and quite capable of punching through bone of this thickness."

Chowder was nodding but still wore a puzzled frown. "A bayonet wound?"

"You're the detective," the doctor said.

"Yeah, well I am that, Doc, but bein' a detective ain't so much about knowin' all the answers as askin' the right questions."

"I suppose you have me there," the coroner agreed as he picked up a scalpel and started to make an incision around the head, starting at the hole. He was cutting with deft, sure strokes that reminded Chowder not of a butcher but an artist.

"So, my questions are these, Doc. First off, could a man make a hole like that with just the bayonet in his hand? Second, if that's possible, and I think it is, then would it kill outright or what? Third . . ." Chowder was ticking off the questions on his fingers one by one. The doctor looked up from his work, raising a curious eyebrow. "Can you tell what angle the blade struck from? This fella wasn't all that tall, maybe five-seven or so. The angle would help to indicate the height, ya see?" Chowder explained.

"Fourth. Let's see, oh, fourth is how long's he been departed? I'm thinkin' no more'n two days. A little hard to tell, him bein' a floater." The body had obviously been in water, a fact so plain that Chowder hadn't even commented on it till now. "Not enough decay for much more than that I reckon. You go right ahead and correct me if I'm wrong there."

The doctor put down the scalpel. It clattered on the steel table, echoing off the cold tiled walls.

"The answer to your first question is yes. Not easy, mind, but yes, quite possible. Hard to say if it killed outright. Maybe, maybe not. I've seen all kinds of head wounds and they're usually fatal. Still, there's a lot about the brain we don't know, Detective, a lot that we can't explain. Had one case in here recently where a construction worker took a fall and impaled himself on a crowbar. He walked into this hospital with the thing sticking out one eye. Went right through his head, too. He lived.

"One thing I can tell you is that there wasn't much water in the lungs, so I'd say he died very shortly after going into the water," the doctor said. "As to angle, it's hard to say until I get a look at the damage to the brain itself. My guess is, and this is judging by the location of the wound in the upper rear area, that it was a slightly downward stroke."

"Hmm," Chowder mused, imagining the height of the attacker.

"And I'd say he's been dead about twenty hours or so," the coroner went on. Chowder started scribbling notes in a little leather-bound book that was worn and curled at the edges. The doctor paused for just an instant, wondering what sorts of things that little book had seen scribbled in its pages over the years. The pencil scratching out hurried words was the only sound.

The coroner picked up his scalpel and resumed his cutting. A little grin skittered about the corners of his mouth. Chowder noticed and wondered at it. Doctors could be damned strange, he thought to himself.

"Lastly, this gentleman was fished out of the Hudson just north of Eighty-fifth Street about two hours ago, and, no, unfortunately I have no idea who he is. Nobody seems to know."

Nine

I tried to slay without rancor, and often succeeded.

—ROBERT PENN WARREN

They all sat together, Duryea, William, and Frederick pulling up chairs once the introductions were made. Tom and William seemed to take an instant liking to each other, especially after William told him he knew Chief Byrnes. Byrnes had been a great help in recovering some jewelry that had been stolen from his mother's townhouse back in '84. Tom chuckled at that.

"Byrnes has always kept a long string of informants, lists of thieves, forgers, safecrackers, confidence men and the like," he told Durant. "Sometimes he'd pay for information or the return of stolen goods. Most times he'd know who the thief was by simply examining the scene and questioning witnesses. Of course, from time to time he'd have to resort to other methods," Tom said with a shrug, thinking of Little Benny Corrigan. "Byrnes almost always got the goods back."

"Well, I don't know how he did it," William said, "but Jay Gould was right in recommending I see him about the matter. He had Mother's jewels back within three days. Delivered them himself as well. Remarkable man."

"I couldn't agree more. I collaborated with him on his book a few years back. Perhaps you've heard of it? *Professional Criminals of America.*

Published in 'eighty-six. Set the standard for the understanding and cataloguing of criminal types and methods," Tom added.

Frederick shrugged but tried to sound enthusiastic. "Fascinating," he ventured. "I regret I can't claim to have read it though. Been busy with my little project here."

"And a wonderful project it is," Mary said. "I can't begin to imagine the planning and work that must have gone into it. It's just staggering."

Frederick looked pleased at the compliment. "Not much more than forest when I got here. Now my guests want for nothing, not even electricity." The pride in his voice was amplified by the evening's drinking.

"I do have one complaint though," Mary said when she sensed that Frederick was about to recite the long list of virtues of the Prospect House.

A frown clouded Frederick's features. "Name it, madam, and it will be addressed if it's in my power to do so. I will not have my guests displeased with any aspect of their stay here," he said, looking at her as if he might jump up and go into action at her slightest word.

Tom knew where Mary was going and figured he'd let her see it through. She was a lot better than him at these things anyway. He never had been much of a diplomat. It wasn't a skill that got much exercise in his line of work. He recognized the gift in her, though. She'd always been able to get more with a few words than he could with an hour of bluster.

"Well, I hesitate to even mention it, Mister Durant."

"Frederick. Call me Frederick, Missus Braddock, Fred actually. I'd be honored if you'd call me Fred."

"Of course. And you must call me Mary," she answered with such self-assured charm it made Tom marvel. "It's that deer of yours," Mary went on. "He's quite bad-tempered."

"Didn't I tell you about that damn buck? Scares more guests than he pleases," Duryea interrupted. Mary smiled at the general. "Exactly, sir. He bit my boy Michael this afternoon."

"Your doctor had to put a couple stitches in it," Tom added. "Beautiful animal, but you should put him in a different enclosure, something where people can't reach in, especially children," Tom said in a low, flat tone that didn't encourage argument.

"It's a wild animal, Fred," William said as if they'd had this discussion before. "I know you don't want my opinion, but he'd be better off free, or better still, hanging on your wall. This caged existence doesn't agree with the nature of the beast. He's not a cow, you know."

Fred seemed none too happy with the advice, but he did the gallant thing and said, "I'm terribly sorry, Mary." He turned to Tom almost as an afterthought. "My sincere apologies to you both," he continued. "Is your boy all right? Is there anything more I can do? Doctor Whelen is really quite good, I can assure you."

Tom and Mary were quick to tell Frederick that Mike had been looked after as well as they could have wished. Frederick seemed pleased, but he wasn't done.

"I want to make this up to you both. I hope you won't mind if I insist on deducting your meals for the duration of your stay," Frederick said, snapping his fingers for a waiter. "I won't have you decline," he said with an upheld hand when he saw Tom about to protest. "Really. I can't have friends of Hiram's chewed upon, and I don't care how long your stay is, nor how much you can eat," he said with a grin.

The waiter appeared and Frederick instructed him about the Braddock dining bill. "And be sure about it, Stephens," he told the man. "I don't want to hear of it showing up on their bill."

The waiter bowed his understanding, mumbling that he'd see to it immediately. Turning back to Tom and Mary, Frederick said, "Now, that's done" with a broad smile. He seemed to cast about the table for something to say or some other topic to change the mood. His eyes rested on the general.

"You know, Hiram we've gotten sort of sidetracked. You never did explain how our Mister Braddock here has risen from the dead."

The general chuckled at that but there was no mirth in it.

"Can't tell you that, Fred. I'll let him tell you that part. I can tell you how I killed him, though."

Mary gave the general a puzzled look, then turned to Tom. The corners of his mouth had tightened and hard lines framed his eyes. Tom rarely spoke about the war. When he did, it was in terms so vague that all feeling was lost, bleached out, leaving only colorless cloth behind. The one sense she'd always had was that Tom had seen and done things too terrible to be told. Whatever those things were, he kept them in a dark corner reserved only for nightmares. Those dreams had not ended with the war. All these years later they still were free to invade their bed in the grave-quiet hours of the morning.

Duryea took a long breath and downed the last of his whiskey. He signaled for another round before he started.

"It was at Chancellorsville, June of 'sixty-three. Bloody awful confusion, once Hooker lost his nerve and went on the defensive. My regiment, I was a colonel then, got separated from the units to our left and right." Duryea took a sip of his drink once it arrived. "No place for a battle, the wilderness of Virginia. Broken ground, low underbrush, scrub pine. Can't see farther than you could throw in most places."

Tom grunted agreement into his glass of port.

"Smoke so damn thick you couldn't see the man next to you sometimes," Duryea continued, staring off as if trying to pierce the haze. "Anyway, we got separated. Had to withdraw or be cut off. Your husband, Mary, had somehow gotten separated from his unit, too, and fought along with my men. Had maybe twenty or thirty with him, if I recall," Duryea said, looking to Tom for confirmation.

Braddock just nodded. He never had a precise count either, though there were those he could still remember.

"Anyway, I called for volunteers to hold our left flank while we withdrew. Sergeant Braddock was willing, if I recall, because that was the direction you figured the Twentieth was."

Tom nodded. "Thought maybe we could work our way back, sort of slide along a creekbed there and link up," he said.

"Right. We could see they'd be coming across a small field bordered by the creek. The sergeant, Tom here, took his men in there, facing at least a regiment. Damned crazy," Duryea mumbled.

"Suppose it was," Tom said with no touch of irony in his voice. "We had the Spencers," he added, as if that was an excuse.

Duryea grunted. "Yes, the Spencers. We had come upon a wagon with three crates bound for the cavalry. Horses were dead, so I guess the teamsters just left it or were killed themselves."

"Never would have tried it without those guns," Tom said.

"Fine rifle," William pitched in. "Had an infantry model once. Shot well. Better than a musket and three times the rate of fire."

"Yup. Liked the cavalry model," Tom said, warming to the discussion of the Spencer's attributes.

"Didn't have the range of the infantry, but better in a close fight. I'd never handled one till then, though I'd seen a few, they were that new. It didn't take a genius to see that they could fire a lot faster than an Enfield. Used to call them the 'horizontal shot-tower.' "

"Exactly," Duryea went on. "They deployed to the left flank, and my Zouaves were withdrawing in the best order we could, when I heard the volleys off your way. Saw them coming with my glass— through the smoke. Charging."

There was a long silence as Duryea took another sip of his whiskey. A cuckoo clock off in the lobby started to chime and chirp the hours. Dishes rattled somewhere in the kitchen.

"Smoke blocked out what happened, but I heard those Spencers barking." Duryea lifted his tumbler to Tom. "And I thanked the Lord for you, Sergeant."

Tom shrugged but didn't say anything. He'd been foolish. He should have died from his foolishness like so many of the men with him. That he hadn't always left the grainy grit of guilt in the back of his throat. Finally, Duryea broke the silence. "Shouldn't have let you do it. When I heard the volleys I figured you could not possibly have survived. Inquired after you once the battle was done, but couldn't get word of you or—anything," Duryea said in a halting voice. "Took you for dead or at best captured. Saved our flank, though."

Mary had been watching Tom while Duryea talked. She watched his eyes. There was a smoky sadness there, a haze of years and bitter experience.

"Wounded," Tom said. He didn't volunteer anything more except, "Spent the next couple of weeks in a hospital. Nothing real serious."

Mary could see there was far more to the story; they all could, but no one asked. Mary didn't think she'd ever know all Tom could tell about those years. She knew how much it pained him to speak of it.

Tom had let her into all the secret places in his life. There were plenty of those—the corruption in the department mostly—but other things, like how he or his men managed to get a confession, or the things he knew went on in Tammany Hall, or even the women before her, everything but this. For this there was a wall, a bitter breastwork so high he could hardly see over it. That barrier had to be assaulted gently or not at all.

Duryea looked at his watch, exclaiming, "Look at the time! I really must be going, but I want you all to dinner tomorrow," he added, extending an invitation like a command with, "I won't hear of anything else."

When they had accepted, the general got up a little wearily, took his leave, and ended with a final, "Come over around four. We'll do some shooting. My boys are crazy for it."

"Well, if it's shooting you want, why don't you all come here for dinner?" Frederick said. "Our range is a sight larger than yours, Hiram, and our chef has no equal north of Albany."

It was agreed and the general shook Tom's hand, saying, "Bring your pistol, Thomas. You can show them how it's done in the police, eh?"

Not nearly enough hours later, Mary rolled over and pried one eye open to squint at the wall clock. Rolling back toward Tom, she nudged him then leaned close to nibble his ear.

"The fish are jumping," she whispered. "Do you know what time it is, sleepyhead?"

Tom rolled away, pulling a pillow over his head.

"Don't tell me. Let me guess." There was a long silence as he pretended to think. "Time to go fishing?"

"No," Mary answered with a poke at his ribs. "It's time for you to spend some time with that boy of ours."

A grunt came from under the pillow, managing to sound guilty and reluctant at the same time.

"What time is it really?" he asked, throwing the pillow off and rubbing the sleep from his eyes.

"It's after nine."

Tom groaned as he rolled his feet out onto the floor and sat up.

"This is supposed to be a vacation, right?" he said as he hauled himself to his feet and stretched. "Damn! I'm sore from all that riding yesterday. Got a bruise on my ribs from the seat on that stage." He rubbed the spot on his back with a grimace.

"No sympathy from me. Now get moving, soldier," Mary said in mock command. Tom grunted as he stood for a moment looking out their window at the morning lake, sparkling in blue-sky reflections. Perhaps it was her pretending to give Tom an order, or the way he looked as he stared off over the water, but Mary found herself asking, "What happened at Chancellorsville, Tommy?" wishing as soon as she said it that she could take the question back.

Tom stood still, silhouetted against the morning light that poured in the window. Mary's question had ambushed him, taken him by the flank, rolling up any resistance before he could mount a proper defense. He found himself back at Chancellorsville, his mind replaying it in fits and starts, the noise and confusion, the smoke thick and stinging in the back of his throat. The volleys crashed over them, clipping branches and throwing up showers of earth. He knew he was telling Mary how it was, but it wasn't him telling it. Some other part of him was there in the hotel room, the rest was back in Virginia, ducking a thundering hail of bullets, so scared he could hardly think. Tom began to sweat as he told her how it was.

He told her how they got into position along the creek. They'd surprised the first assault, cutting down a hundred or more before they knew what hit them. In the lull before the second rush they'd slipped by their left flank along the creek, staying low. When the charge came most of the rebels' first volley tore harmlessly into where they *had* been.

Again, Tom's men had thrown them back but their losses were mounting. Though they shifted position once more, it didn't help.

"Ran right over us. Got in the creek by our right flank. Shot us all to pieces," he told Mary, seeing the small stream running bright red in his mind's eye. The noise and the cries and the splashing of the red water flashed in his head in staccato bursts of sight and sound.

"That's when I got wounded," he said absently. "This scar on my arm," he said, holding up his left forearm. She knew where it was. "Bayonet," he said, rubbing it as if it still hurt.

"He came out of the smoke, running right at me. Held up my arm. I was reloading. Wasn't ready. Bayonet went right through and hit my chest. Bounced off a rib." Tom took a deep breath before he went on. "My Spencer went off under his chin."

There was a long silence. Mary said nothing. The image she had of what that instant must have been like was almost mesmerizing in its horror. Tom just stared out the window at the shimmering blues and greens of the Adirondacks. Mary watched in silence. She knew there was more but dreaded its telling almost as much as Tom.

"You can't imagine what a bullet can do to a boy's face," Tom said at last. "Pieces of bone and blood all over me. Mouth just a big hole. Jaw shattered—hanging. Nose gone. One eye out—like a bloody grape." Tom put his hands to his face as if trying to imagine what it must have been like to be so suddenly and horribly transformed.

"Worst part was it didn't kill him. Stood there face to face, him screaming, holding his face." Tom shivered visibly. "He couldn't have been more than sixteen or so. I ran. Looked back once. He was on his hands and knees in the creek, splashing that red water—screaming."

"Tommy, you were soldiers. He almost killed you," Mary said with perfect logic.

"Oh yes," Tom answered in a low voice. "He would have killed me. I know that," he said turning toward her with a grim smile of gratitude at her try. He was silent for a time and Mary could see he was trying to put words to the things he felt.

"I should have killed him," Tom said slowly. "I should have but . . ." Tom looked at her in a silent appeal for understanding, not of what he'd done but what he hadn't. "What if he lived? He could have, you know. I've seen men survive things you wouldn't believe."

"I don't see how it's possible, Tommy," Mary said gently. It was strange trying to comfort him with the certainty of the death.

"Can't imagine life like that," he mumbled.

"You're a good man, Tommy," Mary said softly. She had gotten out of bed and now pulled him close, cradling his head on her shoulder.

"Bad things sometimes happen to good men," she said with the voice of a mother.

But to her it didn't sound comforting. It sounded trite and patronizing and superficial, a shallow attempt at true understanding. She knew then why Tom had never spoken of these things. She understood for the first time the burden they put on all who heard them. Mary wished she had never heard Tom's story, wished she could unhear it, just wipe it away. Some burdens are best born alone.

Ten

I've always had a great love for the woods and a hunter's life
ever since I could carry a gun and have had a great many narrow escapes
from being torn to pieces by bears, panthers, wolves and moose

—JOHN CHENEY

Chauncey Busher was a teller of tales. They rolled off his tongue in an endless string, like an unraveling ball of yarn. In his slow and easy style he wove that yarn into one story after another, tales of intrepid guides, packs of hungry wolves, prowling mountain lions, giant fish, foolish sports, and most everything in between.

He worked the long, slender oars of the guide boat like a metronome, timing his delivery with his strokes as Tom and Mike trolled for lakers. The big brown trout that prowled the lightless depths of Blue could go fifteen pounds or more. According to Chauncey, who seemed not to take more than a breath or two between stories, there was a laker in this part of Blue that had once towed a boat for hours.

"Fella hooked into 'im and for near three hours he got drug aroun' this lake. Give up at last an' cut the line."

"Really?" Mike asked. "I'd never have done that. Give up on a damn fish? No, sir."

Busher spat a dark stream of tobacco into the tea-brown waters. "Don't know about that," Busher ventured. "Take a damn big fish to tow a boat aroun' this lake. They got teeth, ya know. Not big ones, mind, but they's like needles. Give ya a nasty bite, even the middling ones."

"Guess I know something about bein' bit," Mike replied, chuckling. Tom and the guide laughed too.

"Guess you do at that, son. But you notice there ain't no ducks this side of the lake?" he asked with a more serious edge to his voice. "Well, there ain't. They's skeered. That laker eats 'em. Seen it once myself. Sucked a big, fat drake down with but one feather left. Fish like that'll bite you like you never been bit." Busher paused for emphasis. "And maybe he just never'll let go, neither," he added in a voice that had Mike thinking of being pulled down to the murky depths by the monster of Blue. He laughed a little too loudly.

"Guess I'll let you gaff that one, Mister Busher."

Tom grinned and turned to the guide. "That goes for me too, Chauncey. One thing though," he went on, "why aren't we be using ducks for bait?"

The day flowed by on and endless stream of stories, interrupted from time to time by fish. One was so big it bent Mike's pole nearly double. When it finally gave up and was brought to the net it wouldn't fit, and the guide had to grab him by the gill to drag him in flopping and gasping, "That's a fine big fish," Chauncey said. "Fought him good, too. You got the touch."

Tom and Mike grinned at each other until Mike seemed to remember himself and looked away.

It was late afternoon when Busher bumped the bow of the guide boat into the Prospect House dock. Tom and Mike were tired and sunburned, but neither cared. They'd caught fish and swapped stories. They'd swatted flies and taken turns at the long oars, even though Busher said he'd like it just as well if they didn't. There had been silences too, but the shared kind that grow out of knowing where you are and who you're with and liking it. Tom settled up with Busher and made plans for the next day. Busher took their catch to the kitchens.

"Guess you'll be having trout tonight, Cap'n," Busher said. He'd started calling Tom "Cap'n" as soon as he'd found out what Tom did back in New York. Tom grinned.

"You keep a couple for yourself, Chauncey. We'll see you tomorrow at nine." Tom and Mike walked up the hill to the hotel, noticing how dirty they were once they were among the other guests.

They were in the elevator with a couple of other people that Tom hadn't paid much attention to, when he noticed a furtive glance and a shy smile from Mike. Tom didn't look around until they got off. She was damn pretty in her maid's uniform he had to admit. He recognized her as the one from the pharmacy the day before. She was the only one Mike could have been smiling at, so it didn't take a detective to figure.

The elevator door closed on her sparkling eyes as Tom wondered if he should be concerned. He shook off the thought and put his arm around Mike's shoulder as they headed to their room. "Down, boy," was all he said.

Mike looked surprised. "Huh?" he asked in a puzzled voice. Tom just laughed.

"I'm a detective," he said with a slap on Mike's shoulder. "Once upon a time I was a tomcat too. Before your mother, that is."

"Oh, yeah," Mike mumbled as he rubbed his sunburned shoulder.

Mike and Tom got cleaned up and an hour later they were ready; and, as usual, they waited for Mary, and for Rebecca, who had been fussing about her hair and crying bitter tears over the pigtails Mary had tied. Tom and Mike beat a hasty retreat.

They could hear shooting clearly from the piazza of the Prospect House. The shots thumped and echoed across the lake, the sound bouncing off the mountains beyond. The shooting had started about ten minutes before and hadn't let up. "Sounds like a war," Mike said.

"Sounds like a lot of shooting and not much aiming," Tom answered, saying a silent prayer that Mike would never know what war really sounded like.

"We can take 'em," Mike said to Tom. Tom hadn't wanted to get into a shooting match, but he could see already that it was going to be hard not to. Mike had Tom's Winchester cradled in the crook of his arm and stood at the railing of the piazza for all to see. Tom realized with a start that Mike was posing, probably hoping that little maid would be impressed with his manly handling of firearms. Tom heaved a sigh.

"Don't know, Mike. Sounds like those Duryea boys've been getting plenty of practice. They might give us a run for our money."

Mary, with a sulking Rebecca in tow, came bustling out of the hotel just then and with hardly a pause said, "We're going to be late if we don't get moving, Tommy," as if it had been he who'd held things up. She headed down the broad staircase while Tom and Mike exchanged bewildered frowns.

They walked behind the hotel and up the long hill to the Durant residence. Frederick kept a large but unpretentious house just a few hundred yards away, spending a good deal of his time there during the tourist season. Frederick and his wife greeted them warmly, shooing away Mary's apologies for being late. Frederick introduced his wife, Clara, a charming, cultured woman, well schooled in the social graces, yet still reserved. Tom and Mary were not members of their social circle after all. Until they proved worthy, a certain polite distance would be maintained.

The general came out to greet them, too. "Ah, wonderful," he said when he saw that Mike had brought the Winchester. "I'm afraid my boys have started without you, but that's alright. They'll love to have someone to shoot with." He turned to Tom, saying, "And you too, of course, Sergeant. Oh," he caught himself. "I suppose I should call you Captain now, eh?"

"I'd prefer Tom, if it's all right with you, General."

"Of course, of course. And I'm no general any more either," he replied. "It's Hiram from here on, but my friends call me Hi."

Tom somehow didn't feel comfortable with "Hi," but said, "Fine by me" as he pumped Duryea's hand.

The firing had stopped. The Duryea boys came slouching in to greet them. Chester and Harry appeared to be about the same age as Mike but seemed to have a bit more of a swagger to them, especially Chester. He wore the shadow of a smirk, as if he knew something everyone else didn't. He was well-mannered, though, and well-spoken, too.

"I see you've brought your rifle," he said with an almost fox-in-the-henhouse kind of grin.

"Prepared for a bit of a match? I must warn you, Harry and I have been practicing."

"I heard," Mike replied.

Chester just grinned. "We do enjoy shooting. That a thirty-forty Winchester? We have one, too, but that looks like a newer model. I must have a turn at it."

"Sure," Tom said. "Give it a try."

Mike didn't seem all that happy with letting anyone use his rifle, even if it was really Tom's.

"I think you'll like the balance," Tom went on. "Better muzzle velocity and flatter trajectory than the forty-four forty, but not as much punch. Still plenty good for deer."

"Mister Braddock is a captain in the New York City Police Department, boys," Duryea broke in. "I imagine he knows one end of a pistol from the other as well."

Tom chuckled. "Been on the wrong end of one once or twice, too."

Duryea clapped a hand on Tom's shoulder, steering him after the women, who had headed toward the back of the house. "Never did have a paper target shoot back at me. Prefer it that way."

William West Durant and his wife, Janet, arrived fashionably late. The trip from Raquette Lake was long enough, even by steamboat, that they'd had to start out just after lunch to make it by dinner. No one minded. Once they all settled around the dining table, the talk started to turn to Mary. Frederick, who spent a good deal of time in New York, said with a frown, "You must forgive me, Missus Braddock, but ever since we met last night I have had the feeling we've met before. I really can't place where."

This was just the sort of thing that Tom and Mary lived in dread of. Mary was the sort of woman men remembered. Her long, black hair framed an exotic face that was a blend of her Irish and Cherokee heritage. Her figure and carriage were nothing short of superb, and, as Tom was fond of reminding her, every bit as stunning as before Rebecca was born. She was also a successful woman, one of the few who owned a respectable house, and in her case two.

Many madams fronted for the real owners, who were of course men. Mary ran her own places, and in a twist that she relished had a few years before hired a man to front for her. Tom had insisted on it once they were married. Still, she was at her houses on West Twenty-sixth Street nearly every day. These days, she mostly played hostess in the gaming room.

That had been another change since she and Tom were married.

They'd added a large, tastefully appointed gambling operation to the already successful entertainment that Mary's girls supplied. There were a couple of roulette wheels, tables for dice and faro, and private rooms for high-stakes poker. This was where Mary spent most of her time now, distancing herself from the operation of the "den of iniquity" she'd run for years. This was just for the public.

In reality she was every bit as involved a madam as she had ever been, with the one exception that she no longer entertained clients. She did, however, choose her girls, provide them with the proper clothes, and medical care, and in some cases training. Some in whom she saw potential were schooled in the social graces, the better to cater to her wealthier clientele and out-of-town businessmen seeking a high-toned escort for an evening or two.

It was quite possible that Frederick Durant had been to her place. It was well known amongst the wealthier sporting set, dandies, and fancy men. Perhaps he'd been there to gamble, perhaps more.

"The theater, possibly? Tom and I went to the Grand Opera House just a few weeks ago."

"No," Frederick answered. "That couldn't be it. Haven't been to a play in months. We've been up here since May."

"Delmonico's, then," Tom said. There was just the faintest hint of finality in the way he said this, a whiff of a warning to let the subject drop. Whether Fred picked up on it or not, Tom couldn't be sure, but Frederick said, "Yes, that's probably it. Del's is quite the place to be seen isn't it, darling?" he asked, turning to his wife. Still, Frederick cast a quick glance at Mary, just the corner of an eye, really. Nothing more was said.

"This is a sportsman's paradise, Tom," William said, changing the subject. "Mike here tells me you were out fishing today. Did pretty well, I hear."

"That we did. Mike caught the fattest lake trout I think I've ever seen."

"Really?" Durant asked. "I've been told lately that Blue's fairly fished out. Too many tourists, eh, Fred?"

Frederick didn't rise to the bait. He took a thoughtful bite of trout and pointed his fork at his cousin.

"It's not the number of fish caught, Will, at least that's not what I hear from my chefs."

"Your chefs?" Mary interrupted. "Are they the ones depleting the fish?"

Fred chuckled. "No, no, but they cook them often enough. The guests bring in fish that are barely big enough to fillet."

William grunted. "They catch too many. I've seen whole strings of them thrown away because the sports had more than they could possibly eat."

Fred nodded. "The bears don't seem to mind," he added with a sarcastic grin. 'They come prowling almost every night."

William shrugged but returned to his point. "The fact is that the fish are being depleted, the game too. Some species are simply gone, hunted out."

Duryea nodded. "The guides are saying the same. Most all of them hunt for the market and for the logging outfits, too," he said. "They know something's got to be done, but most of them have families to feed. Hunting puts food on the table. They can't stop."

"If it wasn't for Colvin we wouldn't even have an Adirondacks preserve," William commented.

"Colvin?" Mary asked. "I haven't heard of him, at least not that I recall."

"He's that surveyor, isn't he?" Tom asked. "I think I remember something about him in the *Times*."

"Exactly," William replied. "Verplank Colvin is the surveyor for the state. Never had been a state survey of this area, not till he started in 'seventy-two. You look at an old map of this area from twenty years ago and there's immense swaths of the woods that were unknown. Understand, we're talking about an area the size of Massachusetts."

"People lived here, certainly," Mary said. "And there was logging and things, I suppose."

"Oh, you're quite right, but in terms of knowing precisely what was here and where things were, nobody knew all of it. It was just too big and forbidding a place to map. Colvin's been at it for years, and he's not through yet. Won't stop for anything. Half his guides quit on him.

Still, he loves these woods and he's done more in Albany to see they're protected than any man I know."

"I don't really understand," Mary broke in. "These woods hardly seem to need protecting, especially not if they're as vast as you say. Why can't they be developed?"

William turned to Mary. "That, Missus Braddock, is precisely the question the legislature has been chewing on for years. It's not a simple issue, and there are plenty of reasonable men who have opposing views on it. Take logging. Some say that properly managed, these forests can be logged indefinitely. The problem is with the watersheds for rivers like the Hudson. Men like Colvin argue that logging damages the rivers and reduces the ground's ability to retain moisture, thereby lowering the water level in feeder streams to the Hudson.

"Damage the Hudson and you damage every city and town from here to New York, the Erie Canal included. One thing everyone agrees on is that the Adirondacks a very special place. It is unique. Even the logging companies will tell you that. And, there's a growing sentiment that these forests deserve to be protected. There's been so much damage already, it's clear that if nothing's done this wilderness could be gone in another generation."

Tom, who had been listening to Durant, pointed with his fork and said, "Right now I don't know much about the Adirondacks, but what I have seen is extraordinary. I have one question though. I don't mean to offend anyone, but Frederick and William here—aren't you part of the problem?"

Frederick looked a bit taken aback, but William smiled, holding up his hand to his cousin who appeared about to answer.

"You're quite right, Tom, quite right," William admitted. "You're referring to our development of this area, I take it?"

"Well, yes. Doesn't it work against the preservation interests to be building hotels and putting steamboats on the lakes? You're drawing more people here all the time. They hunt the deer and catch the fish and do plenty of damage in other ways, I'd imagine."

William, who had steepled his fingers and was now peering over them at Tom, wore a satisfied smile.

"Let me explain, Tom, if I may," he began.

"First off, as you know, the Adirondacks are very remote. It takes quite some time and expense to get here. It also means that the people who come must have leisure time, which in turn means they must have money to fund their activities." William tapped his fork on his plate as he made each point, the click, click, click sounding like pieces of his personal puzzle fitting into place.

"You've probably noticed," Frederick added, "that the guests at the Prospect House are from the upper classes. They not only can afford to come, like yourselves, but they are in many ways leaders of society."

"Fred is quite right," Duryea agreed. "You should see the hotel register sometime. The very best; doctors, judges, men of business, lawyers," he nodded at Tom, police captains. Leaders of opinion, Tom."

"Just so, Hi. Just so," William said. "These are the very sort needed here, the sort with influence, political connections, and the economic power to quite literally alter the fate of the Adirondacks."

"So long as there aren't too many of us?"

They looked at Mary, who had voiced what they all were thinking.

"Well, yes. Not to put too fine a point on it. We can't encourage too many to come, and at the same time not too few," William admitted.

"So," Mary said with a wry smile, "you need to have just enough damage to these woods to be noticed in the right circles but not too much to spoil our fun."

William chuckled and shrugged his shoulders with a smile. "Sometimes a part must be lost if the whole is to be saved." William's smile melted then and his face took on an earnest cast. Leaning forward on the table he said, "The whole of this region is worth saving, and it will be saved if it's in my power to do it, even if it's just a few thousand acres. But I pray it will be more, much, much more."

The talk turned to the construction of camps as they drank their coffee, with William talking at length about his ideas on design, architecture, decoration, and furnishing.

"My entire aim is to blend, as far as possible, the structures with the environment they're in. It's a simple concept really, an appreciation and a mirroring of their natural surroundings. It all comes from loving these woods. I want to bring as much of them into my buildings as I can." He paused for a moment, seeming about to explain more, but finally said, "I'd like you to come out to Pine Knot tomorrow. I'll show you what I mean."

When plans were set the entire group went outside, following the sound of the guns. They found the Duryea boys and Mike about a hundred yards in back of the house. A field had been cleared out of the forest here and targets were set out against the rising ground, the natural slope of the hill behind providing a backstop for their bullets. Tom saw right away that Mike was overmatched. Though he took his time and aimed as carefully as he could, Mike wasn't as comfortable with the Winchester as the Duryea boys were with their rifles. One had a Sharps, the other a Model seventy-six Winchester, lever action, with a beautifully grained, checkered stock. They handled them as if they were extensions of their bodies, aiming with the sure eye of long practice.

The firing was deafening up close and Rebecca held her hands over her ears and hunched her shoulders. The Sharps was a .44-40, the Winchester a heavy .45-75. Between them both the effect was like a physical assault. Slaps of sound dizzied the senses and stung the ears. Tom's .30-40 sounded tame by comparison. It was a good shooter and Mike did well with it. His bandaged thumb couldn't have helped. When the boys stopped and they went out to examine their targets, Tom put a hand on his shoulder. "Pretty damn good, Mike. Considering you haven't had much practice, you did some fine shooting here."

Mike shrugged a shoulder at the Duryeas' targets. "Couldn't come close to them."

"Hell," Tom muttered. "You did as good as I could have with that rifle."

Mike straightened out of his slouch a bit and Tom pointed to the target. "Shoots a little high and to the right," he said, circling a cluster of holes with his finger. "Need to adjust the sight a bit. One over, one down, I'd say at this range. By the way, how's that thumb feeling?"

Mike claimed it didn't bother him much. New targets were set up and another twenty-five rounds shot. Most all were in the black. Mike stood a little taller.

Duryea asked if Tom had brought his pistol.

"I happen to have it," Tom admitted while Mary pursed her lips and arched her eyebrows at him. She knew he went nowhere without it and, being a fairly new gun, he'd spent lots of hours at the range "getting the feel of it," as he'd put it, though it was beyond her how one gun was any different from another.

"So, will you treat us to an exhibition of police marksmanship, Captain?" Hiram asked in a way that made Tom forgive the goading. "If you're as good with your Colt as you were with those Spencers, we'll be in for a treat," he said.

Tom frowned as he took out the Colt, a new .41 double action with a five-inch barrel. Opening the cylinder he added one bullet. He always carried the Colt with the hammer on an empty chamber, an old habit that hadn't died despite better safety designs that allowed the hammer to rest in a notch between chambers.

Chester Duryea was about to set out a new target when Tom said, "Haven't done much paper target work in a while actually. You have some cans? I'll show you what I've been working on."

One of the boys ran to fetch a few from the kitchen.

"I figure if I need to use this, my target likely won't be standing still. In fact he'll probably be shooting back, which means I'll be moving, too," he said with a crooked grin. "Conventional target practice isn't worth a damn for that."

Chester came running back with a bag full of cans.

"Good. Now you three boys each take two cans. On my signal I want you to throw them out one after the other."

"Okay," Mike said. He'd practiced this with Tom and knew what was coming.

"I want them in different spots. Spread 'em around." Turning to the rest, he said, "It's more about pointing, like I said, than aiming, exactly. Here, you'll see what I mean. Go!"

Chester threw his cans first, tossing one about twenty feet away, the other much farther. As the first one left his hand, Tom turned and brought the Colt up with both hands. The can hadn't touched the ground before the Colt barked, making the can sing and skitter. Turning, the Colt tracked the second can in the air. Again the pistol cracked and the can jumped. Harry, trying to make it more difficult, tossed his cans farther apart and to the sides but the Colt followed them like a magnet while Tom pivoted behind. Mike threw his in equally difficult locations and at differing speeds, but the results were the same. The four cans were hit one after the other. Mike beamed. Chester and Harry stood dumbstruck.

"The trick," Tom said as he turned back and flipped open the cylin der of the Colt, ejecting the shell casings in a small shower of brass, "is to hurry up slowly."

"Bravo!" Duryea exclaimed. "Bravo. I haven't seen shooting like that outside of Buffalo Bill's show."

The ladies clapped and both the Durants expressed their admiration while the boys collected the cans. Chester was anxious to try the same himself and insisted he go next with a pistol he produced as if by magic. Chester, then Mike, and Harry after him all tried to duplicate Tom's shooting. Only Mike managed to hit more than one and none were hit while still in the air.

When Tom stepped up again at the ladies' insistence, he said to the boys, "Your problem is you've been aiming. Ready?" he asked. With no warning and with Tom facing the wrong direction, Chester, then Harry threw their cans out so fast there was hardly any spacing between them. Tom whirled about. Boom, boom, boom, boom, the Colt struck like a thunderous snake as it swung from target to target. Mike threw his late. The final two hits were like nails in a coffin. Nobody spoke for a full three heartbeats until Tom finally said, "Aiming's one thing. Shooting's another."

Three hundred miles downstate, in the heart of Manhattan there was a knock on the darkened oak of Van Duzer's office door. Without waiting for an answer a clerk scurried in on the balls of his feet and mumbled, "Telegram for you, sir."

Van Duzer didn't look up. He grunted an acknowledgment and continued reading the papers before him while the clerk slid out, the door closing with a soft snick of the latch. The telegram sat for some time as the sun sank, sending a line of shadow creeping across the desk. Van Duzer's pen scratched the papers from time to time while the wall clock ticked off the minutes unnoticed.

When at last the old man looked up from his work, he adjusted his glasses and seemed to see the telegram for the first time. With an age-spotted hand he opened the thing and read the short message, peering over the tops of his spectacles. His eyes tightened as he did and a grim ghost of a smile touched his mouth. HAVE ARRIVED, it said. EVENTS SET IN MOTION STOP ALL GOING AS PLANNED STOP MORE SOON END.

Van Duzer looked through his window up at the fading light. It wouldn't be too late to stop at the club for a late supper. Perhaps he'd see his banker there. He'd need to see more of the man soon, he thought as he let the telegram slip through his fingers and fall to the floor. With a grunt, he bent and retrieved it.

Opening a small drawer in his desk, he rummaged for a box of matches and drawing one out, struck it. The match flared in the grow-ing gloom of the dark-paneled room, casting the old lawyer's face in a ghoulish light as it burned to a steady flame. He set it to the paper and dropped it into an ashtray. Van Duzer sat still as stone and watched as the little fire consumed the message. Going back to his papers, he picked up his pen and scratched out a message of his own.

He'd been lucky to find the man. Van Duzer wasn't a believer in luck though, tending instead toward crediting himself for whatever luck seemed to work in his favor. He believed that a man made his own luck through hard work and shrewd decision. He'd started the search long before Ella Durant walked though his door. Her appearance had sim-ply been a happy coincidence, an added dimension to a scheme he'd been germinating since he'd had his first meeting with J. P.

The Nose had asked him then to look into Durant's dealings upstate, dig through his affairs, and discover his weaknesses. Though Morgan was an acquaintance and perhaps even a friend of William's father, that in no way prevented him from seeking whatever advantage he could. Morgan wasn't one to let friendship interfere with business. He simply sought points of leverage. Once those points were found, pressure would be applied until he got what he wanted and at the lowest possible cost.

So, Van Duzer had done his search and uncovered many an interesting tidbit on William West Durant. In fact, he'd have wagered that he knew as much about the man as he did about himself.

Although Van Duzer had found much of interest, there was one item that caught his attention, a matter of land bought for back taxes, a suit to recover the same, and a family thrown off a place they'd considered theirs since well before the war. He sent a letter and got one in return, a letter hot with hate, even though there'd been years for it to cool. He'd dangled a "business proposition" before the man and an invitation to come to New York to discuss the possibilities in detail.

They had met some weeks ago, before his meeting with Ella. The man was an enterprising fellow, a man of physical action, a man used to work and hardship, a man who would do what was necessary. No genius, but clever enough in his way, clever enough for the work ahead.

Van Duzer didn't want to know how he was going to accomplish their goals, only that he had a clear understanding of their aims. That those aims would coincide once Morgan's deal was done was made very clear. There would be reward far beyond what he and his family had lost. He simply had to apply leverage. How he did that would be of his own choosing. The man had ample motivation, he was sure of that, ample opportunity as well. All Van Duzer asked was to be kept generally informed. Specifics were forbidden. Ignorance would be Van Duzer's best defense.

When Miss Durant had walked into his office, his man was listening in the adjoining room; but it hadn't been that meeting that set him in motion. The next morning's paper had done that; the front page story and the name Tupper.

Eleven

The Edison incandescent electric light plant installed here was started by me June 16th 1882, and has run without interruption every evening since. The lamp which I placed in the elevator car, July 12th, has been lighted every night since successfully. The plant has given complete satisfaction to Mr. Durant, and every one who sees the light is delighted with it.

—G. W. WATERS

Van Duzer's "enterprising fellow" had already settled in for the night when, in another part of the hotel, Rebecca got her second wind. Though it was quite late, she laughed and giggled as she played with Mike in their room. Tom and Mary, who were now in bed, listened to the racket as they read their books, a regular evening ritual. Mary looked at the clock on the wall and shook her head. "You've got to put your foot down, Tommy. That little girl can get away with anything as far as you're concerned."

Tom let out a sigh. He didn't care about 'Becca staying up late and begrudged the interruption of his reading. It was Grant's memoir. The general had been an entirely underestimated man as far as Tom was concerned. "Oh, let her romp. She'll tire out soon enough. Besides it sounds like Mike's just as up as she is."

Mary *humphed,* but shrugged a shoulder. "I don't know what you did with that boy today, but I haven't seen him in that good a mood in months."

Tom grinned. "I told you. It's the father-son fishing ritual. Women aren't supposed to know."

Mary smiled.

"Besides, if I told you I'd be forced to take drastic measures," he said with a mock ominous tone.

"It's part of the code," he said, a sly grin stealing across his lips. "I'd have to eat you to death!"

With that he dove under the covers and in one deft swipe pulled her silk pajamas down to her knees. Mary squealed and laughed, slapping at his head under the sheets as Tom made noises like a bear after honey. His head was just where Mary wanted it to be when, with a crash and a whoop, Rebecca burst in. Bounding across the room, she jumped on the bed and onto Tom's back.

"What are you doing under there, Daddy? You're scaring Mommy!"

Mike, who was just coming through the door, saw Tom as he poked his face out from under the covers.

"Mikey! Mikey! Daddy's scaring Mommy!" Rebecca shrieked. "Help, help." She pushed and pounded at Tom. Playing at beating off his attack. Mike stopped dead. His cheeks turned red and he feigned a cough, but Tom could see Mike grinning.

"You get that bad Daddy, 'Becca!" Mary urged. "He really does scare me sometimes," she said, laughing. Tom just groaned and hid his head under a pillow.

After a minute Rebecca got tired of bouncing on Tom's back while he played dead. She jumped off the bed and bounded to the light switch. She was fascinated with the electric lights. The idea that she could control the magic glass orbs in the ceiling was irresistible.

She was far too young to light the gas lamps at home, but here all she need do was flick a little switch to plunge the room into darkness or bathe it in light. Her small hand grasped the switch and twisted. The light disappeared. The faintly glowing filaments in the bulbs faded fast behind. Another flick and the bulbs burned bright as little suns. Flick, again the room went black. Rebecca laughed each time. They all did.

It was funny and Rebecca's laugh was infectious. Aside from Tom, none of them had ever seen an electric light indoors before, though there were more and more replacing the gas lamps on the streets of New York City. To actually control the bulbs with a little switch from across the room was amazing, even for Tom and Mary.

Rebecca didn't seem to tire of it, not even when Mary, then Tom, and finally Mike stopped laughing at her antics. The bulbs continued to burn and die, burn and die.

"That's enough now, 'Becca," Mary said. Rebecca continued as if she hadn't heard her mother.

"Make her stop, Tommy," Mary said, elbowing him into doing something. Mary had started to worry. Electricity could be dangerous, so she'd heard. She wasn't sure how, only that with each flick of the switch she became more apprehensive.

"Tommy! Tell her to stop. That's enough, 'Becca!" she said with a note in her voice that got Tom's attention. The lights went out.

"'Becca!" Tom said in his best stern voice. "Stop it now, before I—"

The lights went on, but as they did a blue flash jumped from the switch. Rebecca shrieked. A bulb in the ceiling exploded in a shower of sparks and glass. The room was plunged into darkness.

Lettie had waited far longer than she should have. She sat in the moonlight, her feet dangling from the dock. She'd stopped swinging those feet a half hour before. They just hung now, as limp as her spirits. She hadn't noticed the light going on and off in their room. She only knew that he should have been here an hour ago, just as he had last night. He should have come to her in the crisp moonlight, striding down the lawn and into her arms, at least that's how she'd pictured it.

Lettie wanted more. Mike had promised last night to sneak out to her, once his sister and parents were asleep, and he had. They'd sat in the piazza then, rocking together in the cool of the night, laughing and telling each other the things they liked to hear. Lettie had found herself telling him things she had never intended to tell. There was risk in it, she knew.

Still, it felt right to tell him things when he had told her so much. She had believed his tales of the city and his adventures with his gang. They were true, she was sure, and they seemed deliciously dangerous and daring. She'd believed him, too, when he told her he had no girl to call his own. She moved her rocker closer then.

Now it seemed a lie. He was not here as he'd promised, and what they'd done last night had turned from a glow to a dull ache in the pit of her stomach. Even though he'd told her it might be late, since he was going to dine with the bigwigs, he was much more than late. She felt a fool, a feeling she didn't care for. It had never been she who was left waiting. It had always been the over-eager boys, the river drivers, the lumberjacks or occasional tourists. She was the one waiting now, and for the first time she knew what a miserable thing it was.

She kicked a foot at the smooth, black water. There were a series of small answering splashes as startled frogs dove out of sight. Mike was no frog, she told herself as she listened to the splashes fade. He kissed her and she kissed him back, and he had appeared a prince under the Adirondack moon.

Kissing wasn't all they'd done. She thought about that, alone with her feet swinging free. Remembering, she flushed and ached in turns. Though she'd sometimes done more with other boys, this one was the sweetest and the most painful. They'd left the piazza after a while and walked down to the lake, far from the halo cast by the hotel. There, under a small grove of ghostly white birch, they had kissed and lain on the grass. He had surprised her. He was no fumbling novice. Mike knew what to do.

Lettie offered only token resistance, her best imitation of ladylike hesitation. He had seen through that. He had such wonderful hands. Breathless, all she'd managed to do was to rub him through his pants. He'd demanded no more, goddamn him!

Lettie ached all day for the evening to come. She was supposed to be the one making *him* ache. After this night it would be him wanting more and she who would control when and how he got it. She knew how it ought to work.

In her day-long daydream, as she changed sheets and swept carpets, she imagined him anxious and earnest, coming to her on the dock, sweeping her to their little bower. She'd do things, the naughty French things she knew men loved. She'd leave *him* breathless, straining.

Lettie had planned like that all day long, but she'd never planned on his not coming. A short time later Lettie walked up the sloping lawn toward the glow of the hotel. Her heart felt as black as the night, her spirits lower than the bottom of the lake. He was going to pay. No matter what happened when she saw him again, she promised herself that she'd make him pay.

Within twelve hours, Lettie Burman's heart betrayed her head. It hadn't been his fault, she found out in the morning. All the help was talking about the little girl and the accident with the electric lights. Right after breakfast Mike found her as she was changing sheets on the third floor. He'd had to search, she knew. And though she was still disappointed he hadn't come to her the night before and wanted to make him pay at least a little, she knew as soon as she saw him standing in the guest room doorway that she couldn't do any such thing.

"I wanted so much to come last night, Lettie, but my little sister . . . ," he started to say, the words tumbling out in his hurry to explain. The worry in his eyes, the sweet regret on his tongue was all she needed. Any notion of being standoffish melted away.

"I heard," she said. "How is she? The poor little girl must have been scared half to death."

"You don't know the half of it. Scared hell out of all of us, 'specially my folks. Thought my mom was going to take a fit right then and there," he said, coming close as Lettie held a pillowcase absently in one hand.

She couldn't recall exactly what else he said, only that his sister was going to be fine. All conversation ended as she let the pillowcase slip to the floor. Lettie put her arms around his neck. She pulled his hard body against hers. She hadn't wanted to appear so bold, but couldn't quite seem to control it. Mike didn't object, especially once it was clear that explanations were unnecessary. All the tension went right out of him.

A different kind of tension took over. Lettie felt it hardening against her middle. She pushed him away after a few delicious moments. The disappointment in his eyes was so sweet she wanted to close the door and take him right there on the cool, fresh sheets. Instead she whispered.

"Meet me at one. We'll go somewhere," she said in a way that made "somewhere" seem a very delightful place to go. "We'll have a little picnic," she added with a sweet smile that put the lie to her inviting whisper.

They met out of sight of the hotel, away from curious eyes, or so she thought. And now she was here on the blanket she'd brought, staring up through the green temple of the pines on the little peninsula on Eagle Lake, wishing Mike would do what he'd done before.

But he was tentative now, maybe because she'd left a little too much doubt about what they'd be doing. He was gentle and loving, kissing her like a schoolboy and pressing himself against her on their piney mattress. It was achingly romantic she knew, and she should be enjoying his gentle coaxings with ladylike sighs, but she was no lady.

She giggled at the thought, a sign Mike took for encouragement. In an instant she rolled him aside and was unbuttoning his pants, popping one in her haste.

"You just lay back," she told him with a hand on his chest, as it seemed he was about to voice some silly objection. It was his turn to groan as her hands pulled and stroked. Mike forgot any thoughts of objecting as Lettie did the things she told herself she wouldn't do.

Twelve

*In the woods, the mask that society compels one to wear is cast aside,
and the restraints which the thousand eyes and reckless tongues about him
fasten on the heart, are thrown off, and the soul rejoices
in its liberty and again becomes a child in action.*

—JOEL T. HEADLEY

It was the morning of the day before when Tupper found his way to Camp Pine Knot. He needed work, and from what he'd heard Durant was always on the lookout for good men.

"I come down from Saranac looking for work," Tupper told them. "Can lay stone, do most any kind of carpentry. You got that kind of work, I hear."

William West Durant had looked Tupper over as his foreman talked to him. Durant's well-cut suit of gray wool in a light blue windowpane plaid set the man apart from everyone else at Pine Knot. The clothes were fine, but it wasn't the suit that truly set the man apart. He had the look of a *Royaneh*, a chief. He stood above the rest, watching with knife eyes the goings-on below him. Durant didn't need the ceremonial antlers of a chief, he simply clasped his hands behind his back and looked down his nose. Tupper felt weighed and judged at a glance.

He'd heard about Durant of course, though he'd never seen the man. Everyone in the Adirondacks had heard of Durant. Even the rocks and the trees knew his name. It was a name that had come to him back in the Black Maria as it rumbled over the New York cobbles tones. That seemed ages ago, as if his troubles had occurred in another life or to someone else entirely. He'd known then that if he managed to get out of that police wagon it was here he'd come.

He knew he'd need money, enough to disappear if he had to, or start a new life if he didn't. He doubted the New York City cops could ever track him to this place, but if they somehow managed it, he'd need to be prepared.

"You got tools? We don't hire no carpenters without tools," the foreman said, his skepticism building like a logjam.

"Got stolen," Tupper lied.

The foreman hooked officious fingers behind his suspenders. "You're Injun, right?" he said, rather than asked, looking at Tupper hard. "Didn't sell 'em for whiskey, did ya? Got no use fer drunks on this job."

Tupper stiffened. For a fleeting instant he imagined the man with his new knife protruding from his chest. He pictured the eyes, the spasms in the limbs, and the spongy feel of the lungs as he wiggled the blade. The vision passed and, despite being called a liar and a drunk, he answered in a calm, low voice. "I don't drink."

"Even so, ah—what was yer name agin, Littletree was it?" the foreman asked. "Whatever. Even so, I don't figure we got work fer a carpenter with no—"

"You'll hire this man, Eugene," Durant said behind Tupper in a voice as certain as ice in winter. "I judge him a solid fellow," he said. His tone warned against debate. The foreman hesitated before answering, as if he hadn't really understood. "I guess we got use for him on the road, sir," he finally said with a shrug.

"Good man. Get this fellow to work immediately," Durant said as he turned toward the lake. He said nothing more, just walked away with his hands behind his back.

After a growled warning from the foreman about making sure he pulled his weight, he was shown around Pine Knot by another worker. It wasn't out of courtesy, but so he'd know where everything was. The compound sprawled over an untold number of acres, with twenty-seven buildings of various types scattered about.

There was the main lodge and a number of cottages of varying sizes, mainly used by guests of the Durants, a dining hall, a boathouse, a laundry, a five-stall horse barn, two potato cellars, one ice house, and a variety of other structures, including a dog kennel and a dressing room for bathers. The more Tupper saw of it the more he was amazed.

The scale of the place was impressive enough. But it wasn't the size alone, because, individually none of the buildings, not even the main lodge, was all that big. It wasn't their number either, Tupper realized— though he'd lost count of the buildings long before they were through—it was the design of the camp, the way the buildings blended into the trees so that only a few could be seen at any time.

It was the way the natural materials were combined. Stone and bark, logs and twigs all were made to work together, as if these man-made buildings had somehow sprouted from the soil. Tupper felt a comfort here that he had felt nowhere else since he left home years before.

He'd seen the great hotels of New York, had glimpsed the grand parlors of Fifth Avenue through parted curtains. For all their opulence, their crushed velour and fancy brocades, their polished brass and glowing mahogany, none of them spoke to him of home like Pine Knot. This was something new to Tupper, a vision of harmony with nature as different from a hotel like the Prospect House as ice is from water.

Durant's love for the woods showed in every detail of Pine Knot. He had made a conscious effort not to hold the wilderness at bay, but to welcome it home. The variations and textures of the forest were repeated in the stonework, in the ways the logs were joined and fitted, or made to form natural decorations in porch railings or in the eves of the roofs. Most of the buildings still wore bark on the outside, the better to fit with their surroundings.

Inside they were polished, carved, shellacked, and refined. But even inside, natural materials prevailed, with chandeliers of intertwined antlers, walls covered in birch bark, and furnishings of silver birch, varnished to a mellow luster. A warmth was in them that Tupper had felt nowhere else. But it was all illusion, a sophisticated and expensive ruse.

"This is all for one man?" Tupper asked.

"Guess as it is," his guide answered. "Mister Durant and his wife. They got the cousins o' course. They come to visit some. His cousin Fred what owns the Prospect House, I mean. An' there's always guests, lots of guests. Hardly a week goes by they ain't got folks visiting."

Tupper frowned as if he didn't understand, or couldn't grasp what one man could possibly need all this for. Seeing Tupper's look, the fellow continued.

"Mister Durant, he's a dreamer," he said, as if that summed the whole thing up. "Loves these woods. Wants people to love it like he does. Most times, he's plannin' some new thing or other, steamboats or hunting lodges or camps for the likes of some millionaire."

Tupper gave a low whistle, wondering at the riches a man like Durant had to command. There was money to be made from a man like this. Maybe he could stay a while. Some of that money would be sure to find its way to him.

The barn and the buildings that housed the guides and the rest of the staff were ordinary, much like any other farm buildings. Rustic sophistry was not to be wasted on the help. It was a distinction not lost on Tupper when he was assigned a bunk in a bare room that housed five other men. It would be many hours later before he could fully appreciate that hard, narrow bunk. Once his tour was over, he spent the rest of the day with shovel and pick and ax, carving a road through the forest.

In the morning the foreman told him he'd be going to Blue to pick up supplies after breakfast. Tupper figured the man just didn't want him around. Maybe he hoped that if he humiliated him enough he'd force him to quit. Tupper tried not to dwell on it and ate his breakfast with the rest of the men in silence.

A short time later he hitched a team to a handsome new wagon and set out for Blue, some fifteen miles away. He rode alone down the hard-packed dirt road, in no rush, for he knew the round trip would take most of the day. To be in the forest again, breathing fresh air and sweating under the sun like a real man ought to was like a tonic. He wondered why he'd ever left to try his luck in the city. It had been the lure of money.

Now that he was back, money seemed like a damned stupid reason to subject himself to city life. He liked money well enough. But somehow out here it just didn't seem as important. The blackness that had gripped him was fading. It had been part of the city, part of his loathing of the place. His sleep had been dreamless for the last two nights. A faint hope was beginning to take its place and he felt the foul grip of the city lessen. It would be some time yet before it would pass entirely.

He'd have to have time to feel secure from the police, time to become comfortable again with where he was and what he was about; time to heal. He hoped his new boss the foreman wouldn't turn everything bad.

It was late morning, judging from the sun, when Tupper neared Blue. The dirt road was like a snaking canyon, hemmed in by high green walls on either side. Jim had seen deer, red-tailed hawks, ravens, and even an elusive fisher that morning. It had made him glad to see those things. He passed only two other wagons on the road in the four hours since he'd left Pine Knot. He had exchanged short greetings with the other drivers and even a few words with one man who seemed inclined to chat. Neither shunned him or made any comment about his being Indian.

By the time the road took him close by the back of the Duryea camp he was getting hungry. He was told he could get something to eat at the Prospect House if he went around back and asked at the kitchen. Jim figured he'd wait on that till he got his freight settled. The things he was supposed to fetch were at the Prospect House, consisting of a number of crates and an assortment of individual items. He drove for the barn, pulling up in the yard in front of a large wooden, tin-lined trough. The horse was thirsty, as he'd suspected, and his nose was in the water before Tupper set the brake.

A check of the barn yielded nobody but a stableboy, who professed not to know "a damn thing about any damn crates," and suggested Jim go, "'quire by the front desk fer the man-ger." Tupper ambled off, but instead of cutting through the hotel he decided to walk around to the front.

He'd rarely seen its equal, although he'd heard that down south in Lake George, and of course in Saratoga, there were grand hotels that were every bit as big. He'd seen the hotels of New York. They were in another league altogether. Still, the Prospect House, perched as it was on the edge of Blue, with nothing but forest for half a day's ride in any direction was a very impressive sight.

Tupper strolled around it, finding he had to step back from the place to keep it from overflowing his vision. As he turned the corner near the piazza on the east wing of the hotel he heard

"Well, goddamn! If it ain't Jim Tupper!"

Tupper froze and became instantly aware of the knife at his waist. He wished he had the bayonet and wondered how in hell he could have been so foolish as to lose it.

"Jim. It's you, ain't it?"

Tupper looked about but couldn't see who was calling to him, though the voice was familiar. He flexed his knees and came up on the balls of his feet. His eyes darted and his hands knotted.

"Up here, ye darned fool!" the voice called again. Perched on the railing of the piazza was Exeter Owens.

"Hey, Ex!" Tupper called with a wave of his hand that he hoped looked genuine. Inside his gut was a seething icy knot of worms, tumbling and twisting. The last time he'd seen Ex was in New York.

It had been in Madison Square Park. Jim had gone there to eat his lunch away from the construction site. The park was the only place nearby where a man could get some grass under his feet. He'd get away from the steel and stone and dirt of the building site and for a little while imagine he was up north. The noise from the street, the clatter of hooves and wheels on cobbles, the rumble of streetcars, the clanging of their bells, the twittering of cop's whistles and the constant surf of voices beat against its leafy boundaries.

He'd been sitting in the park, head back against a big oak, a tree that had probably been there a hundred years or more, gazing up at the dirty blue sky, trying to imagine he was somewhere else. Ex had been standing in front of him and he hadn't even noticed. A kick at his foot brought Jim back to earth. Ex greeted him like a long-lost relative, which they sort of were. They were displaced Adirondackers swimming the darkened, downstate waters.

They'd had a long talk, mostly about home and the winters they'd spent logging around Tupper and Saranac lakes. They'd met later that night. He and Ex drank watered ale at a cheap saloon on Tenth Avenue, a place that catered to pimps, sneak thieves, confidence men, and a smattering of the dock trade. It stank. The beer was bad. The smoke was thick and clinging.

But they got drunk and had a fine old time, somehow managing not to get their heads bashed in, a common fate of drunks in that part of town. They had planned to meet two nights later in a place not far from the construction site where Jim worked, but that was the night Jim's troubles started.

"Almost didn't recognize ya 'out yer hair. Get yerself scalped?"

Tupper tried to laugh. "Somethin like that, *honio'o*. A fella in the mirror did it. Told me I had to get shed of my old ways. Start fresh as a new man," Tupper said with a straight face. He had to know, Jim thought. He couldn't have been in New York and not have known. For all he knew, Ex might have shown up just as the cops chased after him.

"Stay there. Be right down," Ex called. "Gotta see ya with no hair."

Tupper waited, wondering what to do. The story of the escape had to have been in all the papers. But Ex never had been a big reader, Jim remembered. Maybe he really hadn't heard about the arrest and escape. Tupper waited, his palms damp with worry.

Exeter Owens ambled up with a broad grin.

"Damn! You look a sight changed, Jim-boy. Almost pass for a white man," he said with a joking slap on Tupper's shoulder. "Or at least a Mexican, anyways."

"Hmph. What the hell you know about Mexicans, you ignorant *Honio'o*? You've never been south of New York City," Tupper said, giving Owens's hand a good natured shake. "Speaking of that, where the hell were you last week. Waited for you at the site but you never showed up. Had to drink alone."

"Got myself de-layed on account of a woman," Ex said with a wink. "Time I got there you musta been long gone."

Tupper played the opportunity as if he was landing a ten-pounder on a five pound line. "Wasn't about to cool my heels overlong for the likes of you," he said with a smile. "Decided to head back home the next day. Had to pack my gear an' get accounts settled, that sort o' thing."

Ex nodded. "Damned if I don't know just what you mean. Took off myself a couple days after. Had my fill o' the city. Don't think I'll ever go back neither. A man can't think nor breathe down there. No place for the likes of us, eh, Jim?"

Tupper agreed and asked Owens if he was working and what his plans were.

"Thought I'd do a bit o' guidin' till fall. Then it's back to the woods for me, I guess."

Tupper shook his head. "Not a hell of a lot else to do in winter, 'cept starve. I was lucky. Got a job over ta Pine Knot, working for Durant. Pay's good. Don't know what the prospects are come winter though," he admitted.

They talked like that for some time, never dwelling on the city nor any troubles left behind. They had such a pleasant chat that Tupper found himself forgetting the city altogether. He told Ex about the job and about Durant and Pine Knot. Twenty minutes passed in that fashion when Jim looked up at the sun and said, "Better get going. Got some things I'm picking up, supplies for the Durants."

"Can't keep the big man waiting," Owens said with a sour tone, like he'd just had a bad piece of salt pork. Tupper, suddenly remembering Owens's old land problems, asked, "You got things settled with Durant, right? Seems I recall it working out."

"Oh yeah," Owens said with a dismissive shrug. "Sure. That was years gone."

From what Tupper knew of Owens and what he'd heard from others, he was not in the habit of forgiving a wrong. He treated grudges like children, feeding them and keeping them warm. Owens was not a man you wanted to cross.

Owens had been a popular man at the logging camps, where hard work and close quarters could make some men edgy. He was a good logger and had done just about every kind of logging job from road monkey to river driver. He was tall and strong and he could hold his liquor like he had no bottom. His long, sandy hair and muttonchop sideburns framed a lean, hard face with deep-set eyes under overhanging brows. The eyes could be piercing, but mostly there was a cold kind of fun in them. A wry grin seemed to always flirt with the corners of his mouth, and he could be generous with those who knew him best.

Still, there were rumors about Ex, things said with little to back them up. There had been speculation about a gambling debt and a logging accident. But accidents happened all the time in lumbering. Blame got cast in directions that sometimes it shouldn't. Tupper knew about that, understood it all too well.

"Guess I'll see you around then, Ex?"

"Yup. Waltz some sports around for a month or so, then into the woods for winter."

They shook and wished each other well, promising to get a beer if the opportunity presented itself, and talking vaguely about lumbering together once the flatlanders had gone back home. Tupper walked up the stairs to the piazza and in the main doors, not giving another thought to New York City. It was nearly three hundred miles away, after all.

It was close to two by the time Jim clucked to his horse and got started back towards Pine Knot. He'd found someone who knew about the freight for Pine Knot, and got lunch at the kitchen. A cook threw together a sandwich, giving him a reasonably cold beer as well. All he'd had to say was that he worked for Mister Durant. No other explanation was necessary. He couldn't make it before five-thirty he figured. He had no schedule to keep, but he didn't want to give that foreman any excuses to fire him.

Exeter Owens leaned against the corner of the Prospect House's two-story outhouse, chewing on a long piece off grass and swatting flies. Though the adjoining bathhouse had hot and cold running water, the outhouse had no water at all. The flies seemed to approve. He watched Tupper drive off.

The road was hot and dusty. Tupper was grateful he remembered to stow his bowler under the seat. The Adirondack sun burned like a match head, unfiltered by the soot of the city. Though it was not nearly as oppressive as the city sun, it seemed hotter on the skin. A trickle of sweat leaked down from under the band-of his hat. He reached up to wipe it away when he saw someone cross the road.

A stinging bead of sweat blurred the vision in one eye, but he was sure of what he'd seen. It had been a man and a woman. The woman was dressed as a maid. They'd been perhaps two hundred yards away, but there was no mistaking what he'd seen. The pair crossed the road in a hurry as if they wanted to avoid being seen. The only reason he'd seen them at all was because he'd just rounded a bend at the crest of a small hill.

Aside from Tupper's wagon there was nothing moving on the road. Jim was curious and marked where the couple had crossed, not far from a gnarled, old maple that stretched a sagging, bony limb out toward the sun. In a couple of minutes he came to the spot and stopped. He peered back over his shoulder and again down the road in front. He stood to get a better view. The road was empty.

"Strange," he mumbled to himself. It was about a mile back to the hotel. "No maids out this way changing sheets," Tupper said to the horse nibbling at the grass in the center of the road. "A curious hand sometimes loses a finger," his grandfather used to say. Tupper grinned as he recalled the old man wagging a finger at him, an image that seemed to come to him at just the right moments, as if his spirit watched over him to appear when needed. The old man had power still, almost as much as he had in life. Still, Tupper's curiosity got the better of him.

Pulling the wagon over, he hitched his horse to a tree. There was the trace of a path leading off the road. It looked to be a deer run. Deer were a lot like humans that way. They had their habitual highways through the forest, trails where hooves had carved a delicate passage. Tupper followed the trail and was rewarded with a footprint no more than ten feet from the road. He stood still, listening for any sound not of the forest. He crouched low to probe the undergrowth with his eyes. He heard nothing, but saw the way they'd gone.

They'd followed the deer run. A leaf, snapped off and laying with its light green belly showing, was as clear a sign as he needed. Tupper followed, moving in silence. He figured if he was cautious perhaps he'd see something. It seemed clear they didn't want to be seen. To see them without being seen would be reward enough, a trophy of sorts. Tupper took care with every step.

The toes went first, planted slowly, feeling for twigs that might snap like firecrackers in the silence of the woods. For all his caution he moved fast enough, going hundreds of feet into the forest in a few minutes. Every few steps he'd stop and listen, hearing nothing but his own breathing.

Eagle Lake lay on this side of the road. He wasn't sure how far it was, but judging from the blue gaps that peeked through the trees it couldn't be much farther. In a few minutes more he was near the shore. The lake shimmered between the trees, sunlight dancing on the restless surface. He knew better than to show himself at the shoreline. His grandfather had taught him that on his first hunt.

"See but do not be seen, Jim. That is the way of the hunter," he'd told him. Tupper stood back, concealed by the trees but able to see much of the lake. A noise caught his ear. He couldn't identify it but moved in its direction, somewhere off to his left. A little peninsula jutted into the lake perhaps a hundred yards that way. It was a pretty spot, crowded with towering white pines. It would be shady and cool there, Tupper thought, a perfect spot for lovers to catch a breeze coming off the lake. A broken branch on a beech seedling confirmed where they had gone. Tupper tracked them like a hound on the scent.

He froze at a flash of movement. Something among the trees caught his eye and he focused on it with a hunter's intensity. Something flashed again. He couldn't make it out, just a blur of color through the underbrush. When it didn't change location, he ventured forward, from tree to tree, making no more noise than the breeze in the pines. Keeping a small stand of young aspen between him and the movement he'd seen, he got quite close. He was about sixty feet away before he stopped.

Tupper crouched like a mountain lion, hands on the ground, legs coiled behind. He could see them through a leafy, green window. It had been her head he'd seen, Tupper realized. Her mane of honey-blonde hair rose and fell, rose and fell in slow motion. He could see the young man's hand, her hair cascading through his fingers like a brassy waterfall. He could almost hear them.

The head moved suddenly, the body shifted. There was a brief glimpse of glistening shaft, then a leg, smothered in a maid's uniform, blocked the view. He could see her back arch and her rounded hips descend. Jim Tupper turned away and crept back the way he'd come, his grandfather's voice stern in his head.

Thirteen

The burned buildings were situated not more than thirty feet from the hotel,
in which there were between 200 and 300 people. But for the heavy rain which was
falling at the time the hotel would also have been consumed. The guests were very
much frightened, and turned out of the house in their night-clothes.

—*NEW YORK AND LAKE GEORGE RIPPLE*

Chowder decided to concentrate on finding out whatever he could about Tupper before looking into the case of the floater with the bayonet hole in his head. Though the two were undoubtedly related, at least in Chowder's mind, Tupper had to take priority. A couple of hours spent interviewing the arresting officers, including the one the prisoners had overpowered, hadn't yielded much, except the fact that he was called Jim Tupper.

Most of the time he'd spent in police custody, he'd been either unconscious or in transit, so nothing of any detail was known about him. His wallet and a large, well-sharpened hunting knife were all the police had found. The wallet contained no clues other than his address in New York.

The cops tossed his room soon after he'd escaped, but again had found little of use. Chowder had canvassed the men he'd worked with at the construction site too. About all he had to show for it was a name, a general description, and the fact that he came from somewhere north, near some lake they'd never heard of.

"I expect he'd be going back there, if you were to ask me," one of the construction workers said. "He didn't talk much, but when he did it was mostly about the woods, hunting, logging, that sort of thing. You want to find him, you'd be wise to look there."

Chowder had spent the rest of that day and most of the morning talking to stevedores, captains, clerks, oystermen, stokers, oilers, and deck crews. He'd spoken with the roundsmen who patrolled the dock area. Not one could recall seeing a man with Indian features and black hair, either long or short. The patrolmen hadn't been any more help than the rest, though they'd been alerted to keep a sharp eye for the wild Indian escapee whose picture had been in all the papers.

It had seemed fruitless. Thousands of men worked along the waterfront. Many of those were transients, in port for a day or two, then gone. At any point in time, thousands more might be temporarily ashore. Sailors of every description were commonplace, and unusual looks or dress drew hardly a passing glance. A man who would stand out on Broadway might attract no more attention than a fly at a butcher's shop on West Street.

Compounding the problem was the lack of any identification on the floater. Chowder knew how hard it was too find a man based on just a general description. In his hours working the docks Chowder had turned up five men who'd gone missing. Three of them matched the approximate height and weight of the victim. All of those were sailors. Chowder had little hope that any were his man.

Knowing sailors, those five were probably off on a binge, rollicking with whores, beaten unconscious in some alley, or in jail. Most likely it was some combination of all of that. Still, he had to check them all. He enlisted the help of each of the roundsmen he contacted, asking them to keep a lookout for both the Indian and any one of the missing men who happened to turn up alive and breathing. He hadn't entertained much hope until he got to the office of the Hudson River Night Line.

"Barry Davis," the clerk said. "Barry Davis. Missing from the Albany night boat two nights ago. Captain reported him missing some time after they docked in Albany. Have the telegram right here." The clerk handed it over to Chowder for him to read. Chowder repeated the dead man's description, but it wasn't any help.

"Don't know the man myself, detective. What I do know is that he was a steward on the boat. Been with us since, ah, let's see . . ." The clerk adjusted his glasses and flipped pages in his record books.

"September of 'eighty-one," he said with a note of satisfaction.

"This Barry Davis, he ever disappear before, you know, go off on a spree for a few days or something?"

The clerk looked indignant, adjusting his glasses so he could peer over them at Chowder. "Detective, this is the Hudson River Line, not some oyster barge. If one of our employees misses days without cause, let me assure you he is summarily dismissed. In fact, I processed his termination just this morning."

Chowder grunted in grim amusement. "Looks like somebody terminated him already. He's on a slab in the morgue."

The clerk paled above his starched collar and became quite helpful, quickly arranging for the chief steward of the boat to identify the body. He also looked up Davis's address for Chowder.

"He was a widower, if I recall. Heard somebody say that once, I believe."

Chowder thanked the man, saying, "That's a blessing in a way." He started to leave, when he turned back to the clerk and asked, "One last thing. If I was going to the north woods, what kind of connections would I have to make in Albany?"

"Chief, I've got a body with a hole in his head, an' the coroner says it was the same weapon, a bayonet bought from Fat Bess, most likely," Chowder said as he tried to read Byrnes's reactions. "Fat Bess told me how she sold it to that Indian, and how he changed his appearance. You remember Bess, the one running the operation on Desbrosses Street?"

"Uh-hum," Byrnes answered, nodding. "Prostitution mostly, petty theft, a little bunco here and there, though she was never very good at it, assault, and now receiving stolen goods, though she's never had a conviction on that as I recall."

"That's her," Chowder said. Byrnes had a near photographic memory for the criminals of the city. It didn't surprise Chowder that he could practically recite her sheet. "Tupper paid her a visit. Did a bit o' cleanin' up. Changed clothes, cut his hair to alter his looks. Pile o' black hair in her bedroom was his."

Though there was no way for Chowder to prove that last bit, the color and length were a good enough match.

"Got a steward from the Albany night boat, the one fished out o' North River two days gone? Identified by his boss. Well, he's got damn near the same kind o' hole in his head a bayonet would make. And last, our escapee, this Tupper fella, was from up north, somewhere near Saranac Lake, or maybe Tupper Lake, by some accounts, wherever the hell that is. A little strange, him bein' named like a lake somewhere."

"Adirondacks," Byrnes mumbled half to himself as if he was thinking of something else. "Big tuberculosis sanitarium up there in Saranac. Famous for its cures. A doctor named Trudeau runs the place. He went up there near dead from it, but was cured by the mountain air, or so he said. Read about it in the *Trib*. Anyway, you think he's gone back?" Byrnes said with a puff of cigar smoke. He almost managed to make it sound as if this was his conclusion, not Chowder's.

"Tell you the truth," Chowder said with a shrug, "wouldn't have a clue without him puttin' holes in people's heads on his way."

Byrnes nodded. He took another puff on his cigar, letting the smoke dribble and drift out of his mouth. "The most vicious criminals are often the least intelligent," he said as he looked out the window on Montague Street. "Of course there are exceptions." He took a deep breath and pointed the smoking cigar at Chowder. "Time to send some telegrams."

"Send one to Tommy while I'm at it? He's near there if I recall, ain't he?"

Byrnes just grunted and appeared to think about it, but finally shrugged and said, "Man's on vacation, Chowder. Find out who the local law is up there and put them on alert, send a description." Byrnes paused for a second, then waved his hand at Chowder, saying, "Hell, you know what to do."

"Guess I do at that, sir," Chowder answered. He'd already sent telegrams to Albany, Saratoga, and Glens Falls.

"But don't bother Tommy with this. Not yet, anyway," Byrnes added while cigar smoke went up in little billows. Smoke signals, Chowder thought as he headed for the door.

. . .

Tom, Mary, and Rebecca spent the day with the Duryeas. Mike hadn't wanted to come. Tom figured it could be because he didn't want to shoot against the Duryea boys again. He guessed that instead Mike would be stealing off with Lettie. He gave it no serious consideration. The fact was that Tom didn't care. If the boy was going to have a summer romance, more power to him. Mary seemed to feel the same way and had not questioned Mike too closely when he wanted to stay behind at the hotel. She didn't say anything about it to Tom. They understood that he needed time to himself.

The day had disappeared in a slow and easy way, in good company, good food, and good conversation. They'd taken a row around the lake in the Duryea guide boat and Tom took a turn at the oars. Rebecca caught her first fish from their dock, dipping a dough-covered hook to the little fish below. It had been a relaxing day, but at its end they were all more tired than they thought they'd be. They all went to bed early, Mike, too, though he claimed he hadn't done much all day.

Tom wasn't sure what woke him. It seemed as though he'd just closed his eyes. In fact, he'd been in the kind of deep sleep he had to practically swim out of. Mary shook him just as he was opening his eyes.

"Tommy! Tommy wake up!"

It was the urgency in Mary's voice that did it more than the shaking.

"Fire!" they heard from somewhere down the hall. "Everybody up. Fire!" There was banging on the doors and pounding feet and shouts starting to come from all over the hotel. Tom and Mary rolled out of bed as someone banged on their door.

"We're up," Tom called as he searched for his pants in the dark. "Mike, 'Becca," he bellowed so loud the pictures on the walls seemed to shake. "Get up and get dressed. *Now!*"

Mike opened the door between their rooms almost before the last words had left Tom's mouth. Rebecca followed, shuffling and rubbing her eyes.

"Get dressed. Get dressed," Mary shouted over the growing din in the hallway. "Hurry!"

Rebecca started to tremble. She stood frozen in the doorway with her hands over her ears.

"You're scaring me," she cried. "You're scaring me. Stop scaring me!" Her foot stomped and she began to sob. Mary rushed to her and in an instant whisked her into the other room.

They were all out of the room and into the hall in a matter of minutes, though it seemed much longer. The wide hallway was crowded with sleepy, confused people. Each and every one of them seemed to have something to say, or shout, or cry, or argue about. The area around the elevator was packed ten deep, the press getting deeper by the second.

"The stairs!" Tom shouted to Mike and Mary over the noise. He plowed through the press holding Rebecca high in his arms while Mike and Mary followed. The stairs were crowded, too, but moving. For the first time Tom heard from a hotel employee where exactly the fire was.

"Barn's burning. We'll need help to form a bucket brigade if you're able."

Tom handed Rebecca to Mary once they were out on the wide lawn at the side of the hotel. It was raining hard, but the barn seemed determined to burn. A huge crowd of guests in their nightclothes stood watching. From there the flames could be plainly seen licking at the inside of the barn. Horses screamed and kicked their stalls. Men were racing in and out trying to save them. One horse, a big, black stallion bolted and galloped past them, its eyes wide and white, sparks flying from its singed tail.

A long line of men was forming, stretching down to the lake. Frederick Durant was shouting directions to his staff and all was in confusion. There was no fire department here, no steam engines, no hoses, and little hope. If the fire got hold in earnest all they could do would be to watch the barn burn and maybe keep it from spreading. Maybe. The building was close to the hotel, only thirty feet away. It wouldn't take much to burn the whole place down.

Buckets appeared. Slowly at first, then quicker as the men got the hang of passing them down the line, the water made its way to the fire. Much was spilled. Tom and Mike beside him were soon soaked from spilled water and rain both. They labored and sweated and swore, a long line of men in the dark, lit by the growing orange glow from the barn. They seemed to make progress at first. But perhaps the fire got into the hay, or the men at the head of the line got tired.

Soon it was plain that they were loosing. First the men at the head of the line were driven from the barn by the heat and flames. They were reduced to running up and throwing water through the doors and windows then dashing back, smoldering. The men on the line worked hard. Pails passed full and empty, full and empty.

The line glowed on one side as the fire grew. Features, carved with effort, were outlined in flickering red and orange. Like stokers on a steam engine they burned before the furnace of the barn, shining in fire and sweat. The Prospect House glowed, too, and some of the men started throwing water on it to keep it from catching.

After a time, long after it was obvious that there was nothing to save, the men slowed their buckets, then stopped. They all stood, guests and workers, some still holding buckets, ladies with their hair in disarray, and frightened children in nightclothes, watching the barn go up.

The flames burst from around the sides of the roof, shooting out almost sideways at first. The crowd *ooh*ed and murmured. The whole roof went up, seeming to almost explode into flame, and the crowd took uncertain steps back. The heat could be felt a hundred yards away. Everything, even the trees across the lake and Blue Mountain, seemed to catch fire in the reflected glow as they shot into the chimney of the night.

The fire roared like a beast. It was an oddly silent crowd that watched. They were helpless, all of them.

In small groups, or one by one, the milling crowd started drifting back to their beds. Eventually the sturdy beams gave way and crashed down. Sparks whirled and spun, flying high into the night.

"They look like little stars," Rebecca said, pointing. Tom noticed that there were men with buckets on the roof, ready to douse any sparks that might take hold. Mary and Rebecca turned away. Tom and Mike followed. There were few left behind except hotel employees and Frederick Durant. Tom noticed him standing alone, his eyes fixed on the flames. Tom thought to go to him, to say something by way of comfort or consolation. He realized, after a brief pause, that he had none of either to offer.

Fourteen

*The wilderness guide deserves special note. He is a specimen of
the genus* Homo *that I have nowhere else seen; and, whatever
he may think, destined soon to pass away forever.*

—GEORGE WASHINGTON SEARS

Van Duzer had always been an early riser. Despite his age and weight, both of which were higher than he liked to admit, he was still a vigorous man. He bustled out his front door that opened on Gramercy Park and turned right toward Park Avenue. He cast an appreciative eye at the elegant private park. Its high iron fence preserved the verdant little spot, keeping out the drunks and riffraff.

Van Duzer appreciated a good fence, especially the iron kind with the little spears on top. He glanced across the park at the new Players Club.

Van Duzer huffed to himself as he thought about it. He always figured that Edwin Booth had overextended himself when he built the tall brownstone mansion years before. He'd been flush then, high on his Shakespearean successes. But Booth's success, at least the financial kind, had been fleeting. His theatre failed, and he'd been forced to go to friends a couple of years before.

He and William Tecumseh Sherman, Samuel Clemens, and many other men of high standing in the city's social and artistic circles, had formed the Players, a club for actors and others involved in the theater and arts. They hired the great Stanford White to alter Booth's mansion, making it more suitable for the club.

Edwin Booth still lived in the place, but now he occupied a single, small apartment on the third floor overlooking the park, where he'd retire after the evening's revels. There were always men ready to toast the great actor.

"Actors," Van Duzer mumbled with a shake of his head.

A while later van Duzer got out of a cab in front of his office building. He could well afford a carriage and driver to take him wherever he needed to go, but he was a frugal old Dutchman, and paying a driver full time when he only needed a ride two or three times a day was an extravagance he could not justify.

Van Duzer was in early, but his law clerks were already there. None of them dared be in later than the old man. They greeted him in polite but muted tones as they scurried about the hallways. They all had plenty to do or made it their business to appear to. Most of the partners weren't in yet he noticed as he walked past their dark, paneled doors. There weren't but a handful of them that seemed to know the value of a full day's work. Still, they billed enough hours. He knew how many. He kept a report on each of them, a list of golden hours. Time was money in the law business. No partner wanted to be on the bottom of that list.

Van Duzer hadn't settled in to his office for more than twenty minutes before a telegram came, much as the last one had, on tentative clerk's feet with hushed announcement.

"Tomorrow's paper," was all it said.

"Humph," Van Duzer grunted as he read it a second time. "Man of few words."

He rather liked that. He burned the telegram like he had the last one, tossing the ash into his wastebasket on top of the latest letter from Ella. She was getting cold feet already, just as he'd thought. He watched as the last of the embers died. Ella was out of her depth, had been all along. Her brother had stolen from her and her lawyer was using her. Van Duzer shook his head. "She'll never see a dime," he muttered.

Everyone slept late the next day. The Prospect House was quiet even at 10 A.M. By the time Tom, Mary, Mike, and Rebecca got down to breakfast the big dining room was only part full. Tom picked up a newspaper in the reading room on the way to breakfast and leafed through it before realizing that it was yesterday's edition. He was used to reading his paper in the morning at home. He put it down with a disappointed shrug, but once they'd ordered breakfast he picked it up again.

There wasn't one article about anything outside of the Adirondacks, as far as he could see. Shoehorned between a column about proposed train service to Warrensburg and a story about a wedding in Glens Falls was an article titled, INDIAN LAKE MAN BURNED IN TERRIBLE ACCIDENT, OVERCOME BY SMOKE HE FALLS INTO FIRE.

"Hmph. This is odd," Tom said over the top of the paper. "Says here, ah . . ." He paused as he skimmed through the first paragraphs, "Says here some fella in Indian Lake, a charcoal burner, fell headfirst into his own fire."

"How horrible!" Mary said.

Tom grunted as he read on. "Found him with his feet sticking out. Damn!"

"Just his feet?" Mike asked, a piece of pancake poised midway between plate and mouth. "I don't even want to think about that." What he did think about was Lettie. Mike hadn't seen her last night. In all the confusion he hadn't given her more than a passing thought, and by the time the fire was out and they were back to their rooms he'd been too exhausted to sneak out and look for her. He thought about her now, though, and there was worry in it.

The empty breakfast dishes were taken away as the family talked about what to do that day. They had planned to climb Blue and, even though they were getting a late start they decided to go ahead with it if they could locate Busher. They found him sitting, back against the wall of the boathouse, talking with another guide. He perked up when he saw them coming.

He got to his feet and brushed the grass from his pants while he exchanged a word with the other guide, a handsome fellow with deep-set eyes. The man was dressed in a well-cut vest with a gold watch chain dangling across his middle and a white shirt with a floppy bow tie. His pants were tucked into high boots that were supple and polished.

Busher greeted the family and asked, "What's your pleasure this fine morning?" looking from one to the other.

"Decided not to go fishing today, Chauncey. Thought we'd climb the mountain instead," Tom said, looking up at Blue. They got into a discussion of how long it would take and the kind of footwear and clothes they'd need.

"Can be chilly on top, so you'd be smart to bring something extra," Chauncey said, adding that he'd arrange a carriage to take them up to the trailhead.

"Save a couple miles," he explained. "Might be easier on the little missy here," he said with a pat on Rebecca's head.

"Oh, darn my manners! This here's Mister Exeter Owens," Chauncey said, turning to the man still leaning against the wall. "He's not so good a guide as me, but that still makes him pretty darn good," he said with a straight face, but with a twinkle in his eye.

"Mornin', sir," Owens said to Tom.

Turning to Mary he tipped the brim of his hat, saying, "A pleasure, ma'am," with a rakish grin. "Climbing Blue, eh?" Owens went on with a nod to Mike and Rebecca. "Pretty day for it," he said, looking up at the puffy clouds.

"Got a feeling we might get some weather. Won't be till this evening, though. Still, I wouldn't tarry on the mountain too long." He elbowed Busher. "And don't let Busher get you lost. I'd hate having to go save him."

They had a good laugh at that before the talk turned to the fire. Both of the guides had aided in the effort to put out the blaze. Busher had run through the barn, opening stalls as he went. Owens had been near the head of the bucket line.

"Damn shame," Owens said. "Don't know how it got started. Nobody seems to know."

"Yeah," Busher said. "Got a fishy smell to it. Hell, I'm thinkin' somebody set 'er. Fixed it so's there'd be no puttin' it out."

Tom raised an eyebrow. He'd had some experience with arson investigations, but he was no expert.

"Fire spread quicker than I'd have thought," he agreed.

"Nobody's said so," Owens said with a nod toward the Prospect House, "but something was wrong about that fire."

Tom didn't comment. He stayed silent waiting for more. Silence was a void that talkers liked to fill.

These two seemed like talkers.

"But what the hell do I know?" Owens added.

"Not too damn much, Ex, you ask me," Chauncey replied.

The climb up Blue was harder than they'd imagined. Though Busher hauled a large packbasket slung from his shoulders with leather straps, he surged ahead. He had to stop and wait often while Rebecca caught up. Mary walked with her, happy for the excuse to go slow. Her ankle-length cotton dress, wide-brimmed hat, and too-tight leather boots made for a hot, painful hike. Her feet were aching long before they reached the top. Busher had warned her about the boots before they started, saying, "Them boots're more for the bowlin' alley than the mountain."

They were the closest thing she had to something sturdy, though, so she didn't have much choice. Mary wasn't a woman to let something like shoes get in the way of what she set her mind to.

About two thirds of the way up, the hike went from a steep walk to a rocky climb. Mike ranged ahead with Busher. He and Chauncey went up from rock to rock, matching each other. Busher wasn't about to let his forty-five pound pack make him give up the lead. At a call from Tom, who hung back with Mary and Rebecca, Busher and Mike halted. They'd gotten so far ahead they could hardly be seen between the trees. Rebecca was complaining and almost in tears.

"I'm thiirrrsty," she moaned. "My feet huuurt!"

Chauncey fished out a canteen of water for her once he'd shrugged off the pack.

"When are we going to get there?" and "I want to go hooome," tumbled out of her between gulps at the canteen. Like stones in her pockets, her complaints dragged at her. As they finally got going again, her little feet shuffled and stumbled. Mike couldn't blame her. It was a hard climb for a little girl. He had no doubt she could do it though. She just didn't know it yet. As if reading his thoughts, Busher said.

"Your sister's got spunk. She'll make it sure enough."

A short while later as Mary and Rebecca started to fall behind again, Mike watched as Tom helped Mary up a particularly rough section, then handed Rebecca up to her. Something about the way Tom did that reminded Mike of his father. I was only six years before that his da had been murdered. Looking at Tom, he realized he could hardly remember his father's face. It was almost as if he could not tell where his real father ended and Tom began. It was as if they had blended over the years, becoming one person.

That person was mostly Tom now. It was only now and again that Mike found his da creeping back to his waking thoughts. Mike saw the way Tom picked Rebecca up, how he steadied her. Though she was their own flesh and blood, Mike knew that Tom and Mary had shown him no less love than they had her. He'd always known that, though there'd been times when it had been hard to remember. It was odd that here, on the side of a mountain, he'd feel it more than he had in years.

As he followed Busher, Mike returned in his mind to the grove of pines by Eagle Lake. He thought of Lettie. Thought was too weak a word. He *felt* her, and as he climbed a warm flood of feelings washed over him, some emotional, but mostly physical. She was an ache between his legs and a longing in his heart. She was the rock he didn't see in front of him as he went sprawling into the dirt. Busher looked over his shoulder, hardly slowing.

"You break anything, boy?" he asked with an amused frown. Busher didn't like getting any of his clients hurt, but most of all he didn't want to lug Mike down the mountain, a thing he'd be obliged to do as the guide. Mike picked himself up, dusting the black Adirondack earth from his pants and hands.

"I'm okay," he said. Lettie and the ache of her was replaced by a brighter pain in his knee. Busher stopped and waited. Rebecca scrambled up behind Mike and he held out a hand to help her over a boulder.

"You made it 'Becca," he said, encouraging her with a pat on the head. "See, it's not so bad, right? Mister Busher says we're almost to the top."

"That's right, little missy. Just a spit and a holler left," Busher said.

"We'll just catch our wind here, then it's straight on to the top." He looked at Rebecca, who was alternately huffing and moaning. "Here, sit right down on that rock and I'll recite a little ditty I know. Ought a get yer mind off this hill while you rest up." Busher straightened up, putting his hands behind his back and throwing his chest out.

"*Once a company of beavers, in their engineering fury,*" he began in a tone he seemed to think appropriate to poetry:

> *Took a notion that their mission was to damn the big Missouri.*
> *Under consecrated leaders they assembled in convention*
> *For the instant prosecution of their notable intention.*
> *They were able hardwood biters, they were noble timber topplers.*
> *They beavered down the willows and felled the heavy poplars.*
> *They laid them on the riffle. They were very, very clever.*
> *They were brilliant, but the river paid them no regard whatever.*"

Rebecca, who had been hanging her head in tired self-pity, started to perk up, a small smile creeping across her lips. Busher didn't stop.

> *When we try to curb the surges of unchanging human nature,*
> *Or quench a conflagration with an act of legislature,*
> *Or stem a revolution by the words of quiet thinkers,*
> *Or hold religion static with a martingale and blinkers,*
> *Or stop the steady current of continuous creation,*
> *Or cork the effervescence of a rising generation,*
> *Or stop our zealous doctors from inventing new diseases,*
> *Or keep a wife from doing just exactly what she pleases,*
> *We are every bit as crazy, as I'll prove to any jury,*
> *As those enterprising beavers when they dammed the big Missouri.*

Rebecca, who had stopped huffing and moaning altogether, clapped as Busher finished, they all did.

"Say it again, Mister Busher. Say it again. I like the part about the timber topplers," she said. "That was my favorite."

Busher beamed at her, then glanced up at the sky. A cloud had veiled the sun.

"All righty," he said, picking up and shouldering his pack once more, "but we best be on the move now. I'll tell it again on the way."

It was cool at the top of Blue. Busher had been right to tell them to bring extra clothes. Still, it was a beautiful day and nobody complained. The sun was playing hide-and-seek with the clouds by the time they got there. Looking to the west Busher said, "Guess Owens was right. Got some weather comin'."

The clouds that way were a dull gray sea, but they were still many miles off. The world from the top of Blue rolled away on all sides, covered by an unbroken blanket of green. Deep, blue lakes dotted the landscape, reflecting the sun when it raced between the clouds. The mountains marched away in solid ranks into the blue distance until they finally lost all color, looking like the great, gray, humped backs of whales swimming the forest seas.

They ate a picnic lunch sitting on stumps or on the lichen-covered rocks.

"Colvin cleared this out back about ten, twelve years ago," Busher said, "so's he could have a sight line for his surveyin' 'quipment."

"Hell of a job surveying all this," Tom said, standing atop a stump for a better view. "Wouldn't know where to begin."

"Ain't a thing I'd be likely to know neither," Busher said. "Colvin's got that kinda schoolin' though. Still, he needs a guide when he goes inter the woods, even though there's some says he's seen more o' these hills than any man livin'. There's knowin' the woods and then there's *knowin'* the woods, if you take my meaning."

The tide of cloud rolled in as they clambered down the flanks of Blue an hour later. The woods grew damp with a clinging mist that condensed into a gentle drizzle by the time they were down to the final half-mile. No one complained, not even Rebecca. A carriage was waiting for them when they got to the trailhead. They rode back to the Prospect House as the rain began in earnest.

Tom paid Busher on the way back, $2.50 for his day, 75 cents for the carriage, and a $1 tip. He followed Mike, Mary, and Rebecca into the hotel, shaking the water from his hair when he got under the cover of the piazza. He was walking through the lobby when a voice called from the front desk.

"Mister Braddock? Mister Braddock! Sir, may I have a moment of your time?"

Tom pulled up short, turning toward the clerk who'd called to him. The man came out from behind the front desk, walking with a quick, determined step.

"We've been looking for you, sir."

"We?" Tom asked. "Who would *we* be, and what is it I can do for all of you?"

"I'm sorry, Mister Braddock, but it's a matter of some urgency. Will you come with me?" The clerk put a hand on Tom's arm. The grip was insistent.

"Mary," Tom called. When she looked back, Tom said "There's something I need to attend to. I'll be just a minute."

Mary, who was completely played out, just waved, though she did it with a puzzled frown. Tom turned back to the clerk. He looked down at the hand that clung to his bicep, then up at the clerk.

"I'll thank you to let go of my arm," Tom said when the man didn't take the hint.

"Sorry, sir," the clerk said. "If you'll come with me, Doctor Whelen and Mister Durant would like a word." The clerk wouldn't say more. He just led him out the back of the hotel into the rain. They passed the blackened pile that had been the barn. It was clear that work had already begun on clearing the debris. Even in the rain, Tom could smell the burnt wood. He was lead to what appeared to be an icehouse or root cellar, a low roof projected out from the hillside, flanked by thick stone walls. A heavy door was set three feet back into the stone. The clerk hammered on it with a closed fist. The sound seemed to rumble deep within the hillside, hinting at hidden depths.

The door opened on groaning hinges. The light within was bright, and a cold blast of air pebbled Tom's skin.

"Christ!" Tom grumbled, looking around as he passed through the door. "It's as cold as the grave in here." He rubbed his arms, damp from the rain. "What the hell is all this about?" he demanded, his words falling flat, as if frozen by the walls of ice that lined the place.

"Mister Braddock! Come in sir. I'm glad you've come." It was Doctor Whelen. He looked distracted. His eye would not meet Tom's as he shifted from foot to foot.

The only other person in the icehouse was Frederick Durant. He stood in the center of the room. Lanterns set on big blocks of ice lit the place. The ice, stacked to the rafters, glistened under a blanket of hay.

There were blocks of ice separated from the rest, laid out in roughly a rectangular shape in the center of the room. A sheet covered them.

"Tom," Frederick said, seeming to come to himself, "I'm glad you've come."

"Well, now that everyone's glad I've come, do you care to tell me what this is about?" Tom could guess well enough, but guessing was something he was in no mood for.

"I'm sorry, Mister Braddock. It's just that we wanted to keep this quiet. I'm sure you'll appreciate why," the doctor said.

"That, and the fact that you are a captain of police," Frederick added, "and have experience in these matters."

Tom just frowned. He looked past Frederick and the doctor at the sheet-covered blocks of ice.

"Did you know Letitia Burman, Tom?" Frederick asked in a low voice.

"No. Should I?"

"No," Frederick said. "She was a maid here at the hotel."

"She was in the pharmacy when you came in with your son a few days ago," the doctor added. A cold hand passed down Tom's spine and it seemed as if each hair on his body stood straight out. His teeth clenched so hard that his jaws hurt, but he was determined to show nothing, not until he knew more. He nodded toward the sheet. "Is that her?"

They moved to the center of the room, the doctor at the left side of the ice-block pier, Tom and Frederick on the right.

Doctor Whelen pulled back the sheet, not looking at what lay beneath but at Tom. Tom said nothing and showed nothing. There was nothing to ease the horror of what the fire had done.

"We were able to identify her by this ring," the doctor said, holding up a silvery ring with a small stone. "She was discovered missing once we were able to complete a count this morning."

"My God," Tom said, hardly realizing the words had escaped his mouth. He almost said more, almost thanked them for telling him first, letting him break the news to Mike. Tom waited. He knew there had to be more. The doctor and Durant shuffled, rubbing their hands in the cold. Tom hoped it was just the cold, but hope seemed a lifeless thing in that icy tomb.

After an uncomfortable silence, the doctor finally spoke up.

"There's one more thing, Mister Braddock. And I wanted you to see this, get your professional opinion." The doctor pointed at Letitia's head. The hair was gone, burned away. The flesh hung in blackened flakes. The facial muscles were a deep, brittle red. The eyes, nose, lips and ears had all been consumed. Tom couldn't imagine why he needed to look any more than he already had, but he looked where the doctor pointed.

"She was murdered, sir."

Tom saw it just as the doctor spoke, saw the hole in the temple. Bending close to examine the wound, Tom stared at the hole. He could smell Lettie's charred flesh. After a moment, he straightened and looked at the doctor.

"You're jumping to conclusions, Doctor. That could have been caused by any number of objects commonly found in a barn, anything from a pitchfork to a protruding nail. You saw how that barn collapsed. This," he said, pointing to Lettie's head, "doesn't necessarily prove anything."

"That was my reaction as well, Tom," Frederick said, though Tom could see he was holding back.

"But?" Tom asked.

Frederick shrugged. "Once we found the body, and particularly the damage to the skull, we thought the same thing. Checked very carefully near where she was found, very carefully, I assure you."

"And you found nothing," Tom said, finishing the sentence. "Still inconclusive. You realize she could have moved quite some distance, even with a wound like that."

"I'll tell you what we realized," the doctor said, pointing a finger at Tom. "We realized that your son has been seen with this poor girl on more than one occasion. The dear thing had even confided to others of her feelings for him. And from what we've learned, your son was the last person to see her alive. Apparently, they stole off yesterday afternoon. Were you aware of that?"

Tom glared at the doctor. "So, you put two and two together and came up with murder?" Tom said, not answering the question. "Brilliant!" Tom almost added, "you idiot," but managed to keep it down.

"Two young people have a harmless summer romance and that somehow spells murder to you? Where's your motive, doctor?" Tom laughed at him. There was no mirth in it, just glaring eyes and bared teeth. "I don't presume to tell you how to treat patients. I suggest you do the same when it comes to police work. You're wasting my time and insulting my intelligence. Good night!"

Tom turned his back on the doctor and Frederick. His hand was on the icy latch of the door when the doctor added, "Your son was with Letitia Burman yesterday, *Captain*.

"She did not return last night. I don't need to be a detective to know your son must be a suspect! Telegrams have been sent to the authorities. I have friends in New York as well, Mister Braddock, powerful friends in the judiciary and in political circles. If there's anything we should know about your son it would be better if you told us now," the doctor said with a smug scowl. "There may be no motive, as you say, but certainly you must appreciate that this is a circumstance that must be investigated."

"I'm sorry, Tom," Frederick broke in, "but it's something that we must follow through on. I'm sure it will turn out to be, ah—nothing of any—substance. I'm sure," he said with a sideways glance at the doctor. "But surely you, of all people, must see the necessity of pursuing this."

Tom stood looking from one to the other, wondering if they could somehow find out about Mike, discover his involvement in the fire at the warehouse. The fact that there was no official record couldn't make the incident go away entirely, a fact that Tom hadn't thought would ever haunt them until now. He knew he'd have done the same in their shoes, but, as Mike's father, he knew more than they ever could. He knew Mike.

For a brief, sickening instant, though, the incident of six months before flashed before his eyes, the sight of the watchman lying in the hospital, the smoldering warehouse. He dismissed it. That had nothing to do with this.

"We need to talk to your son, Braddock," the doctor added. Perhaps he took Tom's hesitation as a sign of weakness. "We expect your cooperation. If that is not forthcoming, well—I don't have to tell you how that would look."

Tom smiled at the doctor. It was a sarcastic twist of the mouth that said even more than the words that followed. "I don't give a fuck how it looks!" Tom growled. "You will not be speaking with my son!"

"You arrogant bastard!" the doctor roared, his neck flushing red above his stiff collar. He pointed a righteous finger at Tom. "Your son is a bloody murderer and you're protecting him!"

Tom was surprised at the doctor's reaction. Frederick was as well. He put a hand on the doctor's arm.

"I will not be silenced, Mister Durant. I will speak the truth, as God gives me the vision to see it! This blackguard may imagine he can bully his way out of this, but . . ."

The icehouse door slammed behind Tom with a dull thud that echoed into the hillside.

Tom walked back to the hotel. He was drenched within minutes. He took no note of it. He felt nothing, saw nothing but the image of Letitia Burman's charred body. It hung behind his eyes, refusing to be washed away. Tom wrestled with how he was to break the news to Mike. There was no way to make it easy.

He considered the situation. There was no physical evidence at this point linking Mike to the girl's death, but that was little comfort. Tom refused to think of it as a murder. There was no proof, no weapon, no witnesses, no motive. Mike could still be arrested on suspicion though, and held for God knows how long. Tom didn't want to entertain the notion of this ever coming to trial. He hesitated even thinking about it. It was a possibility that could not be ignored. This was not New York City, home to some of the finest detectives in the country. Tom could only imagine what kind of untrained, hick sheriff might show up tomorrow or the day after to take charge of the investigation. Mike could be railroaded. A bit of flamboyant rhetoric, a bucketful of trumped-up circumstantial evidence, tales of a similar crime in New York, a flow of tearful testimony, and Mike could find himself behind bars for a very long time, or worse.

Braddock had seen it before. He'd done it before. He'd railroaded more than he liked to admit. He hardly knew a cop who hadn't in one way or another. Planted evidence, false or misleading testimony, ambitious prosecutors, witnesses who left town or suffered memory loss, Tom had seen or used them all to get convictions. The fact that he reserved those tactics for career criminals had always been his moral shield, his rational armor.

It was a source of pride in the department. If a cop or detective had a chance to put a known criminal behind bars, he took it, the niceties of the law be damned. As the elevator lurched to his floor, he knew the sickening feeling of being on the wrong side of his moral shield. But as his heels hit the carpeted hallway, sounding like a drumbeat marching toward his door, he knew he was not unarmed. There were things that could be done. He was not without resources, not even there.

If Tom had entertained any doubts, they were erased when he broke the news to Mike. Tom and Mary called him into their room, telling Rebecca they needed to see Mike alone. 'Becca knew something was wrong and she closed the door slowly to catch whatever she could of what was going on. Mike had been unnaturally calm at first, or appeared to be. But it was not calm. It was the draining of all sensation, all feeling that made him seem not to have heard what Tom had told him. He sat on the edge of their bed, stunned and staring, going white as the sheets as the reality of Tom's words sank in.

"I'm sorry, Mike. So sorry," Mary said, a soft hug of words, though she did not take him in her arms. It didn't feel right at that moment, not with the way he sat, pale and hard as a tombstone. His eyes were glazed and unblinking. What he was seeing Mary could only guess. It may have been nothing. He hardly seemed to breathe. After an eternity of minutes, he looked at them, focusing his reddening eyes on Tom and Mary.

"I . . ." he started to say in a voice like a dying man "I loved . . ."

Mike jumped up from the bed and ran to the washbasin in the corner. Doubling over, he vomited up everything that was in him, retching, sobbing, and gasping for air. His stomach heaved long after there was no more to lose.

Mike had known death before. His sister and mother had died in a typhoid epidemic when he was nine. His father had been murdered. He, too, had come close to falling under the knife of one of the men who'd killed his dad, a little animal he'd called "the bow tie man."

It had been then when Tom first entered Mike's life; but not even Tom could save his grandfather from consumption. His grandmother had it, too, by then, and though Tom had paid to send her to the sanitarium at Saranac Lake, she had followed her husband into the grave.

But none of the deaths had wrenched him like this. Lettie was his love. They had shared their bodies and it had been more wonderful than anything he'd ever know. To lose her while their flame burned bright was almost more than he could bear or even comprehend. His mouth was full of ashes.

Mary and Tom stood by Mike, their hands on his shoulders. Mary made no effort to wipe the tears away as they coursed down her cheeks. Mike was as close to her own flesh as another woman's son could be. The storm that wracked him battered her as well. Powerless to stop it, unable to make it better as a mother sometimes could, she could only rub his shoulder and share his pain.

At last he straightened and turned to her. She took him in her arms and held him tight.

"Oh, Mom," was all he was able to say.

It was some time before Mike was back in control of himself. As the storm passed, Tom wrestled with himself about telling Mike the rest. He needed to know. He had a right to know. But there were bigger things at stake than that. It was Tom's responsibility to think ahead, to foresee the possible outcomes and pitfalls of an investigation and perhaps a trial. He thought not so much of Mike and his personal pain, but of what the next step should be. Tom looked at the clock.

"How do you feel about getting something to eat?" Tom said, as if this might make Mike feel a little better.

"We can wash up a bit and go down to supper," he added as Mary and Mike looked at him as if he'd lost his mind. "You'll feel better," he said. "You're exhausted from the climb today, and if you go without food you'll weaken yourself, end up coming down with something."

"Tom, how could you . . ." Mary started to say in precisely the tone he'd expected, but Mike put a hand on her arm.

"It's all right, Mom. I don't know what I can hold down, but I think I need something in my stomach," he said without much enthusiasm. Mary just looked from Tom to Mike, shaking her head.

A while later the family went down to the dining salon. The chandeliers glistened. The china sparkled on snowy, crisp linens. Conversation hummed and waiters hovered. Mike walked through the room as if asleep. His red eyes and stooped shoulders drew a concerned frown from the wine steward, a former slave, who wore the large, brass key to the wine cellar on a chain around his neck.

"Your boy feelin' a bit under the weather, Mista Braddock," he asked with a frown. "Not comin' down wit' somethin', is he?"

Tom nodded, serious and slow. "He had some terrible news this evening, just terrible. Thank you for asking, Mister Erskine."

The wine steward looked at Mike as he, Mary, and Rebecca continued to their table. "Damn shame. Anything I can do, you just let me know," Erskine said so no one but Tom could hear. "There isn't much goes on here I don't know about, sir. I hear things, see things," Erskine said, looking at Tom with knowing, dark eyes. "You take care. Take care o' that boy," and in a louder voice that could be heard at the next table, "The Saint-Émilion, Mista Braddock. An excellent choice, sir."

Dinner passed in a bubble of silence. Even Rebecca was quiet. Food was left half-eaten. Their waiter asked more than once if everything was to their liking. He seemed to pay particular attention to Mike.

Even the busboys appeared to be measuring him as they cleared the table.

Tom watched with grim satisfaction. This was a small step, but an important one. Mary, who had come down to dinner with frosty reserve and black eyes, looked at Tom differently by the meal's end. She understood.

As the family left the dining hall, Tom stopped for a moment and had a word with Erskine. They spoke in hushed tones, their backs to the hall. Tom wasn't sure if he could trust the man, but thought he'd take him up on his earlier offer.

A man like Erskine could know more about what went on at the hotel than the Durants did. Tom hoped he could tell him something about Lettie, what the girl was like, what the rest of the help said about her, anything at all really. He hoped, too, to learn about the Durants and the doctor. Tom didn't know at this point what might be valuable, only that information was far too scarce.

As they shuffled back to their rooms some time later, Mary asked, "How do you want to tell him?"

They were a few steps behind Mike and Rebecca, out of earshot.

"No way but straight out," Tom said, the reluctance clear in his voice. "He's got to understand what we're up against."

Once they were behind locked doors, the electric lights casting the room in stark relief, Tom sat Mike down while Mary got Rebecca ready for bed. "Mike," Tom said, looking at the top of his bowed head. "Son, there's something I haven't told you about Miss Burman—Lettie, I mean."

Mike looked up with a dark, quizzical frown. He didn't say anything. He let the silence do the asking. "The doctor, that Whelen fellow from the pharmacy, he thinks there was foul play."

Mike's frown deepened and he shook his head in a slow arc as if letting the words fall into their proper place. "You know what I'm saying? You know what that means?" Tom said, not quite sure if the words had sunk in. Mike looked up, his red eyes looking fierce and defiant.

"It means Lettie was murdered," he said, almost choking on the word. "And—they think *I* did it."

Fifteen

*So then do not be downcast when I tell you that you
all must die. Listen further to what I say. The name of the one
that steals away your breath is* S'hondowĕk´owa.

—ARTHUR C. PARKER,
THE CODE OF HANDSOME LAKE

Chowder Kelly had always done things his way, a habit that had
become only more pronounced after thirty years on the force. Byrnes
may not have wanted Tom to be bothered with telegrams while he was
off smelling pinecones but Byrnes hadn't said a damn thing about the
mail.

Chowder knew Tom as well as Byrnes did. Some things he knew
better, things shared with Tom across a bar or in the basement of the
precinct house. There were always things the chief didn't need to
know or didn't want to know. Byrnes knew the score. Chowder was
sure Tom would want to know more about this one. There hadn't been
a spectacular escape like this in years. There hadn't even been a string
of murders in a year or so.

To catch a man like Tupper, a man the Tammany bosses wanted
badly, would be a huge feather in Tommy's cap. That kind of success
could carry a lot of weight, the kind of weight a man might put to real
use. With rumors of another police corruption commission forming
soon, it would be useful to be seen the hero. Heroes were damnably
hard to prosecute.

He finished writing a note, adding his thoughts to the copy of the
police report he'd already stuck in a large envelope. Tom would want

to know what he guessed as much as what he knew, so he didn't hold back. Sealing it, he got up from his desk, signed out, and headed for the post office. He knew a clerk there, a man who'd been a useful informant over the years. It was amazing how useful a postal clerk could be. In this case, all Chowder needed was to be sure the envelope got to Tommy without a side trip to the bottom of a bin in the bowels of the postal system. With any luck, it might actually get where it was supposed to go in a day or so. As Chowder handed over the envelope to the clerk, who was grateful he hadn't been asked to do more, he couldn't suppress a satisfied smile.

Tom hadn't been sleeping, at least he thought not. He looked over at Mary, who seemed to be asleep. He thought again about checking on Mike. He'd taken Lettie's death hard and the news that he was a suspect harder still. Through the small hours of the morning Tom had resisted the urge. Now he found himself planting his feet on the cool floor and easing out of bed for fear of waking Mary.

Tom padded softly to the connecting door, opening it halfway. He slipped through, his eyes scanning the twin beds in the moonlight. 'Becca's little form lay buried under the sheets with hardly one curly hair visible. She'd been exhausted after their climb and had collapsed into her bed after dinner, despite her curiosity about Mike. Mike's bed was rumpled, the sheets and pillows bunched up, so that in the darkness it almost appeared that he was there. Tom looked again, then crept to the bed and felt the lumpy sheets. Mike was gone.

Tom was in his pants and shoes a moment later, dressing in haste. He wrote a quick note to Mary, who hadn't stirred, then slipped into the dark hallway. The Prospect House was empty, the hallways echoed. The electricity had been turned off as it was every night, and Tom had to feel as much as see his way through the long, deserted corridors. He saw only one person, floating like a ghost in the dark, the meager glow of a candle lighting the way toward the two-story outhouse in the rear.

Tom wasn't seen. He didn't want to be. He searched the hotel, stalking every corridor, every room, even the bowling alley and the pharmacy, which was unlocked, to Tom's surprise. In his heart he knew where Mike had gone, though he prayed he was wrong.

Tom slipped through the kitchen and out toward the black pile that had been the barn. His eyes strained in the moonlight, which almost seemed bright compared to the tomblike interior of the hotel. He stood motionless for a moment, watching. With a sigh, Tom turned toward the place he feared to go.

As he neared the icehouse door he saw a sliver of light at its edge, a razor cut in the blue-black night. Tom drew close and listened. He felt the cold oozing through, and despite the warmth of the night he shivered. A sob, so soft it seemed to come from the ground, broke the silence. Tom didn't know how long he stood sentinel before that icy door. He only knew that it was not in him to disturb Mike's grieving.

It had to run its course, find its natural release. Tom stood monument-still, listening to the breaking of a young heart. He could not stop his own tears from coming. They coursed down his cheeks, mingling with the rain. The two of them cried together, a heavy oaken door between.

At last Tom put his hand on the wrought iron latch, the city cop in him wondering why nothing ever seemed to be locked here. The latch rattled. The sliver of light disappeared.

"Mike, it's me," Tom said in a soft voice as he pulled the door open. There was no sound at first, just a cascade of deathly cold air, scented with candle wax.

"Mike?" Tom said again as he closed the door behind him. "Mike," he said to the inky blackness, "I know you're here."

There was a rustle of hay and then the awkward clasp of strong arms about his shoulders. It startled Tom, and he flinched at first, but Mike held on, his head against Tom's chest. Neither of them spoke, though for Tom there were volumes to say.

Somehow none of the words seemed adequate and they lingered in his throat, slipping about as he struggled to grasp only the right ones. He felt a coward for not saying them, not even in the dark. He didn't know that, for Mike, just his being there was enough.

They separated at last, Tom saying, "I know how—I mean I can imagine how you must feel, but you can't stay here."

Mike didn't answer.

"You took a chance coming," Tom said. "Who knows what the hell people might think if they saw you. You understand? You've got to go back to the room. Go through the bathhouse. If you're seen there, nobody'll think anything of it."

"Okay," Mike said in a whisper.

Tom patted him on the shoulder. "I'll be back in a few minutes. I need to check a couple of things." The door closed behind Mike with a dull thud and Tom made sure it was pulled tight before he struck a match. Turning to find Mike's candle, he saw Lettie Burman.

"Jesus!" he muttered.

Her fire-ravaged form lay half uncovered on her pier of ice. He thought of Mike, alone with her. He shuddered so hard he had to try twice to light the candle.

"Mike. Mike," he sighed, shaking his head as if to erase the image from his mind. This was the way of madness. He wondered how much damage the boy had done to himself coming here.

As for Tom, he'd seen death before. He was as used to it as a man could be, as if a protective callous had grown around his mind. He needed that defense now. He looked at Lettie, trying to picture her in life, trying to humanize the grizzled form she'd assumed.

"Lettie?" he said, holding the candle close so the shadows moved in her empty sockets. "Lettie, I'm Tom Braddock, Mike's dad." The only sound was the shuffling of Tom's nervous feet in the hay. "He needs your help," Tom said, as if she might hear and come to his aid.

"I'm thinking maybe you can do that," he added. The candle flickered and the corpse seemed to grin in the shadows. "If you don't mind, girl, I'll just have a look at a thing or two," he said with a hand on her shoulder. "I promise not to hurt you," Tom said as he began his examination.

The first gray hint of dawn had begun to light the eastern sky as Tom climbed back into bed. He took the untouched note off the pillow, grateful that Mary had slept through the night. Though he'd washed up before coming back to the room, Tom still felt unclean. Lettie's body had told him two things. He couldn't know yet whether they might prove significant. He'd need to know more before he could make those kind of conclusions. He had guesses, though, and even more questions. He lay awake as the new day crept through the windows. Theories and possibilities banged about inside his head like rocks in a rolling can. Two things he decided: He'd need a microscope and he'd need to talk to Mike.

Chowder couldn't figure what the hell Braddock would want with a microscope. He looked at the telegram once more as if expecting more information to magically appear. A low hum rumbled in the back of Chowder's throat. The damn telegram had been on his desk when he got back from court in the afternoon. For a moment he imagined that Tom had already gotten the envelope he'd sent. He realized as he'd read it that that wasn't possible. It would be tomorrow at best till Tom got that. Tom's message mentioned nothing about Tupper, the escaped murderer. Instead it asked that Chowder send him a microscope as soon as one could be located, or, failing that, the most powerful magnifying glass he could find.

"Not like Tommy at all," Chowder mused as he sat on the corner of his desk. He decided to send Tom a magnifying glass that afternoon. He knew he could borrow one from one of the detectives who specialized in forgeries. A microscope might be a bit more difficult, but that, too, could be had in another day or so. There wasn't much that Chowder Kelly didn't know how to lay hands on in New York, one way or another.

He set to work rounding up a magnifying glass along with a box to ship it in, all the while wondering at the request. Tom hadn't taken a sudden interest in science, he was sure. Chowder knew him better than that. This was about a case. It had to be. But it was not about Tupper. Chowder decided it was time to send Braddock a telegram. Tom was onto something, vacation or no, and once he got Chowder's envelope his vacation was likely to get a lot more complicated.

"Better to give Tommy a bit o' warnin'," he mumbled as he went down to the basement telegraph office.

The morning had passed in unnatural calm. It was hot and sunny and the sky was the clearest pale blue Mary had ever seen. After breakfast Tom said to her and Mike, "I've got to take a look at where Mike and Lettie met that day. I want to see it before any sheriffs go tramping about."

"Wouldn't the rain have washed things away," Mary said, "tracks and whatever?"

"Most likely," Tom said, "but I feel like I've got to do something. I'm gonna go crazy just sitting around waiting for some hick cop to show up."

"I'll go with you," Mike said. "You'll never find it otherwise."

They walked out the road a mile or more. They made no secret of what direction they were headed, and no one seemed to pay them any mind. They reached the spot where the old maple stretched across the road and Mike stopped.

"The path's here someplace. It's hard to spot."

"Hold up a second," Tom said, putting a hand on his arm, the first words he'd said since they left the hotel. "Let's take a look at the ground first."

The side of the road was still a little damp from the rain, the grass retaining some moisture. Tom got down on his knees. There wasn't much to learn from the dried-out roadbed, but he hoped that the earth along the edges might still hold some evidence of Mike and Lettie having been there. Tom grunted as he examined the grassy margin. "Wagon been here," he said. "If you look this way you can see the track where it bent the grass."

Mike looked too. "Pretty well washed away," he said.

Tom got up. "Yeah. Couldn't say whether it stopped here or just went off the side of the road a bit, maybe passing another wagon or something. You don't remember seeing a wagon, do you?"

Mike shook his head.

"Might be nothing," Tom said. "This the path?" He pointed to a faint trail that disappeared into the woods.

"Yeah. I think so." Mike squatted down, looking at the ground as Tom had. "See this?" he said. "I think that's me, my footprint I mean. Rain's washed it mostly away. And that's Lettie."

Tom had a hand on Mike's shoulder, looking where he pointed. "Good work," he said. They're faint, but I think you're right. Hold your foot next to that one." Mike did, and it was a clear match. Tom just nodded, but then he looked closer.

"So, who in hell was that?" he said, pointing to a third track, larger and broader than the other two. It was a few feet further on. "See how the grass is bent under the footprint, the way the dirt's washed away at the edges just like yours? I'd say this was made the same day."

"A fisherman or something," Mike said. "We didn't see anybody though, not all afternoon."

Tom just made a low sound, deep in his throat as he stood up. He looked about, staring up and down the road and across at the woods on the other side. He shrugged his shoulders at last and said, "Let's go look at where you two . . ." He let the words trail off as Mike led the way into the forest.

Tom tried to follow the bigger tracks, but it was next to impossible on the forest floor. They went slow, but all they could see was an occasional ghostly depression, while Mike's and Lettie's prints were somewhat clearer in the center of the faint trail. At last the third set of tracks disappeared entirely.

"You sure you didn't see anyone?" Tom asked, looking about on his knees.

"Nope," Mike said again. "Certain," though he scratched his head and shrugged.

Tom got up. "You were over that way, under those big pines?" he asked, guessing by the pretty look of the spot where Mike and Lettie had gone.

"Yeah. It was nice there. Smelled great. You can see all down the lake from there," Mike said.

Tom didn't say anything. He just moved forward toward the stand of pine. They looked it over carefully, going over the ground on their hands and knees.

"I lost a button here," Mike said after a minute. "Looked for it but didn't find it."

"Where from?"

"My pants," Mike said, not looking at Tom.

"Not here," Tom said. "Must've lost it someplace else."

"No. It was here. Lettie, she . . ." Mike stopped, embarrassed.

"Uh-huh. Well, it isn't here now," Tom said, amused at the color in Mike's cheeks. "Mike, do you know why Lettie wasn't wearing any ah, well any underclothes? I noticed it last night when I looked." Tom stopped, not wanting to give Mike too many details of his examination. "There were remnants of her dress still intact but no pantalets, or— anything."

Mike didn't look directly at Tom. He just shrugged and said, "Maybe whoever killed her—maybe he . . ."

"Yeah," Tom said. "That's probably it."

After a while longer they retraced their steps out to the road. Tom took another look at the wagon tracks, going further up and down the road to see if he could tell anything about them.

"Appears as if the wagon pulled off here. I can't be sure, but I think it stopped. The hoofprints are different here than they are back there. Not as kicked up, like the horse was standing still."

"You can tell that from these tracks?" Mike said, his brow knitting into a frown.

"I'm no goddamn Daniel Boone, if that's what you're asking," Tom said with a wry grin, "but I think it's a fair guess." He showed Mike what he meant about the hoofprints, then looked again at the other side of the road. "May as well check over there, too," he said.

They looked at the margin of the road, not finding anything, then plunged into the verge of trees, checking the ground for any prints. "I don't know why we're doing this. I told you we didn't see anybody else," Mike said after a while.

"Well, you're probably right. Who knows, that wagon could have been here hours after you were gone. No way to be sure. One thing I can tell you, though, is if you find a piece of evidence that's out of place you have to check it. Hardest thing about doing an investigation is keeping an open mind. You gotta let the facts lead *you,* not the other way around."

Mike shrugged and looked around in a disinterested way. He started to walk out toward the road when he stopped. "What's this?" he said.

Tom saw him point to a tree and he walked over to get a better look. There, on the trunk of a young, smooth-skinned oak, was a series of small holes, the yellow wood below the bark showing through. Tom put his nose to the marks.

"I can smell the sap. It's fresh," he said. He looked at the ground and could see a number of footprints at the base of the tree and behind a bigger tree a foot or two away. "Somebody was here," he said.

"Doing what?" Mike said, looking around.

Tom stood behind the tree and looked at the road. There was a clear view, though it was plain that anyone behind the tree would have been hard to spot from the road. "Watching. Maybe watching," Tom said.

He took another look at the marks on the tree.

"And killing time. He stuck his knife into this tree. Bored," Tom said to himself. "Tracks say he was here for a while. How long were you and Lettie over there, Mike?"

"Couple hours, I'd guess."

"Couple hours," Tom said, running a hand through his hair. "He's bored. He's hiding. He's sticking his knife into this tree. Maybe the tree's not the only thing he sticks his knife into," Tom said, regretting it as soon as he saw a dark cloud pass across Mike's face.

"Sorry," Tom said.

"But why? None of this makes any sense. You've got what, two men now—following me and Lettie around, looking to kill us—or her, or *what?* Why? Nobody wanted to kill her, and I know nobody wanted to kill me, so what the hell would somebody be following us for? This is all just guessing. This stuff," he waved his hand at the tracks and the trees, "it just happens to be here. Who knows why? But it don't have anything to do with me and Lettie."

Tom shrugged. "Maybe you're right. Maybe there's nothing to this," he said, looking closely at the marks on the tree while he talked, noticing for the first time their slightly triangular shape, "but, in my experience, coincidence is just a cover for the guilty."

Late in the afternoon Frederick Durant knocked on Tom and Mary's door, apologizing for the intrusion.

"I just wanted to inform you that in all likelihood a sheriff won't be able to get here until tomorrow at the earliest," he told them. "It seems our closest was at Lake George, and he's on a fishing trip somewhere up the lake."

"Hmph," Tom grunted with an annoyed shrug.

"I know how hard this is for you both," Durant went on. "But there's no helping it. I'm truly sorry," Frederick added with formal awkwardness.

Tom nodded, saying nothing at first, but finally he said "Doesn't make me like it any better. That doctor of yours is jumping to conclusions. A man gets a thing fixed in his head in such a way he'll only see things that fit with it."

"I understand, Tom," Frederick replied. "I, too, am more than a little concerned with that. I worry about the, um, how shall I put this— the objectivity of local authorities, if you understand me."

"I do," Tom said. "Your doctor may carry a lot of weight up here, and it seems his mind is made up. God knows what kind of sheriff you've got. And judges, let's face it, backwoods judges are always a roll of the dice, from what I hear."

Frederick nodded. "I'm not without influence, Tom. My cousin also has friends we can rely on for fair treatment before the law."

"That's good to know," Mary said with an appreciative but worried smile.

Frederick nodded, turning to go. "Oh, I almost forgot. You have another telegram." He handed it to Tom. "Came in just a little while ago, I understand."

Tom sat by the window a minute later and read the message.

"What is it, Tommy?" Mary asked, watching him closely.

"Message from Chowder. About that prisoner that escaped the day we left. May be coming our way. Says he mailed me all the information he's got on the case and the magnifying glass I asked for."

"What do you mean? Coming to the Adirondacks?"

"Well, the prisoner, he was an Indian called Tupper, and he used to live up here somewhere, according to Chowder. Chowder thinks he's headed north."

Mary looked increasingly concerned as Tom told her this. It seemed to her that he was taking this telegram too seriously. "You're not thinking of going after him, are you? What are you supposed to do, go off chasing this man and leave Mike to fend for himself?" Mary said.

Tom looked at her in surprise. He hadn't thought to act on the telegram. He'd simply thought it interesting. He could understand her reaction, though. It wouldn't be the first time he'd dropped something for the job. Tom shrugged.

"Normally, you'd be right. There's nothing normal about this situation, though. Mike's my first priority. That's all there is, plain and simple," Tom said, laying the telegram aside. "Besides, there isn't enough here," he added with a nod toward the telegram, "to do much of anything about."

Mary sighed. "I'm sorry Tommy," she said. "I'm just—I mean, this whole situation has got me at sixes and sevens." She came over to him and gave him a quick kiss. "Forgive me?"

"Of course," Tom said. "I'm on edge, too. Who wouldn't be?"

Mary nodded. Still, she had a bad feeling about that little sheet of paper, and was curious about something else.

"What was that about a magnifying glass? Have you been in touch with Chowder."

Tom had held off telling Mary about what he'd found. He wanted to take a closer look and find out more before he told her anything that might raise her hopes prematurely. He abandoned that plan now. "Mary, last night I . . ." He hesitated for a moment, uncertain if he should tell her how he'd found Mike in the icehouse. "Well, I suppose you'll find out anyway," he said.

"Find out what?" she said.

Tom walked her out onto their verandah, where they sat and were able to look out over the lake as they talked. He told her everything of the night before, how he'd searched for Mike and how he'd found him, as well as what his examination had turned up. Mary put her hands up to her face as though she could hold back the image that Tom's words had conjured.

"He was in there—alone with the body—*with* her? Dear God. Oh, dear God," she said, almost sobbing the words. Turning red eyes to Tom, she said, "I hardly thought I slept at all last night. I should have been—I should have known, or something."

Tom put a hand on hers. "You were exhausted. The climb, and then this. I don't know why I went to check on him myself. Listen to me. This is nothing to worry yourself over. What's done is done."

Mary took a deep breath and looked out over the lake.

There was laughter on the broad lawn in front of the hotel. A group of girls played at some game or other. Mary wanted to scream at them. She dabbed at her damp face and asked in as calm a voice as she could muster, "What did you find out?"

He told her all there was, the fact that he'd found no pantalets on the body, and of his other discovery, a piece of plaid cloth that was not part of her clothing.

"I've got my theories about that, of course. That's one reason I wanted a magnifying glass. I need to examine her more closely, scrape under her nails, look at the head wound, and give this a closer look, too," he said.

"There's always something, some piece of the attacker that is left behind—blood, a broken fingernail, flesh scraped off by a nail, something. I can learn more about the weapon, too. I've been trying to work it out, fit the pieces together, and at the same time handle how I'm going to use it once I'm sure. I worry about that doctor. If I tell him things too soon, I mean before I know more, he could dismiss it or invent his own theories, even destroy evidence. Anything's possible."

"You found this in her mouth?" Mary said with a queasy turn of her lip.

Tom nodded. "I think she bit it off in the struggle," he said, looking closely at the piece of cloth in his hand. "You have a better theory on how it got in her mouth?"

The sun sank as Tom and Mary talked. The mountain, towering to their right, glowed orange. A steamboat rounded the point, tooting its whistle and setting the white buck charging about his pen.

"It seems ages ago that Mike got bit," Mary said half to herself.

"Strange how things work out," Tom replied.

"If he hadn't been bit, perhaps he'd never have met that girl."

Mary gave a little start. "I hadn't thought about that. It's true," she admitted, looking down at the animal bounding about his enclosure. They sat and watched the white buck, the blue water, and the orange mountain.

The crack and echo of shooting jolted them out of their thoughts.

"Sounds like the Duryea boys are at it again," Tom said. "Those two do more shooting than any ten men I know, me included."

Mary seemed to be only half listening as the shooting echoed across the lake, bouncing off the mountain in answering volleys.

"We have to talk to him, you know," Mary said at last.

Tom sighed. "I know. I've been putting it off. It's been hard enough on him as it is," Tom said.

"In a way, we've been lucky there's been no sheriff close by. He's had some time to mourn without having to deal with, well—whatever."

"Charges," Tom said, finishing her thought in a grim, low voice. "You're right. We had a pretty good talk today. We'll have to go over it all, though, learn whatever we can."

Mary turned away for a second in a gesture Tom had come to know well. "I don't think I should be there, Tom," she said. "I think he'll be more open with you. I mean about the girl and . . ."

"You're right," Tom said. "He's more likely to tell me about the girl," Tom said. "There're things a boy doesn't tell his mother."

Sixteen

Once again, returning to find in nature's bosom,
A healing for our sorrow, a solace for lost years.
We come Oh Mother Nature as wanderers to the homeland,
Oh grant us benediction, Oh give us peace for tears.

—OLIVE GOOLEY

The men had talked of the fire for most of the day before. In a place where things seemed to move as slowly as the seasons, news of a fire was worth at least a day's conversation. Tupper was amazed the news had traveled so fast. Somehow, he'd never thought of the telegraph. It was Durant's connection to the outside world, a convenience he'd insisted on, running wire all the way from North Creek to Blue, and then on to Raquette some fifty miles or more. Jim couldn't begin to imagine how much it must have cost. It was beyond his reckoning.

Tupper hadn't volunteered much to the talk about the fire, though he'd been asked plenty. Everyone knew he'd been there that day and everyone seemed to think he'd have something to say on the matter, even though he'd been back at Pine Knot by the time the blaze was discovered.

"Barn was standin' when I left," he said when anyone asked, which was quite true. He never spoke of the couple he'd watched. It was one part of his trip to the Prospect House he didn't mention.

He'd settled into a comfortable routine the last couple of days, working and bunking with the rest of the men in a tent camp that moved with the new road as they cut it through the forest. Tupper had no idea where it was going, other than the fact that it would probably not get there for as long as a year. He was content with that and looked forward to the feel of cash in his pocket.

The food was plentiful, the work hard enough to keep his mind from his troubles in the city and from *Segoewat'ha*. "The tormentor," his grandfather used to say, "is in all men. Treat him as you would a serpent. Lock the devil in his cage and let him out only in the face of your enemies."

His grandfather had been wise in the ways of *Segoewat'ha*. His grandfather had once met Handsome Lake, the great Seneca prophet and preacher of the *Gai'wiio*, the code by which all true Iroquois lived. Grandfather had been a young buck of barely sixteen summers in 1814 when Handsome Lake came to his village. Though Tupper had never seen the great Handsome Lake in life, he knew much of him and remembered times when he was young, when preachers came to chant the *Gai'wiio* in his little village. Thinking of Handsome Lake and the code he preached was calming for Jim. He was contented remembering the ceremonies, the throwing of tobacco, and the ritual response, *enia'iehuk*.

Tupper's thoughts were interrupted by the foreman who'd ridden his horse close to him while he was rigging a block and tackle to a stump.

"Mister Durant's expecting guests next week an' the lady says they're low on ice," the foreman said. "Told 'em when they built the place they shoulda made that icehouse bigger. In comes the money, out goes the common sense, I always says," the man added with a chuckle. "Seems they always run short come late August, September. Anyways, need you ta go on over ta Blue again, fetch back a wagonload."

Tupper didn't mind. He figured maybe he'd look up Owens and have a beer or two. He enjoyed the solitude of the long ride, and agreed to set out early the next morning with a large wagon specially prepared to keep the ice insulated. As he drifted off to sleep that night, Tupper was content. Work was good. He was settling into a routine, feeling comfortable, secure and farther than ever from the city.

The next morning Tom and Mike had their talk. They'd walked down to the lake and taken one of the guide boats. Tom rowed while

Mike talked. He held nothing back, but Tom was disappointed anyway. There was nothing in what Mike told him about Lettie, no
spurned or jealous lovers, no enemies that Mike knew of, no unwant-
ed advances from supervisors.

Tom had hoped Mike could somehow point to a suspect, but he
and Lettie had not gotten too deeply into the details of their lives.
They'd shared much, but if Lettie had had any dirty secrets she didn't
share them.

The man who murdered Lettie Burman may have known her or not,
may have loved her or not, may have worked with her or not. All that
remained was that Mike had been with her last, had been intimate with
the girl and would have to remain the primary suspect for anyone
investigating the case. Though Tom had doubted at first that Lettie had
been the victim of a murderer, he'd come to see it as the most likely
scenario, after his examination. So, if it was murder and it wasn't Mike
who'd done it, there had to be something pointing to the one who had.
Tom had one clue, but a small piece of charred cloth was not enough.

Later, Tom and Mike trudged back up the slope to the hotel, no
closer to the truth than they were to the sun. They noticed a shay
draped in black parked near the black pile that had been the barn.

"Wonder if that's the sheriff," Tom said with a glance at Mike, "not
that I'm in any hurry to find out."

"I'll have to talk to him sooner or later," Mike said with a shrug.

Tom eyed the two men who stood beside the shay. It was too far to
get a look at their faces, but he somehow doubted they were the law.
"You're right. But the more time we have before that happens, the
better armed we'll be. No rush right now."

Mary and Rebecca were out when they got back. There was a note
just inside their door when Tom opened it. It was written on hotel stationary. Tom read it and frowned.

"What is it?" Mike asked.

"Says to go to the telegraph office. Man by the name of Clark's got
information on that escaped prisoner from New York." Tom looked
around the room. "Good thing your mother isn't here. She doesn't
much care for the idea of me following up on this, but . . ."

A few minutes later Tom walked to the telegraph office in town. It had been set up by William even before the Prospect House was built. It was a modest, one-room affair, but it served its purpose as the only link to the outside world. "You Clark?" Tom asked as he came through the door. The man behind the only desk in the room looked up.

"And you'd be?"

"Braddock. Thomas Braddock. You send me this note?"

Mr. Clark pushed back in his chair, looking at Tom as if measuring him. "Funny thing about this telegraph, Mister Braddock," he began. "This here's an open line. Means I hear all sorts o' chatter. Everything from here to Pine Knot to North Creek," which he pronounced "crik."

"Saw the one you got yest'day. Natural 'nough, I took it down."

"What's that to me?" Tom said.

"Nothin', nothin' a-tall, 'cept my friend over ta Pine Knot, he sees it, too."

"You've got my attention," Tom said with a puzzled grin.

"Glad o' that, sir," Clark grinned back. "Anyhow, I got a clickety-clack this mornin' from Pine Knot sayin' they got a new man workin' there these last few days. Indian fella, goin' by the name o' Littletree."

Tom couldn't help raising an eyebrow. Remembering the description in Chowder's telegram, he said "Black hair, cut short?"

"Not sure on the hair, cap'n," Clark replied.

"Hmph," Tom said. "Got a pad and pencil?" Tom wrote a quick telegram to William Durant. "Get this out to Pine Knot immediately, if you will." Tom took a silver dollar out of his pocket and slapped it down on the desk. "Keep the change, and let me know as soon as you get a reply."

The telegraph key was clicking before the door closed behind him.

Mike went out a few steps before Tom, letting the screen door slam on its squeaking spring. Tom's hand was on the knob when he saw Mike look to his left. He was hit an instant later.

Tom saw only the fist at first, saw it hit Mike on the side of his face. Another followed as Mike reeled back. There was no other sound, no curses, no shout, just a silent attack seen through a screen door.

By the time Tom opened it, Mike was fending off blows and covering up as best he could, staggered by the sudden onslaught.

He backed across the front porch of the telegraph office, his attacker pressing him hard. As Tom rushed out the door, Mike managed to get in one solid blow to the man's middle that stopped him for a split second. Tom grabbed the man's left arm as it dropped. With a tremendous heave, he pivoted away, dragging the attacker back and around, slamming him into the wall. He drew back his fist but did not strike.

The man, probably not much older than Mike, slid to the floor, his hands to his face. He started to sob between moans of pain. He sat there not moving, weeping uncontrollably. Tom and Mike stood over him. Mike rubbed at his face, smearing a trickle of blood off his eyebrow.

"What the hell's wrong with you?"

"You all right?" the telegraph operator said, poking his head out the door.

"I guess," Tom said with a look at Mike. "Who the hell are you, mister?" he said, realizing this was one of the men he'd seen by the shay.

The man looked up, his red eyes fixed on Mike. He pointed and said, "Killed my sister, you sonofabitch! Killed my little Lettie," he sobbed. "I know who you are, you fucking murderer. I swear to God Almighty I will strike you down for it." He tried to get to his feet but Tom put a foot on his thigh, pinning him to the floor. He put a hand out to hold Mike off, as it looked like he wanted to kick the man right through the wall.

"You don't want to get up just yet, son," Tom said. "What's your name?"

"Lester. I'm Lettie's older brother. Get your goddamn foot offa me," he cried, slapping at Tom's shin. Tom crouched down in front of him. "You've got no right to do this, Lester. My Mike, he didn't kill your sister any more than you did."

"Bullshit! Ever-body says it was him!"

"That's not true!" Mike cried out. His face was red and his hands were balled at his sides. "That's a fucking lie!"

Tom held up a hand to silence him. "Listen to me, Lester. Look at me!" he said, catching his eyes and holding them, "We understand how hurt you are. Mike here is hurting, too."

"Now who's lyin'?" Lester spat. "Huh? Who's doing the lyin' now? You're all the same. Goddamn downstaters, use our women an' go home scot-free."

Tom shook his head in exasperation.

"Sonofabitch!" Mike shouted. "I loved her!"

Both Tom and Lester looked at Mike and for a moment nobody said a word. Tom let Lester roll to his feet.

"That don't mean shit, you lyin' bastard. You love her so much, why'd you kill her, huh? Answer me that?"

Mike said nothing.

Lester spat at his feet. Mike stepped toward him, picking up his fists.

"Thought so." Lester scowled at Tom. "You're gonna lose your boy, here mister. How's that feel like?" Lester turned and stalked away. Tom let him go.

Mary and Rebecca were back in the rooms when Tom and Mike returned. "What happened to you?" Mary said when she saw Mike's face.

"Lettie had a brother," Tom told her. "He jumped Mike outside the telegraph office."

Mary got a washcloth and wet it before putting it on Mike's bloodied eyebrow. She let out a deep, exasperated sigh. "Good Lord, when is this going to end? Are you all right, Mike?"

"Yeah, I'm fine. This is nothing," he said, holding the washcloth to his face.

Mary looked at Tom. "Is this nothing?"

Tom just shook his head. There was no answer that would serve.

"And what were you doing at the telegraph office?" Mary added.

Tom looked at Mike and shrugged. "Got a lead on the whereabouts of that escaped murderer. Can't very well ignore it," Tom said in a way that didn't invite argument.

"No, I suppose not," Mary said, though she was clearly not happy with the idea. She changed the subject and said, "Did you tell Mike about the other evidence you found?"

"What other evidence?" Mike asked.

"The evidence other than these," she said, holding out a pair of pantalets for them both to see. Mike went from white to a bright red. "I found them in his drawer," Mary said to Tom. "Mike, there's blood on them!"

"I know. I know," Mike said. He sat on the bed, rocking back and forth. "I didn't do anything. She gave them to me. The blood, it's . . ."

"What?" Tom said. He was so appalled he could hardly speak. He looked from the blood stains to Mike and back again.

"I'd never hurt her. You have to believe that," Mike said with an intensity that made the words burn. Tom looked at Mike, not sure now what to believe.

"She said I should keep them, like to remember, you know? Said she was getting her friend. That's what she called it, getting a monthly visit from her friend. She noticed after we finished and she didn't want to put them back on."

"Jesus, Mike. You know how this looks? You know how goddamn dangerous this is?" Mary said, shaking her head in disbelief. "I can't decide whether you're crazy or just plain stupid."

"Mike, you should have told me right away!" Tom said. He started pacing the room. "That doctor sees this, or the goddamn sheriff, whenever the hell he gets here, and you're a dead man. You think they'll believe she gave them to you? Hell, I'm not sure I believe it myself. Jesus, what were you thinking?"

"I'm sorry, I'm sorry. Okay?" Mike said, putting his hands against his temples as if his head might burst. "I know I should have told you, but at first I was embarrassed, and then I was afraid of what you'd think. I know it was stupid. I know. I know. I know," he said, bouncing off the bed and going to stare out the window.

"Jesus, Mike. How do we trust you now? You just keep tearing us down, son, whether you mean to or not." Mary put a hand on Tom's arm, stopping his pacing.

"Let's just deal with this, Tommy. Mike's telling the truth. You can see that," she said, concerned about where Tom was heading. "It wasn't smart but it was innocent. Look at him, you can see it."

Tom knew she was right, or at least trusted her judgment. He didn't want to believe anything more. He didn't even want to entertain the idea. Mike was no murderer. He was sure of that.

"We'll make this go away," he said at last. "That's it. We've never seen it and it never existed."

"I suppose you ought to know the rest now, the other evidence I found," Tom said after a long pause. He had been dreading having to get into this with Mike. "You remember I stayed to examine the body?" he said with an almost lecturing slowness. "Well I found something in her mouth, Mike—a bit of cloth."

"You looked in her mouth?" Mike said with a grimace.

"Whose mouth?" Rebecca asked from her room, where she'd been busy listening.

Mary, looking flustered, strode to their connecting door and closed it, saying. "You mind your business, Miss Nosy-pants."

"In her . . ." Mike couldn't continue.

The color drained from his face. His eyes went blank in his ashen face, seeing Tom examining Lettie's corpse. He'd known that Tom would look at Lettie, but somehow the image of him rummaging about in her mouth, and everywhere else, left him weak and sickened. Mike wandered over to the bed and let his knees go slack. He sat with a small bounce, his back to them, framed by their open window, the lake, and the mountains.

Tom had been afraid of Mike's reaction. It was why he had been reluctant to speak of what he'd found unless he had to.

"I'm sorry, Mike but it had to be done," Tom said in a soft voice. "I wasn't about to rely on that doctor."

Mike was shaking his head, but he took a deep breath and said "What about this piece of cloth?" His voice was strained and it was only with a visible effort that he managed to get that much out.

Tom started to explain what his theory was, but he didn't get very far. A knock on their door interrupted him.

"Mail, sir," a clerk said when he opened the door, handing him a large envelope. "I was told you'd want to see any mail immediately."

Tom tipped him a quarter and was ripping at the envelope before the door was closed. He looked at the copied forms, the information from Fat Bess, and the coroner's report on the body of the steward from the Albany night boat.

"Good God!" he growled.

"What?" Mary said. "What is it?"

Mike swiveled about to look at them. Tom went over the information again and scanned Chowder's note while Mike and Mary waited, frozen.

"The same man! Damn it all to hell. It's the same man!" Tom shouted, slapping the wad of forms against his thigh. It cracked like a bullet. "I have to go examine Lettie's body again. I have to see the head wound," Tom said. "Damn, I wish I had that magnifying glass!"

Seventeen

The Eagle Society's ceremony is regarded as most sacred, in this respect next to the Great Feather Dance, O'stowä'gowa. It is believed that the society holds in its songs the most potent charms known.

—ARTHUR C. PARKER,
THE CODE OF HANDSOME LAKE

Tupper was confused by his reception at the Prospect House kitchen.

"Can't give you no ice! For the last time, I don't care if it *is* for Mister Durant. I have been instructed to use no more ice than I have to for our guests. Period. You'll have to try Merwin's or the Blue Mountain House."

Tupper didn't care much where he got the ice, just that he got it, and plenty of it. Coming back empty would likely get him fired. He got back on the wagon, clucked to the team, and was off toward the Blue Mountain House on the other side of town. The Blue Mountain House was smaller and decidedly more rustic than the Prospect, more a collection of added-on buildings in a variety of styles, from log cabin to Victorian.

They catered to a slightly less well heeled crowd who liked to feel as though they were enjoying the simple pleasures of the outdoors, unadorned by the flubdub of the grand hotel across the lake. Tupper got as much ice as the manager thought he could spare. The guarantee of compensation by William West Durant opened the icehouse door quicker than "open sesame."

Still, Tupper's wagon wasn't full. He drove on up the steep ridge at the foot of the mountain to Merwin's. It was the last place he could hope to find ice in any quantity. Merwin's was much like the Blue Mountain House, except that it had a spectacular view of the lake. Perched hundreds of feet up the foot of the mountain, it was a favorite of those who preferred hunting and hiking over the diversions of the lake. Tupper inquired in the main office, a small log building that had been the original hotel, boasting just four, tiny guest rooms upstairs. Again, Durant's request was honored and Tupper was dispatched to the icehouse cut into the side of the mountain to take what he needed. He got to work with a large pair of tongs and an ice pick.

Tom was almost to the telegraph office when a boy came running out, heading for the hotel. "Whoa, son, where you off to in such a hurry?" Tom called.

"Got a message for Mister Braddock," he answered.

"I'm him," Tom replied, holding out a hand for the telegram. He read it quickly, then turned and ran back to the hotel. Bursting into their room minutes later, Tom retrieved his pistol as he told Mary what he knew. The metallic snick of bullets sliding into the cylinder punctuated his words.

"Littletree was at Pine Knot! He's been sent here to fetch ice. He's probably here right now!"

"God, be careful, Tommy," Mary said. "Don't go alone. Get someone to go with you. If you're right about this man, he's already killed three people."

Tom hesitated a moment. He'd been ready to go after Littletree, so anxious to clear Mike that caution did not occur to him, not that it often did. He gave a shrug and a brief, sheepish glance to Mary.

"Mike, run down to the boathouse. See if you can find Mister Busher. Tell him to bring his rifle and meet me in back as soon as he can. I'm going to take another quick look at Lettie's head wound first. I want to be sure about something."

Mike slammed the door on his way out. His feet could be heard pounding down the hall. Tom tucked his pistol into his shoulder holster and turned to Mary.

"Don't worry, I won't take any chances."

"Make sure you don't, Tommy," she said, then, in an attempt to ease the tension, added, "Of course, this might not even be the man."

"True," Tom said, not believing it for a second, but feeling that Mary might like the notion.

"Don't kill him, Tom," Mary warned. She'd seen that look on his face before. "We need him alive. Mike needs him alive."

Tom shrugged and with a dark grin and a bad rustic accent said "Awright, Ma. Ah'll jes kill 'im a leettle bit."

It wasn't Chauncey Busher who rounded the corner of the hotel with Mike about fifteen minutes later, but Exeter Owens. He had his rifle gripped loosely in one hand.

"Your boy said you needed help," he said as he strode up to Tom.

Tom nodded. "Grateful for it. Owens, wasn't it?" Tom said extending his hand. He sketched out who he was looking for and what Littletree was suspected of.

"That ain't Littletree, that's Tupper!" Owens said. "Well it's both actually. Most don't know Littletree's his Indian name. I just saw him a couple of days ago, not more 'n ten feet from this spot."

"The day of the fire," Tom said.

"That's right. Damn! You think he killed that girl, then set the fire? What's got into that boy? Always took him to be a bit edgy, if you know what I'm saying, but never figured him for something like this."

"He's edgy alright. Killed three people between New York City and here. He gives us any trouble, you shoot the sonofabitch. You okay with that?" Tom asked with an appraising squint. Owens shrugged as if it were a given.

"I want him breathing, though," Tom added as they set off. "He's not much use to me dead." Owens gave him a curious look but said nothing.

"Mike, you stay here, okay? Tell your ma we're headed for the Blue Mountain House," Tom said over his shoulder.

"I will Dad. Be careful," Mike called after them.

"I thought Tupper was here," Owens said, puzzled.

"He was, but he went on to the Blue Mountain House for ice."

"Oh," Owens grunted as they broke into a jog toward town.

It was nearly a half hour later when Tom and Owens made their way to Merwin's. They'd missed Tupper at the Blue Mountain House. They crossed the broad lawn, where a group of women in long, full skirts and wide hats played croquet in the afternoon sun. They were laughing and seemed to take no notice of Tom and Ex. Neither their rifles nor their haste drew a second glance. Tom went to the hotel office while Owens waited.

"He's back that way," Tom said as he bounded out, pointing up the ridge behind the hotel. "You ready?" Owens just nodded and checked his rifle, chambering a round and flipping the safety off.

They came upon Tupper at the back of his wagon. He'd backed it up to the icehouse door, so the horse and wagon shielded him slightly. He was chopping at a block of ice, the ice pick tossing up sparkling little sprays with each blow. Tom had a fleeting vision of the thing punching into Lettie Burman's skull.

"Jim Tupper!" Tom said in a way that froze Tupper instantly.

Tupper looked up at Tom and Owens. Ex stood behind Tom, by the horse's hindquarters while Tom advanced. Tupper cursed himself for ever trusting Owens. He could feel a black rage sweep through him. His vision went dark, leaving only a focused circle of brilliant light surrounding Owens and the stranger.

"I'm Tupper," he managed to say.

"Turn around," Tom said. "Put your hands behind—"

He never finished the sentence. A remarkable thing happened, something Tupper would not make head nor tails of for some time. Owens, who was behind Braddock, looked straight at Tupper, then kicked one of the horses with all his might. The horse reared and struck out with his hooves, startling Tom, who turned half about in surprise. It was a stupid mistake, turning his back on Tupper, the sort of thing that got a man killed, even if it was for only a split-second.

Braddock felt the impact, but did not understand that something had hit him until the earth came up to meet his face. He got his hands under him to push himself up, but the grass was turning gray and indistinct. The ground was moving. He couldn't seem to make his arms do what he wanted. He heard a rifle boom above him, so close he was certain he'd been shot. The grass danced before his eyes. His ears rang. Tom felt something wet run down his nose. It dripped black into the gray grass.

Mary heard the shots from across the lake. They rolled like thunder. She felt them to the bottoms of her shoes. One hand went up to her mouth. Mike, who was standing beside her on the verandah saw it. No one else took notice, though there were a number of guests lounging there. Shots in the woods were not uncommon.

"Don't worry. He'll be fine," Mike said. Something in Mike's voice made Mary turn and look at him. Mike knew that it wasn't Tom's pistol they'd heard. He wondered if she knew, too.

"You all right?" said Owens.

"Hell no! Christ, what'd he hit me with?" Blood had stained Tom's shirt and pants in bright streaks and blotches.

"Chunk of ice," Owens said as he helped Tom to sit on the tailgate of the wagon. Tom didn't bother to look around. He wasn't seeing all that well anyway.

"You didn't hit him."

"Don't think so," Owens said. "He's one fast sonofabitch. Off into the trees in two shakes."

Tom heaved himself up, steadying himself with one hand. "Gotta get after him," he said, though he wasn't at all sure how he was going to do it.

Owens put out a hand. "Dogs," he said. "You take it easy for a spell. I know a man's got some fine hounds. Don't worry," Owens said, when it looked like Tom wanted to go after Tupper by himself. "We'll catch him quicker with hounds than without."

Owens headed off at a run. Borrowing a horse from the hotel stable, he galloped toward town, the horse kicking up clods of hotel lawn as he went.

Tom sat with a kerchief wrapped around his head. He held a piece of ice against it as he cursed himself for his stupid lack of attention. A small group of solicitous hotel employees and anxious guests only made him feel more bruised and self-conscious. "Contact my wife at the Prospect House. Tell her I'm all right and going after the suspect," he said to one of the hotel staff. "Could you do that?" He didn't want Mary to worry, though she was bound to anyway. She had been right to worry.

Tom was anxious to get going by the time he heard the dogs. Owens had been gone nearly an hour. He didn't come back alone.

"Brought some help," Owens said. Besides the man with the hounds, three of them, Busher and the two Duryea boys were with him. They were all heavily armed.

"Tried to keep these two from comin'," Busher said with a nod toward the Duryeas. "They wouldn't have none of it." The boys just grinned. Tom shook his head but wasn't about to argue. They were a little older than Mike at least.

"What the hell. Let's go!"

Tupper heard the hounds baying.

When after about fifteen minutes he realized he hadn't been followed, he had started to circle back toward the hotel. He had thought that if he could steal a horse he could get back to Pine Knot and snatch his equipment before they caught up with him. His gear was so important to him, it was worth the risk. He knew that if he had to take to the woods his life might depend on his gear.

All thoughts of going back for his equipment vanished like smoke in a gale, chased off by the baying of the hounds.

Panicked at first, Tupper set off at a run. He gave no thought to how he might elude the dogs. The terrain was rough. Fallen trees, boulders, and dense undergrowth slowed him, still he went as fast as he could. His course meandered through the forest as he navigated the barriers. The dogs, he knew, would not be slowed as much.

He plunged down a steep slope to a small, rocky stream that crossed his path. Slipping down the last few feet, he tumbled into the cold water. Getting up, he stood in the stream, the water rippling around his ankles and dripping from his clothes. He gulped air, his hands on his knees as he looked up the rocky waterbed. The hounds sounded farther off from down in the gully. His panic washed away a little.

"A fish leaves no tracks, Jim," he heard his grandfather say. The voice seemed to come from somewhere up the stream, just out of reach. He followed.

Staying to the water where he could, or jumping rock to rock, he made his way up the stream. The dogs would be slowed by the water, his scent washed away. They'd be confused. He went with confidence, navigating the rocky watercourse with light, sure strides and jumps. If he could trace the stream back to its source, he might be able to hide in the water amidst a marsh or under a sheltering bank. If he could remain hidden until dark he'd disappear.

The thought encouraged him and he smiled as he went. Circling back to Pine Knot was still a goal, though, if he had to do it on foot it would be no use trying. In the time it would take to make the trip afoot, the whole region would be on the lookout for him and certainly everyone at Durant's camp. He could not worry about that now though. Eluding the dogs came first.

Tupper was not slow, not even in the tumbled rock of the stream. He'd gone a bit more than half a mile, when he heard the baying take on a different tone. He knew the sound. The dogs had lost his scent in the water. He'd gain some distance on them, but still they were far too close. He picked up his pace. Though his chest was heaving and his lungs burning with the effort, he sprang like a deer, drawing on his inner reserves of strength and endurance, the legacies of a life in the wilderness. From time to time he listened, barely able to hear the hounds over his own breathing.

Tupper thought of Ex Owens, too. He couldn't figure it. Ex had led them right to him then given him a chance to escape. It made no sense. The only way it seemed to add up was if Ex had somehow been forced to it. Perhaps Ex knew they already had a bead on him, he thought. It could be that Ex had come along to give him his chance if he could. It seemed to fit.

The baying of the hounds, faint now, suddenly changed tone. They'd caught his scent again. Tupper put on an extra burst of speed.

Where's this stream go?" Tom asked between gulps of air.

"Marsh, maybe a couple miles back o' here. Used to be a beaver pond," Owens said. "Might give us some trouble, he gets in there."

Tom nodded. He knew little about hounding, but it seemed obvious how confused the dogs were when they lost the scent in the water. It had been their handler who'd got them on track again, leading them up the stream, talking to the dogs. He kept up a steady banter with the dogs, calling each by name as if they were his children.

"Pick 'im up, Buck! Atta boy. You sniff 'im out, Bear. You ain't fooled, aire ye? Ho Daisy-girl! You show them fellers how it's done, lassy!"

They responded to their master's voice, spurred on by the encouragement. Still, they'd lost precious time while the dogs circled and sniffed in confusion, their noses snuffling through the leaves, over wet stones and mossy logs. It was a slow business. Tom wanted to surge ahead. He started to wade up the stream, the way he knew he would have gone if he were Tupper.

"Stay back o' the dogs, chief," the handler said. "Cain't go no faster."

"He's right," Owens said as the handler turned back to his children, mumbling something under his breath. The one word Tom caught was "city."

"It's slow now, but it's the only sure way," Owens added.

Tom held back. He knew that Tupper had to be widening the gap as the dogs searched for the scent.

Finally the hounds caught the scent again and started up the streambed. Their progress was fitful as the hounds lost then regained Tupper's trail. They went on like that for maybe a mile, alternately bounding after the baying hounds, then waiting as they snuffled and growled in confusion.

After a fitful half hour of progress the dogs lost the scent entirely. They milled about, noses to the ground, making no sound but an occasional, confused yip.

"C'mon, Daisy-girl," the handler said, encouraging the dog with a rough pat on the shoulders, "You can outsniff them two brutes any ol' day."

Daisy cast a doubtful eye at her master but still got back to the task, working the area in widening circles. "Damn strange," the handler said, easing back his slouch hat to scratch at his sweat-matted hairline. "Never seen 'em lose a track like this."

Tom felt his throbbing head as he watched the dogs. "Sure as hell he didn't grow wings and fly away," he said. The Duryea boys laughed. Owens didn't, neither did Busher nor the handler. Owens stood on a large rock, his rifle in the crook of his folded arm. He scanned the forest in silence.

"Get-up there, Bear!" the handler shouted as the dog sat for a moment, looking as confused as the men. "Damnit boys, don't sit down on me now!"

The dogs milled, casting baleful eyes at the men, their tongues dragging. They weren't used to losing a scent either.

Looking back down the stream, Tom noticed something.

He recalled a man he'd once chased through the narrow maze of the Five Points. The fugitive had gone up a drain pipe at the end of an alley and disappeared over the rooftops, a feat that at the time had confounded Tom.

"Think we went by him," Tom said almost to himself. He started back down the stream and stopped under an overhanging branch about a hundred feet away. Tom holstered his pistol. The others didn't pay him much mind, especially not Owens and the dog handler.

"I'll be damned," one of the Duryea boys said. "Hey, Mister Owens, take a look at this," he said, nodding in Tom's direction.

Braddock had picked a good-size rock to stand on, and with a powerful leap grabbed the branch above him. Going hand over hand, he'd been able to get to the main trunk, swinging himself up so that when Owens and the rest turned around, they thought at first he'd disappeared.

"Havin' fun?" Owens called with a bemused grin.

Tom didn't answer. He clambered into the branches of a big pine while the rest watched. From there he swung into the branches of a partially fallen maple, which some recent storm had lain against the pine.

By then the handler was watching too. "C'mon, Buck! Hey, Bear! Ho, Daisy-girl!" he called. He ran to the spot where the trunk of the maple met the ground. A huge semicircle of root and dirt stood out of the forest floor. Tom was working his way down the fallen trunk when the dogs met him near the roots. In an instant they started baying again, picking up the scent where Tupper had hit the ground. Owens grinned at Tom as he jumped down from the reclining trunk.

"Not bad for a flatlander," Owens said in a grudging way. Tom rubbed his hands on his pants, his head was pounding and his palms were scraped from the rough bark. He looked at Owens.

"I don't hunt animals much, Mister Owens, but I *do* hunt men," Tom said with a look at his raw hands. "Let's move!"

The dogs, with the men crashing behind, were already out of sight, lost in the thick undergrowth. Tom and Owens hurried after their racket.

"My boys got a good scent now," the handler huffed when they caught up. "Won't be long, we'll make up fer the time we lost."

The ground was rising steadily the farther they went. Though they crossed another stream the trail did not vary.

"Heading for high ground," Owens commented.

"Have 'im treed proper," the handler added. "Looks to be headed fer Castle Rock."

Owens grunted and wiped sweat from his eyes. "Damn fool thing," he said.

"What the hell's Castle Rock?" Tom asked as they stood for a moment, catching their breath.

"It's nowhere Tupper wants to be, Braddock. I can tell you that."

Tupper knew well enough where he was going. He'd been there before, many years back. He and his grandfather had gone there. He remembered how they'd sat on the massive, sloping boulder at the crown, watching an eagle soar above Blue Mountain Lake far below.

"This is a place of power," he'd been told, "a place where the spirit soars like the eagle. A man becomes light in his body in such a place, light and strong." There had been no hotels then, no steamboats, no electric lights.

Jim's grandfather had been a member of the Eagle Society. He'd dreamt a soaring dream, with visions of mighty wings. To dream such a dream was the only way into the Eagle Society, that, or having been cured of illness by the rites of the society.

"The eagle is our brother," his grandfather had told him. "If you dream as I did, you will come to know the eagle well."

In time, Jim had dreamt of eagles and had been introduced into the mysteries and rituals of the *sha'dotega*, one of many Iroquois secret societies. He had learned the songs and the secret chants, had felt their power, and known the miracles they could perform. He would need a miracle. *tain'tciade*, the "heaven land," would surely await him if he failed.

He began to chant as he ran, preparing himself and invoking the eagle's spirit. The hounds baying in the narrowing distance were a distraction and a spur. He answered their clamor with concentrated power, adding depth and intensity to his invocations. The chants grew stronger as he went, seeming to come from deep within his burning lungs and from somewhere beyond. The fire in him was a sign, a transforming power burning inside. His legs burned, too, as he struggled up the steepening slope.

Huge boulders, thrown off the mountain in ages past, littered the forest floor. He went around them when he had to, used them when he could. The fire in his legs came to equal that in his lungs, but still he went on, never stopping, never resting. He knew the fire for what it was and believed in its power. He felt the chants work their magic.

The crown of Castle Rock loomed above him, a steep, boulder-strewn slope littered with stunted spruce packed together in thrashing masses. He climbed hand over hand, hardly slowing the pace or breaking the rhythm of his incantations. He wished he had his old gourd rattle and calumet fan with the four eagle feathers. They would be a help.

But they were no more, and his only hope lay in his burning lungs and legs and mind. The dogs closed in behind. He could hear them crashing through the undergrowth, their baying triumphant as they sensed him. Tupper's chant reached a crescendo then stopped. It would be no ordinary man the hounds discovered.

"Jesus Christ!" the handler cursed. "What's he doin' to my pups?"

The baying of the hounds hundreds of yards ahead had suddenly changed. A howl pierced the forest, followed by a chorus of confused barks and growls. The howl became a pitiful series of yelps. The dog's pain echoed through the forest, eerie and knifelike.

"That's Daisy! Goddamnit, 'e hurts my dogs, I'll gut him proper, sonofabitch!" the handler shouted.

The rest said nothing. They all stood frozen for an instant, listening to the dog's pain. The Duryea boys peered about uncertainly, gripping their rifles, fingering the triggers. Tom was grim. He wiped his hand on his trousers. He liked a dry grip on his pistol.

The handler cursed a steady stream and they started up again, following the calls through undergrowth so thick they could not see more than thirty feet ahead. They went as fast as they could toward Daisy's yelps. The baying of Buck and Bear seemed to separate from the other dog, going farther up the slope, but the men kept on course for Daisy.

"I'm comin', girl. I'm comin'," the handler called. Daisy seemed to answer. They found the dog on her side, a log lay across her hindquarters. Blood was on the leaves.

"Oh, Daisy-girl! It's all right now. Daddy'll take care o' ye." The handler bent over the battered dog. She licked his face weakly. They pulled the log away. It took both Busher and Owens to do it, lifting it carefully off her.

Then, from high above, the baying of Buck and Bear changed again. They all turned to the sounds, the five of them stunned by what they heard. The baying again turned to angry barks, followed by yelps of pain and a long howl the likes of which none of them had ever heard. An instant later there was a single scream, high-pitched, birdlike, yet human. There were words in that call, but none that any of them understood. Then there was silence.

Eighteen

*These lakes are the highways, the turnpikes, the railroads of these high
and wild regions, and these little boats are the carriages, the stage coaches,
and the cars, in which everybody must travel.*

—SAMUEL H. HAMMOND

The death of the day had come hours before. Mary waited while night
rose up from the forest floor like an incoming tide, drowning everything, even her hopes. The halo of light thrown off by the hotel could
beat back the Adirondack night only so far. Blackness hovered
beyond, waiting to claim its right to all that was. Electricity had its
limits.

Mary heard the wagon long before she saw it. It rumbled and rattled through the little collection of buildings that was the town. It was
the only wagon moving this night and the only sign of life beyond the
sheltering light of the hotel. No one seemed to be venturing far. Not
even the steamboat, which lay tied up and silent by the shore. Mary
took anxious steps forward toward the sounds she had been straining
to hear. She was unwilling to leave the safety of the light entirely. Still,
she walked toward the sound until the hotel behind seemed as if it
existed in a silvery bubble against the blue-black sky.

Slowly the wagon drew closer, though she still could not see it. For
an instant it seemed as if the sound was too close for it not to be seen,
and the hairs on the back of Mary's neck stood on end at the thought
that it was a ghost she heard. But a solid wagon was conjured out of
the night, taking shape just yards away.

"Tommy!" Mary cried. "Thank God. I've been out of my mind with worry."

The wagon pulled up before her and she stepped to its side. "What happened?" was all she could add. When she got close she was shocked by what she saw. Tom sat slumped with exhaustion, his head caked with dried, brown blood. His clothes were filthy, his shoes and legs covered in black mud. His pants and shirt were torn and tattered and he bled from half a dozen scratches and scrapes.

"Tommy, you look a sight!" she said as he got down. She hugged him, heedless of the mud and blood. Owens, who was driving, tipped his drooping hat and said, "Don't we all, ma'am."

Mary noticed for the first time that the guide was as bedraggled as Tom.

"Thanks, Owens," Tom said to the guide, extending a hand, "I'm going out again after a few hours rest. Sorry you can't come."

Owens just nodded and drove off; the Duryea boys, who sat in the back with Busher said nothing, but tipped their hats to Mary as they disappeared.

"Tom, what happened?" Mary said as they started walking back to the hotel. Tom limped and winced as they went.

"He's gone. Disappeared."

"What?" she said, stopping to look at Tom in disbelief.

"Just gone. I don't know," Tom said with a confounded shake of his head and a squint that Mary found disconcerting. She had rarely seen her husband confounded by anything.

"Couldn't find the body after he jumped," he said. "The dogs dead or injured. Bottom of that cliff is a maze of—lots of big, tumbled boulders. He could be down in some crevice somewhere. We just don't know."

"I heard the dogs," Mary said, "howling from across the lake. Gave me chills."

Tom just nodded. "Never seen anything like it. The man hurt two dogs and killed another. Threw one off Castle Rock," he said, then, by way of explanation, "big cliff on the other side of the lake."

After a moment, he added, "Tupper jumped, too."

"My God!" Mary said, shaking her head slowly. Putting a gentle hand on Tom's head she asked, "How'd you do this? Looks nasty."

Tom shrugged and said, "Got hit with a chunk of ice."

"Ice?" Mary said.

"Don't make me explain."

They walked to their rooms in silence, followed by the stares of guests and employees. Conversation ceased as they went by and started up again in their wake. Everyone seemed to have something to share in the light of the hotel lobby.

They hadn't been in their room for more than a few minutes, enough time for Tom to get out of his clothes and into a long robe, when there was a knock at the door. He'd planned on spending a long time in a very hot tub. His shoulders shrank at the interruption, but he squared them as he opened the door. Frederick Durant was on the other side.

"I just heard," he said, looking from Tom to Mary. "I've been at Pine Knot since yesterday evening. Just got back. William told me. Who was this fellow?"

Tom explained how he'd matched the description to Tupper and how he'd quickly examined Lettie's corpse, matching her wound to the one that reportedly killed the steward from the Albany night boat.

"This man was working for William?" Frederick said, shocked that an escaped murderer had come among them so easily.

"No way for William to know," Tom said. "The important thing to me, though, was the descriptions of how this man, Tupper, or Littletree by his Indian name, was killing his victims."

Tom explained how Tupper's other victim shared the same unique wound. A look of surprise and relief washed over Frederick's face.

"He's killed at least two people in precisely the same way," Braddock repeated, "and I can prove it."

"Tom," Durant began quietly, "I'm so glad this has come to light. I mean, well you know, for your sake and your son's. I never really thought that your boy—"

Tom didn't let him finish. "Once your doctor started with his accusations, you had to follow through. I know. I don't like it," Tom added with a direct and piercing look, "but I respect it."

Frederick nodded. "Understood, sir, understood." he said. "You'll understand then that it isn't I who can clear your son, I mean officially. When the sheriff gets here, I'm sure he'll . . ."

"Yes, yes. I know."

"Good," Durant said with a slight smile. "And where is this Tupper fellow now? Where are you holding him?"

Tom and Mary exchanged a quick glance.

"We don't have him," Tom said.

"But, I thought you'd . . ."

"He jumped off Castle Rock," Tom added.

"Castle Rock! Then he's dead, surely," Durant said, looking from Tom to Mary.

"I agree. Don't see how he could have survived a fall like that. Still . . ."

"What?" Frederick asked, clearly puzzled.

"We haven't found the body."

V an Duzer gave an annoyed *'hmph'* from somewhere back in his substantial throat. The Durant woman was already putting restrictions on him. She'd heard the news about the fire, apparently, and seemed to think he had something to do with it.

"The temerity!" he mumbled. Who did she take him for, some rosy-cheeked lad, fresh from the bar exam? He crumpled her telegram, an equivocating message full of self-doubt and guarded words.

The time for second thoughts was over. Though he had to admit that torching barns and murdering maids had not been precisely his instructions, neither had he put any restrictions on his man. Van Duzer had expected damage to the Durants' interests. How to best accomplish that was his man's affair. Van Duzer had been very careful about that, authorizing nothing illegal, at least not in writing.

The man had shown a stroke of genius when he'd used the Indian's escape as he had. He'd shown a violent streak beyond Van Duzer's reckoning, too, a fact that could be a bit disturbing if dwelt on. Van Duzer wasn't one to dwell on things he could not control. Like a force of nature, he'd set the man loose.

Van Duzer's job now was to nail his shutters tight and wait out the storm. Besides, it was not for Miss Durant's interests alone that he worked. He'd been looking for a means to accomplish both the great man's needs as well as his own.

If Van Duzer had been a religious man, he'd have called it Divine destiny, though even he had to admit that "Divine" was a tad too pious a word for what he'd set in motion. But "destiny" was not. How else could one describe the opportunity presented by that Indian? Elizabeth Durant's doubts had no place in his plans. Doubts could be as dangerous as daggers.

He looked at the other telegram that had arrived a few minutes before hers. Things in the Adirondacks were going dangerously well. A raging bull is a hard thing to let go of once you've got him by the tail, Van Duzer thought, and a harder thing to hold on to. But then, that was what lawyers were for, wasn't it? Prudence had gotten him this far, after all, and he was not about to abandon it now.

In the interim there was the Durant woman to consider. Van Duzer set about writing a vague note full of lawyerly double-talk about honoring her wishes and understanding her concerns. It would keep her soothed for a while. He smirked as he wrote.

Tupper floated in the black water of the lake, looking up at the stars. He imagined he was among them, drifting through space, soaring high above the earth on eagle's wings. He *had* flown, but his landing had been hard. His side burned like the belly of a stove on a subzero night. It was scraped raw from hip to shoulder. The huge wound oozed through his tattered clothes. His hands were raw, the skin torn away when he'd clutched at the big spruce that had broken his fall. He was bitten on the legs and hands and arm, where the dogs had gotten him. He mumbled the prayers of healing once more in the darkness as he floated in the shallows of Blue.

He grinned through his pain. The incantations had worked. He had been one with the eagles, if only for an instant. He had flown into the branches of the tree, whose top barely peeked above the edge of the sloping cliff. The men who tracked him had been slowed by their injured dogs and their belief that he could not have survived the fall. He was gone before they climbed down and worked their way to where he'd landed. He heard them calling long after the sun sank, listening as he crouched in the cool water.

He had laughed silently though his side erupted in fire. He could not keep it in. It welled up, triumphant, fueled by the giddy knowledge of what he'd done. It was almost more than he could control, a euphoria that swept him along, washing away the pain that burned him in a dozen places. The best he could do, the only control he had was to keep his laughter silent, no louder than the kiss of the water against the rocks. That laughter never ceased, save for the death of winter's ice.

Tupper had but one regret. He loved dogs.

As the outlines of the shouldering mountains faded and lake turned to black, Tupper saw a small, wispy column of smoke rise above an island out in the lake. He couldn't see the fire. He didn't need to.

"Only man, of all God's creatures, makes fire," his grandfather had told him when he was very small.

"It is an eternal sign of the Creator's love for our people. Fire is a sacred trust. Use it well."

His grandfather's teachings echoed in his head as he gauged the distance across the sleeping water. A quarter of a mile at least, he figured. Tupper stood and stretched, easing his sore muscles, but lighting up his side again. He took his boots off and slung them over his neck by the tied laces. With hardly a ripple he eased into the icy lake and started a slow paddle for the island. With luck, he'd have what he needed and be long gone before *ende'ka gaa'kwa* painted the morning sky.

Braddock rested only a few hours. He'd made plans to go back to Castle Rock and search by lamplight. He was determined to find Tupper, alive if possible.

"Can't sweat a corpse," Chowder used to say.

It was hours before dawn when Tom met Chauncey Busher. The guide stood waiting with two horses and kerosene lamps. Busher had been the only man Tom could get to go back with him. Owens said he had a client in the morning and the Duryea boys were so wrung out he didn't even ask. The other guides were either engaged or oddly reluctant to venture after Tupper. Some made excuses with comments like, "Any man jumps off Castle Rock's just a corpse," which seemed to sum up the prevailing wisdom on the subject. Nobody could explain why Tupper hadn't been found.

"This whole business's got the men spooked," Busher said as they rode. Tom yawned so hard and wide his whole body shuddered. The rest hadn't been nearly enough.

"What with the tales of folks with holes in their noggins," Busher said as he watched Tom yawn, "crazy Indians running about tearin' dogs limb from limb, disappearin' like steam off piss, you know it makes men jumpy."

Braddock understood. Already the stories were overblown.

"He's just a man, Chauncey. Just a man."

The hike to Castle Rock was tough in the dark, but they were able to ride partway in on a trail the horses could navigate. Neither man said much until they got close to the foot of the cliff. Just getting there was a steep, rocky climb and had them breathing hard. They found the spot where Buck had landed, marked by a large pool of smeared blood running across the stone. Busher stood over the spot, looking first left, then right, then up the sloping face of the cliff. It seemed to disappear into the black sky above them, a looming mass against the stars.

"Can't hardly believe he threw a dog off this cliff," Busher said.

They both stood, looking up, their faces yellow in the lamplight. Busher shook his head and turned away. "So, where'd he git to?" the guide mumbled.

They searched for hours, working their way over, around, and under the massive, tumbled boulders. There were many small caves, crevices, and black, inaccessible holes. They peered into each. Again they climbed to the top of the cliff from the other side, retracing the route they'd taken the afternoon before. After a long search of the densely wooded crown they paused at the edge. They both feared that Tupper had somehow hidden himself after killing the dogs, that he hadn't jumped at all, but had somehow gotten by them.

"Woulda been tough to go far," Busher said. "We were close. He couldn't have gone more'n a hundred feet through that stuff," he said, waving back at the densely packed pines. "You'd hear a man in there."

Tom just grunted. The sun was rising behind them by then, painting the forests far off in the west a glowing yellow while the lake below them remained in shadow. An orange reflection in the distance caught Tom's attention.

"That Raquette Lake way off over there?"

Busher nodded. "Pretty view from here," he said. "Want to just suck it all in. Store it away, sorta."

Tom nodded. "Needs an artist to catch the light, the size of it." He shrugged and turned away. "Got no talent with a brush."

Tom turned his attention to the trees below them. A couple poked their heads just above the level of the sloping cliff. Tom tilted his head and squinted at the top of the spruce, then walked down the rock as far as he dared. "You figure you could jump into one of these trees, Chauncey?"

Busher said nothing at first, just walked down beside Tom and gauged the distance.

"Suppose I could, if I was a fuckin' lunatic, which by the way I ain't. But even if I was, I wouldn't expect to make it." Busher looked sideways at Tom. "You lookin' to have a go at 'er?"

Tom laughed, but said, "He didn't have much choice." He peered over the cliff. It gave him a queasy feeling though, and he pulled back and looked away. "I've seen men do all sorts of crazy things, Busher, things you would not believe they'd do."

Busher didn't answer. He took a few steps back, looking once more at the slope and dizzying distance to the treetops that the sun was just then touching with a single golden finger.

"Reckon you'd have to get a runnin' start," he said at last.

Tom and Chauncey rode hard into the little hamlet of Blue Mountain

Lake a couple of hours later. The sun was climbing into the morning sky, chasing drifting wisps of mist from the surface of the lake and from the hollows and vales between the mountains. Tom stopped at the telegraph office. Busher kept on toward the hotel.

"I'll be there in ten minutes," Tom called after him. He stomped into the little building, which had just opened. Minutes later the telegraph key was clicking out a message for Chowder Kelly.

Tom found Mary, Mike, and Rebecca just before they went down for breakfast. They had just opened their door as Tom strode down the hall.

"He's alive!" he said as he rushed into the room. "Or at least he was. Found a blood trail down to the lake," Tom said as he grabbed some things and threw them into a small satchel. "Must have missed it in the dark last night."

"You're going after him?" Mike said, the excitement in his voice crackling. Before Tom answered, he said, "I'm coming!"

That brought Tom up short. Tom and Mary rounded on him.

"Whoa, son. I can't allow that!" Tom said.

Mike was ready for the objections. "Dad, you'll need me. I'm good with a gun. I'm tough and I won't slow you down any more than those Duryea boys." Tom didn't have an immediate response to this, nor did Mary, so Mike added, "And I need to do something, you know, for Lettie's sake."

"Mike, you can't," Mary said. "It's precisely because of Lettie you shouldn't go. If you take off into the woods now, even though it's with your father, it'll only raise suspicions. That doctor has it in for you. He's already shown he's willing to jump at straws. You can't give him more ammunition. Suppose you did find him? Suppose you kill him? What's it going to look like, like you're trying to erase your crime with this man's blood."

"Mom! That's not . . ."

"That's what it'll look like to them, to that doctor and maybe Durant, too."

"Mike, listen to your mother," Tom said. "She's talking sense. You aren't."

Mike was good with a rifle and a tough kid, hardened by his years with his gang on the Lower East Side. But this wasn't the old neighborhood, and the man Tom was after was no ordinary man. The fact that he'd survived the jump from Castle Rock spooked Tom, though he would not admit it.

Beyond that, he still thought of Mike as a boy, regardless of all evidence to the contrary. He could not accept that Mike was ready for something like this. He wasn't so sure about himself, for that matter. Without a guide like Busher or Owens he wouldn't attempt it.

"This man, I don't know what he is," Tom said. "He's insane, a lunatic, capable of God knows what. He's butchered people, escaped from five men with dogs, and jumped off a goddamn cliff, for Christ sake," Tom said, shaking his head as he stuffed socks into his satchel.

"I know all that, but—"

"Mike!" Tom shouted. The lack of sleep, exhaustion, and his still-throbbing head had Tom at the edge. "No, goddamnit! No! Are you crazy, too?" he growled. "All you'd do is get yourself killed, maybe me, too. That what you want?"

He tried to erase the glare from his eyes, but it was too late.

Mike's expression went from shock to hurt to rage in the space of a few heartbeats. Tom caught Mary's look of reproach, saw Mike's cheeks redden and his eyes water. He wished immediately that he could take back what he'd said. He knew the damage he'd done. Before his eyes Mike seemed to retreat, turning back into the sullen young man of a week before. Mike turned without a word and stalked out of the room, slamming the door behind him. The silence was not even broken by Rebecca, who stood tight-lipped in one corner, fingering the corner of her dress. Mary didn't say a word. She didn't have to.

"Be careful, Tommy," Mary said as they parted in the hallway. "Don't worry about Mike. I'll talk to him. You just worry about yourself. I want you coming home to me, and in one piece this time," she said with a forced smile.

Tom grinned. "The only one coming back in pieces is Tupper," he said. He kissed her hard and added, "Don't worry. And listen—tell Mike I'm sorry, okay? Promise you'll do that for me? I don't think he wants to hear it from me right now."

As he strode through the lobby he noticed a crowd at the front desk. There was a quantity of luggage piled about and some raised voices among the guests. Tom distinctly heard the words "checking out." As he walked down to the boathouse he glanced back at the verandah outside their rooms. Rebecca and Mary waved goodbye.

"Let's go, Chauncey," Tom called as he neared the dock. Busher was talking to Owens and some others who made no move to follow. Tom figured the only reason Busher was going was because he'd been promised double his rate to do it. Tom knew the chief would approve the expense.

Tom threw his gear into the guide boat and lay his rifle near the stern. Busher's gear was already stowed. They set off in silence, the guide pulling the oars in a slow rhythm that still seemed to propel the craft at a considerable speed.

"Guess we'll check the islands," Busher said. They had already searched the shore around where Tupper's trail ended. It was possible that Tupper had thrown them off by wading around the shoreline and taking to the woods again somewhere on the far side of Blue, but, for some reason, Busher didn't think Tupper would have done that.

"A man crazy enough to jump from that cliff might make the swim," Busher said. "Oftimes parties camp on them islands. Besides, this lake's got maybe twenty miles of shoreline. We go searchin' the whole thing, it'll take all day. That big island," Busher said with a jerk of his head over his shoulder, "it's got caves. Hardly anybody knows that. He might try to hide there."

Busher wasn't heading directly to the island, though, but skirting to one side, coming at it from the side. Busher saw the question in Tom's eyes. "Can't go straight across. Rocks all around there. Seen many a boat busted up out there. Besides, we can check a couple of the smaller islands on the way."

Tom sat in the stern in silence as the dark waters swam by.

"*Somebody's* camped out there," Tom said as they approached one of the two islands nearest where Tupper's trail had disappeared. Busher craned about, holding the oars up out of the water.

"See the smoke?"

"Yup. Ain't our man, but whoever it is might be a help," Busher said as he started to pull toward the smoke. They were still two hundred yards from the island when they heard shouting and saw two men emerge from the trees at the shoreline. Tom put his rifle across his knees. As they drew closer the men called to them.

"Stole our boat!" one shouted. "And most of our gear," the other added.

"Sonofabitch!" Busher said with a violent shake of his head. "Ain't that a fine mess o' beans. Damn it all to hell." He stopped rowing, dragging the oars so the boat eased to a stop a hundred feet from shore.

"When you notice the boat gone?" Tom asked.

"An hour or so back. Searched the whole damn island. It's gone for sure," was the reply.

"What'd it look like?" Busher put in.

"Same as yours 'cept dark blue."

"Let's go, Busher," Tom said in a low voice. Busher just stroked with one oar, turning the bow away from shore. He said nothing.

"Say! Ain't you gonna help us?"

"We'll have somebody pick you up," Tom called back across the widening distance. "Hey!" he added. You didn't have your rifles in that boat, did you?"

"What you take us for, mister? We ain't fools," one answered.

Tom said nothing, but when they were almost out of earshot he called, "Got enough food?"

The two just waved in reply.

As their boat left the men in its wake, Busher said, "You know, Tupper could've stole that boat maybe ten, twelve hours ago."

Tom looked at his pocket watch. It was 10:10. He snapped the case shut as if shutting out the import of Busher's words.

"You know how much distance one o' these boats can make in that kinda time?" Busher said.

Tom looked about them at the long, unbroken expanse of water and its dense border of trees. He thought not of Tupper or of how far he might have traveled, but of Mike.

For a long moment Tom considered turning back. He thought of taking Mike with him or of somehow building a bridge over the gap between them. He wanted to do it, wanted to go back and set things right. How he might do that, he didn't know. And what good would it do, if Mike wasn't cleared of the cloud he was under? Tom had his limitations. He was no magician. Tom trusted in the kind of magic born of muscle and steel and determination, the kind that could move mountains or bring a man to justice no matter how far he'd rowed in the night.

"I don't want to know," he said at last.

They'd been rowing for maybe ten minutes before Tom asked, "How long you figure it'll be before somebody finds them?" with a nod back toward the island.

"Not long," Busher said. "Today sometime, likely enough. T'morrer fer sure."

"So, where we headed?" Tom asked. It was clear that Busher had no doubts, from the steady way he pulled at the oars.

"If'n it was me got that boat, I'd been rowin' till sunup."

"Hide out during the day," Tom said.

"About the size of it. Reckon he wouldn't take to bein' seen much."

Tom did some quick figuring. "He'd be somewhere in Raquette Lake then, right?"

Busher just smiled.

"Let me know when you need a break at the oars," Tom said as he eased back on his hard caned seat.

As it turned out, Tom was in luck. He didn't have to row a stroke all the way to Raquette. The *Killoquah,* one of Durant's little steamers, overtook them in the channel between Blue and Eagle. They hailed it and within minutes had their boat stowed on the roof and their gear at their feet. Tom and Chauncey dozed most of the way, with just an hour's interruption to change steamers at the Marrion River carry. They were both well-rested by the time the silvery expanse of Raquette opened before them.

A brief stop at Pine Knot revealed nothing at first, except how nervous William was. He was expecting an important guest in the next few days, he told them. It was a man whose name was never mentioned, an omission not lost on Tom.

Tom had seen Erskine for a few minutes before he left the hotel. They'd had a private chat in the empty dining hall. Erskine didn't tell him much about Lettie Burman that he didn't already know, except for the interesting fact that the doctor had been "pining" for her, according to the girls she worked with. Perhaps even more interesting was what Erskine told him about the Durants, particularly William.

"They say he cheated his sister outa big money. Say she's gonna sue, maybe. Not the first time Mister William's had trouble neither. Had land troubles on an' off. Bought some land around the Raquette, an island an' such, for back taxes. The folks that owned it didn' wanna go. Lot o' bad blood over that. The Owens clan."

"Exeter Owens?"

"Sure 'nough. Him an' his dad's family. His daddy owned the land."

Tom had had to hurry, so he wasn't able to get into the details of what Erskine had told him. It was interesting to know that William West Durant was not exactly the patrician father of the Adirondacks that he appeared to be.

Tom thought about this as William told him what he'd heard concerning Mike and Tupper. Durant had seen copies of the telegrams and knew of the suspicions surrounding the death of Lettie Burman.

"Tom, I'm sure there's nothing to this doctor's accusations," William told him. "It's this maniac, Littletree, or should I say Tupper, who's obviously to blame. For that I blame myself. If I had known somehow," he said with a slow shake of his head. "My foreman didn't want to hire the man. Did you know that?"

"Not your fault, William."

Durant nodded in appreciation then offered, "Is there anything I can do for you, Tom? Do you have enough provisions, food, ammunition? Name it and it's yours."

At first Tom declined, but then remembered that he had but one box of ammunition for his rifle.

"Easily remedied," William said. "Follow me."

They went to Durant's cottage. Tom waited in the front room while William went to his gun rack in the bedroom.

"That was a thirty-forty, right, Tom?" William called. But before Tom answered he heard William mumble, "Damned odd," followed by the sound of drawers and doors opening and closing in a hasty clatter.

"William?" Tom called, taking a step toward the door.

William West Durant appeared in the doorway, two boxes of cartridges in his hand. He wore a puzzled expression.

"I'm afraid I have only two to give you, Tom."

Bradock shrugged. "That's more than enough. I—"

Durant interrupted him. "It seems I've been robbed."

Busher was glum as they rowed away from Pine Knot a while later. He'd been a good deal more enthusiastic when he thought they were chasing an unarmed man.

"Gotta have a care, now he's got a rifle," Chauncey said. "That feller could pick us off from the shore like we was birds on a wire. Gotta have a care."

Tom didn't disagree. Tupper had proven dangerous enough armed only with an old bayonet. Now, as the dense wall of trees and brush stalked by, Tom began to imagine how easy it would be to lay in wait. The thought sent chills down his back. It was not striking back that worried him, but the thought that his fate might not be of his own making. He dreaded that above all else. Tom wiped his palms on his pant legs and gripped his rifle a bit more tightly.

Tom and Busher settled on a plan after a bit of discussion. They'd keep well out from shore, two hundred yards or so. It was a distance that would make any shot chancey, yet close enough so Tom could scan the shore with his field glasses for anything suspicious. The glasses would bridge the gap; not perfect, but close enough.

"Trouble is this lake's got—maybe ninety or more miles o' shoreline," Busher said. "'Course we ain't gonna search her all, just the likeliest spots."

Tom just grunted.

"You're gonna have to spell me on the oars," Busher added, then, almost as an afterthought, said, "And about my time," he stopped rowing as he said this. "You know it's a sight more valuable now Tupper's got that rifle."

Tom heaved a sigh and said, "Six dollars a day. How's that fit?"

Busher just nodded and started rowing again. It was more than double his regular rate. Tom picked up the glasses and watched the shore. "Looks like it'll be a longish day," he said to the trees.

Nineteen

Darkness falls suddenly. Outside the ring of light from our conflagration the woods are black. There is a tremendous impression of isolation and lonesomeness in our situation. We are the prisoners of the night.

—CHARLES DUDLEY WARNER,
IN THE WILDERNESS

Mary didn't know precisely when Mike left his room. She had gone out with Rebecca some time around ten, killing time and trying to keep the girl happy. They had searched the shoreline for frogs, which 'Becca begged Mary to catch but wouldn't touch when she did. They'd gone bowling, too, and stopped back at their rooms just before noon. Mary didn't think much of it at first, figuring Mike had just gone out for a bit of air. Where could he go after all, she'd reasoned.

She took a quick walk around the grounds before lunch, hoping they could eat together; but he was nowhere to be seen. She went down to the dock where she saw Owens loading his guide boat on a steamer. He tipped his hat and Mary waved back.

"Have you seen Mike?" she said.

Owens said no, but ambled over to chat for a moment.

"Been getting set for a trip over to Raquette. Got a client wants to fish," he said. Mary smiled and made small talk.

Owens drank her in as she walked back toward the hotel. The low-waisted summer dress she wore, a rose-colored thing, just a bit tighter and thinner than strictly proper, swayed with each step up the rolling lawn. Owens turned back to his packing, but his mind wasn't in it.

Mary and Rebecca went to lunch. It was nearly two by the time they were back in their rooms and well after three once Rebecca got up from her nap. Though Mary laid on the bed in only her light shift, letting the cool lake breeze wash over her, she could not sleep. She thought of Mike.

After the way Tom had acted she could understand how he might want to be alone. She bit her lip in frustration. Mike had begun to show much of his old self, but now the gulfs were back and wider than before. The more she worried the blacker her thoughts became. She imagined he might not return, that he'd drowned or was lost in the wilderness. And what if the sheriff arrived and Mike couldn't be found? She did not want to entertain those thoughts, but they came nonetheless, playing over and over in her head like scenes from a penny dreadful. None turned out well.

Late that afternoon Mary and Rebecca again went out searching. The hotel, the little town with its scattered buildings and tiny church, the other hotels; all showed no sign of him. They were out for hours.

Heading back toward the Prospect House, Mary debated whether she should notify anyone. Mike could be in desperate trouble, lying injured in the forest. In her imagination, he'd tripped over a log or fallen in some rocky streambed. His leg was broken. It was cool in the woods despite the late August sun and the sweat of his pain turned to a deathly chill. He was hungry and scared and the night was coming on fast. His calls went unanswered, attracting only the attention of hungry eyes as the darkness engulfed him.

She was torn. What if she did notify someone, what would they think? Surely they'd figure he was on the run, that the evidence pointing to Tupper was a sham by a big city cop to pull the wool over their rustic eyes. They'd search for Mike, but it would not be the sort of search she'd want. Mary decided to wait until around supper, and then to tell only Frederick, relying on him to handle the situation.

With Tom gone and out of reach for God knows how long, she didn't see an alternative. She'd take her chances with the Durants. Regardless of where that decision might lead, finding Mike had to take precedence over all else.

As she neared the hotel with a sulky, complaining Rebecca in tow,

Mary was brought up short. Two men were on the broad steps leading up to the verandah. One was the doctor. The other she didn't know, but something in his manner put her on alert. It wasn't anything she could put a name to, but she knew that this was not someone she wanted to meet just then. Turning, she steered Rebecca toward the back of the hotel. "'Becca," she said, "wouldn't you like to go bowling?"

Tom's hands felt like they'd swollen to twice their size. His palms were chafed red and his fingers seemed like little sausages, ready to split if he bent them too far. Every hour or so he'd spelled Busher at the oars, pulling their little craft smoothly in and around the countless coves and points of land that made up the Raquette Lake shoreline. "Damn lake goes on forever," Tom said after hours of poking into every crevice.

Busher grunted. "Wouldn't be such a chore if I wasn't 'spectin' to get shot every time I see a leaf move."

Tom didn't answer. He'd felt like he was wearing a target too. He didn't like it any more than Chauncey.

"Didn't sign on to get any extra holes in me. The holes I got suit me fine," Busher added.

Tom wanted to tell him to shut one of his, but thought better of it. The chances of finding Tupper were slim enough as it was without losing his guide. Tom looked at him hard. "You'll get double your regular rate and then some. I gave you my *word* on it," Tom said. He knew his emphasis on *word* wasn't lost on Busher, and hoped that the guide was a man of his.

Tom knew well enough how Chauncey felt. Tom's stomach was knotted up and his jaw ached with the constant tension. Several times they put ashore to check likely spots more thoroughly than they could with the binoculars. They stalked the woods, moving with silent steps, crouching low, but found nothing but squirrels and one partridge that burst almost from under Tom's feet in a flurry of wings and feathers. Tom had almost fired at it and his heart raced for minutes after, feeling like it made enough noise to be heard clear to Albany.

Despite their efforts, they'd found no sign of Tupper. It was as if the lake had swallowed him whole.

The end of the day crept over the mountains to the east. It was still a couple of hours until dark, and fatigue had at last dulled their edgy nerves.

"He's here," Busher said as Tom put down his glasses with a grunt of frustration. Tom had been glassing the shoreline as if he wouldn't give up the search even in darkness.

"I know it," Tom said, though, in truth, Tupper could be miles behind them.

"No doubt he knows we're here, too. But if you're willin', I have a thought on how we might just surprise our Indian friend."

Tom rubbed the swollen lump on his head. It ached and had throbbed whenever he'd taken a turn at the oars. He shrugged it off. "Let's hear it," he said.

Tupper rowed all night, resting only when his muscles screamed or his bleeding hands needed tending. Though his hands were raw and slippery with blood, he'd kept to the oars. Though his body ached and his wounded side bled through his shirt, he would not stop. Tupper had no doubt that he would be followed. Sooner or later they'd give up trying to find his body. They'd round up some more hounds and they'd track him to the lake. He was almost delirious. Fatigue, pain, and blood loss had left him reeling. Still, he goaded himself on.

He saw them searching as he lay concealed during the day, had watched as they rowed by his hiding place. The boat lay submerged in just four feet of water, enough so it wouldn't be seen unless a man was right on top of it. Now that the sun had set, it was again time to move.

He smiled as he lifted out the stones that had kept her concealed on the bottom. The boat rolled and bobbed as he lightened the load. Like an otter, it could not be kept down.

He'd need her speed that night. He'd chosen his hiding place well, a place that was mostly open with little underbrush to shelter him. It was the sort of place that any pursuer would tend to pass over. That had been the way of it. He'd slept most of the day away, never moving unless he had to, and even then not before he was certain there was no one near.

Tupper had seen the two men moving slowly, well out from shore, late in the afternoon. He'd caught the glint of glass from the big one and knew they were using binoculars. Tupper had remained motionless behind a log that lay behind a thin screen of young beech. He didn't raise the rifle he'd stolen from Durant, though he was tempted. The shot would have been a long one, a thing he wouldn't chance with a gun he'd never fired.

As he thought this, he realized with a start that they knew he was armed. It was the only reason those two would have stayed so far from shore. Tupper cursed and his temples throbbed with the effort not to scream. It was bad enough they'd tracked him this quickly, but to know too that he'd stolen the rifle seemed almost supernatural to Tupper.

"The devil is with them, *Segoewa'tha* himself," he growled through clenched teeth.

His side seemed to burn brighter as he said this, the pain running deeper than the ruined skin and the bruised muscle. His hopes of eluding them or catching them flat-footed with the rifle were illusions. He'd have to play a different game now. They were ahead of him, waiting in some narrow place where they could shoot him from shore or block his escape and capture him. Outlet Bay, or the carry to Forked Lake were likeliest. That was not going to happen, Tupper told himself.

"Stupid white men," he said, spitting on the ground. "Fools to think they can catch an *Ongwe'onwe* that easily."

Tupper began to plan as he lifted the last few rocks out of the boat in the deepening gloom. He emptied the water and packed his gear, stopping before he set off only to empty his bowels. He was careful to bury his shit under the leaves before he went. What he didn't see was the lone guide boat far out in the lake. It had disappeared behind a point of land before he was ready to push off.

Busher had set about making a lean-to almost immediately after they'd gotten into position. In short order he had a small shelter with a pole frame roofed in bark and hemlock boughs. A soft bed of boughs covered the ground as well. As night fell Busher kindled a small fire and set a pot to boil.

"I know," Busher said as he caught Tom's look, "but I figure he knows we're here anyhow."

"Still no point giving him any more goddamned advantage than he's got already, Chauncey."

Busher shrugged. "You like your pork'n' beans cold, that's fine by me. 'Sides, since we made the portage, we're way ahead of him and the trees will cover our smoke. He won't be along for some time yet."

"Shit," Tom said. Busher grinned. He didn't care much for cold beans either.

"Burn the right wood an' a man can be on top of it before he'll see the smoke," he said.

Tom had to admit the fire hardly threw off any smoke, and what there was of it was being carried off by the breeze, which was picking up. Tom shrugged and walked off. Busher seemed to know what he was about, so he let it go.

Braddock sat on a rock at the shoreline, his boots almost in the water. This was a good spot. The lake was narrow here, though still wide enough that a boat hugging the far shore would be tough to spot once the night set in. Busher was betting that Tupper would have to either come this way or abandon the boat and take to the woods. There were other options open to a man like Tupper, they just weren't as likely.

"He could haul his damn boat over a mountain, if he was crazy enough I suppose," Busher said when they talked about it. "A man can do lots of things, if he sets his mind to it. All we can do is take our best guess."

This hadn't been much assurance to Tom, though he had to admit that out here, with the world virtually empty in every direction, a compass could point, there wasn't much else to be done. Braddock hoped Tupper wouldn't take to the woods. Finding him out there without dogs was a job he did not relish.

"Damn near to impossible," Busher had said. "Damn near. There's probably over two hundred thousand acres of forest back o' this lake.

Miles an' miles to anywhere. He gets in there, you might not see 'im, ever.'"

After a quick meal, Tom waited by the shore, the .30-40 Winchester across his knees and lukewarm pork and beans in his belly. He watched as the moon scaled the mountains and sent a silvery stream flowing across the lake. A gusting breeze blew, ruffling his hair. Busher had said it would bring some weather by morning.

Already the stars way off in the south and east were hooded by a low, brooding mass of black sky. Tom hoped that the guide had put enough bark on the lean-to. He hated a wet night in the woods.

The thought set him in mind of the many wet nights he'd spent in the army. There was no recalling them all. They ran into one another in an endless stream of mud, spongy boots, and soaked blankets. Even now, twenty-five years later, he couldn't smell wet wool without it coming to mind. So, as he watched the lake he thought not of Tupper but of those few years a lifetime gone when a wet bed seemed an adventure.

He was able to shake it off then. Like a sleek young retriever with a duck in his mouth, he'd gripped those years and shaken off their miseries, most of them. Still, they had left their mark as they had on everyone who'd served.

Braddock shrugged off his memories. He wasn't sitting on a rock in the middle of nowhere so he could reminisce, he told himself. But in the stillness of the night thoughts speak loudly.

As he watched the empty lake it was Mike who spoke to him. It was as if the boy were there beside him, telling him the things he'd been too deaf to hear. Tom knew how he'd have felt if he'd been stopped, treated like a boy, a hindrance to real men. But, the truth was that Mike wasn't a boy at all, Mike was only a few months younger than most of the men Tom had served with in the Twentieth New York.

Tom's head throbbed. He shifted his rifle on his knee. He wished Mike was there, wished he could tell him how he felt, how wrong he'd been to treat him like a boy. But that wouldn't happen. Mike was twenty miles away, safe in the Prospect House, and hating him.

Braddock checked his watch. He had to hold it up almost to the tip of his nose to see the hands, and only then once he'd angled it toward the moon's faint light. It was 10:15. He'd wake Busher in another hour. They'd agreed to watch in shifts until the early morning hours, when they figured it was likeliest Tupper would try to slip by. They'd both stand guard then.

Tom got up off the rock and rubbed his rump, gone numb from the cold, hard stone. He leaned against a birch whose bark seemed to glow, magnifying the moonlight in a spectral kind of way. He listened to the breeze in the branches, the lake lapping the shore, the hollow sound of their boat bumping against unseen rocks. It had been many years since he'd been out in the natural world at night. He didn't count the city as the natural world, though he'd seen plenty of it by gaslight. Not realizing it, he had missed the great outdoors. He hadn't known it was so. Thinking back, it was one of the things he recalled fondly from the war, the solitary hours standing guard under the stars, the sharpening of the senses when the world lay still.

Braddock didn't realize at first that the hollow bump, bump, bump he heard was not entirely of their boats' making. Other boatlike sounds had crept in on the lapping waves. Perhaps it was the breeze that was picking up. It blended the sounds so they became almost one.

The craft was upon him before he knew it was there, sliding by just a couple hundred feet from shore. Startled, Braddock raised his rifle. He strained to see the sights but couldn't and cursed as he aimed. He thumbed back the hammer and nestled his finger on the trigger, tightening as he focused on his target. The rifle boomed, a tongue of flame lighting the scene for a fraction of a heartbeat. In that brief instant of Winchester lightning, Tom saw it was Mike he'd shot at.

Tupper heard the shot. His head snapped around and he cocked an ear to catch the echoes. His neck ached with the sudden movement and his head swam.

"What you make of that?" he asked his grandfather's spirit sitting silently in the stern. He knew the shot was not directed at him. It had been too far off. He knew, too, that his pursuers would not have given away their position like that.

"Some things a man knows, some he believes. The rest he guesses," the spirit said as Tupper held the oars still. "What a man knows is but a drop in an ocean of knowing."

"Hmph," Tupper grunted. The old man's spirit said nothing.

"Shot was over ta Forked Lake," Tupper said at last, as if the old man was really there. The fact that the spirit was no longer just inside his head, but sitting in the back of his boat, made no impression on him at all. It seemed a natural enough thing, a manifestation that was just as real in its way as the physical, simply different. He gave it no thought.

The shot convinced him he'd done the right thing to double back. Whether it was the men he'd seen, the big cop and the guide, or just a hunter, the way to Forked Lake was blocked. He cursed his luck. If he'd been able to gain just a few more hours on them he'd be halfway to Long Lake by now.

"Goddamn steamers!" he said. "No man rowing could have caught me up like that."

"Fire and water," his grandfather said. "White men turn the world against us. The beaver in the pond and the trees in the forest are weapons in their hands."

Tupper's shoulders slumped over his oars. He wilted under his grandfather's words and his aching body sent waves of pain coursing through him. His head hung and his oars dragged as he thought of the truth in those words. But it was a momentary thing, a passing thunderhead of despair.

His boat rocked in the breeze that swept in gusting breaths across the lake. Tupper looked about. There was nothing to be seen, save a pinprick of light where he knew a camp to be. He was alone.

"Ain't caught yet, goddamnit," he said aloud. He flexed his arms at the oars, feeling the bruises and scrapes, but also feeling the strength that was in them. His grandfather's spirit smiled.

"Quiet old man! Heard enough from you," Tupper said with a warning frown. The old man seemed to laugh.

"Good. Good," he said. "The trout does not jump into the boat, Jim."

Tupper had to smile at that as he picked up his oars again. He remembered his grandfather saying that in another lifetime, when his pants were short and his hair long. "No, he doesn't," Tupper said as he started to row again. "The *Honio'o* may think they have me, but they do not. Not all the steamboats on all the lakes can make it so. They must catch me man-to-man, in the forest or on the water. Here I am strong and they are weak." The long oars groaned as Tupper pulled. The craft sliced through the water. Tupper knew where he was going.

Mike! Mike!"

Busher came at a run, his rifle ready.

Tom held a hand out. "It's my son. Don't shoot," he said, wading into the lake as if he might walk out to the boat. He'd only meant to fire a warning shot, to capture Tupper alive, but in the dark the best he'd been able to do was point somewhere ahead of the boat. He couldn't be sure.

"Dad?"

"Jesus, Mike, you all right?" Tom called as he splashed into the lake up to his waist, his voice cracking. The boat turned toward shore, a deeper shadow on the blue-black water.

"Don't shoot! It's me. It's Mike."

Tom caught the bow of the boat without a word, reaching for Mike with groping arms. An oar bumped him as he caught Mike's hand. He pulled the boy to him, rocking the boat and nearly capsizing it in his haste. He hugged him in the dark, an awkward embrace with the hard edge of the boat digging into his middle.

"Dear God, Mike I thought I killed you," Tom said, gripping him in vicelike arms. Mike hugged him back. Tom could feel him tremble.

"I'm okay, Dad."

"You're sure you're all right?" Tom asked, squinting in the dark, holding him at arm's length. "I—" he started to say, but Busher interrupted. He pulled at the bow of the boat, saying, "Best get you dried off, cap'n. I'll stoke the fire."

Once the boat was beached and Busher had added wood to the fire, Tom started stripping off his wet clothes. Mike took off his boots, propping them on sticks near the fire. Tom hung his wet pants from a nearby branch and, like Mike, propped his boots and socks as close to the fire as he dared. All was done in a silence punctuated only by the snap and pop of the fire. The flames grew, casting them in shifting reds and yellows so that at last they could see each other. Neither of them looked. The sides away from the flames were all in shadow.

When they had taken care of their wet clothes and Tom had rummaged in his pack for dry things for himself and a fresh pair of socks for Mike, he stood on the opposite side of the fire as Mike put the socks on.

"What the hell are you doing here, Mike?" Tom asked. There was no anger in his voice, only fatherly exasperation and a hint of something else. Mike picked up his head and looked straight at Tom. He could have sworn there was a touch of pride in the question. His jaw almost dropped. The fire crackled, sending a flock of sparks up into the blackness.

"I had to," Mike said, rubbing his hands by the fire.

A grim pursing of his lips and a nod were Tom's only reactions. He noticed Mike's hands in the firelight. They were red and raw.

"You rowed all that way, didn't you? Didn't take a steamer."

"Yeah," Mike said. "Didn't want anybody to see me."

"Your mother know?" Tom asked. He figured he knew the answer.

Mike shrugged with a guilty twist of his head. It was the one thing he wished he'd done.

"If I left a note . . . ," Mike began.

"You figured she'd have sent them after you," Tom said. He took a deep breath. "She'd have been right to. You know that, don't you?"

Mike didn't say anything. He didn't have to. Tom heaved a sigh and shook his head slowly.

"We're gonna have to get word to her," he said as he rubbed his temple. It had been throbbing since he'd taken that shot. "She'll be crazy with worry. You know how she can get."

Mike, who had been watching Tom with quiet intensity, allowed a tight grin to play across his lips. "Yeah, I know," he said.

Busher got up another pot of beans, cutting chunks of pork and tossing them in as the pot began to simmer. He tossed a can behind him. It bounced and clanked in the darkness.

"You didn't eat much, I figure," he said, squinting an eye at Mike. "Long pull from Blue." He stirred his pot for a moment as they stood watching the fire. "Got somethin' for them hands," he said. "Get it for ya after you sup."

Ten minutes later Mike was gulping down his dinner as fast as he could shovel it. Tom and Busher watched in silence, Tom with a furrowed brow, but the hint of a grin, Busher with a look of puzzlement. When he was done, Mike told them how he'd taken a boat when nobody was looking and pulled at the oars all day while keeping an eye out for them and for any pursuit.

"How'd you figure to find us, boy? You never been on these lakes before, have ye?" Busher asked. Mike grinned in a way that told them he knew how foolish he'd been, then said, "Didn't have much of a plan, I guess. I wasn't so worried about finding you as I was of finding Tupper."

Tom barked a grim laugh. "Lucky you didn't."

"Yeah," Mike said. "Came near to getting shot just finding you."

"Aw, now you know that was . . . ," Tom started to say, but Busher and Mike laughed him past his apology until he laughed, too. "I swear," Tom said, "I doubt you'll ever let me live that down."

Mike nodded in mock seriousness. "Not any time soon," he said grinning.

Tom grinned, too, and said, "That's my boy."

It wasn't long before exhaustion crept up on them all. The fire burned low, swallowed by their yawns. At last Busher got up, fetched his rifle, and as the darkness closed in on the dying fire, said, "I'll just take a turn for a while. Wake you in a couple hours."

Tom grunted a reply and he and Mike were soon lying curled in their blankets under the lean-to Busher had built. Sleep overcame them in minutes. The blackness of the deep woods blanketed them as they slept.

Tom didn't know what woke him. It was not a pleasant awakening. It was a jolt, a sudden, violent shift of reality that jacked his eyes wide and set his senses crackling. He strained his eyes and ears for the thing that had stolen his sleep. Lying still in the womb of the night, his senses slowly filled the void around him. He heard Mike's even snoring. He smelled the hemlock boughs that made his bed. He heard the gentle kiss of the lake as it lapped the rocky shore, the restless rustle of the forest as the wind stirred the treetops. He smelled their dead fire and the damp loam of the forest floor. Under that carpet of leaves and moss and withered vegetation, the earth was black, blacker than the night.

None of these things had broken his sleep. He knew that, or rather sensed it. Tom strained his eyes to take in whatever light and contrast they could. The only light that was plain and true was the light of the stars. He could see some through breaks in the trees. He thought, too, that he could make out a bit of the ghostly reflection of the moon on the lake, a scattered blur of silver through the trees. He lifted his hand before his face, moving it back and forth. He couldn't see it.

Living in the city, where gaslight and electric street lamps shooed away the dark, he'd forgotten how black the night could be. Usually that would not have bothered Tom. He wasn't one to fear the dark or fill it with demons. It was not superstitious dread that put the butt of the Colt in his palm, it was the sense of a presence, of watching eyes. He pointed the blued-steel barrel at the night. It was little comfort.

Slowly, Tom rolled to his knees, letting the blanket fall away. Again he spent minutes testing the air, listening, motionless. The wind breathed hard for a moment, setting the forest whispering, swaying, creaking. There might have been rustling steps down toward the shoreline. Tom couldn't be sure. He pointed the Colt in that direction, but when the wind subsided the rustling died too.

There was one noise that didn't stop with the wind, though. Tom couldn't identify it at first. It was a rhythmic creaking that he at first took for branches rubbing together. But there was something not right about that guess. He knew that sound, had heard it before, but here out of the context of the city noises he knew, he could not place it, though it was oddly familiar. The creaking subsided and was still, leaving him guessing. Tom came up to a low crouch, balanced on the balls of his feet. He thought to wake Mike but decided against it. He didn't want to risk the noise Mike might make and he didn't want to turn his back on whatever was out there.

Busher lay sleeping on the other side of the campfire. It felt like more than a couple of hours had passed and he imagined that the guide had fallen off, forgetting to wake him. Busher disdained sleeping in shelters like a sport, he'd said. He preferred to sleep in the open "whilst the weather cooperates." Tom suspected there was more than a little boast in it, a way to let a flatlander know who was the guide and who was the sport, even if their quarry ran on two legs.

There was no sound from where Busher lay. Tom couldn't make out his form either. Stepping around the dead remains of their fire, he figured he might risk waking the guide. Tom was prepared to give Busher hell for falling asleep. Busher'd been reluctant to watch through the night and confident that Tupper wouldn't attempt to attack the camp.

"He can count, I guess. Three of us don't make good odds fer him. We can sleep easy on that account."

As Tom stepped past the fire in its small circle of stones, he could feel the faint heat of the still-smoldering coals. A smoky, orange ball glowed up at him like the devil's own eye. Tom didn't care for the image. There was too much of the devil in the man they were after.

Tom moved to where he thought the guide lay, crouching low and groping like a blind man. Busher wasn't there. Puzzled, Tom kept searching, feeling the forest floor. He thought to strike a match, but the thought of making himself a target didn't appeal much.

"Hell," Tom mumbled, "Tupper could be standing right beside me, I'd never know it. Busher," Tom called in a hoarse whisper. "Busher, where the hell are you, man?"

The wind kicked up again, sending a shiver down his back.

"Busher, goddamnit! Where'd you get off to?"

The familiar creaking commenced again, started by the wind. It was off to the left a bit, but not far by the sound of it. Tom listened. It came to him then. "Damned if that don't sound like a hawser."

When the tide ran full or when the winds whipped across the harbor, the ships docked along the East River would tug at their moorings, setting the big ropes to groaning and squeaking. That's what this sounded like, except smaller somehow. Tom remembered they'd hung their food in a tree.

"Don't need 'coons nor b'ars eatin' my pork. Like bacon too much to feed it to the critters." Busher had said. But this sound wasn't coming from the right direction as far as he could tell, though he didn't really trust his senses in the night.

Tom groped forward, deciding to investigate the creaking rope, if that's what it was. He advanced, left hand extended, right holding the Colt close by his side. Branches tugged at his clothes and arms. Leaves and twigs crackled under foot. He cursed under his breath, knowing he was making too much noise, but unable to do anything else.

"Wouldn't take a goddamn Davy Crockett to hear me coming," he mumbled.

Still, he went forward, trusting to the pistol if need arose. He stopped after a few more steps, standing still, straining to see whatever he could and to take his bearings from the sound of the groaning rope. With a few more steps he figured to be right on it. Maybe then he'd risk a match.

Tom took a number of blind steps forward, feeling with his feet before setting them down, but as he did one foot caught on a fallen branch. He tried to pull free but somehow the other foot caught too. He stumbled forward, thrashing against the branches clutching at his legs. Tom made a desperate effort to keep from falling. All hope of stealth gone, he crashed through the underbrush, stumbling as he went, bouncing off one tree, then another until he ran into something.

The impact was abrupt. He could smell the damp wool, and the unwashed flannel of the man. Groping arms encircled him. His attacker yielded to the impact, giving way to Tom's forward momentum, holding him in a limp embrace.

"Christ!" Braddock said, pushing the Colt into the man's middle. Something stayed his hand, something not right. The man made no sound and seemed to sway as Tom wrestled with him.

"Busher? Busher, that you?" Tom said in a hoarse whipser. "Goddamnit. You scared the shit out of me." There was no answer. "This is no fucking joke. Damn it all, I nearly blew you in half. Busher?" No answer. The silence scared Tom worse than running into the man. "Busher. Come on. Fun's over."

Sweat ran in an icy trickle down Braddock's back. He reached out and touched the damp flannel of the man's shirt, feeling his way up until he reached his legs.

"Jesus Christ!" Tom grunted, the shock grabbing at his throat. The man was upside down. A rope creaked somewhere above.

Tom's hands trembled as he searched his pockets for a match. He fumbled them out, dropping a bunch in the process. He tucked the Colt in his waistband and after a moment's hesitation struck a match. It spluttered and flared before settling into a constant flame in Tom's cupped hands. His hands were red in the flame's glow, as red as blood. It took an instant to realize his hands were smeared in it.

"Shit! What the . . ."

Tom held the faint light closer to the body, cupping his hands to keep the flame alive in the growling wind. A long gust rolled through the trees, snuffing his light and plunging him again into darkness. The body swayed before him, bumping him. The rope creaked and groaned.

Tom lit another match after three attempts. This time he got a long look. It was Busher, hung by his feet about four feet off the ground. He was hard to recognize. His face was a red mask. His crimson mouth, hung open in a ghastly, cavernous way but it was too big to be a mouth. A closer look showed him it was his throat, cut wide and deep, gaping with the weight of Busher's head. The match burnt down to Tom's fingers and again he was plunged into the dark. The image of Busher's nearly severed head floated before him where the light had been.

Tom crouched low, the Colt appearing in his hand. He knew that the man who'd butchered Busher was there with him, feet away or hundreds of yards off, he couldn't tell. Like the hot breath of the coming storm it pebbled his skin and rustled the leaves. Tom was as close to panic as he could remember, but he didn't give in to his fears. Though his stomach knotted and his mouth seemed filled with sand, he held firm. Tupper couldn't see any better in the dark than he could, he reasoned. It was some consolation to think that, though he wasn't sure he believed it. The Colt was consolation too. Tom trusted his skill with it as completely as any man could. As the walnut of the grips warmed to his hand his nerves calmed. Then he thought of Mike.

A rustling off toward the camp galvanized him. In a hot flash he threw away all caution.

"Mike! Wake up! Get your gun!" he yelled at the top of his lungs. Tom ran, not caring for the noise or the branches that slapped at his face and caught his legs. "Mike, get up!" he called as he came crashing toward the camp. He almost ran into the lean-to. Mike was rolling to his knees, groping for the rifle.

"Jesus Christ! You scared the shit out of me!"

"You all right? Got the rifle?" Tom said, relieved but wasting no time. "Busher's dead!"

"Wha?"

"Murdered. Let's go!"

"Murdered? How? Where?"

"Not now. Get your pack," Tom said. "Gotta find a defensive position," he said, reverting to his war vocabulary, remembering in a flash the times when he could not seem to dig fast enough nor build breastworks high enough.

"Can't stay here."

"Where we going? Can't see a hand in front of my face. Can't hardly see you," Mike said. Tom stood still for a moment. In truth, he wasn't sure where they should go.

Blundering around the forest wasn't much of an option. They'd be easy game. They'd need cover if they were to see the next sun.

"Tree," Tom said, knowing they couldn't take to the boats, where they'd be easy targets from the shore until they got far enough out. They went to a large, white pine, not far from the shore.

"Climb," Tom said. "I'll cover till you get up."

Mike climbed for some minutes before Tom started up.

"High enough yet?" Mike said, when Tom caught up.

"Hard to tell," Tom said. "Can't see the ground. A bit more." The branches of the big pine were like the rungs of a ladder and they climbed with relative ease for another ten feet or so before stopping. "This is good," Tom said. "Better than waiting to get shot in that lean-to." The dense screen of branches and needles hid them completely.

"Long as we stay quiet, we'll have the advantage," Tom said. "Get comfortable. We'll wait out the dawn. Maybe surprise him if he comes in again. Keep that rifle ready."

They sat long in silence. The big tree moved and swayed as the growing wind grabbed at its branches. Tom drank in the smell of the pine. The scent was a tonic, reaching places in his lungs that city air never touched. He was gradually lulled in its embrace, his nerves soothed. Mike sat silently near, straddling a branch with his back against the rough trunk.

Tom thanked God he was all right. With a little bit of guilt for his selfishness, Tom realized how glad he was to have him near. How foolish he'd been to doubt the man. The *man,* Tom repeated in his mind. Though one part of him was angry that he'd come, another was grateful beyond speaking for his being there.

The rain started sometime around 4 A.M. They could hear it pattering on the roof of leaves around them. For a while their pine kept them dry enough, but as the upper boughs became soaked, a steady bombardment started. It wasn't long before it soaked them through, despite turned-up collars and snugged-down hats. The wind shook the tree with great, shivering gusts, pelting them. In their hurry they hadn't thought to fetch their oilcloths.

"Cold," Mike said as he shifted on his perch, one hand gripping the trunk for support.

Tom grunted agreement. Though he doubted it was much cooler than the mid-sixties, it felt twenty degrees colder in his soaked clothing.

"Colder still for Busher," Tom said.

"You're sure? I mean he wasn't just—"

"I'm sure," Tom said.

"Huh?" Mike said. His teeth had begun to chatter and talking was becoming a chore.

"For one thing," Tom said just above the noise of the wind, "Busher had his throat cut. The others Tupper killed with a bayonet, Lettie and the man from the Albany boat, according to Chowder. And this has been bothering me all day. Tupper hit me with a chunk of ice."

Mike chuckled. "Can see how that might bother you."

Tom chuckled too, though his head hurt at the memory. "No. I mean, there he was with an ice pick in his hand but he doesn't stick me with it. He hits me with the ice."

Mike was silent for a long moment while the wind moaned through the forest. "So you're saying?" he said, not sure of what conclusions to draw.

"Saying here's a man's supposed to have killed people with a long, sharp metal object to the head, but when he's got the chance to do just that he hits me with an ice cube. Don't add up."

Mike twisted on his branch to get a better look at Tom. He couldn't see his face. Tom was just a lump of deeper black on the nearby branch. A gust of wind shook their tree and, like a wet dog, it shook off the rain, pelting them. An icy river ran under Mike's collar and down his back. He shivered in the darkness. Mike pulled his collar tighter. He sat in silence. How much of his shivering was from the cold and wet was hard to say. There was enough in their situation to make a warm man shiver.

Twenty

There is a breed in the Adirondacks today that calls itself guide.
Let the outlander beware. The last genuine article passed over the hills . . .
years ago . . . Around 1900 he disappeared from the landscape with the
earlier wolf and the panther, and the woods never saw his like again.

—MARY MACKENZIE

Mitchell Sabattis sat near a small campfire, burning low. Buttermilk Falls roared behind him, tumbling down its steep, rocky channel then dropping ten feet to the quiet pool below. The rocks he lay on still held a little heat from the sun, but the night air was chill and the rain beat hard against his little shelter. Mitchell had left late that day, once he'd packed his client off to Boston, where the streets were cobbled and houses so close they shared walls with their neighbors.

Mitchell had no good reason to leave his home in Long Lake. He had no client, no tracking to do, nor gear to lug. What he had was a feeling, a need to be in the wild. He loved the woods, had spent his life in the open. His earliest recollections were of forest and water, fish and game. The cathedral of trees that stretched for days in all directions was as much a home to him and as much a church as any roof he'd ever known. It had been calling him for days, as it did from time to time, pulling him from the comforts of a hot stove and clean sheets. His wife knew those moods. She'd said nothing when he left, not even when he didn't say how long he'd be gone. Her husband always returned, but she couldn't always say when.

Mitchell sniffed the breeze. The rain would stop before morning. He hadn't bothered building shelter, preferring to rest under his overturned boat. A mattress of hemlock cushioned the ground. He'd stay drier under the boat than in just about anything else. He had his oilcloth and food enough to last through days of wet weather. He'd even stowed dry wood under the boat, in case the rain decided to linger. It often did. Storms could squat in the mountains for days, feeding off the lakes and the currents of air swirling among the peaks.

Mitchell lay on his back, looking up at the ribs of the boat, ribs he had made with his own hands, cut from spruce stumps, where the roots spread into the ground. He'd sheathed the boat with pine planks just five-sixteenths of an inch thick. The spruce root ribs gave them strength far beyond their weight. Mitchell liked to harvest his pine from high elevation, north-facing slopes, conditions that made for slow growth, tight rings, and strong wood. He let them cure for years. Mitchell was a patient man.

His boats could carry three men and enough gear for weeks in the woods, travel hundreds of miles, portaging from one lake to the next. Water was the highway of the Adirondacks and boats the best way to travel. They were fast. The long oars could drive one at speeds no two paddlers could match. They were simple, elegant, their knife-edged lines pleasing to the eye.

Mitchell liked to keep things simple, mostly because simple just seemed right. There was something in the forest that demanded simplicity. Things had a way of getting boiled down in the wilderness. The woods would get hold of a man and slow him enough so he could see the world around him, slow enough so he could see himself.

There had been a time when alcohol had blurred Mitchell's vision, back when his sap was high, before the word of God had gotten through. He was slower now in the ways that counted and saw himself with an unclouded eye. He saw the woods and waters as few others did. He knew his place in them and them in him.

Sabattis settled in to wait. He lay under the boat and watched the last of his little fire flicker and die, drowned by the steady rain. The night stalked in. The roar of the falls lulled him, weighing his eyelids and loosening his limbs. Still, he waited. He'd had the waiting feeling for days, the sense that something was approaching. He closed his eyes. He'd need his rest, he figured. He'd seen sixty summers pass under the Adirondack stars. He wasn't as young as he once was.

Tom's got this Tupper fella on the run, Chief," Chowder said as he burst into Byrnes's office. It was barely seven o'clock, but Byrnes was already half through his first cigar. Byrnes looked up from his desk with a frown wreathed in smoke. He hated when Chowder didn't knock first. It set a bad example for the rest of the men. Byrnes flicked the ash off his cigar and held out a hand for the telegram. Though he was happy to get the news, he'd be damned if he'd give Chowder any encouragement.

"Got in last night," Chowder said as he handed it over.

Byrnes read in silence. "Sounds like he's got his hands full." He looked up at Chowder and grinned. It was not a pleasant sort of smile, and Chowder knew what was coming. "Pack what you need and get up there, Kelly. I want this bastard back in a box or in irons. Don't care which."

Chowder Kelly threw out his chest and did his best, snappy salute. "Sir!" he said before turning and marching out the door.

"And close my goddamn . . ." Byrnes said as Chowder disappeared, leaving the door wide open. "Sonofabitch!" Byrnes said, blowing smoke. Still, he grinned in a rueful sort of way.

"Too close to retirement to teach that bastard any respect," he mumbled. Byrnes didn't really mind. Chowder was worth two of any of the rest of his men, but he could be a burr under his saddle, too. A little time stomping about the woods would do him some good.

Twenty-One

Man is nothing here, his very shouts die on his lips.

—JOEL T. HEADLEY

"I can't see the boats," Tom said as he craned to see around the branches. "Damn! I think they're gone!" It was finally light enough to make things out through the mists that the sun had yet to burn off the lake. They could see a bit of their camp and pewter-gray slices of water, but not much more. "To hell with this," Tom said. My ass is so damn sore, I don't give a shit if it gets shot. I'm going down." He heard a click as Mike thumbed back the hammer on the Winchester.

Tom climbed down slowly. His stiff limbs and back wouldn't allow for any fast moves. He stopped at each descending branch, scanning the dripping forest. He saw nothing, but continued at a careful pace, dropping to the ground at last, his pistol ready and his back to the wide trunk.

"C'mon slow, Mike," Tom called in a hoarse whisper. "Watch your footing."

Mike was down a couple of minutes later.

The boats were gone. Tom and Mike stood at the shore for a long moment, staring out at the empty lake. Nothing moved in any direction. No other boats could be seen, no steamers, no guides, nothing.

"Shit," Tom muttered. "Looks like we've got some walking to do."

They checked the camp. It seemed undisturbed at first, but on closer inspection Tom found that most of their provisions were gone.

"Bastard cleaned us out," Tom said. Mike just looked about, his hands gripping the stock of the rifle so hard his knuckles were white.

"How could he do this?" Mike asked, shivering in his damp clothes. "I didn't hear anything, didn't see anything. It's like he could fly or something."

Tom grinned, though there was nothing funny about what Mike had said. "How was it we were the ones up in the tree then?" he said, trying to ease Mike's nerves. "Tupper's no bird," he went on, "though I'll admit there's some evidence to the contrary. Trouble is, we're in his element, and as long as we are . . . ," Tom said, trailing off, not needing to finish the thought.

"Figured with Busher we'd have an even chance. Now . . ." Tom gestured in the direction where their "even chance" hung with his throat cut. "Gotta see about him," he said with a resigned sigh.

They cut the guide down, easing his body onto the blood-soaked carpet of leaves. Mike, whose hands started to shake when he first saw Busher's gaping throat, managed to steady himself and carry on much like Tom did. Mike didn't want to let his father down, not even in this.

They wrapped Busher's body in a blanket, then collected enough stones to cover him. Without a shovel it was the best they could do.

"Keep the animals from taking him, at least," Tom said when they were done, though he wasn't so sure of that.

They collected their remaining gear, dividing it between them. There wasn't all that much, and very little of it food. They searched the shoreline, hoping the boats had only been cut loose and had drifted away.

They were on a long, wide finger of land that jutted out into the lake opposite the carry from Raquette. The lake ran in a long bay to the east for what looked like two or three miles. To the north the lake disappeared behind ragged peninsulas that hid bays of untold size. What appeared to be the north end was at least two miles off. Though they trudged and scrambled about for what seemed like miles, they found nothing. They stopped finally at a low, wide marsh that blocked their way.

"Damn," Tom said, shielding his eyes to look into the distance. "Long hike to get around this."

It was an area of muddy pools, tall grasses, and thick cattails, bordered by dense stands of brush. A lone heron, standing like a statue on long orange legs, was all they could see. "We're not gonna find them. My guess is he either sunk them or towed them across."

"Either way, they're no good to us," Mike said. "Anybody live out here? Haven't seen a thing all morning."

"Thought I heard Frederick say something about building a house out here. Can't recall if he'd actually done it. Tell you the truth, I think we're better off going back to the carry. More likely to find someone there."

Mike nodded, looking at the impenetrable marsh and the surrounding army of trees. "Beats wandering around."

There was a whining buzz then that seemed to pass between Tom and Mike, followed by the boom of a rifle. Tom was down on the ground in an instant, the Colt in his hand. Mike stood where he was frowning down at Tom.

"Get down!" Tom shouted. Mike awoke from his stupor and crouched as a second shot whistled where his head had been.

"Where? Where's it coming from?" Mike said. There was fear in his voice now. "Don't know," Tom said. "Maybe somewhere off that way." He pointed toward the forest away from the marsh. "He's got us caught." Another shot snicked through the branches above them.

"Did you see anything that time?" Mike asked.

"Thought I saw something the top o' that little hill," Tom said, pointing the Colt. Another shot sent up a shower of earth and leaves an inch from Tom's shoulder, throwing dirt in his eyes. Tom shouted in surprise and pain.

"That's him!" Mike said as Tom rolled to his left, pawing at his eyes. Tom heard Mike's Winchester boom three times in quick succession. Tom could barely see Mike through the dirt and tears.

"Dad, you okay?" Mike shouted. "You're not shot, are you?"

"No, I'm okay, just got some dirt in my eyes," Tom said, still struggling to clear them. He was seeing double out of the right one, which had gotten the worst of it. "See him? Hit anything?" Tom said, trying to see up the hill.

"Don't know," Mike said. Think I might have flushed him. They waited in silence straining to see. Tom couldn't get his right eye to clear. It felt like a small boulder had lodged under the upper lid. He looked around, measuring the terrain and the safest avenue of escape.

"Mike, we gotta get better cover." He was looking at the marsh, with its thick border of brush and cattails. "We get in there, he won't be able to see us. We work our way down his flank, come at him from the west."

Mike just nodded, though with a twist of his mouth that said he wasn't happy about the prospect of wading through the muddy tangle. There hadn't been another shot in a couple of minutes. Mike began to relax and he lifted his head to see up the hill.

"Maybe I hit him," he said. There was no sound except the breeze.

"Stay down!" Tom said. "No way to be sure. Listen, you fire a couple shots up there, I'll run for the marsh. When I whistle, I'll cover you from there, okay?"

Tom rolled into a crouch and gave Mike a nod. The Winchester boomed and Tom was off at a run. The Winchester boomed again as he crashed through the heavy brush. But it caught at him and tripped him, and he went down on one knee. He thought he heard another shot buzz by him, but he couldn't be sure. He kept going as the Winchester boomed again. He dropped behind a heavy clump of cattails, his legs in the black water. A shot ripped through the cattails somewhere to his left but not close.

"Mike," Tom called.

"Yeah?"

"Stay low!" Tom checked the Colt for mud or any other obstructions, then rose up and fired. The Colt barked as he sprayed the woods, trying to place each shot in a slightly different location, hoping that one would be close enough to keep Tupper's head down. Mike came crashing through the brush a moment later. There wasn't any answering fire.

Mike was breathing hard as he splashed down beside Tom. They both crouched low, up to their waists in water. Tom peered along the fringe of the marsh. "We keep along here, behind the brush," he said, pointing, "then come out maybe a quarter mile down. Work our way up the hill and come at him from the side and rear." Mike just nodded.

They started moving, keeping well separated and staying low. They waded through black, stinking water, sometimes sinking to their knees in sucking mud. They scrambled over logs and boulders. They swatted at mosquitoes and deer flies that swarmed up in clouds at every step. All the while Tom rubbed at his eye. There were no more shots. Nothing but silence followed them.

It took half an hour to work their way through the marsh to a spot where Tom thought it would be safe to reenter the woods. They stopped at a large deadfall, a tree that had fallen into the marsh, its branches forming a nearly impenetrable tangle. Beaver had chewed some of the branches.

"Okay. I'll go out this way," Tom said, pointing along the trunk of the tree. "You come out a little further down. Give me a few minutes. I'll whistle when I think it's clear."

Tom pushed his way through the tangle of brush, branches, and cattails, disappearing in a few yards. Mike waited until the noise of his passage lessened, figuring he'd passed through the worst of the tangle. When he didn't hear any firing he started to move around to the other side of the deadfall. He waded around the ends of the branches. The water was deeper there, coming up above his waist. He had to hold the Winchester up to keep it dry.

Mike was nearly around and getting into shallower water, when his feet caught on some submerged branches. His left foot slid between two and he fell forward. His foot twisted as he went, locking it in. Mike was under water before he realized what had happened. He tried to get his feet under him but he couldn't kick free. He pushed up from the muddy bottom, but the best he could do was get his nose above the water. Panic set in quickly. His feet thrashed.

He twisted onto his back, hoping to work free, but all that did was send a searing pain up from his ankle that had him screaming under water, gulping for air and getting only liquid. He lunged up for another gulp of air but sank back as he sucked in water with it, choking and coughing, taking in more and more water with each passing second. Mike fought with everything that was in him, reaching down to pull at the branches that gripped his ankle.

He dropped the rifle to fight with both hands. His leg screamed as the skin was torn on the rough bark. He lunged for another gulp of air but he was weakening and barely got a mouthful. He grabbed the branches and thrashed like a madman, but they were too strong, still supple from being under water. With a final lunge, he tried to call for help, but managed only a strangled gurgling before he sank below the surface again.

He couldn't breathe. His lungs were full. The black water filled with mud choked off the last of his consciousness and he started to relax, sinking to the bottom as the last of his sight narrowed to a pinpoint. His oxygen-starved brain flashed brilliant images in bursts of color, Tom, Mary, 'Becca, his fight with the bow tie man on the Lower East Side, a cat he kept when he was little, Lettie's hair with the sun shining through.

Nothing.

Mike didn't feel the hand that grabbed him, didn't know how he'd been pulled from the water. His first conscious thought was of pain, as a rough stub of cattail dug into his cheek. More pain followed, as coughing and retching wracked him. Water spewed out of his mouth along with everything he'd eaten in his entire life. He curled into a ball, gasping and retching, unaware of who had saved him or how.

When at last he opened his eyes enough to focus, he looked up at a face he'd never before seen. The face was small and deeply furrowed. Like an old, brown glove or a carving in well-aged wood, the visage was creased and worn. There was a steadiness, a constancy about it, almost as if the mountains had taken human form. It was an Indian face. It looked at him from under the brim of a small round hat, almost like a yarmulke the Jews on Hester Street wore, except with a narrow brim. The Indian grunted and smiled.

Tom had scouted ahead into the forest, sliding from tree to tree, keeping low but still blinking and rubbing his eye. It was running tears like a leaky faucet and still feeling like something had lodged under the lid. He went perhaps fifty yards, taking a long sweep across their front. He didn't see or hear anything.

Working his way back to the area where he expected Mike to

emerge from the marsh he crouched waiting. He planned their next movements while he checked the Colt once more, breaking open the cylinder and looking down the barrel. A bit of dirt, a twig, a piece of marsh grass was all it might take to jam it or even blow it up in his hand. He had it back together in thirty seconds, but by then was wondering where Mike was.

He figured he'd be behind him by no more than a couple of minutes. Tom started to scan the marsh and the dense brush, taking his eyes off the forest. He didn't want to risk calling. Impatience and worry mixed in him as the seconds ticked by. With a final glance over his shoulder at what he hoped was the empty forest, he started to push his way back into the marsh. As he fought through the broad border of brush, he became more worried.

Had Tupper taken to the water, paddling up on Mike through the narrow channels? Tom doubted it, but the fact that he hadn't considered the possibility before made it seem all the more plausible. Tom was sweating heavily within seconds, the exertions of his struggle through the brush and tall grasses adding to his anxiety. He tried to run, grunting with the effort of fighting the clutching branches. His clothes tore. Scratches marked his face and arms and hands. He held tight to the Colt as he bulled through, tripping and thrashing.

He burst through at last and slid into waist-deep water before he could stop himself. The first thing he saw as he slid down the muddy bank was an Indian standing over Mike not more than ten yards away. Tom slid to a stop, the Colt held on the man with both hands.

"Stop!" Tom said in heaving, breathless growl, though he wasn't sure exactly what the Indian should stop doing. Tom saw the shotgun, held in the crook of an arm.

"Hello," the man said, seemingly unconcerned about the pistol pointed at his middle. "You need help." It was not a question but a statement of fact, a distinction not lost on Tom. "Heard the shooting."

"It's okay," Mike choked out. "Saved me." Mike couldn't finish as a series of wet coughs had him holding his middle and spitting up more water. Tom noticed the boat for the first time, noticed, too, that the man was drenched and dripping.

"Fished the boy out. Pretty near drowned in there," he said with a look at the black water.

Mike nodded with an emphatic shake of his head, though he still choked and coughed.

"Skittish for sports," the Indian said, as he looked at the pistol Tom held on him, the man's shotgun never wavering from its rest.

The Winchester, Tom noticed, lay beside Mike. Tom took a hard look at the man. It was clearly not Tupper. This man was older, shorter, and of slighter build. Tom let his pistol drop to the grass. "We've got our reasons," he said, but when the Indian didn't ask, he went on, "I'm Tom Braddock. This is my son, Mike. Our guide's been murdered and somebody's been shooting at us."

A frown furrowed the Indian's leathery features. The eyes sharpened. Mitchell Sabattis could remember only a handful of murders in all his years in the Adirondacks. They were a rarity, though death from other causes was common enough.

"Your guide?" Mitchell said. There wasn't a guide in the north country he didn't know or had heard of. They were like family, some of them, a fraternity of men who'd chosen the way of woods and water.

"Busher," Tom said, watching Sabattis closely. "And you'd be?"

"That Ole, or one o' the other brothers, Chauncey or—"

"Chauncey," Tom said.

Mitchell shifted the shotgun and stuck out a small, brown hand. "Mitchell Sabattis," he said.

"Sabattis," Tom said, remembering the story he'd heard in the hotel bar. "Heard o' you." Tom sloshed through the marsh and shook with him. The little man's grip was like iron.

"Who was it shooting at you?" Mitchell asked with a nod of his head toward the forest.

"Man named Tupper," Tom said. "Escaped murderer from down in the city. He killed Busher."

"Don't know the Tuppers that much," Mitchell said. "Mohawks, from up around Saranac and Tupper Lake?"

Tom nodded.

"Littletree's their real name. Not many of 'em left. The grandfather died just a year or so ago, from what I heard. He was the last of the old family." Mitchell looked hard at Tom. "And you say he murdered somebody in the city?"

Tom explained how he knew that and how he'd come to be in a marsh on Forked Lake getting shot at. Tom skipped a bunch of inconvenient details in the telling. He wasn't sure if Mitchell believed it all, but the man didn't give any indication either way.

"And he's out there?" Mitchell asked.

"Well, if it wasn't him shootin' at us, I'd damn sure like to know who else."

Mitchell shrugged and picked up his shotgun. "Let's go see."

The three of them fanned out as they went through the brush. Mitchell insisted he be in front a few yards, Mike to his right and Tom at the other end, about a hundred feet away. They worked their way through the woods, going very slowly, pausing with every few steps. Tom indicated with hand signals where he though Tupper had been and they circled back in that direction. The cover was thick. Leaves and dead branches made it almost impossible to walk silently, although Tom noticed after a while that Mitchell seemed to make no noise whatsoever. Mike made enough for both of them.

At last, sweating and tense, they approached the hill, going up from tree to tree. They crested the top and had a relatively clear view of the surrounding woods. Tupper wasn't there.

"Somebody was here," Mitchell said, kneeling to examine the ground. "Behind this log." A tree had fallen, breaking off a few feet above the ground, leaving the trunk lying at an angle with a space underneath. "He shot from here. Good cover." Tom bent and picked up a shell casing.

"A thirty-thirty Winchester," Tom said. Mitchell and Mike both looked at it, but Mitchell was more interested in the ground.

"He came in this way," he said, pointing at tracks Tom and Mike could hardly see. "See the way the prints go? Heavy on the toes. Stalking," Mitchell said. He pointed to one of the clearer tracks and the way the front of the foot had left a deeper impression. "He was on one knee for a bit," Mitchell went on, "then he laid down to shoot."

Mitchell turned and examined the ground again, bending low, almost like a hound. "Left this way," he said after a while. "In a hurry."

"Why do you say that?" Mike asked.

Mitchell looked at him as if he were blind. "Look," he said. "Tracks are clearer. He took no care in how he went. See the scuff mark where he kicked the moss off that rock?" Mitchell said, pointing to a rock a few yards away, "This man didn't do that on the way in. Could be, he saw me coming in the boat. I'd have been out of range."

Tom grunted. It made sense. This was not so much different from the way he went about investigating a crime scene back in the city. The differences were critical though, the signs much more subtle. But the signs were there for Mitchell.

"This man was right-handed," Mitchell said with a look at Tom. Tom nodded but didn't say anything, waiting for Mitchell to explain. Mitchell said nothing more, so Tom went back to the leaning tree trunk. Kneeling, he examined the ground closely. He saw it then, the combined impression of right knee and left foot.

"He kneeled behind here."

"So?" Mike said. "Most people are right-handed."

"Not Tupper," Mitchell said. "His whole family was left-handed. Everybody knew that."

They didn't linger long. Mitchell led them back to his boat and rowed them the mile or so back to their camp site of the night before. They'd come into shore with both the Winchester and the Colt trained on the trees. The three of them scoured the area around the camp ranging well back into the forest, but Tupper was not there.

"Knew Ole better than his brothers," Mitchell said later as they stood over Chauncey's grave. Sabattis examined everything he could, every sign and print and broken twig. "One man," he said after a while. "Just one."

They went back to the grave and the tree where Busher had hung. "Chauncey and Goose were younger. Old man Busher's second wife's," Mitchell said. "Good people mostly, even if they are Baptists. Guiding at the Prospect?"

"Yup," Tom said as Mitchell pulled some stones away from

Busher's head. He crouched low for some minutes, looking at the corpse. Finally, without standing or even looking at Tom, he said, "Tell me again."

Tom did. He held nothing back, sensing that if he did Sabattis would somehow know it. The guide listened in silence. His dark eyes gleamed, though, and one eyebrow raised when Tom told what happened at Castle Rock.

"You heard cries? What they sound like?" He merely grunted when Tom told him as close as he could, and he didn't question Mike at all, just watched him with eyes like deep, black mirrors as Tom explained that Mike was a suspect in Lettie Burman's death, though it was going to be clear now, even to the doctor, that Mike had nothing to do with that. At last, when Tom was done and had told what he could, including their night in the tree, Mitchell asked, "What will you do?"

The question caught Tom off guard. He'd expected something different—doubts, hostility, or at least skepticism. He hesitated before answering.

"Go back or go forward," Mitchell said, as if either were of no consequence to him.

"Hell!" Tom said, balling his hands into fists. "I'm going to catch this sonofabitch, *we're* going to," he said, nodding toward Mike. "We're not about to back off, not even for this; especially not for this."

Mitchell nodded, looking from Tom to Mike.

"Tupper will not catch easy. Won't give up," Mitchell said.

"You're going to help us?" Mike asked.

Mitchell looked at him almost as if he didn't understand the question. "You've told me the truth. Anyone could see. And my own eyes have seen what was done to Busher."

"Thanks," Tom said.

Mitchell shrugged. "Not you I'm helping, not really," he said as he started to pile the rocks back over the body.

"One thing bothers me," he said as Tom helped with the stones.

"I know," Tom said. "You're thinking about his throat and why he wasn't killed like the others."

Mitchell grunted and stood, stretching his back. Looking down at the pile of stones, he said, "Every critter kills in his own way. Maybe when a man becomes an animal he kills like an animal." He shrugged, rolling another stone into place. "I don't know," he added, "I guess you've got more experience with killers than me, at least the two-legged kind. Makes me wonder, though."

A half hour later they were in Mitchell's boat, heading for the Raquette River.

"He's not on the river yet," Mitchell explained. "Just came from Long Lake. I would see if he was."

Tom took this at face value, though Mike gave a small frown of doubt. Mitchell took no note of it.

"Couldn't he have taken a boat that way?" Mike asked.

"I came that way," Mitchell said. "I saw no one. The only other way is by land, and that's a long way around, miles, with a river to cross. If he went that way and then heads for the Raquette River, we'll still be way ahead."

"Then we've got maybe four, five hours on him," Tom said, looking at the sun. Tom's curiosity was up, though, and he had to ask, "If he's not on the river, then what do you figure he did?"

Mitchell didn't answer immediately. This had been bothering him, too, so much so that he almost doubted that Tupper hadn't been able to get by on the river without being seen. If he was Tupper, he'd have gone downriver as fast as his boat could go.

"He could have doubled back," Tom said. "Wait for the right time. He maybe took to the woods and God knows where."

Mitchell considered another possibility that Tom hadn't voiced, but, as he looked at Tom and Mike again and considered what they'd told him, he dismissed the thought. He was a good judge of people, always had been. Their words were true. He was sure of it. There was one more possibility.

"He's not running because he's not finished," Mitchell said. "He's waiting."

Twenty-Two

So rapid was the passage of the boat, that the water,
as it parted before it, rose up on each side as high
as his shoulders, and foamed like a torrent past me.

—JOEL T. HEADLEY

The search hadn't started officially until just before dawn. Though Frederick had quietly sent out some of his men the evening before, they'd come back with no sign of Mike. By late that night, when Mary could no longer avoid the sheriff or the doctor, she had to give in and tell them Mike had vanished. Mary, with Frederick Durant at her side, met with the sheriff in Frederick's office. The sheriff, a Scott named MacDougal, was not pleased.

"Ma'am, wi' all due respect to you, your laddie looks guilty as a fox in a chicken coop. Him running like he has don't look good. No' good a' tall."

"Now, Mister MacDougal," Frederick broke in, "we don't know that Mike is running. You can't assume that and have no definitive proof to make such a statement."

Despite Durant's manner, MacDougal didn't budge much.

"I know who you are, Mister Durant. Know who your cousin is, too. But the fact is a man gets to thinkin' on his deeds an' his legs just can't keep still. Aven't seen a runner yet wasn't guilty," MacDougal said with a mixture of skepticism and deference. He shrugged and went on. "Canno' prove it yet, I'll grant ye, but if he's lost, it'd be damned bad timing, I'd say."

Much of the rest of the interview went the same way, with a thick bedrock of suspicion underlying most of the sheriff's questions. What Mary hadn't paid as much attention to was that MacDougal had asked a number of salient questions about Tupper, the method by which he'd killed the man in New York and the steward on the Albany night boat. He still thought it was damned suspicious that Mike had disappeared when he had, but if it wasn't for Mary's fear and anger she'd have noticed that he seemed to have a good many questions for the doctor as well.

Mary didn't know what to think by the time she left. She'd kept her temper though. She'd had too many dealings with cops over the years not to know how to handle them. There wasn't much she could do, anyway. She felt powerless, helpless, lost. Her city-bred self-assurance had been stripped away.

In New York, with her money, her discreet influence, and her police captain husband, there was little she couldn't accomplish, few she couldn't bend to her will one way or another. Here, she was just another tourist, albeit one who had Durant's ear. Durant was her only card, and perhaps Duryea, too; though, of him she wasn't as sure. Mary had learned by hard experience to work with the cards she'd been dealt. But this was a bad hand, a loser's hand.

She was relieved, though, that she'd been able to dispose of Lettie's pantalets before the sheriff arrived. There had been too much else to try to explain without having to deal with that little question, too. The thought of them made her wonder. She didn't like to even entertain the thought, but sometimes her mind took her places she didn't want to go. Mary suppressed a shiver and bent her thoughts to how to find Mike.

She got Frederick's promise to again send some of his guides in search of Mike and asked if he thought Duryea could help.

"The general's not in the best shape for a prolonged search," Durant said with an absent look in the direction of the Duryea camp. His attention seemed riveted on a stage as it left the hotel. It was piled high with luggage, and passengers clinging to every available perch. The top-heavy coach rumbled off slowly, wallowing and pitching as it went.

"His boys might pitch in, though," Durant went on, regaining his thoughts with a small sigh. "They're a high-spirited pair and could be of some help, I suppose."

Mary nodded. "It appears I'll need all the help I can get," she said. She didn't like to think what might happen if MacDougal found Mike first.

"Can I get a boat to the general's, Frederick?"

Durant watched a few minutes later as Mary, with Rebecca at her knees, was rowed around the point. He fingered the telegram in his pocket. He'd have to tell her, he knew. But with all the attention focused on her son, adding to her worries for her husband hardly seemed fair. He hadn't thought it wise to tell her before her talk with the sheriff. MacDougal had been very curious on that point, and he'd worried that Mary would have revealed his whereabouts.

The message from William had been ominous, but at least it was clear that Tom was somewhere near Raquette Lake. Frederick had already sent a man to find him and tell him about Mike's disappearance. He'd hoped to send Owens in search of Tom, but the man was said to be at Raquette already, with a client.

He'd told his man to find Owens, too, if he could. With a little luck, perhaps one of them would be able to catch up to Tom. Turning back toward the hotel, he saw MacDougal standing on the lawn below the verandah. He was gazing at the point of land where Mary had just disappeared.

Tupper watched from the top of the ridge. He had a good view, could see the carry, the long, narrow outlet from Raquette and a bit of the river beyond. His long-laker lay nearby. He'd hauled it up the ridge, a thing nobody would expect and never think to look for.

"A warrior who does what his enemies expect wins no battles," his grandfather said as he'd looked up the steep ridge.

"Only a man with *hanisse'ono* on his heels would drag a boat up this ridge, old man."

Tupper had muttered, but he'd done it anyway, making up his mind to watch and wait from the top. Tomorrow or the day after he'd try the river, once he was sure he'd thrown off pursuit.

Tupper puzzled again on how damnably persistent the cops had been. He hadn't counted on them tracking him so far. Maybe that cop he'd fallen on had died. Maybe that was the reason. Somehow he doubted that the New York cops could care all that much about the foreman he'd knifed. "Maybe they just don't like their prisoners escaping on them," he mumbled.

"The fisherman always tries hardest for the one that gets away, Jim," his grandfather said in his ear.

Tupper nodded at the wisdom of that, but turned to his grandfather's spirit and asked, "Who they were shootin' at then?"

He'd heard the shooting hours before, the echoes rolling from somewhere over by Forked Lake. There had been too much shooting for hunters, although you could never tell about sports. They'd get out into the woods and lose all sense. He'd known them to drink, play at shooting, and generally act like schoolboys, once they got away from the lights of the city. He figured he'd never have an answer to all that shooting, so he thought he'd just sit tight. The extra time would throw them off, make them think he'd already slipped by. But it was all guessing and little knowing. In the meantime, he could rest, ease his aching muscles, and soothe his scraped side.

He found the herbs he needed near the edge of the lake, plants whose names he could not remember. He'd taken them without the appropriate prayers, he knew, which required a small fire and burning tobacco. He regretted that, but hoped that by removing the seed pods and planting them as the rituals required, that at least some of the medicine in the plants remained to him.

They seemed to work, though his side still burned like fire and cut like knives when the scab cracked. He opened a pack and fished about, coming up with a mason jar of preserved peaches. Tupper eased back against a log. Tomorrow would be soon enough to move, maybe even the day after.

Half empty, and it's the last week in August," Frederick said to William as they picked at the last of their strawberry shortcakes in the hotel dining hall. The setting sun painted the lake in hazy hues of yellow and orange outside the open windows.

"Saw the coach leave," William said, "thought the springs would bust from the weight."

Frederick's grin was far from merry. "This murderer's got them spooked. The stories I've heard would curl your hair. You'd think the man was killing dozens of women, flying off mountains, stealing children in their sleep."

"Damn shame," William said, shaking his head.

Frederick tried to brighten the mood, though, and added, "Once Braddock catches him, it'll put the whole thing right."

"I pray you're right, cousin, but I'm beginning to wonder. Braddock's been chasing him two days, going on three. Thought he'd be caught by now."

Frederick stopped picking at his shortcake and pointed a fork at William. A strawberry was impaled on it, dripping bright red juice.

"I wouldn't underestimate him, Will. He's the sort who does what he sets out to do. A lot like Colvin that way. He will not stop, not for anything. I know he doesn't know these woods, but I sure as hell wouldn't want him after me, not if he's the man I think he is."

William heaved a sigh. "I believe you're right, but I hope you're right sooner than later. I need this over with soon," he said with an urgent tone to his voice. "I need . . ."

William seemed to catch himself and tried to shrug it off with an apologetic smile. He'd taken a look at his balance sheet the night before and didn't like what he saw. Although he still had cash on hand, it was going out far quicker than it was coming in. In fact, it was hardly coming in at all. Almost everything he was doing was speculative, which made his hoped-for deal with Morgan all the more critical. Another bill for the construction on the yacht had arrived, too, a fact that did nothing to improve his mood.

"What, Will? Can I help in some way?" Frederick said. "Is everything all right with you?"

William shrugged. "Oh fine, Fred. It's just that this all comes at a damned inconvenient time." William shook his head slowly. "Nothing you can do, Fred. Nothing anyone can do."

Frederick was silent. He rarely heard his cousin speak like this. Ever the optimist, he had let very little stand in his way while he carved his empire out of the wilderness.

"Will, surely there's something. Is it Ella that's got you down?"

William looked across the table at Frederick with a grim set to his mouth.

"Telegram this morning," he said. "Morgan's getting cold feet."

"He'll come 'round, Will. Once this all calms down he'll be back, and hotter than ever," Frederick said, trying to cheer his cousin, but not so sure he could. He'd heard that Will's money was going out faster than it came in. He didn't realize how fast.

They camped in the same spot Sabattis had been the night before. There was no sign that anyone had been through the carry around the falls in the last day.

"So, he's got to be behind us," Tom said when Mitchell finished searching for signs.

"Can't say. Most I can say is he hasn't been here."

"We could wait for him here. Set up an ambush," Tom said.

"River's narrow. We'd have a good shot at him," Mike added.

The guide seemed to consider this, standing by the rapids, looking back at the calm stretch of tea-brown water above it.

"No," he said. "Tupper, or whoever it was shot at you, would be expecting that. I would."

They watched all night, taking turns but staying close by the camp. Tom and Mitchell had agreed on it. They had no way of knowing if Tupper or anyone else had seen where they'd gone or had followed, but in the absence of that knowledge it was best to be prepared. Sabattis shrugged. "Always best to think your game knows more than you think. We keep watch."

They stayed beyond first light, watching by turns, weary from sleepless hours. More than once during the night they each had the feeling they were being watched. Mitchell got a fire going, boiling coffee and frying ham. They ate, packed their gear in silence and, once the fire was doused, Mitchell went to fetch the boat. Fitting a small yolk between the thwarts, he heaved the boat up, and in one smooth motion had the yolk positioned on his shoulders. He carried the boat, bottom up, looking like a long wooden turtle. They hadn't taken two steps when Mitchell stopped.

"What?" Tom asked, watching the guide's eyes in the shade of the boat. With a small flick of his head he said, "Somebody comin'."

From some distance below the falls there was a flash of color and movement between the trees. Tom put a hand on the butt of his pistol, Mike thumbed the safety on the Winchester.

Mitchell started walking down toward the pool at the bottom of the falls, making his way over the tumbled rocks. He seemed unconcerned. Tom and Mike followed.

Soon, two men appeared through the trees. One was clearly a guide. He was lugging a large packbasket and what appeared to be an easel. A rifle was slung over one shoulder. The second man carried nothing but a slim wooden box on a strap slung across his shoulders and a stout hiking stick. He was well-dressed in new linen breeches, tucked into high, polished boots. He wore a vest over a crisp white shirt and a wide-brimmed felt hat with a broad leather band. A heavy gold watch fob dangled across his middle. Mitchell set down the boat and waited.

"G'mornin'," he said when they got close. The guide gave a small wave. The other looked surprised and a bit annoyed. He cast the guide a disapproving look, but managed a civil, "Good morning, gentlemen."

"Word, Barney," Mitchell said to the guide, motioning that he wanted to talk privately.

They stepped away and spoke in low tones.

"Are you an artist, sir?" Tom asked after a brief, awkward silence.

"Yes," was all the man said as he looked at the falls.

"You'll want to be careful out here," Tom said. "Not entirely safe."

"What place in this world is?" The man said in a distracted mumble.

"We're in pursuit of an escaped murderer. Have reason to think he may come down this river."

The artist looked at Tom with a distracted frown, as if talk of escaped murderers was an inconvenience he'd rather not deal with. He looked from Tom to Mike, and then to the guides, as if seeing them for the first time.

"I'm sorry," he said, turning back to Tom. "You are?"

"Captain Thomas Braddock, New York City Police."

The artist cocked his head and gave a slight smile. "A bit out of your bailiwick, aren't you?" He extended a hand. "Homer. Winslow Homer."

A light of recognition went on in Tom's eyes. "You worked for *Harper's* during the war," he said. "I remember your work, the picture of the sniper, the Confederate prisoners, you'll forgive me if I don't recall the names."

Homer nodded. "Yes, those were mine," he said with no visible reaction at being recognized in the middle of the wilderness.

"Oh, and my favorite is the one of the veteran in the field cutting wheat," Tom said. "But that was after the war, wasn't it?"

"Right again. Good of you to remember," Homer said. "One of my favorites, too; but, listen, about this murderer thing—I've come to paint," as if that fact somehow excluded him from all earthly concerns. "I'm not going anywhere. Barney here is armed, so am I, for that matter," he said, pulling his vest up to reveal a small Stevens single-shot .32 poking out of his pocket.

"I'll be fine." He stuck out his hand to Tom. "Pleased to meet you, I'm sure, and, ah, thanks for the warning," he said almost dismissively, then strode off toward the base of the falls. His guide shrugged and followed.

"Barney knows how to look after himself," Mitchell said as he turned to pick up the boat.

As they walked downriver Tom saw Homer unfolding his case as he sat on a large rock.

He had an excellent view of the falls.

It was near noon when they reached the small hamlet of Long Lake.

"Stop at my place," Mitchell said as they rowed up the lake, a narrow body of water not much more than a mile wide. It was nestled between undulating hills on the left and a mountain on the right.

Ahead it disappeared, with no end in sight. The hills near the scattered buildings that Mitchell called the town were bare, except for an army of stumps and little plots of garden, none more than an acre or so.

"Telegraph here?" Tom said.

"Uh-huh. Been in a few years now. Not the most reliable, though," Mitchell said. "Not more 'n twelve miles to Blue. Only takes half a day to deliver a message in person."

"But we rowed for days, forty, fifty miles, I'd guess," Mike said.

"You'd guess," Mitchell said.

"We started off heading more or less west from Blue, Mike. But now we're heading northeast. Came in a big circle," Tom said. He'd been studying his map as they went, a somewhat sketchy thing based on the Colvin survey of '76. Turning to Mitchell, he said, "Need to get word to my wife."

Mitchell nodded and said, "Busher?"

Tom had been worrying about that. Sending word of Busher back to the Prospect House but not coming in person would only raise more suspicions; yet, in going back Mike would surely be arrested, assuming the sheriff had arrived. And if they went back, Tupper's trail would go cold as a lake in February. There seemed to be a choice only between lesser evils.

"I'll take care of Busher," Mitchell said. "Send some men to fetch 'im back."

Tom looked at Mitchell and nodded. "I thank you for that," he said. Mitchell nodded, then looked over his shoulder at the smoke drifting from the chimney of a modest house set well back from the lake. "Wife's been bakin'," he said with a deep pull at the air.

"We can afford to take a bit of food. If Tupper comes, it won't be till late. He's hours behind."

"What makes you so sure he'll come this way, Mitchell?" Tom asked. "He could just go into the woods, right?"

"He could, sure. But that's rough goin', even for somebody who knows these woods. This lake, it leads to the Raquette River on the other end. That goes on up ta Tupper Lake an' even further."

"Tupper Lake?" Mike said. "How'd he get a lake named after him?"

Mitchell smiled. "Other way around. His family took that name 'cause they been hunting there for generations. When havin' an Indian name got cumbersome years ago, they just started callin' themselves Tupper." They beached the boat then and walked on up to the house.

The Sabattis house smelled of bread fresh from the oven, of cakes and pies set out on windowsills to cool. They were welcomed by Mitchell's wife, a small woman with a round face and dark eyes who came to the back door when she heard them coming through the yard. She didn't appear surprised to find her husband home unexpected and in the company of two strangers.

A few words with Mitchell in a tongue Tom had never before heard was all that passed between them, that, and a short introduction for Tom and Mike. She bustled off moments later, wordlessly setting the table and getting up a quick meal for the three of them. Mitchell fetched an enamelware bucket and a bar of brown soap from under the dry sink, and with a nod toward the backyard said, "Pump's out back. There's rooms up the stairs."

Simple though it was, Tom couldn't remember a better meal. It was eaten in haste though, gulped down with cider and cool spring water.

"No time to dawdle," Mitchell told them. "Tupper'll be on the lake tonight." With that Mitchell went out the back door with Tom's note to Mary stuffed in a pocket and a promise to have it in her hand by nightfall. Tom had decided against the telegraph. He didn't want to share his message with any loose-lipped operators.

"I'll see if my brother's free," Mitchell said. "He'll take this to your wife."

Tom nodded. "Thanks."

Mitchell returned an hour later, nodding to Tom that he'd seen to the chore.

As the day died, bleeding across the sky in pastels of orange and yellow and salmon and blue, the guide boat bumped ashore. The lake was narrow near the southern end, a couple of miles below the town. An island split the lake, leaving relatively narrow channels on either side not more than a couple hundred yards wide.

"Moose Island," Mitchell said. "No moose now. Hunted out," he said as they hid the boat on the north shore. Sabattis threw some branches on it to hide its outline. Mitchell had said this was the best spot on the whole lake to cut Tupper off. If he took this route he had to pass the island. "Might be tonight. Might be tomorrow, but I'd bet anything he's heading this way."

"Hope so," Tom said. "Any luck, we'll spot him in the narrows, then be in position to cut him off. Either way we've got him." Tom looked back down the lake to where the Raquette flowed in, about a mile off.

"How long is this lake anyway?" Mike asked, craning north. "Can't see the other end."

"Some fourteen fifteen miles, give or take. Plenty o' lake," he said with a wave.

They settled in to wait, picking their spots while they could still see well enough and making sure of their route to the boat. They were all on the south end, Mitchell in the middle, Tom off to the west and Mike to the east. Mitchell accepted Mike's role in the hunt without a word, never questioning his right or ability to be there.

The night was long. Minutes crawled like hours and hours didn't seem to move at all. Though they were all rested, the night lulled them. The lake, as smooth as black glass, stretched into the distance, merging into the deeper black of the forest. Off to the north a light or two twinkled between the trees, but soon even those died. All that was left was the night sky, the stars, and ghostly, motionless puffs of cloud. It didn't take long for Mike's thoughts to turn to Lettie.

He never had time to grieve. Things had happened far too fast. It was all still unreal, her death, the suspicions surrounding him, Busher's murder; all of it felt as if it had happened to someone else. The image of Lettie's blackened corpse laid out on the ice seemed to float to the surface whenever he thought of her, blotting out everything else. Try as he would to remember her flowing hair or the soft porcelain of her skin, it would not last. A corpse was all she had become. Mike shuddered, though the night was warm.

Tom had been right. He should not have gone to see her that last time. Tom had been right about a lot of things.

Mike looked up at the blue-black sky. The Milky Way stretched away in points of light uncountable. He imagined that from somewhere beyond the moon Lettie could see him, and that some part of her was with him. Mike smeared tears from his cheeks with the sleeve of his shirt. Through one clouded eye he saw movement. Rubbing his eyes, he looked at the twinkling canopy. A silver streak slashed across the sky, then another, and a third, burning so briefly he almost doubted what he'd seen. More came in ones and twos. He was dazzled. It was a sign, a shower of stars for him alone. His eyes ran again at the thought.

As he wiped away the tears he almost missed Tupper.

Mike pulled a kerchief from his pocket. He turned as he did, reaching back and twisting half about. It was then he saw the movement on the shore, a brief black-on-black thing he couldn't identify. It was some distance north of the island. He thought at first it might be a deer, but when the shape separated from the shore he knew it was no deer, not unless deer had oars.

"Tupper! Dad, he's got 'round us!"

Mike brought the rifle up when he saw the man double his strokes, putting his back into it. The boat shot away, so that even from over two hundred yards he could see the lake turn white at the bow. Mike fired once, twice, jacking bullets into the chamber as fast as he could work the lever. He couldn't see his sights, couldn't see where his shots went. The rifle cracked again before Tom and Mitchell came up, crashing through the woods.

"There he goes!"

"Where? I don't see a—"

"There. There!" Mike said, pointing at the swiftly diminishing boat. Mike was about to take another shot when Mitchell said, "Waste of lead. Come!" Sabattis took off through the wooded island, dodging trees, branches, undergrowth, and logs with uncanny ease. Tom and Mike stumbled behind. Soon all they could do was follow the sound of his running.

The boat was uncovered and ready to shove off when Tom and Mike got there. Mitchell waited at the oars. He sat, saying nothing while they clambered in. Then Mitchell Sabattis started to row. Tom had never seen anything like it. The small, brown guide seemed to have the power of ten men. The boat surged forward like a thorough-bred charging from the gate. The lake foamed at the bow, sending up a small fountain on either side. The oars dipped and rose, reaching back in graceful arcs before dipping again. They made hardly a splash but dug deep into the water, leaving swirling, black whirlpools in their wake. Mitchell worked the long oars in silence, his breathing falling into cadence with his strokes. Mike sat behind him in the middle, Tom at the stern.

"Carried his boat right by us," Tom said. "How in hell he figure that?"

"Hell of a lead, too," Mike said, craning around Mitchell for a better look. "Three, four hundred yards, but damned if we aren't gaining."

"Won't catch," Mitchell said between strokes. "Too much weight."

They'd gone over a mile by then, and even in the dark they could see the sweat shining on Mitchell's face. "Switch when we get to the bridge. You row," Mitchell said to Tom.

There was a narrow point a couple of miles up the lake spanned by a floating bridge. Tupper would still be out of range by the time they got there, but it was a perfect opportunity to switch at the oars. Tom was still fresh, while Tupper would be starting to tire. Mitchell slowed some from the inhuman pace he'd set, but he still worked the oars with vigor and efficiency. He showed little sign of fatigue beyond the running sweat on his leathery features.

Nearly another mile went by before Mitchell said, "Take shotgun."

Mike picked it up. "Why not the rifle? He's in range and . . ."

They'd narrowed the gap to maybe two hundred yards, but at night, with a single shot, the odds of hitting anything were remote at best.

"Shotgun!" Mitchell said again. "Fire when we stop. Maybe get lucky."

Mitchell took another series of strokes, pulling with everything that was in him. The loaded long-laker seemed to leap half out of the water and the gap narrowed further. With a flick of one oar he turned the boat nearly half around, slowing it at the same time so it hit the bridge with a glancing blow, stopping almost immediately. Mike jumped out and knelt on the floating bridge, which bobbed and rolled under him.

"Both barrels," Mitchell said, gasping out the words. The old shotgun boomed twice, sending out sheets of flame and smoke. None of them could see if they'd hit anything. They didn't take the time.

Tom and Mitchell dragged the boat across the rough log bridge and jumped back in, Tom at the oars, Mike in the middle again, and Mitchell at the stern. Tom laid hold of the oars. Mitchell took up the paddle.

"Pull! Pull like the devil!" Mitchell shouted. "Pull!"

Tupper cursed. His wounded side had opened up, the scab cracking and oozing with each stroke. How had they seen him? He'd been so fucking careful, carrying the damn boat until he could carry it no more. Still they'd seen him. He'd expected a trap at every narrow spot on the river, and especially at Moose Island, and had gone well around; but still they'd seen him. When he neared the bridge, he was sure there'd be men waiting there to stop him. When he saw there weren't, he was grateful for at least that small stroke of luck.

His grandfather could not explain it. He sat in the stern, not looking back or to either side.

Tupper fought through the pain and weariness. He'd rested all the day prior, watching from his perch atop the ridge by the outlet of Raquette Lake, but it was still not enough. He'd been on the move since sundown, carrying the boat down from his hiding place, rowing for miles downriver, carrying again around rapids and falls, and finally past the island at the south end of the lake.

He was bruised, blistered and bleeding but he went on, knowing the lake was his best hope. If he'd been able to slip by, a highway of rivers and lakes went clear to the St. Lawrence. But that chance was gone. He was in a race now, a race he was losing.

Tupper could not seem to keep the other boat from closing. He fell into a chant, one of the Eagle Society songs that had always held power for him. It helped. His pain was slowly lessened, chased away to a place not of himself. He rowed and chanted and rowed and chanted and rowed. His eyes became fixed on the dark horizon. He scrambled over the bridge, hardly aware of how he did it.

He didn't watch the boat as it came on behind. He knew they were heavier. He knew, too, that the men who could match him at the oars numbered no more than the fingers on his hand. Still they gained, but Tupper did not alter his stroke. He thought he could outlast them, even as hurt as he was. They gained despite his strength and his trancelike concentration. Then they fired.

He saw the flash. The noise jolted Tupper, breaking his trance. An instant later a hail pattered around him, splashing in the lake, bouncing against the boat, grazing one arm and one hitting him square in the chest. Like a rock thrown hard it delivered a stinging blow, then bounced off rattling in the bottom of the boat. Tupper cried out but hardly broke stroke.

He screamed a long, triumphant call that echoed through the night, bouncing off the shouldering mountains. It was the call his ancestors made when they'd fought the French and their Huron dogs, a whooping shriek of victory and power. Tupper's grandfather was smiling.

"Their bullets have no power," the spirit said. "No power. It is you who have the power! Row now. Row while they are in dismay."

Tom didn't bother to look. He knew the range was long for a shotgun. He just gripped the oars and got to work. On his first stroke the long maple oars groaned and flexed. The boat shot forward. But on his second stroke his hands banged together. The oars splashed the lake and the boat slowed.

"Left over right," Mitchell said. It was always hard for a novice to get the hang of the overlapping sweep of the handles, more like a racing scull than a rowboat. Mitchell worked the paddle, trying to compensate for Tom's inexperience. He paddled and steered. An experienced guide could do both with the oars alone. Mitchell knew Tom could not do that.

But he could row. By sheer strength and will, Tom had the boat going even faster than it had before. The more comfortable he became, the faster they went. Mitchell eyed the oars, watching them flex.

"Easy," he said, "not so much back."

Tom eased off a bit. He knew he couldn't keep up that pace anyway. Mike reloaded and was staring ahead.

"Must've missed," he said. "He's rowing like the devil himself."

He cocked the shotgun.

"Don't waste ammunition," Mitchell grunted. "Need—closer."

He dug hard with his paddle and Tom kept up a powerful stroke. Between them they had the boat moving as fast as any steamer, or so it seemed to Mike. Still, they could not seem to catch up.

"You have their power now," his grandfather said. "They struck too soon. Their power is yours." It did seem that way. Tupper had widened the gap. It was as if the shotgun pellet, a .32-caliber ball that now rolled in the bottom of the boat, had given him a new surge of energy. He focused on the stinging lump on his chest, seeing it in his mind as a source of strength, a symbol of his true power. It had bounced off. In all his years he'd never heard of such a thing. He had flown like an eagle. Now he was harder than stone.

Time stood still while the lake raced past. The only sounds were the creak of the oars, the rush of black water, and his own heavy breathing. Another mile went by. The town disappeared behind. The lake widened on either side. The end was still nowhere in sight, lost in the blue-black distance. Tupper's side still burned. His bruises ached. But none of that seemed to be his concern.

It was as if they had become someone else's pain. He was aware of them, but they were not his. What was his was the water, the stars, the breeze that cooled his scalp, and the thrill of the chase. He was confident now. The buckshot had made it so. The lump on his chest radiated power throughout his body, running down his arms in a warm, electric glow. He grinned at the thought. For a man who hated electricity, it was an irony, but true.

He snuck a quick look over his shoulder. Big Brook would be coming up on his right soon. For a moment he thought about trying to duck into the mouth of the river, maybe even follow it all the way up to Slim Pond. He could get to Little Tupper from there, but it was a nasty carry and the lake didn't take him where he needed to go. He looked again at the boat that followed. In the darkness he had to squint hard to see it, but it was still in sight. Hiding in the mouth of Big Brook would not work. They were too close. The oars dipped and groaned and dipped again. Powerful or not, he was only one man and had not put enough distance between them.

He'd make for the Raquette. There was no other way. The river, which continued at the outlet of Long Lake, was a maze of twists and turns, oxbows, islands, and sandbars. It was made for ambush. Tupper began to plan as Big Brook materialized on his right.

"Six miles more," Tupper grunted. "Then they'll see what an *ongwe'onwe* can do."

Tupper rowed on. Sweat rolled off him in rivulets. He worked hard to keep his hands from slipping on the blood-soaked oars. He hadn't rowed like this in months. His hands were not tough enough. He had scraped one in his flight from Castle Rock, too. His hands felt as if they were on fire. This too he pushed to some faraway corner of his brain.

"The *nia'gwai* is known to chew off his own paw to be free of the trap," Tupper remembered his grandfather telling him. The old man's spirit sat in the back of the boat, nodding. "Imagine that power," the spirit said. "A man who can do that is a man above men. To such a man, pain is nothing."

Tupper knew that was so, though he had no intention of chewing off his hand to prove it. Coming out of his thoughts, he checked again on the boat behind. At first he didn't see it and thought he'd lost them altogether. Then they materialized from the deeper shadow of the trees. They were closer. At first he thought it was a trick of the light, but that wasn't it. They'd made up the distance he'd gained. He could see the one in the stern working the paddle, saw the other with the shotgun.

It was at least another six miles to the outlet of the lake. He knew in an instant he would not make it. Their extra weight was overcome by the man on the paddle, and the big man who worked the oars had at least his strength and more. Tupper made his decision.

"He's turning in!" Mike shouted. "Going for shore."

Mitchell stopped in midstroke.

"Shore. Now!" he said in a low but urgent voice. He used the paddle to turn the boat, while Tom worked the left oar. "Big Brook," Mitchell said. It was about all he could get out, he was breathing so hard. Tupper's boat shot toward the north shore of the river. He'd make it to land before them.

"Fuck!" Tom growled with a look over his shoulder. "Puttin' the river between us."

Tupper's guide boat disappeared into the shadows. He'd be on land and ready to fire in a heartbeat. Mike knew there wasn't much chance, but he let go with both barrels, hoping for a lucky shot. Tom pulled hard. Mitchell steered.

"Go slower," Mitchell said. "Careful! There's rocks hereabouts."

They were still twenty yards from shore when the boat lurched with a sickening crunch. Something ripped at the bottom. Wood splintered. The boat seemed to scream. Mike was in the water before he knew what had happened. He went under. Tom saw him disappear as if in slow motion, hardly believing it. He shot up from his seat without thinking and the crippled boat threw him over the side.

The water was cold and black. Down seemed the same as up. His clothes and boots and pistol pulled him under. Something jabbed at his leg. His boot caught on a submerged branch. For a long, horrible moment he thought he would not break free. He struggled to reach the surface.

When at last he came up, gasping and struggling, he saw Mike clinging to the side of the boat. Mitchell was paddling for shore. The boat sat low in the water. Bullets whistled about them. They heard them first, followed by the crack of the rifle.

Zing-boom! Zing-boom! One splashed close by, skipping like a stone. Another went high. A third, then a fourth sang about their ears before they could scramble up on shore. Tom collapsed against a tree, breathing hard.

"Sonofabitch! Everybody okay?"

His Colt was in his hand. His hair hung about his eyes and he was sucking air like a landed fish. But when he caught Mike's eye, there was a light there that Mike had never before seen. Mike felt that light like an electric shock, and he could not stand to look long. Bullets continued to rip through the trees, thunking into trunks, rustling through the leaves.

"Where's the shotgun?"

"Lost it," Mike said between gasping breaths.

Tom just nodded.

"I'll get the Winchester." Mike crawled to the boat, which lay half submerged by the shore. Mitchell stood and waded back out into the lake. Without a word he dove in.

"Jesus Christ! You'll never find it. Come back," Tom shouted.

Mitchell paid him no mind. He swam out, then ducked beneath the surface.

"Damnit!" Tom growled. Looking at Mike, he said, "Ready?"

Mike thought he knew what "ready" meant. He nodded. He'd chambered a round and drained the water from the gun as bullets bit the trees above them, raining little bits of bark and twigs.

"C'mon!" The light in Tom's eyes said the rest.

Tom got up, crouched low, then dashed forward toward the shore of Big Brook. They weren't more than twenty yards from it, and Tom had covered half the distance, before Mike realized what he was doing. Mike stumbled after Tom's shadow as it flitted from tree to tree. The bullets stopped for a moment.

"Behind that tree!" Tom called back to Mike, pointing to his right. Tom ducked behind a big maple. "Wait. He's reloading," Tom said in a hoarse whisper. "Fire at the muzzle flash."

Big Brook was maybe one hundred yards wide at its mouth, but Tom wasn't thinking of crossing. He had no idea of how deep it might be and no intention of exposing himself and Mike on the open water, not even under cover of night.

"Tupper knew what he was doing, putting this creek between us," Tom said while he tried to catch his breath. "Bastard knows a thing or—"

Tupper's rifle boomed again.

"There. See it?" Tom said, steadying his Colt against the tree. It barked, lighting Tom's face in a brief burst of flame. He fired slow and steady, taking his time and aiming each shot. It was a long shot for the pistol. Mike tried to do the same. Tupper's firing ceased after just two shots, then started again from a different location.

Tom and Mike kept up a deliberate, withering fire, driving Tupper from one hiding place to the next. They took turns firing and reloading, not letting up. Shots still whistled back at them, though none seemed to come near. In a brief lull, while Mike reloaded and Tupper's fire had ceased, Mitchell came trotting through the blackness. He was dripping from head to toe, except for his hat, which he'd apparently left onshore. The shotgun was in his hand.

He took position behind a boulder. When Tupper fired again, all three cut loose at once, the shotgun bellowing and belching smoke, the Colt and Winchester ripping holes in the night. All fire from the other side of Big Brook ceased. Smoke settled over the oily, black water. The silence rang.

They waited while the minutes crawled by. None spoke. No sound came from the opposite shore.

"Dad," Mike said. "We must've hit him, had to. What do we do?"

"Stay put," Tom said, "at least for now. Could be trying to come at our flank."

Mitchell got up and, in a low crouch, faded back into the trees.

"Where's he going?"

"Watching our backs, maybe. Checking the boat, I don't know." Tom craned to see what he could of the lake. "Can you see Tupper's boat?"

Mike said he couldn't. "I'll work over to the shore to get a better look."

They were perhaps sixty feet or more from the lake shore. Their view of the shore on the other side of the stream was limited.

"Careful," Tom said. "I'll watch our flank."

Mike went from tree to tree, making sure of his cover. Tom kept the pistol ready. From off behind he could hear a hollow bumping and scraping. Tom hoped it was Mitchell checking their boat. He hoped too that it wasn't beyond repair.

Mike's rifle shattered the silence. "He's getting away!"

The rifle boomed again. Tom jumped up and scrambled to where Mike stood, firing. The boat was already well away and moving fast. They'd have missed it entirely, if Mike hadn't changed position. Tupper was hugging the shadows close to shore, risking the rocks. Tom didn't fire. Tupper was already out of pistol range.

"Brace the rifle against the tree," Tom said. "Aim high. I'm going to check on the boat."

When Tom turned back he could see a light through the trees.

"How's it look?" Tom asked when he got back to where Mitchell stood over the stricken craft. It was on the shore, turned bottom up. Even in the weak lamplight, Tom could see the splintered wood. Mitchell was working fast with a hammer and a chisel. Tom didn't bother to ask where the tools had come from. He'd come to expect the unusual from Sabattis.

"Be some time," Mitchell mumbled, more concerned with the boat than with Tupper or whether Mike had gotten in a lucky shot.

"How long?"

"Less 'n we got. More 'n I like," he said as he fished out a piece of canvas, some copper sheathing, a jar of copper nails, and a jar of spruce gum. Tom started to say something, but stopped himself and shrugged.

"What can I do?" he asked, tucking the Colt away.

"Find me a spruce branch. Two feet long, half-inch diameter," Mitchell mumbled as he studied the damage. The Winchester went silent. Mike materialized in the lamplight. "He's gone."

Twenty-Three

But the Adirondacks are quite another affair. There you do not visit Nature,
you are enveloped by her. You lie on her breast, and her arms are around you.
She mixes your blood with the balsam of her caresses. All that she loves—
her happy solitude, the floor of glassy lakes, her woodland song and odors—
she gives you. In the Adirondacks you are wholly American.

—THOMAS GOLD APPLETON

The bullets had not bounced off this time. Whatever magic had been his was lost. His grandfather had nothing to say about that. In fact, the old man had been nowhere in sight when the bullets started flying. Tupper winced at his wounded leg. He'd bandaged it in haste with a white shirt he'd pulled from the pack of one of the fishermen.

He knew better than to use colored cloth. The dye would kill him as sure as any bullet once it got into the wound. He moved his foot, stretching the calf muscle, which had a four-inch furrow carved in it. The leg would stiffen up if he let it. He'd be slowed. Slow was something he could not afford to be.

He flexed his hands. They still tingled. When his rifle had been shot away, his hands had gone numb. It was an evil magic, and Tupper thanked *Hodianok'doo Hedi´-iohe´* that his hands were returning to him. He looked at the rifle. It was of little use now. The forearm was shattered, the loading tube bent.

When it had happened, he was knocked on his back, dazed. He'd crawled back to the boat dragging the broken rifle. More stunned than he realized, he knew his grandfather must have been with him for him to even make it that far. His luck held, though, and he'd gotten well away, pulling with hands that could not feel the oars. Even when the bullets started again, he'd been hopeful. The range was long, the night black.

Then the boat erupted in splinters. There was a burning slash across his leg, like a rope of fire. He could see through a hole in the stern. Water was running in. The lake bled through another hole beside him. Blood and water mixed in the bottom as shots splashed close by, or whistled past.

Still, he did not stop rowing. A shot cracked into the blade of an oar. splintering the tough wood lengthwise, ripping the oar from his hand, and tearing open his blistered fingers. Tupper regained it as best he could, but he slowed, his rhythm thrown off. He went slower once he got himself going again, for fear of breaking the oar altogether. His bleeding hand slipped on the handle. The boat filled, though he stuffed clothes in the holes. Finally he pulled for shore just before the lake smothered the craft entirely. As he stuffed a packbasket, he considered himself lucky. Pursuit was nowhere in sight. He didn't understand it. He didn't question it. He just started walking.

Later that morning Mary and Rebecca sat on one of the stumps that dotted the broad lawn of the Prospect House. They'd eaten early, then gone down to the pen to feed the white buck. He'd been restless, but ate from Rebecca's hand once he'd settled down.

"Remember when Snowflake bit Mikey?" Rebecca asked. She'd taken a notion to name the deer a couple of days before, and had called him by it so many times since that Mary could swear he was starting to answer to it.

"His hand was all bloody. Snowflake was bad then, but now he's good. When Mikey and Daddy come back they'll be surprised."

"Yes they will, 'Becca," Mary said, though her throat tightened almost too much to speak. Rebecca had somehow come up with the idea that Mike was with Tom. She seemed quite convinced and had mentioned it more than once. Mary prayed that repetition would make it so.

Once the deer lost interest in food, they went to sit and watch the lake, while Rebecca's heels beat an uneasy rhythm on the stump. They sat like that for some time watching, as if Tom and Mike might come rowing up to the dock at any minute. They were there when a man rode up to the Prospect House from the direction of town. He tied his horse to one of the posts of the verandah and came ambling across the lawn toward them with an intent but curious cock to his head.

"Would you be Mary Braddock, ma'am?" he asked.

"I am," she answered, standing to meet him.

"Have a message for you. Your husband described you well," he said, holding out a folded piece of paper. "I'm Sol Sabattis, Mitchell's brother."

"My husband?" Mary said, brightening but confused. "But who's Mitchell? I'm sorry, I don't know any Mitchell. What was the last name again?"

"Sabattis, ma'am."

"I don't understand. What does this have to do . . . ," she said, but stopped when she saw the writing in the note. Rebecca watched Sol as Mary read.

"You're an Indian," Rebecca said. Sol just nodded. "Do you live in a tepee?"

" 'Becca!"

"It's all right, ma'am," Sol said with a grin, then, to 'Becca, "I live in a regular house, with a porch and a green door; but when I was a boy my granddad used to say how he lived in a long house when he was little. It was covered with bark."

"Like a tree?"

"Just like a tree. It was as snug as could be, according to him."

"That sounds like fun," Rebecca said, and started asking lots of questions while Mary read the note with fumbling fingers. It was dated the day before and read:

My dearest Mary,

 Mike is with me. He is well. We have had some setbacks, but Mitchell says we should catch Tupper tonight. I think of you often. Do not worry for us. We are in good company. Kiss 'Becca for me. Your devoted husband,

 Tom

Mary let out a long sigh and for a moment she actually felt as if she might fall down. "Thank God," she whispered, her fears for Mike at least partly assuaged. She let the note drop to her side as she looked out at the lake, momentarily forgetting Rebecca and Sol.

They were safe, or at least they were a day ago. Relief drained the high color from her face, and she shook her head at her foolishness for ever doubting either Tom or Mike. She smiled at Rebecca and patted her head. Turning back to Sol, she said, "I can't thank you enough, sir. This is most welcome news. You were right, 'Becca," Mary said. "Mike *is* with Daddy."

"Told you, Mommy," she replied, as if she'd read the note herself.

"Tell me about Mitchell," Mary asked Sol. "Anything you can about what he's doing with my husband. And what happened to Mister Busher? There's so much I don't understand. I'd be most grateful for anything you can add."

It didn't take long. Sol wasn't any more of a talker than his brother, and didn't know all that much about the situation. He only said, "My brother is the best guide at Long Lake. Not a thing that walks, crawls, or swims he can't track and kill, ma'am. He ran into your husband on Forked Lake, from what I hear. They been after this Tupper fella ever since. Couldn't tell what happened to Busher," he added, not meeting her eye.

Mary noticed, but didn't ask more. There was a part of her that didn't want to know. As she got over her initial relief, she still worried about Tom and Mike. Whatever had happened to Busher, it hadn't been good. Tupper, it seemed, was every bit as dangerous as Tom had said, and perhaps more. Though Mary asked a lot more questions, she didn't get many more answers. Finally, with a sigh, she asked if Sol could take back a note.

"Be glad to take the note ta Long Lake. Can't promise it'll find Mitchell or your husband, ma'am."

"I know," Mary said with a frown. "I'm relying on you completely." Mary scribbled a note on the other side of Tom's.

Tom,

I love you more than words can say. You can't imagine how relieved I am to hear that Mike is with you. Please be careful! Sol

won't tell me what happened to Chauncey. I suspect the worst.
Take no chances, and take care of Mike. Come back to me and
'Becca. All my love,
   Mary
P.S. The sheriff is here, a man named MacDougal. He'll arrest
Mike if he finds you. Avoid him if you can.

After Sol had gone, Mary went with Rebecca down to the water's edge. 'Becca liked to throw pieces of bread to the fish and seemed to have a bottomless supply stuffed in a little pocket. "I told you, Mommy. I told you Mike was with Daddy," she said as she started throwing bread into the water.

"You were right. Right all along," Mary said. "You are soooooo smart, you little daisy-face. Oh, I almost forgot. Daddy said to give you this." Mary kneeled and gave her little girl the longest hug she could remember, and a kiss just the way Tom always did, one on both cheeks and one on the nose. Mary had just gotten to her feet when she saw a boat rounding the point. There was only one man in it, so she paid it no mind until it was almost at the dock.

"Ah, Missus Braddock," she heard a voice say. Looking up, she noticed it was Owens at the oars.

"Why, Mister Owens, back from Raquette Lake?"

"Yes ma'am. Did what I set out to. Send the clients home happy, I always say."

"I'm sure you do," Mary answered.

Owens gave Mary a devilish smile as he tied up his boat. "Why, yes I do, Missus Braddock," he said. His tone was suggestive, and he held her eye longer than was proper. Turning to get his gear out of the boat he said, "Saw your husband a couple days ago. Didn't see me, though."

"Really?" Mary said.

"Yup. Pretty dark at the time. Busher was with 'im."

"I see. No one else? No sign of that maniac, Tupper?"

"Nope. Suppose he was makin' himself small. Then again, wasn't me looking for 'im," Owens said, making it sound as if he'd have caught Tupper already if he was. Rebecca giggled as a little school of fish rose up from the shadow of the dock to fight for bits of bread.

"Used to like that when I was a tyke," Owens said with a nod toward Rebecca. "You want to go catch some real fish, missy?"

"Oh yes! Could we, Mommy? I would love that sooo, sooo much! Could I *feel* one?"

"Sure. Eat one, too, if you like," Owens said.

Mary paused to consider that. "I don't know, Mr. Owens. We never did fishing before."

"Catching fish is a thing I know. I'd even take you for free, as a treat to the little miss here."

"My name's Rebecca, but my mommy and daddy call me 'Becca; Mike, too."

They made plans then for later in the day, after lunch. Mary figured she wasn't going to do much before Chowder arrived, anyway, so it could do no harm.

"Anyway, been out in the woods a few days," Owens said, rubbing his hands on dirt-shiny pants lags. "Imagine I might be a tad offensive, 'less I scrub off a layer or two."

They pushed off before the sun crested the mountains on the eastern shore. The boat leaked.

"She's sprung," Mitchell said. "Joints're loose." He'd never said a word about Tom running it up on the rocks, though Tom could see he cared about the thing like a father for a child. Mike fished out an old shirt and started sopping up water, while Mitchell and Tom rearranged their gear to keep it dry. They hadn't gone all that far when Tom spotted something in the water. It was a piece of Tupper's oar blade, a long, narrow sliver with a jagged furrow dug into one edge.

"Bullet," Tom said when they fished it out.

Mitchell nodded. "Good."

Mitchell pulled for another half mile or so, while Tom worked the paddle and Mike glassed the shoreline and sopped water. Looking ahead, he said to Mitchell, "Rock coming up on your right."

Mitchell looked puzzled and glanced about as if taking his bearings. "No rocks here."

"Well, I'm looking at one," Mike said, glassing the water again.

"Not a rock," Mitchell said without looking. He pulled toward the thing, which was no more than fifty yards off by then. Waves were lapping over whatever it was, showing something just below the surface.

"It's a boat!" Mike shouted. "It's Tupper's boat!"

They pulled alongside the submerged craft. Just a bit of the stem and stern poked above the surface. A few rocks sat in the bottom, enough to keep it down, but not enough to sink the buoyant spruce boat entirely.

"Hasty," Mitchell grunted.

Tom agreed, but said, "Never would have seen that at night. Would've been miles beyond here if we hadn't waited till first light." Mitchell said nothing. He just pulled for the shore.

"He's gone on foot then," Tom said, looking at the line of tress stretching for unbroken miles in either direction. "Wonderful!"

"Not wonderful," Mitchell said as they beached the boat. "Not wonderful at all." He shook his head, but he was clearly resigned to what they had to do. He managed a grin, though, and added, "Still, even a breeze leaves tracks in the forest."

"Maybe so, Mister Sabattis," Mike said, "but it's a damn big forest. Busher said Tupper could disappear in there and never be seen again."

Mitchell shouldered his pack with a grunt. Shrugging into the heavy leather straps, he said, "That's how I think about the city, but I know that ain't so. Besides, Busher ain't me."

They started by inspecting the shoreline north of where they'd landed. Mitchell led, his dark eyes scanning the shore and the forest floor. He talked as he went.

"Everything leaves tracks, if you know what to look for," he said. "Twigs don't break themselves. Leaves lie natural-like if undisturbed. Moss bruises easy. You have an eye for those things, they'll tell you all you need to know." He went so fast that Tom and Mike wondered how he could spot anything. They made no comment, trusting that he knew what he was about.

After a short while Mitchell stopped, then kneeled, looking left and right. Pointing to the ground he grunted, "Blood." Turning left, he plunged into the forest. Tom followed. Mike knelt where Mitchell had, trying to see what he'd seen. A bit of moss scraped from a rock was all he noticed.

For the rest of the morning the three stalked Tupper's trail. It took them through dense undergrowth and groves of birch so white they lit the forest floor. They followed a meandering trail that only Mitchell saw, through endless stands of hardwoods and tangled, stumpy ground where loggers had taken the spruce and pine. They scrambled around downed trees, over rocks and hills, ravines and bogs, while the sun climbed to its zenith.

From time to time Mitchell would stop to check for sign. He never seemed unsure or doubtful, not even when the trail led up a rocky creek bed where water gurgled unseen, rising up in little dark pools here and there. He'd stop and kneel to read the moss or leaves or rocks, as if he was reading a book at the library. He had the look of a scholar at these times, a man accustomed to a life of study and acute observation.

They walked hard, but rested frequently. The stops were only enough to catch their breath and perhaps chew on a bit of dried, smoked venison. They walked in silence, spread well apart, Mitchell first, Mike in the middle, and Tom behind. Tom often stopped to watch the trail, waiting hidden for Tupper to come stalking up behind. He'd wait behind cover until Mike and Mitchell were lost to sight. Sometimes the forest held its breath, sometimes it seemed to whisper. Tom's pistol grew hot in his hand, but he saw nothing.

As they walked deeper into the forest, Tom began to realize how lost he was. The trail had twisted and turned around swamps and streams, rocky ridges and tangled windfalls. The only thing he was at all sure of was that they were headed generally west. He began to appreciate how much they were depending on Mitchell. It was not a good feeling, considering what had happened to their last guide. At least on the water there were borders, ends and beginnings. Here all was the same, or so it seemed to Tom. The trees marched away in all directions, infinitely varied but essentially the same, one direction no different from the next. It was like a Coney Island house of mirrors, except the mirrors were trees.

The ground they crossed became low, with swampy areas thick with alder, balsam, and silver birch. Mitchell went on following an invisible trail as though he were on a city sidewalk. Though he'd stop to read the signs, he seemed to know exactly where he was going. He followed the trail through heavy brush, where the earth went from spongy loam to sucking mud. There, for the first time, Tom saw a clear footprint of the man they were after.

"This man has at least one wound," Mitchell said, "maybe two. He's favoring the left leg. You can see by how he sets his feet and the depth of the tracks." He pointed to a set of three and Tom could see, now that Mitchell had pointed it out, that indeed the left track was lighter, the right deeper.

"Not slowing him much," Tom said. "We've been moving pretty fast." Mitchell just nodded.

They waded a muddy, sluggish stream bordered by high grass dotted with delicate harebell and blind gentian, with its clusters of blue flowers. Tom went first, charging across the open space, while Mike and Mitchell covered him from hiding.

Tupper had been there, but he'd moved on. Clouds of thirsty mosquitoes were all they found. Tom and Mike slapped at them. Mitchell took no notice. After a while he stopped and fished in his pack.

"Try this," he said. "Make it myself."

He handed Tom a corked bottle half full of a viscous, black liquid that left a greasy ring on the inside of the glass. Tom pulled the cork and sniffed at it.

"Ach! For the love o' Christ, what's in this?"

Mitchell grinned. "Can't say. Keeps the skeeters off though."

Tom and Mike daubed it on, trying to hold their breath.

"Smells like coal tar, turpentine, and bear shit," Mike grumbled. He held his hands out at his sides not knowing what to do with them. He finally shrugged and wiped them on his pants.

"Pretty close," Mitchell said, corking the bottle before putting it back. "Works," he added with a shrug.

They started to climb then, going up a steady incline that got steeper as they went. The trail ran straight up and over a small mountain.

"What mountain is this?" Mike asked the next time they stopped.

"Got no name I know of," Mitchell said.

"You know where you are?"

Mitchell didn't speak at first. He crunched some hard crackers as if he hadn't heard the question. "We are in the hunting ground of the Mohawk, keepers of the eastern door to the Iroquois nation," Mitchell said at last, "Land that was theirs for as long as the stars were bright. My father, Captain Peter, fought here with the Yankees against the British. It is the land I've known since I was a boy."

Mary sat on the verandah, Rebecca at her side. She fingered the bit of cloth in her pocket. Since Tom had started chasing Tupper, she'd kept it with her. It wasn't much, just a small patch of plaid flannel, with blue and green and brown threads hanging loose where it had been torn. When the sheriff had arrived, she wondered if she shouldn't turn it over. It was evidence, after all, but she worried what the reaction would be. Coming from her, a woman who'd never even seen the body, and whose son was the prime suspect, she thought she knew. Her word would never be respected, as much because of he sex as for the more obvious reasons.

The piece of cloth Tom had found in the Burman girl's mouth would mean nothing coming from her. It might even be "lost," or dismissed outright, its value and meaning gone forever.

Mary prayed again that Tom and Mike would come back with the murderer in irons. It would be the only way to put all their worries to rest. Anything short of that left too much open, too many possibilities. If Tupper wasn't caught, the piece of flannel might be Mike's only defense. He had no such shirt, never had. Tom had told her to keep it safe. Safe it would stay until he returned.

"When are we going fishing, Mommy?" Rebecca said, shaking Mary out of her thoughts. "I see Mister Owens by the dock. See him? See? He's waving." Rebecca waved back. "Let's go. I want to catch fishes now."

They did catch fishes, "long ones with fins and little spots," as 'Becca described them. Owens baited their hooks and told them what to do if they got a bite. He took care of everything else, netting when they got one in close, pulling hooks, and rowing the boat. Most of all, he was entertaining. He sang funny tunes, like "Bile 'em Cabbage Down":

Jaybird died with the whooping cough
Sparrow died with the colic
Along came the frog with a fiddle on his back
Inquirin' his way to the frolic.

His voice was rough and his pitch was off, but it only seemed to add to the fun when he went into a rendition of "Blue-Tailed Fly"—

They laid him 'neath a 'simmon tree
His epitaph is there to see:
"Beneath this stone I'm forced to lie
A victim of the blue-tailed fly."

Rebecca caught a fish then. She squealed and clapped as Owens brought it in. She wanted to touch it, so Owens held it for her. She felt its side with just one finger.

"He's so smooth, Mommy, and he's cold," she said with a giggle. She looked closely at the fluttering gills and open, doll-like eye.

"He looks sad, Mister Owens. Do you think he's sad?"

"Couldn't say. Never gave a thought to such a thing. Could be so, I guess," Owens said with a look at the fish. "Plenty of things in this world to make a body sad."

"We should throw him back," Rebecca said in her gentlest voice. "Right, little fishy? You need your family, don't you? You miss your home and your Mommy."

"Throw him back, Mister Owens," Mary said. "Maybe he's sad at that."

Owens smiled and let the fish slip into the water.

The hours passed, marked by stories and fish. Owens told how Robert Rogers made his slide down a cliff on Lake George to escape the Indians; how three men in a jamboat got swept away by a river full of logs, and then dug out of a sandbar days later and miles downstream; of how a famous Indian guide from Long Lake chased a mountain lion out of hiding, prodding him with a stick till his sport could get a shot, and when the sport missed, how he killed the lion himself.

"Every word's true," Owens insisted more than once. There were tales of bears shot, fish caught, and men lost in logging accidents. Not once did Owens talk about Tupper. He never mentioned Mike or Tom. Mary was glad of it. For a few hours she had been made to forget. Rebecca had wonderful fun, even though they released almost all the fish they caught.

And Owens was a charming companion and storyteller. He had an eye for Mary, of that she was certain; and when, at the dock he gave her his hand to help her out of the boat and she'd slipped, he'd caught her waist. His hands had lingered ever so slightly. And when Mary raised her dark eyes to thank him for the day, he'd not looked away.

"Mary!" someone called. A waving figure from up on the verandah caught her eye. A moment later Chowder Kelly stumped down the lawn.

"Uncle Chowder!" Rebecca cried as she ran to him.

"'Becca. How's my favorite little daisy?" Chowder picked her up like a feather and whirled her about, skirts flying. "Oh, but you're gettin' so heavy. What're they feedin' you up here?" he said as he put her down. "Looks like you sprouted another inch, or I'm an Orangeman."

"I eat pancakes every day," Rebecca said. "They make them sooo big, and I can have as many as I want."

"Chowder," Mary said as she came up to them, "you are a sight for sore eyes. I'm so glad you've come."

Chowder shrugged. "Gets me out of the city and away from the chief."

Mary gave him a hug and a peck on the cheek.

"Are you going to find Mike, Uncle Chowder? He's with Daddy you know, and Daddy always knows where *he* is."

Owens came up just then. Mary wondered with a start whether he'd heard what Rebecca said about Tom and Mike. Owens's expression didn't give anything away if he had. He carried Rebecca's bonnet in one hand, a string of trout in the other.

"The little miss forgot her bonnet," he said, handing it to Rebecca. "I'll see these fish 're ready for dinner."

Mary thanked him and turned to Chowder, who Owens had been eyeing.

"Detective Sergeant Kelly, at your service," Chowder said, extending a hand.

"Owens 's the name. You're up from the city to help find the killer, then?"

Chowder nodded.

"Yeah. Wish I could help s' more, but this is our busy time. Have to be off for Long Lake this evening. Got work up there tomorrow."

"Mister Owens has been very helpful already," Mary said to Chowder. "He helped Tom when they first went after Tupper."

"Oh? You are to be thanked then, Mister Owens. I'm sure I speak for the commissioner himself when I give you your due on behalf of the department. It's a fine, hardy man who pitches in on the side of the law when there's a pinch."

"Nothin' at all, Sergeant. Wish I could help more, like I say, but my idle afternoons 're scarce as hen's teeth now," he said with a nod toward Mary, "but none more pleasantly spent, ma'am."

They parted, Mary, Rebecca, and Chowder heading for the verandah. "Hell of a place, this," Chowder said. "The very devil to get to, though." He looked down the length of the verandah, then out at the lawns, the lake, and the boathouse. "Hardly a soul about. Them guides," he said with a nod toward an idle group by the boathouse, "they don't look overbusy. Stage was near full heading out, too."

"Can't blame people," Mary said. "Everybody's jittery over the murder."

"Oh, to be sure. I just wonder what's keepin' Mister Owens so busy, is all."

Mary laughed. "Not here two minutes and you're busy detecting. Relax Chowder. Owens isn't your man." The laugh faded, the smile too. "It's that lunatic, Tupper," she said. "That's why nobody's around.

Everybody's scared to death. Tommy would be, too, if he had any sense, which we both know he doesn't," she said with a rueful smile that was still part pride.

Before Chowder could ask the obvious question, Mary answered it for him. "Mike's with him, just like 'Becca says," she said in a low voice. "You don't know that, and I didn't tell you, but he is." She fingered the swatch of cloth in her pocket. "Hmm," Chowder rumbled. "We obviously need to talk."

In low tones, Mary told Chowder all she knew. She even told him about the piece of cloth.

"I suppose you should have this," she said, handing it to him.

"Bit it off the attacker?" Chowder mumbled, examining it closely. "Arm about the neck, she struggles, bites."

"That's what Tommy thought." Mary turned and called out, " 'Becca! Stay where I can see you."

Rebecca had strayed on the lawn while Mary and Chowder sat talking.

"I am, Mommy."

Mary waved back.

Chowder waved too. "That sheriff you told me about, he doesn't know about this?"

"No. He hadn't arrived when Tom went after Tupper, so Tom left it with me. Tom didn't trust that doctor."

"Where's the sheriff now?" Chowder wanted to know.

"Haven't seen him today at all. Out searching, I suppose." Chowder stretched and got up from his chair. "Think I'll just go an' ask."

Chowder came back a few minutes later, clumping fast down the echoing wooden verandah. "He's gone someplace called Long Lake with a party of deputies, according to the clerk at the desk. Got word there was lots o' firing on the lake last night, a regular battle."

Mary jumped up. "I'm going with you!"

Chowder was about to protest, but hesitated a moment then shrugged and said, "Better pack some things."

They had bushwhacked for hours since their early lunch, a stop that hadn't lasted more than ten minutes.

"He wasn't wounded bad," Mitchell said. "No more blood on the trail."

"How far ahead you think he is?" Tom asked. "We must've made up some distance on him."

"Maybe," Mitchell said. "A trail don't change much in a couple hours. Couple days is another tale. We're close, though."

"Close enough to catch him today?"

Mitchell shrugged. "Depends. He's heading for an area that's seen lots o' logging. We're lucky, he might get spotted. If we're not, we might lose his trail. Logging chews up the forest. Could be tough tracking."

"Great," Tom said, spitting out the word. "Let's go."

A few minutes more and Mitchell stopped dead. Tom ducked down on one knee. Mike stood watching, too tired to recognize the danger. Tom waved him low. Mitchell bent and circled in a widening radius. When Tom felt it was safe, he advanced to where Mitchell was searching.

"He stopped here," Mitchell said, not taking his eye from the ground. "He's careless." Mitchell poked at some leaves with his toe, turning up a mason jar buried there. He picked it up and sniffed at the open lid. "Peaches."

"Peaches?"

"Peaches. See for yourself," Mitchell said, holding the jar for Tom to inspect. "Probably doesn't know we're behind him. If he did he would've been more careful."

Tom didn't see how. The jar had been buried. Mitchell seemed to sense his skepticism. "There's other sign he didn't bother to cover. Crumbs there by the log," he said, pointing them out, "and this." He held up a piece of brown paper no bigger than a postage stamp.

"Need to be careful, but move fast. He's not more 'n a mile ahead, maybe less. Run when we can."

"Let's go," Tom said, waving Mike to follow.

They moved at a grueling pace, walking fast most of the time, and running when the way was clear. Mitchell didn't seem to tire, though he went fast enough that he slowly widened the gap between him and Mike. They were going at a jog, Mitchell well ahead, when something caught his eye and he skidded to a stop. He peered at a large hemlock just to the right as Mike and Tom jogged up.

Mitchell cocked his head and was frowning, when suddenly he called out, "Stop!" Mike skidded on the leaves, his feet going out from under him. He felt his foot hit a root under the leaves, felt and heard something snap. There was a whoosh as a limb of the hemlock swept above him like a scythe.

"Sonofabitch!" Tom said, the big branch just missing him. "You all right?"

Mike got up as the branch swayed back and forth above him. He brushed himself, unhurt but scared.

"Sorry," Mitchell said. "Moving too fast to spot it. You okay?"

Tom examined the branch, which had been held back with a length of rope rigged as a tripwire and buried under the leaves. "Damn lucky, I'd say. Might not have killed, but it sure would have done some damage, enough to slow us down at least."

"He knows we're here," Mitchell said, "or he's just being careful. We'll need to go slower. Gotta be close."

By the time they took their next break they were all breathing hard and dripping sweat onto the brown carpet of leaves.

"Holding up okay?" Tom asked when he saw Mike shuck off his pack and drop onto a log.

Mike wiped his forehead with a damp kerchief. "Sure," he said with a gulp of air. "Besides, can't let a couple of old guys get the better of me."

Tom laughed but kept it low, just a rumble in his chest. "Got news for you. Mitchell could run us both into the ground."

They took a quick drink and started again. The terrain became more rolling, the forest thicker, spotted with pine and spruce. The forest floor was cooler, the air more fragrant. They jogged, the packbaskets bumping on their backs, straps chafing shoulders. Mitchell stopped once more, Mike and Tom after. He stood listening, head cocked to one side.

"What is it?" Tom asked when he came up.

"Loggers. Thought I heard axes. We need to close up on Tupper if we can," Mitchell said. "Keep spread out. Have a care." He started again at a trot, following Tupper's invisible trail along the side of a long ridge.

The pines were thicker, their needles sometimes slippery under foot. As they went, the sound of lumbering became louder. They could hear the chunk of axes and the calls of men from somewhere above them, up on the ridge. Still, the trail they followed seemed to skirt the logging, keeping within earshot but out of sight. Then a shout echoed from above. It carried like the ringing of a bell.

"Timber, timber, timber!"

They heard a long creaking groan as some giant of the forest went over. There was a whoosh, an impact, and a second, long, groaning shriek, another whoosh, an impact and another groan of tearing wood.

Each falling tree seemed closer than the last, marching down the ridge. Tom, Mike, and Mitchell stood frozen as the shrieking wood and crashing limbs thrashed toward them. They gathered speed. The third tree, then the fourth rocked the trees above and shook the ground beneath their feet. A wind went before, like a tornado it whistled around them.

"Run!" Mitchell had to shout over the noise. "Run!"

Tom followed Mitchell as he bounded ahead. They ducked behind a huge maple. The forest erupted behind them. Branches, bark, leaves, bunches of needles and pinecones rained down as an enormous white pine exploded where they had been. A cloud of dust rolled over them. Shafts of light stabbed through the forest canopy. "Mike!"

Tupper heard the crashing of the trees behind him. He grinned. With luck his trail would be lost in the carnage. He wasn't sure he'd been followed, but he'd expected it and had moved as fast as he could despite his wounded leg. He told himself that only an expert, a man born to the woods would be able to pick up his trail. But such men could be found and were maybe already behind him. It was wise to go and go quickly.

As his grandfather had reminded him, "The rabbit does not stop to see if the fox still follows." Like a ghost, Tupper flitted from tree to tree, until the noise of the loggers was lost in the distance.

Twenty-Four

One mornin' 'fore daylight, Jim Lou he got mad
Knocked hell out of Mitchell and the boys was all glad
His wife, she stood there, and the truth I will tell
She was tickled to death to see Mitchell catch hell
Derry down, down, down derry down.

—"THE RACKETS 'ROUND BLUE MOUNTAIN LAKE"

"Are we there yet, Uncle Chowder?" Rebecca asked in a weary little voice from the back of the shay.

"Pretty soon I think, 'Becca," he said, though he wasn't all that sure.

They'd been on the road nearly three hours. The sun was strong, the road rutted and dusty. Like brown talcum power, it rose up as they passed, settling on everything. Their throats were dry. In their haste, they'd forgotten to bring water. Rounding a bend in the road they saw the silvery flash of water and a lone house amid a field of stumps.

"Hey there," Chowder said. "See, what did Uncle Chowder tell ya? There's the town."

Rebecca jumped up. "That's not a town. A town has lots of houses, lots and lots."

She was right. They drove another mile and more before they came to anything that looked like a town, passing a few cabins and houses on the way, none of which looked too prosperous.

Cresting a rise in the road, they saw a scattered cluster of houses, a church in the distance, and what appeared to be a general store.

The town did not hold their attention, though. A small group of men were milling about the shore of the lake. Two seemed to be examining a pair of boats.

"Oh," Mary said, putting a hand on Chowder's arm, "that's the sheriff, MacDougal, the one in suspenders, with the high boots. Sol Sabattis, the one I told you about, he's the one kneeling."

They pulled to a stop a moment later. The sheriff walked toward the shay, squinting at Chowder once he'd recognized Mary.

"What good you think you'll do here, I'll be damned if I ken," MacDougal said to Mary.

"It's no help you'll be, that's certain."

Rebecca gave the sheriff a sour look.

"Och, an' ye brought your little missy with ya, too. Ain't that just grand."

"It's my right to be here," Mary said. She had her hand on the whip and looked as if she might use it.

MacDougal ignored her. Looking at Chowder, he said, "And you'd be Sergeant Kelly." He extended a hand as he looked Chowder up and down.

"At your service, boyo," Chowder said with a smile that was no smile at all.

"A Mick! Don't that beat all. Come to show us rustics how things're done," MacDougal said with a wry grin. "Suppose I won't hold that agin ya. Glad of the help, if ya gotta know. Not much of a pool o' trained detectives up this way," he said, throwing a thumb over his shoulder at the deputies behind him.

"Detective Sergeant Kelly," Chowder said, trying figure whether or not he should take offense. "Here to help. That's all. What's your interest in those boats?"

MacDougal hooked his thumbs behind his suspenders and set his legs apart.

"Well, *Detective Sergeant Kelly,* this is how matters stand. Missus Braddock's boy is on the run. There's those that say he killed a pretty, young maid, but I suppose you ken that."

MacDougal paused, but when Chowder said nothing he went on. "Seems he's joined up with his father an' Mitchell Sabattis. Don't suppose you knew that. The three o' them're chasin' this Tupper fella all over hell's half acre. Was a gun battle on the lake last night. Found one boat shot up, the other bashed, an' three kinds o' shell casings. That's how I know Mike was there," MacDougal said, as if this were proof of his detective skills.

"Exemplary police work," Chowder said, as if he meant it.

MacDougal huffed. "Well, it sure didn't come from Sol. He can be one dumb Indian when it suits 'im."

"I'm sure," Chowder said without inflection.

"An' another thing, Chauncey Busher's dead. He's the guide Braddock set out wi' after Tupper."

"Mister Busher's dead?" Mary said. She tried to sound shocked, but wasn't sure she pulled it off. She'd certainly suspected as much.

"He told me the beaver poem," Rebecca said. "He's not dead. I saw him last week."

She looked up at Mary for confirmation, but all Mary could do was offer a distracted frown. Though Mary knew that going after Tupper was a thing fraught with danger, she somehow never believed that anyone but Tupper might be losing his life because of it.

"When did it happen? How?" Mary asked.

"Not real clear on the details. Don't have the body yet, just the report. Sol tol' me that much."

"Tupper's a maniac," Chowder said. "You should be grateful Braddock's taking a hand in this."

"Braddock's got his son in mind more 'n anything about catchin' Tupper, with all due respect, ma'am," he said with a nod toward Mary. "Not that I blame him. Done enough pokin' around the last day or so to know a thing or two. I ken that your son an' Lettie were not alone that last day when they were—" MacDougal caught himself, then thought of a more delicate way to phrase it, "when they went for a walk. I ken there was someone spyin on 'em, and not one, but maybe two."

"What do you mean not alone? Who else was there?" Mary said, frowning.

"Have a good idea it was Tupper. Matched a wagon track to the one he left at Merwin's; got a big nick in the rim. But someone else maybe was watchin', maybe somebody even Tupper didn' ken was there. Hard to tell."

"What would Tupper have been watching Mike for, and someone else besides? This is bizarre!" Mary said. She was frowning and pacing beside the carriage.

"Couldn't agree more, ma'am. I'd like knowin' a few things myself," MacDougal said. "But you're not helpin' here, Missus Braddock. We need ta get a move on. We're off ta Tupper Lake to head them off. Signs point to them headin' there."

"The three of you?" Chowder said with a nod to the other men.

"Ey."

"You could use a fourth. I'm coming along, if you don't mind."

"I don't," MacDougal said.

Chowder half expected a different response and was caught off guard.

"I . . ." Chowder started off, before he realized he wasn't getting an argument. "I'm glad to be of service," he said with a shrug.

"That's grand, then!" MacDougal chuckled. "You ready to go?"

Mike! Mike!" Tom shouted as he ran back to where the tree lay in a settling cloud. There were shouts from the ridge above and the sound of running feet.

"Mike!" Tom clambered over the tree, fighting his way through the splintered, twisted branches. Broken boughs lay thick on the ground. Tom kept calling and digging, Mitchell too. He saw a flash of color and doubled his efforts, digging and clawing with frantic strength. The taste of fear rose in his throat. Mike lay motionless.

Tom bent low over Mike, feeling at his neck for a pulse, putting an ear to his chest. Loggers came running.

"Mike," Tom said, shaking him and slapping his face.

"Fuckin' fools!" someone said.

"What the hell you doin' down 'ere?" another man grumbled.

"Who's hurt? Not one of ours, is it?" another asked.

"My boy, goddamnit," Tom said. "You dropped a fucking tree on him."

Four men stood over them talking at once.

"You crazy? Can't ya hear when we call *timber?*" one said.

"If 'n he's stupid enough ta stand under a fallin' tree, well—"

Mike began to rouse. His eyes fluttered.

"Serve 'im right, he got his head busted. Stupid sport. Can't take a shit in the woods 'out a tourist poppin up."

Mike groaned and opened his eyes. A couple of the men laughed. Mike looked up at Tom. "Sorry—I . . . ," he started to say, wheezing, his words almost lost in the laughter.

Tom was on his feet. He turned to one of the men and with a snarl, kicked him in the stomach, a sideways kick that would have pleased old Master Kwan. The man went down like a tree. Pivoting to his left, he caught a second startled logger with a slashing chop to the neck and a right to the solar plexus. He spun again, lashing out with a foot, taking the legs from under a third, dumping him in a heap with a tremendous blow to the chest. He ducked under a fist, grabbed a shirt and, using the man's momentum, threw him to the ground. Mitchell stood to the side, leaning on his shotgun, a faint grin painting his creased features. Tom turned back to Mike

"Ribs," Mike said, holding his side.

"Okay, Mike, just lie still. We'll get you taken care of."

"Tom," Mitchell said, hardly raising his voice.

A logger charged from behind. Tom, still in a crouch, didn't rise to meet him. He dove at the feet, sending the man tumbling forward into the fallen tree. Tom rolled to his feet. The biggest of the four was almost on top of him. He aimed a vicious kick at Tom, his boot whistling so close to his head he could smell wet leather. Tom diverted the blow, letting it glance off his arm, which threw the man off balance just a little. Tom came out of his crouch and hit the man square in the nose, a blow that splattered red across them both and knocked him hard on his back.

Tom turned to face the others. Two were up but showing no fight. A third rolled on the ground, groaning and holding his stomach. A glance at Mitchell showed he'd shifted the shotgun to the crook of his arm and his finger to the trigger.

Another knot of loggers was coming down the ridge.

"Got a man hurt down here," Tom shouted. "Need a doctor."

"Only man's gonna need a doctor's you, mister," one of the loggers said.

"Hell, 'Brose, give it up," another said, holding his stomach. "That your boy, mister?"

"Yeah."

"Who gives a shit?" the one called 'Brose said. "Sonofabitch's got a whuppin' comin'."

"Oh, shut yer yap, 'Brose. You can have your whuppin' later, if you've a mind. The boy needs help. Go fetch Mama Dupree." Turning to Tom, he said, "She's the closest we got to a doctor."

The other loggers had gathered about by then. The man who appeared to be the foreman looked from Mike to the loggers. "How many o' you got hit by the tree? What the hell went on here?"

'Brose started shouting. He was hopping mad, literally jumping from one foot to the other, pointing and swinging his fists, saying how, "That big fella jus' up an' lit inter us fer no call at all."

Now that 'Brose had a bigger audience he was getting brave again. Tom let him spout, restraining an urge to silence him for good. He turned back to Mike, ignoring 'Brose, which only seemed to make him louder. Mike's breathing was quick and shallow, his skin pasty pale.

The foreman cut through 'Brose's shouting. "Anybody call for Mama Dupree?"

"Tol' 'Brose ta fetch 'er," the one logger said.

Looking at 'Brose, the foreman shouted, "Then what the fuck're you doin' here? Get goin'!"

"But that bastard . . ."

"I don't give a shit, 'Brose," the foreman shouted back. "Your gang boss says go, you fuckin' better well go, goddamnit!"

"This ain't over, mister," 'Brose said, pointing at Tom. "Got a reckonin' comin'.

"Run, you bastard," the foreman shouted, after him. "Run or you'll spend the winter ice fishin'."

'Brose broke into a trot, followed by a shoal of laughter.

Turning back to Tom and Mitchell, the man said, "How's he doin'?"

"He's not dead," Tom said. "More than that I can't say. Got some busted ribs, looks like."

Mike nodded, holding his side. The foreman looked at Mitchell and nodded with a grin.

"Hey, Mitch."

Mitchell grinned back.

"Boys," the foreman said to the rest, "this is Mitchell Sabattis, best darn guide an' boatbuilder in the North Country." There was a murmur of recognition from the crowd. Tom cast a quick glance at Mitchell, who now stood against a tree, leaning on the muzzle of his grounded shotgun.

"We can sort out what happened later, not that I believe this fella kicked hell outa you fine specimens," he said, laughing. They all laughed, except the three. "Meantime, we'll see to the boy. Rest o' you get back to work."

The crowd melted as the foreman knelt beside Tom. "At least he ain't bleedin' much," which was true enough. Aside from a few scrapes and a couple of rents in his clothes, Mike didn't look all that bad. "Considering you got a tree dropped on you, you're doin' fair ta middlin'," he said to Mike with a pat on the shoulder.

"Anything hurt besides the ribs?" Tom asked.

"Everything," Mike said, doing his best to grin through the pain.

"Least his sense o' humor ain't hurt," the foreman said. He stood a few minutes later as he saw a woman come rolling through the forest. She was six feet tall if she was an inch, and must have gone well over two hundred pounds. Her arms were huge and they swung freely from a massive set of shoulders, as she stumped through the woods with a black bag dangling like an afterthought. She had no visible neck, her head appearing to have been put on without one. Wiry hair was pulled back in a helmetlike bun. The legs that supported her were pink tree trunks framed by black boots and a line of brown lace at her hem.

"Christ," Tom whispered.

"Not much to look at, I'd agree," the foreman said under his breath, "but it don't pay ta have a pretty woman out here, not with my lot."

A dirty apron hung down her front, covered in grease and smeared, brown blood. She wiped her hands on it as she came. She bent beside Mike, ordering Tom and the foreman to "Gimme room, you two."

"Hello, sweetie," she said to Mike in a very different tone. "Why, look at you. You ain't hardly hurt at all." Pulling open her kit, she added softly, "We'll just patch you up a bit. Have you doin a jig in no time. Here, have a drink," she said, offering Mike a flask. "Doctor's orders."

It wasn't long before Mama Dupree had Mike on his feet, though he looked ghastly pale doing it. With Tom's help he hobbled toward the logging camp. It was on the other side of the ridge, about a half mile away. Mike was spent by the time they got there.

"Twisted my ankle when I turned to run," Mike told Tom. "Fell on my face. Lucky for me it was beside a rock. A branch whacked me good before I could get up, but I think the rock saved me from the worst of it."

"Seen men crushed like a bug," the foreman said. "You was lucky." Turning to Mitchell he asked, "What were you boys doing down there, anyway?" Mitchell said nothing. He just turned to Tom, who gave the man a shortened version of their story. "Damned bad luck then for you," the man observed. "Don't suppose you'll catch 'im any time soon."

Tom looked at Mike. "I don't know. I'd say our luck was pretty good."

Mama Dupree wasn't a doctor, but she did as good a job of doctoring as any doctor could.

"Ribs ain't broke bad," was her diagnosis to Tom after she'd had a chance to "see to 'im proper."

She rigged up a brace around his middle, a corset, really, with some added whalebone extending up the torso. She wrapped it tight and fixed a poultice for his twisted ankle, too, putting a bandage where he'd ripped the skin back in the marsh.

"Can't thank you enough, ma'am," Tom said late that afternoon as she bustled about the crude kitchen, working up the dinner meal.

"Sure, sure," she said. "Give 'im some rest; he'll bounce back fine. The young ones always do. Now git on outa here. Got work ta do."

"How's the boy?" The foreman asked as the men started filing in late in the day. "Better," Tom said "He's anxious to get moving. The man we're after, he's on the move, I can tell you that."

The foreman grunted, "Guess I'd be too, if I'd killed a girl. The boy good enough to travel?"

Tom shrugged. "Says he is. Not real sure though. One thing's certain, he won't sit still for long. That girl that was killed, she was his—you know, ah, girlfriend."

"Oh!" the man said, "I understand now. Won't get far tonight, though. May 's well stay here, get some food in ya."

"I appreciate the offer," Tom said. "I wouldn't mind a hot meal, but we gotta go. We're losing ground every second we sit here." Tom saw 'Brose come in along with the other man who'd taken exception to getting beat. He nodded in their direction. "They won't give us any trouble, will they?"

The foreman smiled. "Nah. They just like ta fight. And from what they say, you really did beat the tar outa them boys."

"Guess I did," Tom said.

The foreman laughed. "Them two don't really mean no harm. Just got too much piss an' vinegar, that's all. C'mon, you two," he said over his shoulder. "You got whupped square," he said, "now shake an' have done with it."

The one called 'Brose shoved a hand at Tom. His nose was purple and both eyes were blackened. Tom stood and shook with him.

"No hard feelin's," 'Brose said, cotton balls stuffed up his nose.

"Sure," Tom said, uncertain of how to take the peacemaking. "You okay?"

'Brose touched his face and winced. "Ain't the first time had my nose broke. Reckon I'll live."

Tom smiled. "Had my nose busted twice," he said. "Hurt like a sonofabitch."

'Brose grinned. "Hell, I'm jus' glad my head's still 'tached. Hope the boy mends up," he said, then turned and walked out. The other one shook without a word, then turned and limped away.

"That'll keep 'em quiet a couple o' days, I reckon," the foreman said. "You're the first man ever licked both of 'em."

Mike winced as he rolled out onto his side a few minutes later, then pushed himself upright. He gripped the edge of the bed and clenched his teeth.

"Okay?" Tom asked, his eyes narrowing.

Mike nodded.

"Take it slow."

"Mama Dupree's got some things fixed up for you. Keep you goin'," the foreman said, shaking with them when they were ready. "Good luck."

Tom, Mike, and Mitchell set off into the growing gloom, the logging camp fading into the woods in a feeble glow. Disembodied voices singing along with a screeching fiddle echoed for a few minutes before the forest swallowed them whole.

Twenty-Five

We should turn wild so as not to surrender to our own
wildness, but rather to acquire in that way a consciousness
of our selves as tamed, as cultural beings.

—HANS PETER DUERR

Mike was afraid to tell Tom how bad he was hurting, afraid if he showed his pain he'd be left behind. Every breath was a deep ache and sometimes a sharp stab that seemed to lock his lungs up so he could hardly breathe at all. He felt bruised all over, as if someone had taken a bat to him. When they set out, all Mike carried was the Winchester. Tom split Mike's load between him and Mitchell. Mike was grateful, but still barely able to keep up.

It didn't take Mitchell long to find Tupper's trail. He went to where they had been stopped by the falling trees, then searched the ground in the direction Tupper had been heading. Somehow, in the gray light Mitchell sniffed out the trail. They were far behind Tupper now, so far they had little hope, unless he stopped. Still they plodded forward, trusting whatever luck was theirs. None of them spoke of giving up.

The forest was cool. The sky brooded like a leaden sea, hovering so low it seemed they might bump their heads on it. They trudged through the woods as in a netherworld, a place not quite of this earth, where outlines faded one into the other. Shapes and shadows in the trees seemed to be more than they were, as if another forest lurked just behind the one they could see. It had become a cold unsettling place.

The warm browns and greens of the day were warm no longer. Spirits sagged as the hours wore on.

Even Mitchell seemed weighed down. He went forward bent double, trying to see Tupper's prints. Mike's ribs ached so bad he couldn't bend much at all, and he was panting like a dog. Still, there was no complaining. Though Tupper had melted into the heart of the forest primeval, they would follow. Though the forest was vast and deep, so deep no man could know it all, they knew in time he would surface. When he did, they would be there. They were his shadow, dogging his steps, nipping at his heels. Only a dead man loses his shadow.

They passed through the forest like shadows, a bent fern, the snap of a twig, the scuff of a boot their only markers. When the sun had given up the last of its light, Mitchell stopped.

"We can go no further," he said, shucking off his pack, "not without light."

He rummaged in his pack, pulling out a kerosene lamp. "I figure we're about three hours behind," he said. He lit the lamp and adjusted the wick to get the best light. "We can track him for that long before we'll have to camp. I don't know about you, but I don't care for the idea of coming upon him with a lantern in my hand."

"No argument here," Tom said. "Best to get after him again at first light." He looked at Mike, who was pale and sweating. "Maybe we better take a rest for a few minutes, though."

Mitchell agreed. He turned out the lamp and they sat for a while in the darkness, nibbling at the food Mama Dupree had given them. They rested only fifteen minutes, but Mike felt better for it.

In fact, it was he who got up first. He picked up the Winchester and said, "Ready?"

They trudged on through the night, following the yellow halo of Mitchell's lamp. More than once Tom imagined it was a ghost they followed, a spirit of the forest, leading them farther away from all they had ever known. He tried not to think that way, but it was hard not to.

When at last they stopped, it was a cold camp they made. They lit no fire, cooked no food. They bedded down together in the shadow of a big boulder, crawling into their blankets spread on a bed of hemlock.

Mitchell extinguished the light and they were asleep within minutes. Wisely or not, they kept no watch. They were too exhausted. They did, however, sleep with their weapons.

The sun had started to paint the horizon a pale rose when Tom woke. Mitchell was already up, standing with his back to Tom, looking at the lightening forest as the trees emerged from the morning mist. Tom studied the old Indian. There was something timeless about the way he stood, silent and watchful. Tom felt as if he saw Mitchell's elemental self, the culmination of a long, unbroken line of forest men, centuries of knowledge and lore and skill passed down from father to son. He seemed ageless, timeless, a man not entirely of this world. Mitchell unbuttoned his pants and sighed as he urinated on the leaves.

They came upon Tupper's camp within an hour. It wasn't more than a mile and a half from where they'd slept. Tupper had made no fire. Like them, he'd slept on the ground. Mitchell examined the site. He dug under the leaves and came up with a white bandage caked with dried blood, with a bright red center.

"Changed bandages. There's some blood here and there. Nothing serious." Mitchell felt the ground, a shallow depression in the leaves where Tupper had slept. "Cold. He was up at first light, just like us."

"At least we've gained on him," Tom said. "Might be as close as we were before the tree fell on Mike."

Mike smiled. "That'd be good," he said. Part of him was feeling guilty for getting in the way of that tree and ruining their chances. "Let's keep going."

It was late in the afternoon when they stumbled across a road. There was no way to know it was there. It just appeared before them, a narrow tunnel in the trees, rutted, with high grass down the middle. They stood there for several heartbeats, heads swiveling left and right as if they'd never seen such a thing in their lives.

"Logging road," Mitchell said. Though it was barely a whisper, it seemed loud, and Mike imagined the words echoing down the tunnel for miles. "Probably goes back to the camp that way," he said, pointing to his right.

"You think he took this?" Tom asked, looking at the ground. It hadn't rained for days, and the sandy soil would not hold a track well.

"Maybe," Mitchell said. "I would. That way heads to Tupper Lake," he said with a nod to the left. "Stay here. I'll check for signs."

Mitchell stepped across the road. The way he did it reminded Tom of a man crossing train tracks, with a care for what might be coming around the bend.

"Nothing," Mitchell said. He came back to stand in the road. Slowly he walked in the direction of Tupper Lake. He stopped twice, checking the ground and grass, then without a backward glance waved for them to follow.

The road wound through the forest for miles. At times it did not seem like a road at all where the grass grew thick, or where a rocky runoff crossed. Still, it had seen use. Wagon tracks were visible and the occasional pile of manure was recent.

They were stopped for a short rest when Mitchell turned to look back the way they'd come. Tom and Mike looked too. There was nothing to see.

"What is it?" Tom asked. Though his ears had grown sharp, they were still city ears.

"Someone coming," Mitchell said. "Wagon."

Movement through the trees became a horse. A buggy came behind. Four men rode in it, rifles bristling. Tom checked his pistol, flicking off the safety. Mike did the same. They stood still, letting the buggy come to them.

"That's Uncle Chowder in the back," Mike said, amazed. Tom grunted agreement.

Though he was glad to see Chowder, he knew who the other men must be.

"Put up your weapons," MacDougal called. Tom saw three rifles swivel toward them.

"Dinna move!"

"Do what he says, Mike," Tom said. "Don't worry."

Mike propped the Winchester against a tree, feeling suddenly naked.

"You too. Both o' you," MacDougal said, waving his rifle at Tom and Mitchell. "Pistols, too."

The buggy was close then. It stopped and MacDougal hopped down followed by Chowder and the two deputies. Chowder hung back, eyeing the others, one hand hooked on his belt. He winked at Tom and Mike.

"You're Braddock?" MacDougal said. Not waiting for an answer, he added, "And this'd be your murdering rapist of a boy," but in a tone that Tom took to be sarcastic, as if the man didn't believe it. Tom bristled anyway, baring his teeth in a low snarl.

"Don't look like such to me, from the looks of 'im," MacDougal added. "But then, we don't get much o' that kind up here." He threw open his jacket, showing his badge. "Sheriff MacDougal," he said. "Been lookin' for you, but I expect you figured that."

When neither Tom nor Mike answered, he shrugged and said, "You dinna look surprised to see me. Put your hands out, Laddie."

The rifles didn't waver. There was a long moment of silence. Mike looked to Tom, who gave him a slight nod. MacDougal pulled a pair of cuffs from a back pocket. "Hands in front," he said. Mike watched in a trance as the steel clicked shut around his wrists.

"Sorry for this," MacDougal said, "but it's a thing that's got to get done. You'll be going back wi' one o' the deputies to stand before a magistrate."

He turned to Tom and Mitchell. "An' your part in this is done, you two. You've got no jurisdiction here. Anyway, I suppose you'll be wantin' to go back with your boy."

Tom nodded. He might do more for Mike in the courts than in the woods, but giving up was not a thing Tom had a taste for. He swallowed it whole for now, the bitter flavor of defeat nearly gagging him.

"You still going after Tupper?" Tom asked.

"Aye. He's an escaped murderer, if reports are to be believed, and we can't have none o' them mucking around in our woods, scaring tourists an' such."

Tom looked at Chowder. MacDougal followed his gaze.

"An' he's going with me. Just him, mind you. One o' you city cops're more trouble than I need. 'Sides, you're too damn close to this. No telling what ye might do."

Turning to Mitchell, he said, "Sabattis, you're welcome to come if you like."

Mitchell shrugged. "Guess I won't," he said.

They started off again, Mike riding handcuffed with MacDougal and the deputies, Tom and Chowder walking behind. Mitchell walked ahead, tracking.

"How the hell you find us?" Tom asked. "I couldn't even find myself in these damn woods."

Chowder chuckled. "A good guess and some luck. The sheriff found the boats on the lake. He had a report of all the shooting and checked it out," Chowder said. "A clever enough fella for local law, by the way."

Tom shrugged. He wasn't in the mood to hear how good the sheriff was just then.

"Found the spot where you went into the woods after Tupper," Chowder went on. "He figured you'd be going more or less for Tupper Lake, so he tried to head you off. MacDougal knew about that logging camp. His cousin's the foreman. MacDougal thought there was a chance you might have been there. We were there this morning. They told us about you," Chowder said.

Tom nodded. "So you were trying to get ahead of us?"

"Something like that. MacDougal figured it might be easier than trying to catch up to you. Oh!" Chowder said, suddenly remembering, "Mary gave me this." Chowder handed the swatch of cloth to Tom.

"Hmph. Damn near forgot about this. Seems years since I found it." Tom said, turning it over in his hand, imagining the man who'd worn it. "Listen, Chowder, be careful with this one. He's dangerous. Tell you the truth, it might be more than one man. Mitchell, our guide, he says the man who shot at us back at Forked Lake was right-handed. Tupper's left-handed."

Chowder shook his head. "Wait a minute. Who the hell shot at you?"

"Same man killed our last guide," Tom said. "Might've been Tupper. Might not. We never saw him."

Chowder frowned. "You've been havin' all the fun without me again," he said, wagging a finger at him.

Tom smiled. "Not exactly. Listen, I've got to have a talk with MacDougal."

Chowder grinned and said, "He knows there might be another man. Told me he found evidence of a second man near where Mike and the girl had their little tryst."

Tom looked surprised. "How in hell?"

"Seems that was a popular spot with the help," Chowder said. "One o' the maids told him. Mike's girl told her she was going to take him there. Besides," he added with a nod of his head toward where MacDougal walked with Mitchell, the two deep in conversation, "I think he knows most o' that by now."

Tom nodded. "Maybe MacDougal's okay," he allowed. It made Tom feel a little better, knowing MacDougal wasn't the buffoon he'd feared he'd be. Still, Tom was afraid to fully voice his fear to Chowder, afraid of sounding weak to his old friend.

He needn't have worried. Chowder knew Tom better than to ever think him weak. He understood Tom's concern.

"Don't worry," Chowder said, trying to make light of Tom's warning. "That's what we do, catch the dangerous ones."

"Yeah I know, I know. But this one—you didn't see what happened to our other guide," Tom said, looking straight at Chowder, catching his eye. "The man who wore this shirt," he said, holding up the cloth as if it might poison him, "is capable of anything. Don't take chances. If you see him, shoot him. And watch your back."

"But he's worth more to you alive, I mean to Mike and all."

"Well sure, but so are you."

Chowder chuckled. "Hell, Tommy, the bad guys haven't killed me yet. Too much of a damn, stubborn Irishman."

Tom wasn't laughing.

The wagon stopped ahead. Tom and Chowder caught up. Mitchell had disappeared. They heard him in a thick patch of beech. He emerged in a minute and waved.

"Gone off the road here," he said, pointing to signs neither Tom nor Chowder could see. The rest grunted as if they could read the trail as clearly as Mitchell.

MacDougal, Chowder, and one of the deputies split off once they shouldered their packs. Mitchell, Tom, and the second deputy rode with Mike in the wagon.

Tom put his hand out to Chowder. "See ya," he said. Chowder grinned in reply and turned to follow MacDougal. Tom watched him check his pistol as he disappeared into the trees.

Twenty-Six

This is a horrible place for a man to die.

—DAVID HENDERSON

"We'll stop at Long Lake," the deputy said, once he'd clucked to the horse. "Mind if we stay with you, Mitchell?"

"Plenty of room," Mitchell said.

They hit the road to Long Lake in about a half mile. It wasn't much different than the logging road, a little more rutted, a little less rocky. Nothing moved on the road. In fact they didn't see another soul.

Nearly an hour later they stopped to let the horse water at a little stream. Nobody spoke. Mike sat in the wagon, his head down. Tom cast one glance at him, then at Mitchell. Neither met his gaze. Tom had become more and more uneasy since parting with Chowder. He'd said nothing to Mitchell or Mike. In fact they rode in almost total silence. When they stopped, Tom got down and paced, looking back down the road from the direction they'd come. Mitchell watched him from the back of the buggy, his shotgun across his knees.

"You know, Dad," Mike said, breaking the silence, "Mom will be there when I get back. It's not like I'll be alone."

Tom turned to him, cocking his head to one side. Mitchell watched them both.

"Besides, we can prove I didn't kill Lettie. That's gotta be clear to everybody, once they hear about what happened at Forked Lake."

Tom slowly shook his head. "What you know and I know might not be so clear to a judge up here, Mike. We have to be sure. You'll need a good lawyer, a proper investigation."

"Sure, but Mom can take care of that, and we can get help from the Durants, right?"

"I suppose Mike, but—"

"Just go, Dad. Go back and catch him. I'll be all right." Tom and Mitchell and the deputy, too, looked at Mike. "I won't really be cleared until Tupper is caught, anyway," Mike added.

Tom didn't say anything. He dropped his head in thought and kicked at the dirt.

"Damnit, Mike, I want to go with you!" he said finally. "It's my place to be with you," he added, almost as if trying to convince himself.

"I'm not a boy," Mike said.

Tom stopped his pacing and looked straight at him. A grim smile crept across Tom's face, a light kindled in his eyes. "No, you're not. Haven't been for some time, though I've been late to see it."

Mike smiled back. "Go!" he said.

Without a word, the sheriff handed Tom his rifle. Tom looked at Mike as he hefted the Winchester in one hand. "I'll be back," he said at last.

"I know," Mike answered.

Tom and Mitchell watched as the wagon rumbled away. Mike turned once and waved, raising both hands to do it. Tom waved back, almost shouting for them to stop. Sending Mike back alone hurt like nothing he could remember. It put him in mind of amputees during the war, and how they'd complain of the pain in their lost limbs. For the first time he thought he knew what they meant.

Tom and Mitchell turned and walked back. They were miles behind, with little hope of catching up. Neither of them mentioned that or even gave it a thought. They didn't need hope. They had everything they needed.

For the next two hours they alternately jogged and walked, going quickly along the hard-packed road, nearly as fast as the wagon had gone, so that they were approaching where the sheriff and Chowder had split off. The sun was dipping below the treetops by then, the cool of the forest creeping out from under the trees.

Then, miles off, they heard shooting, heavy firing, booming, echoing. They stopped, frozen by the sound, counting the shots that slowed quickly, sputtering, then dying. Tom and Mitchell looked once at each other and broke again into a trot. Another report rolled across the trees, followed by a long silence and then a second shot. Neither Tom nor Mitchell slowed as the forest settled into uneasy silence.

Mike and the deputy arrived at Mitchell's house late that night. It seemed to materialize out of the fabric of the night, a lighter patch of dark with edges and corners. No lights were on. No dog barked as they rode up. The buggy rattled into the yard.

There was a rustling and the noise of hooves in the yard in back.

"Damn deer after Mitchell's corn," the deputy said. "Can't shoot enough of 'em."

They walked into the darkened kitchen through the unlocked back door. The deputy struck a match and lit a lamp that he'd gotten from the back of the buggy, his face cast for a moment in yellow relief.

"Anybody home?" The deputy called. "Hello?"

Mike sat at a table in the center of the kitchen. He stared at the steel around his wrists. "Say, Vern," Mike said. "Can't we take the cuffs off for now? I give you my word I won't leave the house."

Vern seemed sympathetic, but said, "Waaall, ah don' know. Mac-Dougal tol' me ta keep a tight rein, you bein' a runner an' all."

Mike tried not to show how he felt about that. He had half a mind to throttle Vern a little till he changed his mind, or whatever passed for a mind in his case. But in a reasonable tone he said, "I got ya. I'm your responsibility."

The stove clattered as the deputy got a fire going. A puff of smoke blew back into the room where it rolled to the ceiling, scenting the place in a way that had Mike thinking of his parents' kitchen when he was a boy.

"But MacDougal's not here," he went on, "and . . ."

There were footsteps on the stairs somewhere off in the darkened house. Mrs. Sabattis emerged from the gloom into the light of the kitchen, wearing a long nightshirt and slippers. She looked once around the room, staring for an instant at the deputy and Mike, where her eyes flickered over the glint of the handcuffs. She shooed the deputy away from the stove.

"I'll get some water," he said, fetching a bucket from under the sink. More footsteps could be heard, a pair of them.

"Anyway Vern, MacDougal's not here," Mike continued. "I'd take it as a personal favor if . . ." Mike stopped and turned. Rebecca came running.

"Mikey!"

She jumped into his lap, knocking him back and almost upsetting the chair. Mike hugged her as best he could with his shackled hands. She gripped his neck in a fierce hug.

"You little ginger snap! I've missed you!" he said, amazed at himself for saying it, because he'd never thought he'd miss the little pest.

"Ew! Your face is scratchy," she said, pulling away, "and you smell bad! You need a bubble bath!"

Mike laughed and let her slip to the floor.

"Mom!"

Mary came down the stairs behind Rebecca, her thoughts doing somersaults. She didn't know what to expect. What she hoped was that Tupper's body was in the back of a wagon, covered with a sheet. Thinking of Tupper, she prayed that Tom and Mike were unhurt. For a horrible moment she imagined all sorts of things, but she put them out of her head almost as quickly as they sprang up. Those things were unthinkable.

She yearned to see Tom and Mike again, to hold them and know they were back. Anything else wasn't worth thinking. Little butterflies were let loose in her belly and made her head feel light. Mary set her jaw when she got to the bottom of the stairs, ready for whatever might come. But she wasn't ready for what she saw.

Mike seemed to have aged years. His face looked drawn, burned by the sun, and blotched with insect bites. A spotty growth of beard gave him a grizzled look. There were dark circles under his eyes and his clothes were dirty and torn. She tried to hide her shock, but she wasn't sure she did.

The pans clattered on the stove. The deputy went to fetch water. Mary stood for a moment, her hand going to her mouth in shock. She held her arms out to Mike, but as she did, Rebecca turned away from him with a trembling mouth and tears running down her cheeks. She ran and clung to Mary's leg, stopping her as Mike stood. Mary didn't see the cuffs at first. Rebecca's tears distracted her. She though perhaps Rebecca was so happy to see Mike that she'd been overcome. That notion died when she saw the glint of steel, the short length of chain.

Chowder had let MacDougal do the tracking, not that he had much choice. He could not fathom how anything could be tracked through the dense undergrowth in these forests. In many places he couldn't even see the ground, it was so thick with ferns or grasses or other sorts of low-growing things he didn't have a name for. The going was rough and exhausting. Where they passed through areas that had been logged it was worse. The limbs and branches left by the loggers formed an impenetrable tangle on the ground. New growth of birch and poplar and beech formed thickets only slightly less dense than hedges. Thorny blackberry tore at their clothes.

Chowder was grateful the trail stuck mostly to the logging roads in those areas. It seemed not even Tupper wanted to fight through if he didn't have to.

The sun became an orange glow behind the trees as the afternoon wore on. Chowder couldn't tell for sure if it had set, but it was close. It had been hours since he'd parted with Tom and Mike. He wondered how long it would take them to make it back to Long Lake. He hadn't told Tom that Mary was there, figuring he'd enjoy the surprise. He grinned. Mary had been quite a catch, and he'd always been more than a little jealous of Tommy for doing the catching.

Shaking Tom and Mary out of his thoughts, Chowder watched the thickets and dense patches of young spruce where the shadows were starting to gather. The light was changing by the minute, and even the open areas were becoming fuzzy. MacDougal hadn't slowed. In fact, the sheriff had only stopped for a few minutes in the hours of tramping they'd done. Chowder was beginning to wonder if they'd stop at all. He couldn't imagine how they'd track by lamplight.

They were working their way up a narrow draw. MacDougal was in front, the deputy behind, and Chowder in the rear. There were boulders to the right and a steep slope to the left hemming them in. The ground at the bottom was all in shadow.

For Chowder there was no difference between the deafening boom of the rifles and the impact that knocked him off his feet. It was as if he'd been hit by the sound. He was stunned to find himself on his hands and knees. For a split second his brain could not register what had happened. His left leg didn't seem to work as it should, and a searing pain started to replace the numbness there. He felt his thigh. His hand came away bright red. This passed in no more than two seconds, but it seemed much longer. More shots came from left and right. MacDougal had disappeared, the deputy too. Chowder pulled out his pistol, but couldn't see what to shoot at. He was alone, kneeling in the open.

Chowder tried to get to his feet and run, but the best he could do was hobble, dragging his burning leg. A bullet whistled past, hitting a tree in front of him, splattering little pieces of bark. Chowder tried for the tree, the closest cover.

Something hit him in the shoulder, exploding out the top of his chest. He fell into the leaves, his face digging into the crinkling, soft bed. He could not get enough air. His breathing was labored and something bubbled and burned in his lung. When he tried to lift himself his shoulder moved in a way it never was meant to, grinding and burning so bad he fell on his face. The firing stopped.

Chowder rolled onto his back, his head propped against a log. He fumbled with his good hand, rustling the leaves for his pistol. He looked down at the hole in his shirt. He was glad it wasn't his best one.

Sitting up a little, he managed to shuck off his pack, though the pain of moving his shoulder reduced his vision to a small speck of light, with sparkling stars flitting around in the blackness. Somehow he managed to get a kerchief out of his pack and tie off the wound in his thigh. Another shot boomed, then a second, but they didn't seem directed at him. Chowder collapsed against the log, trying to catch his breath.

He closed his eyes and floated in a swirling red mist. He was spinning through the forest, the trees rotating above his head. He'd have to get that under control if he ever expected to walk out. He'd make himself a crutch come morning, he figured, trying to plan, to focus on something beyond the pain, the spinning, and the bubbling.

When Chowder opened his eyes someone was there. He didn't think it was McDougal or the deputy, so he shot him. He just brought up the pistol at his side and blasted him dead center. The man didn't fall down or drop his rifle, though he doubled over like he'd been kicked by a horse.

Chowder shot him again. The man just said "Damn!" and stumbled away, holding his gut. Chowder started to feel better. Movement caught his eye off to the left somewhere. Someone was running. Chowder shot at him, too, shot until the pistol clicked and clicked. A rifle boomed. Something hit him. He couldn't see. Something was in his eyes and he was so dizzy he had to close them. He didn't see the man standing over him, didn't feel anything more.

Tupper heard the shooting. He stopped and listened. At least three or four people firing, one a pistol, the rest rifles. He doubted it was more than a mile or so back.

"What the hell's that about," he said. His grandfather didn't answer. The spirit seemed puzzled, just standing there.

Tupper took a step back, the first backward step he'd taken in weeks. He took another, not knowing why exactly. All the shooting—it was about him. There was no way he could know that.

He wasn't even certain anyone was on his trail, though he'd traveled as though someone was. He looked at his broken rifle, good for only one shot, and that iffy. It might even blow up in his face. He wasn't sure. There was a lot he wasn't sure about.

But if men were shooting at each other, someone might have been hit, someone might have dropped a rifle or pistol. He thought about his food, which was running low. He'd have to start eating bunchberries soon.

He told himself these things, and they were true, but there was another truth; he'd been chased by men he'd never seen, men who were probably behind him now, shooting at something. He wanted to see them, know what sort of men they were. They'd come closer than he liked to admit. Knowing who they were was a thing worth a risk, a thing of great value when he went into town. Tupper took another step back, but stopped when he heard more shooting.

"Sure you want to do this?" he heard his grandfather say. "The trout does not jump into—"

"Told me that one already," Tupper interrupted.

"—the bear."

"Give it up old man. I'll be careful," Tupper said, shrugging the old ghost out of his head.

He started retracing his steps. Night was falling. He didn't have much time.

Tupper made his way back, going with extra care and using the trees and undergrowth to cover him. He did not follow his old trail, but a parallel course, so he'd stand little chance of running into someone head-on. In about half an hour he came to the edge of a ravine. It was almost pitch-dark in the bottom and not much better above. Tupper sniffed the air.

There was the smell of death down there, and he recoiled as from a hot stove. Tupper made sure of his rifle, and wedged an extra three bullets between the fingers of his left hand, ready to reload. A groan came up from the darkness. The hair on the back of Tupper's neck stood straight up and gooseflesh pebbled his arms.

"Two dead white men. Another soon. *Shondowek´owa*, the death herald, is waiting," his grandfather said close beside him, which startled Tupper almost as much as the groaning. "I see their spirits. They are confused."

Another groan drifted up out of the ravine. Though Tupper shuddered, he went forward. He was almost upon the first body before he stopped. Kneeling close, he examined it, a man he'd never seen before, a man with half his head gone and a brass star pinned to his vest. A Winchester .44-40 lay beside him.

Tupper dropped his rifle and rummaged in the man's pack, coming up with a box of shells. He checked the rifle, which was loaded and looking as though it was working perfectly. Tupper grinned while he searched the pack for food. Once he had whatever he could use, including cash from the sheriff s pockets, he went to see about the one who was groaning.

Tupper started forward, but instead of going further into the ravine he skirted it, working his way down the edge from tree to tree. Outlines were indistinct. Regardless of what his grandfather had said, he couldn't see any bodies. He didn't have to see them to know they were there, though. He could smell the gun smoke and the stink of loosed bowels.

The groans continued. They seemed to follow, calling him; but he wasn't about to rush in. That was the way of the fool. There would not be much he could do for the man, anyway, except perhaps to put him out of his misery. Tupper thought these things as he worked his way around the ravine.

Maybe his thoughts distracted his attention for an instant, but Owens was there, seeming to materialize from the gloom. He was bent over a body, checking the man's pockets. Tupper put his rifle to his shoulder without really aiming it, thinking Owens was a friend, but taking no chances.

Owens straightened, bringing his rifle around, perhaps seeing Tupper's movement from the corner of his eye. He had his rifle on Tupper for a split second then he hesitated. He recognized Tupper. Letting the muzzle drop a fraction, he smiled and nodded. Tupper nodded back, dropping his rifle from his shoulder. When he did, Owens fired.

Tom and Mitchell ducked down. The reports cracked through the dark forest, seeming so close the shots might have been directed at them. In a second it became clear they weren't. Although close, they were not that close. Mitchell stood and signaled to Tom, who came and stood beside the guide.

"Not far. Maybe quarter mile or so. We go slow."

Tom just nodded and followed Mitchell, who now seemed to measure every step and place each foot with exaggerated care. Tom tried to do the same, as sweat rolled down his back in little rivulets. He wondered if Mitchell was as scared as he was. Mitchell didn't show it, but only a fool wouldn't be scared.

It was further than Tom had imagined from the sound of the shots. It took at least a half hour before they came to the ravine. It was becoming so dark, they were in it before realizing they were hemmed in on either side. Mitchell held up one hand and Tom stopped behind him.

They listened, and Tom thought he could smell the residue of gun smoke. Mitchell sniffed too, peering into the dark as he did, crouching then for a better sight line, but seeing nothing. It was then they heard a long groan. It seemed to come up from just beneath their feet. The sweat on Tom's back went suddenly cold and every hair on his body seemed to stand straight out. He couldn't see Mitchell's reaction, but after a second he signaled again and they went forward.

The groaning man was a little way down the ravine, propped against a rock. Mitchell approached him with great caution, circling behind, keeping the shotgun on him. When he got close enough to see, it was clear the man was near gone. From his belly on down he was red with blood. His head hung on his chest. His hands gripped his middle.

"Who the hell's this?" Tom whispered. "This isn't the deputy, nor the sheriff, either."

Mitchell prodded him with his shotgun but got no response. Bending low, looking at the face, he thought the man looked familiar. Mitchell got out a match. He struck it, holding it close.

"Zion Smith!" Mitchell said.

The eyes fluttered open. "Fuckin' right," Smith said.

Mitchell jumped back out of his crouch. The match went out.

"Skeered ya, huh?" Smith wheezed. "Don' worry. 'Bout dead, I guess."

Mitchell bent close again, striking another match. Tom was at his side, holding a pistol on the man.

"Zion, what happened?"

"You know this man?" Tom asked. Mitchell nodded. He had known Smith in the logging camps. Though Mitchell had never warmed to the man, he knew him as a solid hand in the woods and a steady man on a hunt.

"Got shot," Smith said. "Water."

Mitchell got his canteen and gave it to Smith, who sucked at it, letting half pour down his chest. Smith collapsed against the rock. The canteen fell into his lap.

"Thanks," Smith said, then added, "Sorry."

"What?" Tom said.

"Zion, who shot you?" Mitchell asked. Smith said nothing at first. His head hung low, so they could hardly see his eyes, and it almost seemed as though he'd died right then. After a moment, though, he picked is head up and pulled his hands away from his belly. They looked as though he'd dipped them in red paint. He looked down at himself as if there was an answer in the red apron around his middle. Smith shrugged and held his hands out with his palms up.

"What the hell," he said, wheezing out the words, "I'm dead already. May's well tell it true. I was with Owens."

"Huh? Owens left us two days ago, said he had a client," Tom said.

Smith ignored this. "He got the sheriff. I shot the other one, but ended up he got me."

"Owens? Ex Owens?"

Smith nodded.

"But what were you two—" Tom stopped, unable to understand what had gone on.

"How the hell you shooting at the sheriff?" Mitchell said.

"It was Tupper shot the sheriff," Smith said. "That's how Owens wanted it to look."

"What?"

"Owens," Smith said, raising his voice. "He killed the girl and Busher, too. Some fella in New York. Not sure who else."

"What the hell girl are you talking about?" Tom growled. "Lettie Burman, the maid at the Prospect?"

"Owens," Smith groaned, nodding. "He done 'em. Makin' it look like Tupper."

Tom sat back on his heels. His mouth hung open, his eyes went blank. He could not grasp what Smith had just told them. Mitchell, too, was confused, and he took off his hat to wipe the sweat from his forehead. Things seemed loose in his head, swirling like bits of grass in a tornado. Smith coughed, holding his middle.

"Oh shit," Smith said, "pissed my pants."

Tom gave him another drink. Smith revived a bit.

"What about the girl and Busher?" Tom said.

Zion looked at Tom. "You're the city police, ain't ya? That boy's yours? The one they think killed her?"

"Yeah," Tom said.

Smith groaned again and there was a gurgling in the back of his throat. "Damn, but he shot me good. My own fault. Thought he was gone."

"Zion, you helped Owens ambush the sheriff, make it look like Tupper done it?" Mitchell said. "Is that what you're tellin' us?"

Smith just nodded, not looking Mitchell or Tom in the eye. "Ex said he'd cut me in. He's got a deal with some lawyer in the city. One got away, I think. Ex might be shot, too. Dunno."

Coming out of his shock, Tom said, "Which one got away?" his brain screeching to a halt like a train braking hard, his thoughts turning to Chowder. "Where's the other deputy?"

"Other deputy? Ain't seen 'im."

"Zion, why?" Mitchell said. Smith didn't try to explain. He probably didn't have the breath for it.

"You got somethin' ta write with?" Zion said, his voice sounding weaker.

"Huh? What you gonna write?"

"Confession. This my dead-bed. That'd make it legal in court. God damn Owens fer getting' me inter this. Not gettin' a cut o' anything 'cept perdition now. Do good while I'm able."

Mitchell and Tom rummaged in their packbaskets but found no paper or anything to write with. Tom went to check the sheriff's pack and came back a few minutes later with a map. "This's all I could find," Tom said. "No pencils, ink, or nothing."

"Whittle me a stick," Smith whispered. "Little one, like a quill."

"There's no ink, though," Mitchell said, then stopped himself, understanding what Zion was thinking.

It took some time for Smith to write his story. Tom and Mitchell huddled close while the night engulfed them, lighting matches for Smith to see by. Zion's hand was none too steady, and the pen none too good. It left lots of drops and blotches before he got the hang of just how much blood to use. When he needed fresh he'd take his hand away from his belly and dip the makeshift quill into one of the oozing holes.

Smith and Mitchell both held the map steady, and soon there was a border of bloody fingerprints all around the edges. In the feeble light it almost looked pretty, like pictures of flowers on fancy stationary.

Tom could see that Smith was fading fast. His words ran in hills and valleys across the map. His eyes fluttered as he tried to concentrate. Tom gave him water, but its effect to revive Smith became less and less. When Smith was close to done, he looked up for a moment in thought, maybe searching for the right word or bit of information. His face in the flickering light was gaunt, almost insubstantial, as if his body was fading, too.

"Who's the old man?" he said, his body swaying as in a storm at sea. Tom glanced over his shoulder.

"Who? There's nobody there," Tom said. Smith shook his head. The match went out.

Tupper didn't know exactly what happened at first. He found himself on his back, looking up into a dark canopy of leaves and sky, so dark he almost thought he couldn't see. His head ached and pounded. He had no idea how long he'd been there, nor at first why he was there at all. When he moved to sit up, the trees started to spin and blood dripped down the front of his shirt. He put a hand to his scalp and felt a burning furrow maybe two inches long on the right side.

There was hardly any dried blood, so he reasoned he couldn't have been down for long. He tried to remember what had happened, how he'd been hurt, when suddenly he remembered Owens's face, the smile and the nod of recognition. The shot he didn't remember, but checking his rifle, he found that he'd let loose a round, too. Owens was nowhere to be seen, so Tupper figured he hadn't hit anything.

He got to his feet and stumbled off in the night. He didn't know exactly where he was going, didn't really care just then. It seemed important to go, though, and not be caught with the dead sheriff and the others his grandfather had said were there.

There was a point when he thought he heard a twig snap some-where off to his left. He crouched low, nearly falling over his head spun so much. There were other sounds that he took for men in the woods. He waited for some time until there was total silence, then he got up and moved away as quietly as he could. He walked for some time, his head clearing little by little, but still throbbing and bleeding. He put a bandana around his temple and that seemed to help.

Over and over he asked why, repeating the word like a chant, an incantation. If his grandfather knew, he wasn't saying. He stood in the blackness, a wisp of gray, no more substantial than a moonbeam, motionless, mute.

"Why, old man?" he asked his grandfather. "Speak to the dead. Tell me," Tupper said, his hands held out like a beggar. "You can speak to them, Grandfather. You can learn the truth."

The spirit seemed to shift, becoming ragged as if blown by an unseen wind.

"There was one who was Owens's friend. Has gone where I cannot follow," his grandfather said, the words like a bell in his head.

"You are spirit, Grandfather. Surely you can—"

The old man held up a white hand and Tupper's voice left him.

"He has gone to *ganos´ge,* the house of the tormentor, the abode of *Hanisee´ono,* where there is no end to pain." Tupper shuddered as he stood on wobbly legs. The hair on the back of his neck bristled. He said a prayer and felt better for it.

Though he could not understand why, it was clear enough that Owens was behind his troubles. Owens had wanted him to escape, wanted him to run. That's why he'd kicked the damn horse to help him get away from the cop. Again, *why* was a thing he couldn't fathom, but it appeared true.

The more Tupper thought about it, the more confusing it seemed. If Owens had wanted him to escape, why shoot at him now? Why kill the sheriff? Though Tupper hadn't actually seen it himself, it appeared clear that Owens had done it. And how had Owens even found the sheriff? Tupper figured he'd have to have set an ambush, so he must have known where they were heading.

If he'd known where the sheriff was heading, he knew where he was heading, too. None of it made sense to him, but one thing was clear. Owens had shot him, left him for dead in the middle of the forest. For that alone he had a reckoning coming.

Tupper began to plan. His steps began to have purpose. Despite his pounding head, he set a determined course, gritted his teeth, and forced his legs to go as fast as they could.

Tupper felt the forest watching, saw how the trees tried to hem him in and block off his escape. Trees and rocks, unseen roots and undergrowth grabbed at his feet or blocked his way. When at last he burst into the moonlit logging road he was drenched with sweat and gasping for air. He gripped the sheriff's pistol in one hand and the Winchester in the other. He started to run down the uneven road, settling into a mile-eating jog.

It was a long road back, but nothing compared to the unending torment he planned for Exeter Owens.

Twenty-Seven

I have traveled in foreign lands; have been twice to the
Amazon valley; and I rise to remark that there is but one
Adirondack Wilderness on the face of the earth.

—GEORGE WASHINGTON SEARS

They found Chowder after a few minutes of searching. He seemed to rise up from the forest floor before them, materializing from the rocks and leaves, a bloody apparition that stopped them in their tracks. Tom wasn't sure it was him at first, not till he set his lantern down and knelt beside the body did he recognize his old friend.

"Oh, Chowder," Tom mumbled, his shoulders slumping, "Not here. Not in this godforsaken wilderness."

Mitchell stood at Tom's side. He put a hand on his shoulder.

"You're wrong, Tom. God is everywhere here. It is His garden. To die here is to die on God's doorstep."

Tom turned his face to Mitchell. "God's doorstep? Chowder'd have had a good laugh at that."

Mitchell smiled. "It's only the living God forsakes. The dead he gathers in love."

Tom wept, though he tried to hold it back. Tears streamed down his face, carving little rivers through the dust and stubble. His shoulders shook under Mitchell's hand.

Weariness and grief weighed him down, and for a while he let them crush him, wring him out, till his eyes had wept the last drop of tears in him. Tom took out a kerchief then, wiped his eyes, and blew his nose.

Tom bent and kissed Chowder Kelly twice on the top of his forehead.

"For Mary and 'Becca," he whispered.

From behind him, Mitchell said, "Our Father, who art in Heaven, Hallowed be thy name." He didn't know the proper Catholic prayer, but figured The Lord's Prayer cut across just about every religion he knew of. "Thy kingdom come, thy will be done . . ." He said the words with gentleness and spirit so that Tom heard them as if for the first time. It seemed, too, as if the feeble light of their lanterns grew a little stronger, pushing back the darkness.

"Though I walk through the valley of the shadow of death, I shall fear no evil."

When Mitchell finished Tom got to his feet. "I'll be back, old friend," he said to Chowder.

They went in search of MacDougal, moving farther up the draw. They heard rustling steps beyond the reach of their lanterns. "Coyote," Mitchell said. They came upon MacDougal a few yards further on. His shirt and vest were torn open and the stomach lacerated.

"Critters eat the guts first," Mitchell said.

Tom grunted as he bent to look at the body. "Took half his head off." He looked around at the sheriff's equipment strewn about the body. "Somebody's been through his stuff," Tom said. "It appears not every animal goes on four feet."

Tom looked the body over with great care, searching for any lingering clues. "Definitely shot from a distance," he said. "No powder burns. Rifle. Didn't know what hit him." Tom looked around. "Had a rifle and pistol, too, right, Mitchell?"

"Yup."

"Well, they're gone, ammunition too," he added, checking the sheriff's pack. Mitchell started to search in a slow circle while Tom did his examination. A few yards away he bent with a grunt and picked up a Winchester. Its forearm and loading tube were smashed and bent.

"What you make of this?" Mitchell said.

"Hmph. Maybe MacDougal got off a shot. Let's take a look at that. Hold up the light a bit." Tom checked the rifle, holding it inches from his face. "Pistol did the damage, I think. Hard to say for sure. Hold it!"

Tom moved the rifle so the light shone on the action. There on the side of the receiver, engraved in silvery script were the letters W. W. D.

"Durant!" Tom said. "This is the gun that was stolen from Pine Knot. Tupper! Sonofabitch!" Tom held the rifle as if he might break it over his knee. "He was here! How the hell was he here, if Owens and Smith were the ones who did the ambushing?" Tom shook his head. "The only way that's possible is if Tupper came later."

"Couldn't have been much later," Mitchell said. "We only got here a half hour after the last shot."

"Damn it!" Tom growled.

They searched further after that, looking for clues to who the second shooter might be. Tom went back and checked Chowder's pistol, finding it empty at his side.

"You were shooting at something," Tom said to the body. "He was a pretty good man with a pistol, too," he said to Mitchell. They spread out and continued to search. Minutes later, Mitchell heard Tom call. He found Tom crouched over a body that was slumped against a log.

"The deputy," Mitchell said.

"Fucking Owens! Three men dead! The bastard." Tom's heart pounded, his head swam.

He thought of Chowder and his anger doubled. All of the pressure of the last few weeks seemed to be boiling up. His hands balled into white-knuckled fists, and for the first time he could ever recall, he actually shook with rage. Tom stood stiffly, as with a conscious effort to control unwilling joints. He stared off into the black void of the forest, quivering, his eyes dead and unseeing.

He seemed to sway as he put his head back and let out a scream. It burst out of him, an explosion beyond words. The chords in his neck stood out like red wires, veins bulged at his temples. He screamed again, more of a roar this time, then again, and again, until he was weak and light-headed. He felt the pressure lift, though he still boiled.

Mitchell, who'd stood silent, watching, said, "Good to let it go. A man can bust if he don't let it out. Used to use the bottle myself. No more."

Tom grunted agreement. He'd tried that, too, when he was younger.

"We'll carry Chowder out, then get help with the rest," he said. "Gonna be a long night."

They fashioned a stretcher from some beach saplings and a sheet of rubberized canvas Tom found in MacDougal's packbasket. It was a long, hard carry, close to three miles, Tom guessed. The going was slow and they needed to put the stretcher down every few hundred feet. It was exhausting work carrying Chowder through the forest over fallen trees, around boulders or dense brush.

Within a mile they were both soaked with sweat and breathing hard. Though Mitchell didn't complain, Tom could see he was close to the end of his rope. They'd hiked over twenty miles that day, not slept in over twenty hours, and now were carrying a body three miles more through rough terrain at night. Tom was amazed that a man Mitchell's age was still on his feet. Tom wasn't sure how much further he could go, himself. But every time he doubted himself, every time he had to set Chowder's body down when his back and arms screamed for rest, he remembered Owens.

Owens might be back at the Prospect House within a day. Owens would have no way to know that his accomplice had written his confession and signed Owens's death warrant. The thought of Owens that close to Mary and Rebecca drove Tom on.

His only solace and hope was that Owens had no reason to hurt them. But then, what reason did he have for what he'd done? Whatever the reason, there seemed no rationale to the crimes, no thread tying the murders together. Tom and Mitchell talked the problem up and down on the long haul out of the woods, and they were no closer to an answer at the end than at the beginning. Neither of them could figure why Tupper had been the target, what he had done to set the rampage in motion, or whether he even knew what had really happened.

"For all we know, Tupper thinks we're after him for the escape in New York," Tom said. "How would he know otherwise?"

One thing Tom and Mitchell agreed on was that there were too many questions and too many miles ahead before they'd see any answers. They concentrated on putting one foot in front of the other, leaving the answers for later.

It took nearly four hours to carry Chowder's body out. Tom and Mitchell sat on the ground, too tired to move. After a while, when his heart stopped racing and the sweat on his back started to dry in the night air, Tom mumbled, "We need help with the rest." Mitchell nodded. He looked ghostly pale in the moonlight.

"Mitchell," Tom said, concern painting his voice. "You all right?"

"Old," he said. "Just old."

"Listen," Tom said, "I haven't thanked you for all you've done."

Mitchell held up a hand.

"No. No," Tom said, refusing to be deterred. "You've done more than any man could be expected to do. Never a complaint, never a question. You've been a true friend through this whole damn thing. Just wanted you to know I appreciate it."

Mitchell looked at Tom, though neither could see the other clearly in the faint moonlight.

"A man does what he can," was all he said. He shrugged and got up. "Let's go. Get help at the lumber camp."

Tom looked at Chowder's body laying in the moonlight. "I don't want him to be, I mean I don't want the animals to get at him," Tom said.

Mitchell nodded. "I know. He was your friend. I'll go. Stay with him," he said.

Without another word, Mitchell took up his shotgun and disappeared into the night.

Tom sat on a small boulder by the side of the road. The Winchester was across his knees. The silence was complete. On either side, the blue-black night made the road seem like a tunnel with no end, stretching into the future and the past. The high grass in the middle was a ghostly gray.

"Strange roads we've taken here, Chowder," Tom said. "Strange roads, old friend."

It somehow didn't seem right to sit with Chowder and not talk to him. Through so many years of precinct banter and barroom bullshit, they had always had something to say. Now, though it was only Tom doing the talking, they had a conversation. In the long hours before dawn, Tom Braddock spoke his heart and soul to the body of Chowder Kelly. He told him things he hadn't told anyone, not even Mary.

He spoke of life, and of God, and of whether or not there was a heaven or hell, things he and Chowder had philosophized on over many a pint. But mostly he spoke of the things they had done, the cops and criminals they had known, the shared experiences of a lifetime. He told him, too, of how he would miss him, how Rebecca and Mary would, too, of how there would always be a seat at their table reserved for him.

As the dawn began to color the tips of the trees and the road became a lighter gray, Tom could see his old friend congeal in the light, growing more distinct. Tom didn't like to look at him.

"Told you to be careful," he said with a sigh. "But you never did listen to me, did you? Too old to change your ways, eh?" He chuckled. "Well, you did good, Chowder. You died the way you lived, and a man can't wish for more than that, I guess. And, you got me Zion Smith."

The sun was past it's zenith before Tom and Mitchell started back toward Long Lake. It had taken another six hours to fetch help and carry the bodies out. By that time they were staggering like drunken men, and despite his anxieties about getting after Owens, Tom knew he had to rest. He and Mitchell were persuaded to return to the logging camp, bunk there for a few hours, and get a hot meal into them before heading on.

They slept like dead men, though the sky was bright with morning sunlight when they collapsed, fully clothed, onto hard bunks. They were sore and tired when they got back up on the wagon some hours later, but at least they could keep their eyes open. It would be another five- or six-hour ride back to Long Lake. Tom hoped he'd have the strength to go straight on to Blue, but a big part of him doubted it. The accumulated fatigue of the last weeks had taken its toll. He ached down to his bones and in his joints.

"'Bout the only thing doesn't hurt is my hair," Tom grumbled as he hauled his stiff body up into the wagon. His feet were blistered from walking and his mind numb from long days without rest. His body needed more than just the couple hours he'd grabbed. He almost envied Chowder, lying under a blanket in the back. His pain was done, his burden laid down. Tom took a deep breath. He was going to need a long, long rest when this was over.

After walking all night, Tupper slept in a grove of beech not far from the road. All the next day, as Tom and Mitchell labored to recover the bodies of MacDougal, Chowder, and the deputy, Tupper watched the lake, looking for his opportunity. He'd decided that taking the road, though it was only a fraction of the distance, was far too dangerous. He had no way of knowing how many might be out scouring the countryside for him. It was best to assume the entire county was on alert. He imagined a farmer with a shotgun hiding behind every tree, and felt safer on the water, where a man could keep his distance. Even if seen he might not be recognized, so he was glad at last when he saw a boat left untended at the shoreline.

He watched all that day and into the evening before he took it. Tupper slipped away with hardly a ripple. His hands had healed some in the last couple of days, the open blisters had scabbed over. They ached, though, as he wrapped them around the oars, and bright blades of pain cut him where his scabs opened. Still, it felt good to pull at the oars again.

Tupper didn't have a firm notion of what he was going to do. One advantage to taking a boat back to Blue, aside from the fact that he would never be expected to return that way, was that it would take him longer.

Time was working for him now. Owens must have thought he'd killed him. Ex would figure that it would be only a matter of time before the sheriff and his posse was discovered, along with his body. The natural conclusion would be that they'd killed each other in a shoot-out.

A riot of violent images tumbled through Tupper's head when he though of Owens. When his thinking side took over, he knew it wouldn't do to kill the man. There were answers only Owens could give, and unfortunately he needed to be alive to give them.

"Then again, maybe not," he said to his grandfather, whose spirit had appeared in the back of the boat as soon as he pushed off. "Maybe Owens's conscience will not let him go on," Tupper said with a raised eyebrow, testing the notion on the old man.

His grandfather looked skeptical. He could see into his grandson's mind. Pain. Blood. Revenge. The old man saw them all, an angry kaleidoscope of reds and oranges, shot with bolts of black, an aura of negative energy floating around him. The images bounced around inside Tupper's head, painting lurid pictures behind his eyes.

They all showed Owens in hopeless agony, suffering beyond endurance, until at last he'd beg to confess. Tupper remembered the stories of how his ancestors tortured captives, of feet split open, fingers, noses, or ears bitten off, and of roasting captives over hot coals. Tupper smiled at the thought. There should be no end of suffering for someone like Owens, no words that didn't end in screams.

Tupper indulged his fantasies as he rowed. That's all they were, really. Though he savored them as if to make them real, he knew they were only dreams. Not that he wasn't planning on hurting Owens; he didn't rule that out at all. He'd hurt the man, hurt him bad and deep. But torture and murder? Tupper's heart was not in that. His grandfather had taught him to revere life, the gift of *Hodianok'doo Hed'iohe*. The taking of life was not to be done lightly.

He knew, too, that Exeter Owens alive was his key out of the mess he was in, at least the Adirondack part of his mess. The city part was another problem. But that seemed to pale in significance when he thought of Owens pulling the trigger on him. That image blotted out all others.

The problem was how to capture Owens alive. On that point Tupper didn't have a clue. What he did have was determination. He'd find Owens wherever he was. He'd catch him. The wheres and the hows didn't concern him yet.

He carried with him a legacy of lore and knowledge and magic, gifts that had carried him beyond the reach of the most determined hunters. They would see him through this, too. He rowed into the mouth of the Raquette River where it emptied into Long Lake. From there it was all upstream.

It was in the early morning hours, after he'd rowed and carried his boat to Forked lake, that Tupper came near to stepping on the biggest snapping turtle he'd ever seen. It was lumbering through the night, going from lake to lake under the cover of darkness, moving much like himself, out of sight of predatory eyes. It snapped and hissed at him, holding open its powerful beak, its neck pulled back into the shell and ready to strike. The hoary shell was well over a foot wide and twice as long. A snakelike tail dragged behind.

An idea came to Tupper once he got over his surprise. He recalled seeing bullets bounce right off turtles of this size. He'd learned when he was young to shoot for the neck if he wanted turtle soup. Here, he thought, was a breastplate to stop any bullet. He found a dead branch and held it out for the monster to strike at, but when it did the branch snapped in its jaws. Tupper tried again with a thicker branch, letting the turtle grab onto the wood for a moment to make sure it would hold. He reached in then and cut the thing's throat. This was a gift from the Creator, and he said a prayer of thanks as he rolled the carcass over and went to work.

Twenty-Eight

That same look, it comes in their eyes when you give 'em the business.
It's something a man can hang on to, come black-frost or sun.

—ROBERT PENN WARREN

The deputy had decided to wait one day at the Prospect House. Mary was glad of it. It saved her having to decide whether to wait for Tom or go on with Mike.

"Don't know much what MacDougal wanted done with yer boy," the deputy told her. "If he don't come back, or I don't hear from him, I s'pose I'll have ta wire Glens Falls, see what they want ta do."

Mary and Rebecca ate in the dining hall. Mike had to eat in their room, his ankle shackled to the bed. He'd insisted on them going down to eat, as if all was normal, preferring to eat in his room, staying away from curious eyes and whispered remarks.

Mary thought he was holding up remarkably well, considering. He might have easily slipped into a dark mood and be forgiven for it, but he seemed serene instead. Mary didn't understand it. She figured he was just hiding his true feelings, or perhaps trying to be strong for her and 'Becca, putting on a confident face.

She'd asked him about it the night before as she adjusted the wrapping around his ribs. She wanted him to open up, to tell her how he really felt, give him a shoulder to cry on, if he needed it. She didn't get what she expected.

"You weren't there, Mom. You didn't see Mitchell and Dad. They wouldn't give up, no matter what. If you'd been with us you'd know."

Mary had nodded as if she understood. She knew well enough how determined Tom could be, but that was nothing new, at least not to her.

"The only reason I'm sad is I'm not out there. These . . . ," Mike said, holding up a leg and jingling the chain, "these'll come off when Dad catches Tupper." Mike grinned. "Like Mitchell said once, 'It's when the lakes are low that I know the rain will come.' "

"I'm not sure I follow you," Mary said.

"I suppose you kinda had to be there, but it means that when things are looking low and at their worst, it's then that things are about to turn for the better. Don't worry," Mike said with a reassuring smile, "they'll catch him."

Mary sat on the verandah while Rebecca threw pieces of bread to the fish down by the dock. She thought about Mike and the things he'd said. He'd never in all the last six years been an optimistic boy. There had been too much hardship in his life, too much tragedy. But something had changed. Somewhere in the forest something had happened. Mary did not begin to understand what, or how it had taken hold so completely, but it was plain that even in chains Mike was free. Mary wished that she could see with the same clarity.

Mary came out of her reverie. Rebecca was calling to her. Mary laughed and waved. She saw Owens then, coming up the lawn. He gave her a tip of his hat, as if she'd waved at *him,* and came up the broad stairs. He clumped down the nearly empty verandah, his boots sounding heavy.

"Afternoon, ma'am," he said. "Heard you were back. How's the boy? Sorry to say I heard about him, too."

Owens wore a concerned look, but there was something in his tone Mary couldn't put her finger on. She thanked him for his concern, though, and asked him to join her. It was lonely at the hotel now with most of the guests gone. Even Durant's little steamers seemed to whistle sadly as they carried one or two passengers between the lakes.

"Did I notice you limping, Mister Owens? Are you quite all right?"

Mary asked. Though it wasn't polite for a woman to comment on a personal matter with an unattached man, Mary didn't much care. She certainly didn't want to discuss Mike's predicament, nor Tom's failure to capture Tupper, so she latched onto the first thing that came into her head.

"You have a sharp eye, Missus Braddock," Owens said. "A sport damn near shot my leg off. Tripped and dropped his rifle." He pulled up his pants leg to show her the bandage on his calf. "Came this close," he said, holding up a thumb and forefinger an inch apart, "to hitting the bone. Lucky though. Ended up with just a scratch."

"That is lucky," Mary said in an absent sort of way. Something about Owens had struck a chord with her. She wasn't sure what it was, but the notion that there was something oddly familiar about him seemed to wash her other thoughts away.

"Does it hurt much?" she asked, looking at his leg. Perhaps it was the boots, she thought. They seemed to remind her of something.

"Been hurt worse. A little tender is all."

"I see," Mary said. She'd decided it wasn't the boots and tried to put the notion out of her mind. "I suppose it can be a dangerous business, hunting."

"Hunting's not dangerous. It's fools that're dangerous," Owens said, waggling a finger. "Guides see plenty of fools."

Their conversation continued for some time, as the sun started to settle toward the mountaintops. From time to time the odd feeling returned, and Mary found herself watching Owens for some clue to its cause. Rebecca came running up, saying she was out of bread and was going to ask a waiter if she could have more. She waved at Owens, who waved back as she turned and skipped off.

As if for the first time, Mary saw the shirt, the mended tear in the sleeve. Her heart stopped, then fluttered in her chest like a bird in hand. She could not seem to draw the next breath. The fabric!

Mary's eyes went wide and she gripped the arms of her chair as if she might be blown away if she didn't. Owens noticed and gave her a curious frown.

"Missus Braddock, you look like you've seen a ghost," Owens said with a narrow-eyed look that mimicked concern. It was a cold look, though the voice was soothing, "Are you all right?"

Flustered, Mary said, "Oh, oh yes. I'm fine. I just remembered something, that's all," she mumbled.

Mary's palms started to sweat and a cold trickle of fear crept down her spine. She got up without thinking, finding herself standing before she thought of a plausible explanation. She flushed, and her fingers fumbled at her waist.

"I—I promised my husband I'd send a telegram for him," she said.

Owens just raised an eyebrow. "I'd be happy to take it to the telegraph office for you, if you like," he said, which flustered Mary even more.

"Oh no! I mean I wouldn't dream of imposing," she said. "It is a private communication, as well," she added, regaining her command a bit. "I'm afraid I've been a goose. Tom will be so mad if I forget," she said, adding some urgency to her excuse.

"How any man could stay mad at a wife as charming as you, Mary, I don't know," Owens said as he stood.

He put out a hand, catching one of hers before she knew it. His palm was as cool as the skin of a snake and he barely restrained his finger's crushing power. He looked into her eyes, holding her spellbound for a horrible instant. Mary felt like a mouse before the strike. Owens's eyes were dead. His voice was caring, but it was a carefully contrived imitation of how a caring man might sound.

"Is there nothing I can do to help?" he was saying, though Mary hardly heard the words. "I'd be happy to help you, Mary, in any way I could."

"Goodness, no! It's really something I must see to myself," Mary said, avoiding his eye.

Her skin crawled at Owens's touch, and for a horrifying instant she let herself imagine what those hands had done. "Thank you, Mister Owens. You're too kind," Mary forced herself to say, "but I must go."

She slipped her hand from his with the best smile she could muster. "Sorry to run off. Now, where is that daughter of mine?"

Mary walked into the shelter of the lobby, wishing there were more people about. She tried to tell herself that she could be mistaken, that there must be hundreds of shirts just like that in the Adirondacks. Surely, she had to be wrong.

Tupper was the murderer: Hadn't Chowder and Tom been sure of it? What difference did a shirt make after all, when all the evidence pointed to Tupper? Mary's heels echoed through the lobby as she hurried to find Rebecca.

Rebecca was in the kitchen, playing with one of the many cats who kept the mice at bay.

"'Becca! There you are! We have to go."

"Go where, Mommy? I'm playing with the kitty."

"Maybe you can do that again a little later, sweetie. We need to send a telegram to Daddy now," Mary said, taking her hand.

"Oh good, a telegram. I love to watch the key go clickety-clackety."

Mary smiled, "That is fun, isn't it?" she said, though her mind was elsewhere.

Mary thought for a moment to tell Frederick or William, but had to dismiss the idea. She had no proof. She'd given the swatch of fabric to Chowder. If she told the Durants, they'd surely confront Owens, but without the evidence they'd be unable to hold him. Flushing him before they were ready to arrest him would only result in another chase.

The only way was to get a message to Tom, if she could, and stay away from Owens until Tom got back. She was thinking of just how to word the telegram. She'd need to be very careful, she decided. There was no telling if some friend of Owens's might see it.

It could be days before Tom got it, and half the Adirondacks might know of it before then. By the time she got to the telegraph office she'd made up her mind. She hoped Tom would understand.

Owens watched as Mary and Rebecca disappeared back into the Prospect House a few minutes later, their telegram sent. He ambled into the telegraph office once they were gone.

The telegram was waiting for Tom when he woke. It had been near noon when he and Mitchell rumbled up to the Sabattis place. Though he'd wanted to keep on to the Prospect House, he was dead-tired

and unsteady in his seat. He and Mitchell collapsed with orders to
Mrs. Sabattis to wake Tom in an hour. She'd let him sleep a half hour
longer. He read the telegram with foggy eyes and an even foggier brain.

I FOUND THE SHIRT YOU WERE LOOKING FOR STOP
CHOWDER HAS ONE LIKE IT STOP COME QUICK STOP

Tom read it again, "What the hell," he muttered. He rubbed his eyes
and tried to focus as the words swam in front of him. "A shirt?"

Steaming bowls of biscuits and fresh corn pulled his attention away
and the sizzle of frying steaks had him frothing at the mouth. He put
the telegram down and dug in. For fifteen minutes Tom shoveled food
without a break. Only when he took a moment to butter his third biscuit did he glance at the telegram again.

"Why she all on fire about a shirt?" he mumbled with his mouth
full. "Fuck!" he shouted, bits of biscuit flying. He jumped up from the
table as if he'd been kicked out of his chair. "Sonofabitch!"

"What the hell?" Mitchell said, staring in amazement. Tom offered
a stammered apology to Mrs. Sabattis and said, "Owens, he's at the
Prospect House! Mary's seen him! I gotta go!"

Mitchell jumped up and ran out the back door. Tom was close behind.

"Mitchell," Tom said. He'd scribbled a message on the back of the
telegram. "Can you get this sent to Mary? I'll go ahead."

"Sure, Tom. I'll be fifteen, twenty minutes behind you. Go!"

It paid to have friends who, like himself, had no love for the Durants.
Owens crumpled Tom's telegram as he put it in his pocket and walked
out of the telegraph office. He looked around at the deepening gloom.
The sun had set a half hour before. Hardly anyone was about. There
was a low rumble off to the west, and the sky flickered, outlining the
black trees in blue-white lightning. The storm was still some distance off,
but rolling in fast. Owens smiled. Perfect cover for the night's work.
He figured he had about an hour to get ready. Lights were coming on
in the hotel.

"Thank you, Mister Edison," he mumbled, grinning in the glow.

. . .

It had been hours since Mary sent her telegram. She'd stayed in her room with the doors bolted while the hours ticked away. They'd taken their dinner in their rooms, too. The only time the door had opened was to let the waiter in with his cart. Rebecca grumbled about being cooped up for hours, but Mike had helped occupy her as best he could.

Mary told him about Owens. Mike agreed that they were best to stay behind locked doors until Tom returned. For now she'd have to wait, like bait in a trap.

A rap at the door interrupted her thoughts. The waiter announced himself. "Picking up the trays, ma'am," he said through the door.

Mary threw the bolt and opened it a crack. She was about to peer out before opening it all the way when the door was shoved hard, cracking her in the head, sending her staggering back.

"Sorry, Mary, but I really must intrude," Owens said, as if he were interrupting dinner conversation. He gripped her arm as she started to turn, and with the other hand punched her on the side of the head.

Mary opened her eyes and looked at Owens's boot just inches from her face. The world had turned on its side and the room towered above her. The floor pressed against her face and something sharp dug into her temple.

"The boy, he's in the next room?" Owens asked, "And Rebecca, too?" When Mary didn't answer immediately, Owens slapped her and said, "Don't make me kill you, Mary. Really, don't."

The way he said it froze the blood in her veins, but helped bring her to her senses.

"They're asleep," she managed to say.

"Good. Good," Owens said, seeming quite satisfied. "Now I'm going to let you up. Do you understand? Yes?" Owens helped her to her feet but held his bone-handled bayonet ready at his side. "Well then, now that that's over," he said in an impossibly friendly tone that frightened Mary more than the length of steel in his hand, "we can go. You do want to see Tom, don't you?"

Mary stiffened, her eyes widening under a small trickle of blood from her forehead.

"Tom?" she managed to say.

"Oh yes," Owens said with a dead-eyed smile as he handed her a kerchief, "he'll be along shortly."

The connecting door opened. Rebecca slid in with a finger to her mouth. "Mikey's sleeping," she whispered.

Mary looked from her to Owens, whose eyes had narrowed to black slits over a toothy smile. She felt the tip of the bayonet press against her back.

"Oh, hello, Mister Owens," Rebecca said when she realized he was there. She walked to them, her small pink feet tiptoeing.

"Say anything and I'll butcher her right here," Owens whispered in Mary's ear. Mary's world rocked and screamed. The room may as well have been on fire, her precious little girl wading through he flames. Mary's voice croaked. No words came out.

"Hello, 'Becca," Owens said. "We're going to see your daddy. Do you want to come?"

They made their way through the deserted hallways of the near-empty hotel, their footsteps echoing. With each step Mary's mind raced. She tried to plan, tried to imagine how she might escape, raise an alarm, or at least save Rebecca. She thought of Tom and prayed he wasn't already dead. As long as he'd gotten her telegram, there was a chance. She knew that as long as he was alive he'd come for them, and no force on earth would stand in his way.

Owens took them through a back door, out through the rain, which had just started. Lightning lit the way to the small building that housed the dynamo, the Long-waisted Maryann. They rushed inside, out of the rain.

The room was empty. A boiler hissed. A steam engine spun wheels. A long, leather belt ran to the dynamo, which hummed in time with the *thumpeta-thumpeta* rhythm of the engine. There was a horrible smell to the place, a burnt-flesh smell, mixed with oil, wood smoke, and ozone.

"Where's Daddy?" Rebecca said, looking around. "This is a scary place. I don't like that thing." She pointed to the Long-waisted Maryann, it's copper-wrapped coils standing well over her head. Owens paid her no mind. He looked at his watch.

"I think we have some time," he said, as if waiting for a train. "Give me your hands, Mary," he added, once he'd bolted the door. Mary put her shaking hands out. Owens, who had lengths of rope ready in his pocket, tied her hands in front of her. It was done so quickly Rebecca didn't say a word, just stared in confusion.

"Mommy?" she said when Owens was done. "What game are we playing?"

Owens grabbed Rebecca's hand and pulled her to a chair in the corner of the room.

"You stay here, 'Becca," Owens said. "We're playing a scary game. But don't worry, your daddy will be here soon."

Owens went back to Mary and pulled her to the other side of the room. The thumping steam engine hid them from Rebecca.

"The woodpile," Owens pointed. "Bend over." He shoved her down across the wood and pulled up her skirts.

"No! No! No! You can't!" Mary cried, but not so loud as to scare Rebecca. She started to rise but Owens hit her, and a moment later she felt the tip of the bayonet at her temple.

"Someone's bound to come in," she said, trying to reason with him, buy time. "The man who runs the dynamo."

Owens chuckled. "He's too busy cooking. Don't you smell him? Chopped him up and stuffed him in the boiler. Now, either I fuck you in front of her or I kill you in front of her. Your choice."

Mary couldn't say anything.

"Cat got your tongue?" he whispered in her ear. "Well, suppose I was to do her first? Not a bad idea, now I think about it."

"Mommy?"

"It's all right, 'Becca," Mary forced herself to say in a strong voice. "You stay right there. Just close your eyes and wish for Daddy to come."

Under the noise of the steam engine and the storm beating on the roof, Mary turned her head and said, "Go ahead and fuck me, you pathetic bastard. When Tom gets here, we'll see who gets fucked."

Owens slammed her down onto the woodpile. Mary felt him pressing hard between her legs. A hard hand felt for her sex, pulling her underclothes away.

"Fuck you like I did that little maid," Owens growled in her ear. "See how you like that. Stuck her in one end then stuck her in the other." He pressed the bayonet against her temple. A trickle of blood ran down her face, dripping off her chin into the wood.

"Shoulda seen her squirm," he said, chuckling.

Mary gagged in horror. Bile rose in her throat.

"Get away from my mommy," Rebecca said. Mary felt a rush of water on her legs and back.

Owens jumped off, turning on 'Becca, who stood defiantly with a bucket in her hand. Owens kicked it away, sending it bouncing across the room. He raised a fist, but before he could strike, Mary grabbed a length of firewood and with both hands swung it against Owens's skull.

It was a glancing blow, but it opened a gash that fountained blood as Owens staggered to his left. Mary swung again but missed, the wood whistling inches from his face. Owens struck out with his bayonet. It went through Mary's left arm, just above the elbow and punched into her side, grating on a rib.

Mary stared, frozen in shock, looking at the length of steel skewering her flesh. Owens grinned through the blood streaming off his head. He twisted the blade. Mary screamed and dropped the wood.

"That's right. Scream!" Owens yelled, his eyes bulging and the veins standing out on his neck like blue wires. He brought his face close to hers. Blood from his head wound dripped off his nose, falling between her breasts. "Nobody's gonna hear you," he whispered. Mary felt the room wobble and her vision swirl with tiny lights and moving shadows. The floor came up to meet her face.

"Be here any time now," was the first thing Mary heard. She woke looking at her knees, her head hanging down. She tried to focus. "Won't they be surprised," Owens was saying to himself.

"What was it about the shirt?" Owens said when he saw Mary coming to. She was bound to a chair, her arms tied tight. "Huh? Why the shirt? You know, if you hadn't sent that telegram, I'd have been done with it. So, tell me," he said, tilting her head up to give her some water. Mary was dizzy and her arm felt like a bolt of fire had been shot through it. She looked at Owens through the screen of her hanging, black hair. He looked ghastly. Blood was smeared all over his face and the scalp wound continued to trickle.

"Go fuck yourself," she mumbled once she saw that Rebecca was still all right.

"Hmm. Well, we'll just see about that, won't we?"

Owens fished in his pocket. "Like to see what your Tommy wrote back? It says STAY IN YOUR ROOM, STOP. THERE IN TWO HOURS, STOP." Owens looked at his watch. "That would make it any minute now." Owens smiled but clucked at Mary.

"You know, you really did complicate matters with your little telegram. Forced me to change plans rather drastically. Now I'll have to get rid of your Tommy, too. Very inconvenient, Mary." Owens shook his head almost regretfully. "I'm afraid you'll be paying rather dearly for that."

Mary, looking about, thought the room had changed, then noticed the light in the ceiling was shining in one direction. Some sort of shield had been rigged on it so it left half the room in shadow. Owens had what she thought was a towel in one hand, the bayonet in the other. When she looked closer she saw that the towel was wrapped around a pistol. "Only question," Owens continued, "is who gets here first."

Mary frowned and Owens smiled at her confusion.

"Tupper's on his way to our little party, too. Thought I killed him, but I guess I didn't. Friend o' mine saw him stealin' a boat over ta Long Lake," Owens said with a frown. "So, you see, this will all work out very nicely. Tupper was headin' this way. Guess he thinks he'll get even."

Owens chuckled at that and shook his head as if the notion was unbelievably stupid. "So, Tupper will kill you and little Rebecca here," he said, running a hand through Rebecca's golden curls, "and of course, poor, noble Tom. Happily, I will be able to dispatch the obviously insane Tupper. He really is crazy, you know," Owens whispered as if confiding some great secret, "and then all will be well."

Owens beamed at the simple genius of his plan, then just as quickly his mouth turned down in a pouting parody of a frown.

"Regrettably, I'll be too late to save you from the same fate as the unfortunate Lettie Burman. Such a sweet thing. I really could not resist, not after I saw her with your son, the lucky dog."

Mary spat at him. Owens looked at the bloody, pink spit with blank eyes as it slid down his leg. "I take it you approve of the plan."

He bent down and forced a wadded-up kerchief into her mouth, tying another over it and knotting that one at the back of her head. "Not too tight now, is it?" Owens asked when he was done. Mary just glared at him.

Rebecca was already bound and gagged in the chair next to her. Owens walked to the other side of the boiler then and waited, facing the door. The room thumped and hummed. The world outside crashed and flickered. Rain beat on the roof and rattled at the windows that Owens had covered with blankets.

Minutes crawled by while Mary fought to stay conscious, stay focused, keep thinking of what she might do. Here eyes locked with 'Becca's. Mary did her best to comfort her with only her eyes. For the longest time, longer than Mary could remember since Rebecca was just an infant, she held her with her eyes. Rebecca looked back and, despite their red rims, the tears, the fear, Mary saw there was still strength there.

A click of the latch brought their heads around.

The sudden movement had Mary's vision swimming. A wave of nausea swept over her. She felt her stomach rise in her throat. In a panic, she fought it back, fearing she'd drown behind her gag. She locked her eyes on the door and tried to concentrate as the room wobbled and rolled. The door, which Owens had apparently unlocked, swung slowly open. The night shouldered it aside, a solid, black wall streaked with rain. Nothing stirred. The door swung until it bounced softly off the wall. The rain hissed and splattered on the threshold.

Tupper had been watching the hotel for hours. He'd seen Mary and Rebecca go back and forth to the telegraph office, though he had no idea who they were. He watched as Owens crept into the office, too.

He saw how Owens had watched the woman and girl. The hill behind the hotel was a perfect vantage point, and the field glasses Tupper had taken from the sheriff's pack were excellent. Tupper had seen Owens go into the small building behind the hotel perhaps an hour before.

He wondered why the man had changed clothes inside. He'd been tempted to shoot him then, had peered down the barrel of the Winchester, nestling the front blade sight on Owens's chest. His finger had caressed the trigger for a moment, but he had not fired.

Putting a bullet through the man was not enough, no matter how good it might have felt to do it. He'd put the rifle down then, and settled in to wait and watch. He knew there would be an opportunity, knew that, like the sky in the west, things were coming to a boil. The rain had started a little while later as he lay under a bush on the hilltop. He'd watched as Owens disappeared back into the hotel.

It had almost been too dark to see. The rain and the black night had nearly made them invisible. He saw them though, Owens and the woman, the little girl, running for the door of the building through the rain as lightning lit them, froze them as if in a photographer's studio. As the door had slammed shut, Tupper gathered up his things. He had no choice now.

It was clear from Owens's actions that the woman and girl were a part of his plan. Tupper felt, rather than knew, it was not a good part. There was no good reason for Owens to be spiriting them into an outbuilding in the rain. Tupper wished he'd taken the shot, grumbling under his breath at his foolishness.

"You cannot unmake the past, Jim," his grandfather said at his side. "You chose well with what you knew."

"But now I must go in after him. He's going to kill them, I can feel it. He has the advantage now. All I have is this," he said, knocking his knuckles against his chest, making a hard, hollow sound.

"You have more, Jim. Much more. The future is not given to me. I do not see it. But his advantage may only be in your head."

It had been his grandfather who'd pushed open the door. "He is in the corner, behind the machine," he said. "You must be careful."

With a whoop, Tupper burst in, a pistol in one hand, the rifle in the other, tucked against his hip. He fired blindly, the light throwing off his aim. The bullet clanged off the Long-waisted Maryann, throwing off sparks. *Thud, thud, thud, thud.*

They didn't sound like shots at first. Mary wasn't sure what had happened, only that the man who must have been Tupper was now on his back and blood was on the wall.

Owens came out of the shadows. The towel-wrapped pistol smoked in his hand. He stood over Tupper for a moment, then kicked his foot aside, closed the door, and threw the bolt once more.

"Well, that went well, don't you think?" Owens said, grinning, not talking to Mary so much as himself. He grabbed Tupper's boots and dragged him across the room.

"Crazy, murdering Indian, running about, leaving bodies wherever he goes." Owens made a whoop like an Indian and hopped once or twice in a mock war dance. Tupper's legs jiggled in Owens's grip.

"Scared shit outa the tourists. Cost the Durants a bloody fortune, but not near enough yet. Fucking William stole my land," Owens said as he dropped Tupper's boots with a thud on the floor.

"My family's land since before I was born, my island, right smack in Raquette Lake." Owens kicked at Tupper's legs. "Forced me off." He booted him again. The body flopped and jiggled. "Goddamn sheriff came with a shotgun." Owens's foot thumped into Tupper again. "Cleared me outa my own island!"

Mary was shaking her head. None of this made sense to her. Rebecca was silent, her eyes wide and red.

"Heard his sister was gonna sue him, how he cheated her like he cheated me." Owens walked back and picked up Tupper's pistol and tucked it in his belt. The rifle he held in the crook of one arm. "That lawyer, he's a crazy old coot, crazier than me, maybe. He had some millionaire about to buy a camp from Durant, lot o' land, too.

" 'Drive the price down, son,' " Owens said, imitating the gravely voice of an old man and sticking out his gut. " 'Hurt William West in the bargain, you can name your price.' "

Switching back to his own voice, Owens said, "Didn't give a shit how I got it done. Didn't want details. So I don't give him no details," he went on in a sing-song tone.

Mary still wasn't sure if he was talking to her or not. He seemed to be in a trance. His eyes were unseeing. Blood dripped down his face, yet he made no move to wipe it away. "Just luck Jim here decided to stick his foreman," he said, kicking a leg again.

"Shoulda seen the headlines: MURDERING INDIAN ESCAPES POLICE," Owens chuckled with a wave of his hand. "Didn't have an idea till I heard about him. It all fell into place after that. Like a sign from the Great God Almighty himself, a big ol' finger from on high, saying *this here is your instrument, Ex, use him any way you like.*"

Owens looked at Mary, who wore an uncomprehending expression. For an instant, he seemed to falter. He looked from her to Rebecca and his eyes flickered and a deep crease stole across his forehead.

"The first one was the hardest," he said. "After that it got easier, till I got to liking it, especially that little maid." Owens seemed to catch himself, as if he saw what he'd become and didn't much like it.

"Sorry you had to get caught in this," he said softly. "But hell, what's done is done." He shrugged, his turn of conscience seemingly gone as quickly as it had come. Then he added, "What I said before about doing you like I did Lettie, well, I won't do that, I guess. Kill you quick. No pain or nothing. Once your husband gets here we'll get this all done an' put behind us."

Twenty-Nine

If you die for Right that fact is your dearest requital, But you
find it disturbing when others die who simply haven't the right.

—ROBERT PENN WARREN

Tom rode hard from Long Lake, as hard as his plow horse could go. That turned out to be not very fast; still, he managed to keep the animal at a trot most of the way. Once night fell, he had to slow for fear of having the horse fall over a rock or root in the darkness. The rain had started maybe a half hour before he got to the hotel. Exhausted, drenched, and muddy, he bounded through the lobby and took the stairs up to their floor. Tom knocked on his door, then tried the knob, surprised to find it was open.

"Mary? 'Becca?" he called. Looking around he saw they were not there and went to the connecting door. He saw Mike was asleep on the bed. The light was off and he flicked the switch with a loud click that woke the boy.

"Dad!"

"Mike. You all right?"

"Sure. You got him? You got him, right?"

"No. Where's your mother? She's not in the room, 'Becca either. I sent a telegram, told them to stay put," Tom said, his tone worried enough to bring a frown to Mike's face.

"What's wrong, Dad? What is it? I was sleeping. I don't know where they went."

"It was Owens all along, Mike. Not Tupper, but Owens who killed Lettie, Busher, and the rest." Tom hesitated for a moment before adding, "And Chowder, too."

Mike's eyes went wide. Chowder was one of the men Mike had always thought of as being indestructible, a tough-as-nails cop whose nightstick had bruised half the male population below Houston Street.

"Uncle Chowder?" Mike said in disbelief.

"Yeah. He's gone, Mike. Don't believe it myself. Where's the deputy? We have to get you out of those irons. Owens is here. Your mother wired me. I don't know where he is, but we can't have you cuffed, not now."

"The deputy's just down the hall, room two twenty-three," Mike said.

Tom was out the door before Mike had finished. Mike heard him pounding on the door.

"Keep yer britches on, goddamnit," Tom heard the deputy call. "I'm comin'."

When the door opened, Tom pushed it aside and barged in.

"Hey!" the deputy said.

"Listen, the sheriff's dead, the other deputy and Chowder, too. Ambushed! All of them! Tupper didn't do it. It's been Owens, Exeter Owens all along. Man named Zion Smith was with him. He confessed to it. Now, give me the key to Mike's cuffs. Owens is here at the hotel and I think he might be after my family."

"What the—?" the deputy said. "I can't. I can't do that. How do I know you're tellin' the truth?"

"Oh, for Christ's sake!" Tom said through gritted teeth "Give me the fucking key!"

"Well, You got no right to get—"

Tom didn't let him finish. He chopped at the man's neck and he went down like the legs had been cut from under him. Tom picked him up by the shirt and looked into his fluttering eyes.

"The key, goddamnit!"

The deputy waved a hand toward a chair where his pants hung.

"Thanks," Tom said before smashing a fist into the man's temple. A quick search of the pants yielded the key. Tom took his pistol and locked the door behind him, leaving the deputy unconscious on the floor.

"Listen, Mitchell is not far behind me," Tom told Mike as he unlocked him. "Take this pistol. Tuck it in your belt under your shirt, just in case."

They went into the other room with Tom mumbling about having told Mary to stay behind closed doors. He did a quick search, finding nothing until he looked under the bed. There was nothing there, but as he got to his feet Tom noticed two small splotches of blood on the carpet. They had blended in with the reds and yellows of the weave so as not to be visible from more than a few feet away.

"Shit! Look at this."

Mike bent down to look.

"You sure you didn't hear anything?" Tom asked Mike.

Mike's face screwed into a worried frown, but he shook his head.

"Damn! No. I should have been more careful, I—"

"Not your fault," Tom said, putting a hand on his shoulder, half to steady himself. When he stood, a wave of dizziness swept over him. He rubbed his eyes and blinked to clear his head, but he still felt strange.

"Listen, go down to the lobby. Keep an eye out for Mitchell. When he comes, start searching. Don't go on your own, you hear me?"

Mike nodded as they opened the door and headed out.

"I'm going down to the bunkhouse first. Maybe get lucky and find Owens asleep in his bed," Tom said with a sarcastic twist of the mouth.

They split up then, Mike heading for the elevator, Tom trotting off in the opposite direction. It took a minute or so for the elevator to arrive. Mike paced back and forth as he listened to the clunk and whirr of machinery as the contraption arrived. The door opened and the brass gate was slid aside by the sleepy operator.

Mike had taken one step inside when he heard a rush of feet behind. He was only half turned when he was hit, tackled and hurled into the elevator. He crashed into the opposite wall, his broken ribs screaming, robbing him of all breath as they stabbed deep into his side. He crumpled to the floor as he heard the operator say, "What the hell? You can't do—"

Mike heard an impact and saw the operator go down, holding his head.

"You killed my sister, you goddamn, bloody bastard!" Mike heard a voice say above his head. "Swore I'd 'venge her. You got this comin'!"

"I didn't kill her," Mike managed to say. "I loved her."

He earned a vicious kick for that.

"Don't you say that! Don't you say a goddamn word, you! I'm doin' the talking! You're a fuckin' murderer, you weasely bastard, an' you ain't getting away with it."

Mike looked up and saw a knife, large and red with blood. He realized then that he'd been stabbed.

"Send you straight to hell, may God guide my hand."

Lester crouched to strike, lifting the blade as he did. Mike didn't think, he just kicked out as hard as he could. He caught Lester in the stomach, pushing him back. Off balance, he stumbled half out of the elevator, falling on his back. The operator, who had regained his senses, kicked his feet away and slammed the brass gate closed. With a blood-slicked hand he slammed the lift mechanism to the down position and the little room started to lower.

Mike pulled himself up, hanging onto the gate, the pain in his side so intense he could hardly stand. But Lester had regained his feet, too, much faster than Mike imagined he would. Lester dove at the gate, first trying to wrench it aside, then plunging his arm through. He cut the operator's hand, sending blood splattering across the car as the man yelped and pulled it away.

The car was small and Lester's blade almost reached Mike as well, but the elevator was half down and Lester was crouching to reach them. Mike pulled the pistol from the back of his pants, suddenly remembering he had it. But he held his fire as a strange thing happened. The elevator operator put a foot against Lester's arm, pinning it within the gate. Lester yelled and cut at the leg, but couldn't manage to get it off, despite the gash he inflicted. The operator gritted his teeth and braced himself against the wall. The elevator descended. Lester went from his knees to his belly as he tried to pull his arm out, panic making his eyes big as saucers.

"No! No! Lemme go! Damn you!"

The operator paid him no mind. He ground his foot against Lester's arm as the gap between the car and the floor narrowed to a couple of feet, then a foot. The knife dropped, clattering into the car.

"Stop!" Mike yelled. "Let him go!" But it was too late.

Lester's scream echoed through the deserted hallways as his arm was crushed in the narrow gap. It disappeared through the brass grate. Blood followed the elevator down. Lester could no longer be seen, but his screams followed them, echoing down the shaft. They turned to howls, then ceased altogether.

Tom didn't hear the screams. He was out in the storm by that time, the rain pelting his shoulders, thunder shaking the ground beneath his feet. He didn't find Owens in the bunkhouse, nor did he find anyone who claimed to know where he was. He circled around toward the rear of the hotel, not knowing where to look first, but feeling it was wise to check the outbuildings, structures that Owens would be likely to know well and be more comfortable using.

It was as he was checking the icehouse that Tom saw a figure in the distance enter one of the buildings behind the hotel. It was too dark to see who it was. It was even difficult to make out exactly what building it was. They seemed to huddle together in the dark, their outlines indistinct.

He thought he heard a shot, but the thunder and pelting rain made him uncertain. It took a few minutes for Tom to locate the small building. He padded around the outside, peering through the windows, but finding each of them covered from within. None of the other utility buildings had coverings on the windows of any sort.

There was light, but visible only as bright slashes on either side of the curtains, or whatever they were. There may have been a voice, too, but the pounding rain made it all but impossible to tell. Tom didn't know what building this was but he approached the door with caution.

He felt the latch, finding it unlocked. Tom stood in the rain for a moment, collecting himself, taking a few deep breaths and checking his pistol. He figured he'd go in hard, try to surprise whoever was inside. If it wasn't Owens the worst that could happen was that he'd scare the bejesus out of one of the help.

Tom kicked the door open, rolling across the threshold and coming up in a crouch, his pistol ready. The light was in his eyes, leaving the back of the room in darkness. The only thing he saw clearly was Mary and Rebecca, tied to chairs, the light on them as if they were actors on a Broadway stage. Tom saw movement in the dark, but a moment too late.

The thuds of a pistol and the impacts on his body were indistinguishable. His arm went numb and blossomed in red. His pistol clattered across the floor. An instant later he was doubled over by a blinding impact in his stomach. He dropped to one knee, gasping for air, not even certain what had happened. He heard a click and looked up to see Owens standing a few feet away, a towel-wrapped pistol in his hand.

Mary was trying to scream. Here eyes were wide and the veins in her temples stood out with the strain. Rebecca was screaming, too, but behind their gags they sounded so distant, so very far away, as if they were in a dream. Owens took another step and Tom heard the pistol click on another empty cylinder. Owens seemed confused, but not concerned. He threw the pistol aside, keeping the towel. He started to reach for the gun in his belt. He was sure of himself, in no hurry.

Tom didn't think. He was dead already. He charged at Owens, hitting him low with a shoulder under the ribs. Owens's pistol skittered off into the darkness as he crashed into the wall. The building shook and wood splintered.

Owens let out a gasp, but tried to grapple. Tom was operating on instinct. He wanted to drive his fist through Owens's head, break every bone that could be broken. Tom drove a left into Owens's jaw that snapped his head half around. He instinctively threw a right, but he pain was blinding, stealing what little breath he had. He kicked at Owens's leg, crumpling him backward, but Owens was caught by the wall and somehow remained on his feet. A rain of lefts poured down on Owens's head as lightning flashed at the windows.

Owens's head bounced like a rag doll's. His nose was smashed. Teeth tumbled from his mouth like red and white kernels of corn. He flailed back, dazed. Tom felt nothing. Another left crushed Owens's cheekbone and eye socket. Tom felt the bone collapse under his fist. Owens went down on one knee and Tom bashed him with a knee to the face, snapping his head back into the wall.

But Tom was barely able to stand himself. Each breath was an agony, and his vision was down to a small circle of light, surrounded by blackness. He could hardly breathe, feeling his stomach might burst if he did. He reeled, finding himself falling against the wall above Owens.

He somehow caught himself and was about to stomp down on him, when Owens hit Tom with a piece of firewood, the piece Mary had dropped. It hit Tom on his wounded arm, and for the first time he screamed. Something hit him in the stomach as he staggered back, his vision black and starry as an Adirondack night. He was hit again, though he didn't feel it. Mary screamed behind her gag as Tom fell at her feet. She stared down as his eyes rolled back in his head, showing nothing but white.

Mary rose up, throwing herself forward on top of Tom, her only thought to cover his body with hers.

Owens stood over them, sucking air, gasping for each bubbling breath. Mary felt his blood spatter her back. He said nothing. His face was a jellied mass of red and he labored for each breath, his hands braced on shaking knees. Glacial minutes crawled past.

Mary heard him above her, expecting to feel the bayonet plunge through her skull. She could feel Tom breathe beneath her and knowing there was still life in him gave her strength.

"Wanna die t'gether, huh?" Owens gurgled above them at last, his broken face making the words come out in a slurry of blood and spit.

Mary heard Owens turn and lifted her head to watch him stagger off, looking blindly for a weapon. Mary saw something else out of the corner of her eye. Tupper's boot moved.

"Get yer wish. Promise," Owens slurred. "Watch little 'Becca get it first." He spat blood and it ran down his chin. "Whersh foockn' pisto?"

Mary saw Tupper rise until it seemed he towered above her. His head and shoulders were covered in blood and one ear hung off, dangling by a thread of flesh. His left leg was dipped in red too.

"Dere," Owens grunted as he bent for the pistol. Tupper stumped after him. Mary heard him mumbling something she could not understand. It sounded like a chant, the words coming in a definite cadence. Owens heard him too. He had gone down on one knee to pick up the pistol. Owens turned and fired as he stood on wobbling legs. Point-blank, he blasted at Tupper, the shots sounding impossibly loud in the enclosed space.

Tupper kept coming. He didn't slow, didn't seem to feel the bullets ripping into him. Mary swore she could hear him chant, even after he'd been hit. Tupper rushed the last few steps, crashing into Owens and carrying them both into the Long-waisted Maryann. The dynamo rocked. Sparks flashed. Blue arcs of electricity leapt out of its coils and terminals. Tupper and Owens went stiff, like insects, electric pins skewered them in place.

Tupper's shoes began to smoke and blue flames jumped from his fingertips, disappearing into Owens's twitching flesh. Low moans escaped them, as they stood, locked together. The steam engine thumped its relentless rhythm, eating the forest a stick at a time, feeding power to the dynamo. Wood become electric. The light in the ceiling went out.

Mary rolled off Tom and watched as the two men sizzled. Tom stirred. Tupper fell first. Smoke leaked from his eyes and hair. Owens fell too. He seemed to melt into the floor as if his bones had turned to jelly. For a long time nothing moved. The smell of burnt flesh and singed hair hung heavy, settling in a low mist along the floor. In the occasional flashes of lightning, Mary could see the bodies by the dynamo. They did not move.

Mary began working on her bonds, working her hands back and forth. Her wounded arm screamed with every movement. It seemed to take forever, but it was only a few minutes before she got one hand loose. A moment later her gag was gone.

"It's over, 'Becca. It's over, sweetheart," she said. "I'll untie you in a second."

At last she got the second rope loose, and she reached for Tom, slapping his face and calling his name. "Tommy! Tommy! Stay with me. Hang on. You're gonna be all right."

His eyes flickered. He could barely see Mary, but he knew she was there. "Sorry," he said.

Mary laughed and cried and kissed his cheek. "Save your sorries for someone who needs them. You just hold on, I've got to get 'Becca loose." Mary rushed to her, pulled off her gag and hugged her.

"You are so brave. Such a brave little girl!" Mary said in her ear as she hugged her tight. Rebecca cried, unable to say anything. Mary worked on her bonds. The knots were tight. She got one off and was pulling at the other when Rebecca's eyes went wide. She shrieked and pointed with her free hand.

A black shadow oozing gray smoke swayed in the dark. Owens staggered, then went to pick up something from the floor. A shot split the darkness like a bolt of lightning. Tom had somehow gotten to his backup pistol and was firing from the floor. Mary didn't know if he'd hit anything.

Tom's arm was waving around like a reed in a storm. He fired again, but Owens seemed to pay no attention. He stood slowly, the length of steel glinting in his hand. Mary dove for the floor as Tom's pistol cracked again. Owens stumbled, then regained his footing; but when he did, Mary was there with Tupper's Winchester thrust up under his chin. She pulled the trigger.

Thirty

Mike and Mitchell were at the door when Owens went down. Mary came close to shooting them, too, when they pounded into the room. She screamed, but then Mike was there holding her, and suddenly the room seemed to be filled with people, waiters, maids, guides, and guests all jostling at the door and trying to peer in at the windows. Mary fell beside Tom, and Mike scooped Rebecca into his arms where she buried her face in his shoulder.

"Tommy. It's over," Mary whispered. "Can you hear me? He's dead."

"Oughta be," Tom wheezed. "Blew his fucking head off."

Mary laughed gratefully, hysterically, like a string of Chinese firecrackers exploding.

"He'll live, I think," Doctor Whelen told Mary sometime near 1 A.M. The doctor had been working on Tom for hours. He ran a hand through his hair as he spoke with her and blinked the fatigue from his eyes. "I've done about all I can for now. He's unconscious but stable." He looked at Mary from under heavy brows, as if measuring her.

"I can see there's more," Mary said. "Tell me. What is it?"

Whelen shrugged. "He's in a weakened state, Missus Braddock. He can't be moved. In a few days perhaps we'll see, but right now he would not survive the trip to North Creek, let alone Albany, where he'd be able to get the best of care. And . . . ," the doctor hesitated a moment before continuing, "if an infection sets in, well there's limited resources at my disposal, as you might imagine."

"So he might still die?" Mary said.

"I'm afraid so," the doctor replied, not looking Mary in the eye. "He's a strong man, though, with a vital will, so I am hopeful."

Mary shook her head. "You have no idea, Doctor. No idea."

As he described it to Frederick and General Duryea at an early breakfast many hours later, "Though I'm certain he was in the utmost pain imaginable, he hardly showed it."

"He's still alive then?" Duryea said.

"Oh yes. Quite, though I'm damned if I can say how, gentlemen. Surely, he might not survive much longer. The man has been through hell. He was in a weakened state to begin with. I'm certain he had a concussion, probably sustained from before the fight last night. He was dehydrated and about as close to exhaustion as a man can be. He'd lost almost half his blood, or I'm a veterinarian, yet he was talking to me while I worked. Remarkable!"

"Indeed! I told you," Frederick said. "The man is as tough as roots."

Doctor Whelen nodded. "He's so full of opium, he's not aware of much pain at this point. But when he awakes, well . . ." Whelen shrugged. "We'll just have to keep him dosed."

"Did you see Owens?" Duryea said with a shudder. "Not even an animal deserves such a fate."

"Normally I'd agree with you, General," William West Durant said as he sat down with them. He'd traveled through the night to lend whatever support he could to Tom and Mary and had just come from Tom's bedside. He'd seen Owens as well. "But, in this case, I'd have to say that Exeter Owens received exactly what he earned."

Within a few days Tom seemed well enough to travel, although he was in a great deal of pain. Still, he managed to sit up in bed and sip the clear broth that Mary fed him with her good arm. The doctor had seen to her as well, finding the wound to be a clean puncture through the bicep.

"You were fortunate, Missus Braddock," Dr. Whelen told her as he fixed a sling for her arm. "There appears to be no nerve damage and relatively little blood loss. This could have been much worse. Your son was lucky, too. He's got a nasty cut, but apparently, when his ribs were set in that lumber camp, the woman bound in some whalebone for stiffening."

Mary smiled. "I almost took them out, but Mike wouldn't let me, said they helped ease the ache, especially when he slept."

"Be glad of that. The bandages and the whalebone deflected the worst of the blow. He might be dead right now, if not for that."

The decision was made to try to get Tom to Albany, or at least to Saratoga. He was given an extra dose of laudanum that had him seeing double but feeling little pain. He was bundled in blankets against the autumn chill, which had gripped the region after the rain.

Mitchell was there as they loaded Tom into a carriage that William had provided. He stood to one side, his shotgun leaning against his side like a third leg. His hat looked as well-used as ever. Mitchell's deep-set eyes sparkled when he saw Tom, and the creases at the corners of his mouth deepened into a smile.

"Mitchell," Tom said, extending a hand from under his blanket. "Good to see you."

The old Abanaki Indian took Tom's hand. "And you too," he said with a small grin. They clasped hands for a long moment until they both felt awkward.

"Be back come spring," Tom said through the opiate haze. "I'll write."

"Good," Mitchell said with a nod. "Next time we just go fishing."

One by one, Frederick, General Duryea, and finally William said their good-byes, wishing Tom well, making him promise to write, saying that he must come back when he was well, and many other things he figured they mostly didn't mean, but said because they were gentlemen.

"If you don't mind, I'll call on you in a month or so, when I'm back in town," William said. "We are all in your debt, Tom and I hope you don't mind if I look into ways of repaying you in some small way for the good you've done."

Tom just smiled. He'd been fed so much laudanum that he wasn't at all sure what William was saying. But he gripped Durant's hand and managed, "Thanks," though he wasn't sure for what. They put him in the carriage then and Tom closed his eyes. He didn't know about coming back, or fishing, or anything. He wasn't sure even he'd make it home, though he tried not to show it to Mary.

They all shook Mike's hand, too, and they all said how happy they were that he'd been cleared, and how they'd never believed he'd done such a terrible thing, and that they hoped he'd not remember them unkindly. Mike held no grudges. That surprised him. He thought he probably should, especially against the doctor; but, somehow, he just did not feel that way. What he felt, now that he had the time to feel was a slow sadness.

He mourned Lettie Burman still. The pain of losing her had withered to a dull ache, a suit of sadness he put on each day with the opening of his eyes. But that sadness did not rule him, not as it would have a month before, a lifetime before. He tried to bear it as he figured Tom would, or as Mitchell bore things.

He felt no less deeply. He simply carried the hurt in ways he hadn't before. He could not have explained how that came to be. It simply was. When he shook hands with Mitchell, the old guide held him with his ancient eyes, his small hand gripping Mike's like roots on rock.

"A man leaves much behind when he leaves these woods," Mitchell said. "You take much, too. I will be here when you return."

The trip to Albany nearly killed Tom.

It was three weeks and two operations later before Tom started to come out of his haze of pain and opium. It was many weeks more before he felt anything like his old self.

September leaves blazed around Blue Mountain Lake, and on clear, bright mornings, when the waters were still, they danced with liquid fire. October frosts sparkled, and November ice stilled the shoreline before Tom got back to the job and the case.

There had been much left to do, and he kept two detectives busy on the legwork while he was laid up. When he at last had what he needed, he went to Byrnes to set things in motion.

That evening, as Tom and Mary lay in bed, he told her what he planned to do in the morning. She approved. Though complete justice was a virtual impossibility in this case, she knew Tom was doing all that was possible. It was more than Van Duzer would expect, she was certain of that.

The gaslight was turned off and Tom kissed Mary good night. There was a long silence before Mary spoke.

"Tom, what does '*ganos gay*' mean?"

"What?"

"*Ganos gay*. You said it over and over after you were shot. You were only semi-conscious. I couldn't tell if you knew what you were saying or not. '*Tain cha day.*' You said that, too. Do you remember?"

Tom didn't respond, though he sat up and propped himself against the headboard.

"It was just so odd. I've always wondered," Mary said. "It sounded like Indian words. Did you learn them from Mitchell?"

"No, not from Mitchell," Tom said softly. "God, I thought that was a dream." He ran his hands through his hair and sighed. "It *was* a dream, I'm sure. Seemed real, though, so damn real." He looked at her closely. "I said that stuff?"

"You were delirious," Mary said. "The doctor wasn't sure you'd live through the night at first."

"Yeah, But it was as if they were right there. Like I could reach out and touch them. They spoke to me and I could hear them. Really strange."

"Who?"

"Tupper and his grandfather," Tom said, suppressing a chill.

"But that's not possible," Mary whispered.

"I don't know what's possible or what's not possible, Mary. I know what I saw, what it felt like. And—I know what they said to me."

"Why didn't you say anything? Why didn't you tell me?"

"You'd have believed me? Later, after I woke up I thought it was just a dream," Tom said. "I didn't know I'd said anything."

"What do they mean, those words?"

Tom sighed. "Near as I know, *Ganos'ge'* means 'house of the tormentor.' It's hell, I guess, or something like it, to an Indian. They said the words, but didn't tell me what they meant. The strange thing is I understood them. The other word means 'heaven world.' It's Iroquois, I guess."

Mary sat up next to Tom in the darkness. She took hold of his hand, knowing there was more. She didn't ask. She just caressed his hand and listened to his steady breathing. It was many minutes later before Tom continued.

"They were doing something to Owens," Tom said. "Holding him down or something. But it wasn't him exactly. It was his spirit, or what I knew was his spirit. It was strange, blurry. Like there was two of him, Owens I mean. He was struggling. He wanted to get away. And there was a place. I couldn't see it but I could sort of feel it and I knew they were making him go there. Then they hauled him up and took him, and the old man kept saying, *'Ganos'ge.'* He said other things, too, but I can't remember. He chanted that word so that I almost imagined I could see it. Owens was screaming," Tom said. "The other word the old man said to me. He said *'Tain 'tchiade* is yours in the living world, if you desire. Only you can say.' It was almost as if he was leaving it up to me if I wanted to live or die. My decision."

Mary was silent, the full import of Tom's story sinking slowly, like a leaf in water. Her thoughts swirled and she thought to say a thousand things, none of which came to her lips. It was Tom who finally broke the silence.

"I guess I knew what I desired," he said.

Van Duzer sat back for a moment, his high, deep-tufted leather chair creaking in a comfortable way. He'd have to have a talk with Morgan soon. They'd made Durant wait long enough, he calculated. With winter coming on, and the tourists gone, there would be no way for Durant to recoup his losses before next summer. Land values were at the lowest levels in years. Morgan could name his price and Durant would have little alternative but to take it.

The old lawyer smiled as he looked about the office. The mahogany was waxed to a mellow red glow. The brass was buffed. The carpets were the deepest plush wool, and swallowed noise like a well-bribed judge swallows lies. Perhaps a new painting for the spot near the window, he thought, considering how to reward himself for his coming success.

Van Duzer leaned forward and picked up a gold-quilled pen. He was about to write a note to Morgan when he was stopped by a commotion outside his door, voices raised. The door burst open, revealing a tall, broad man with a full mustache and a derby under one arm.

"Who in blazes are you?" Van Duzer grunted in surprise. "Hopkins! Hopkins! See this man out!"

The clerk poked a head around the threshold. "Terribly sorry, sir, but I—"

Tom closed the door, silencing Hopkins's groveling.

"Not his fault," Tom said. "I insisted."

Van Duzer started to rise from his chair, a red flush blossoming at his collar.

"Explain yourself, sir!" the lawyer roared. "By what right do you presume to barge in here? This is not one of your Bowery saloons, you—you . . ."

"Sit down!" Tom said, pulling his vest aside to show the badge on his chest. He'd come unofficially, out of uniform. "Captain Braddock," Tom added, knowing that would be all the introduction he'd need. The story of his adventures in the Adirondacks, thrillingly embellished by journalism's finest, had been plastered across the papers for weeks back in September.

Van Duzer went silent, hesitating.

"Do it! I will not say it again," Tom said in a low voice that sent a chill down the lawyer's spine.

Van Duzer seemed to collect himself, and settled back into his throne, crossing his hands on his ample belly, even leaning back a bit. He glowered at Braddock from under bushy brows, a courtroom glare that had struck fear into many an opposing counsel or witness.

Tom walked to a chair facing the desk, wincing slightly as he settled himself into it and wondering just how long it would take before the ache of his wounds would finally leave him. He stared back at the lawyer for a moment, then put his feet up on the edge of the desk. Van Duzer's lip quivered and Tom could see a vein throb at his temple.

"Explain yourself, I say again," Van Duzer said with low menace. "If you imagine that you can walk out of this office with whatever it is you came for, you will be sadly disappointed."

Tom was silent and appeared to be listening with interest and an almost clinical curiosity, an attitude that unsettled Van Duzer. He was used to a very different reaction to his words and august presence.

"I am not a man to trifle with, nor am I easily intimidated," he said, but the words had a hollow ring.

Braddock smiled. "You will not be trifled with, I can assure you," he said. "Nope. No trifling here."

"You know who I am, and where I stand in this city?" Van Duzer said. "I have many powerful friends, sir. Your badge will not protect you."

"No, ordinarily I'd have to agree with you, Rupert."

Van Duzer stiffened at the use of his first name.

"But these are not ordinary times. You're confused, I can see. Let me explain," Tom said. "You will not set foot again in any court in New York State. If you do, you will be arrested. Do you understand me so far?"

Van Duzer's brows lowered even further and a sneer crept across his lips.

"You will leave this office within the hour. You will not return, not under any circumstances. If you do, you will be arrested."

"On what charge?" Van Duzer erupted. "On whose authority? This is absurd! This interview is at an end, Braddock. Get out of my office. Now!"

"Morgan is no longer a client of yours," Tom continued unchecked, "not since we told him what you'd done. I wouldn't bother trying to contact him. He won't be available to you. In fact, you have no clients. Not even your friends at the Wigwam," Tom said, referring to Tammany Hall. "They won't come near you now."

"But I've done nothing! Where's your indictment? Where's your evidence? What is it you imagine I've done?" Van Duzer said, doing his best not to raise his voice or lose command. "I have heard quite enough from you. By the time you get back to your dingy little police office and your small-time cop concerns, you will find out who holds the real power in this city." Van Duzer rose and strode to the door as he said this. Tom didn't rise, didn't take his feet off the desk.

"Good day to you, sir!" the lawyer said as he opened the door. But he stopped and went silent when he saw a uniformed officer stationed outside in the hall. Tom sighed.

"The only reason you will not be leaving this room in handcuffs is because of the influence of your friends," Tom said. "We've had talks with them all, all the important ones. Inspector Byrnes and I have been busy these last few days. Once they saw what we had to show them, they all fell in line, the judges, the Fifth Avenue clients, the lawyers, your political friends at City Hall and the Wigwam.

"They were all quite astonished. They were equally anxious to protect one of their own, though, and I regret to say they prevailed upon Byrnes and the mayor to let you go quietly. Been too many messy scandals lately, too many inconveniences," Tom said with a tone of regret.

"Personally, I would just as soon break every bone in your body and toss you in the river to drown." Tom sighed again. "But that's just me."

Van Duzer closed the door. Tom reached into his inside jacket pocket, pulling out a stuffed envelope. He threw it on the desk. "You'll want to look at those," Tom said. "Copies of telegrams from Owens to you, a copy of a deathbed confession implicating a certain New York lawyer, with Morgan for a client, copies of bank deposits to an account under Owens's name, copies of letters to Ella Durant. Do I need to go on?"

Van Duzer looked about the office as if seeking a means of escape. He picked up the envelope though, frowning at its contents as they unfolded before his eyes. "You were working both sides, Rupert, playing on Durant's troubles, his sister's suit, and Morgan's deal. For what? That I don't know and can't understand. I don't imagine you're about to tell me either, are you?"

Tom sat in silence as Van Duzer read. Minutes passed as a tall clock in the corner ticked away the seconds. "Was it a percentage, a few hundred acres, your own estate in the wilderness?" Tom asked at last. "Something like that, right?"

Van Duzer sat back down in his high-backed chair, seeming much smaller than he had before.

"Whatever," Tom said. "Let me make something clear to you." Something in the way he said this made Van Duzer look up. "My blood is on those papers, my blood, the blood of my wife, the blood of my children, the blood of my friend." Tom rose to his feet and leaned on the desk, planting his hands and hunching his massive shoulders. "Do you understand me? Listen closely, you fat bastard. This is the last time we will see each other. If I see you again, I will kill you, whether it's at the opera, the Broadway stage, the Bowery dance halls, anywhere. I will kill you. On sight! In the worst fucking way imaginable! Your friends have bought you this one opportunity. Only one. Take advantage of it. Disappear. Never come back and never cross my path again!"

Tom left Van Duzer's office feeling better than he had in a very long time. He smiled as he walked past Gramercy Park, watching the governesses pushing prams about in the bracing November air. The last of the brittle, brown leaves huddled in the gutters and bunched against the corners of the high fence.

Tom pulled his collar up. Within the hour, the roundsman he'd left with Van Duzer would escort him out. Braddock would have preferred to simply make Van Duzer disappear. It was a thing easily accomplished, if he'd been allowed.

He'd argued for it with Byrnes, who'd lent a sympathetic ear.

The chief had chewed the end of his cigar to a slimy stub, puffing thunderheads of smoke, but in the end said, "Can't do it, Tommy. Don't get me wrong. I'd like nothing more than to see him floating in the river, for Chowder's sake at the very least."

Byrnes held up a hand when he saw Tom about to argue again. "No, Tom, don't bother. We've gone over it up and down. He's got too many important friends. Can't kill the sonofabitch, and can't convict either. All things considered, I think we've pursued the right course."

Tom knew it was true. If they tried to bring Van Duzer to trial on the strength of a few one-sided telegrams and a dubious confession, they'd never have gotten anywhere. So they'd decided to use his own prominence against Van Duzer, to blacken his character and reputation to such an extent that none of his cronies or clients would come near him.

Byrnes had predicted they'd rather cut him loose than suffer the embarrassment of his continued acquaintance. Men like Morgan needed to cling to appearances as much as the next man, and perhaps more. In fact, convincing them that Van Duzer was a man to be scorned was easier than Tom had imagined. It became quickly apparent, in fact, that he was not loved, but feared. Tom had enjoyed the shows of high moral indignation as his "friends" got in line to cast him out.

"At least you'll have the satisfaction of doing it in person," Byrnes had said. Tom grinned at that.

"Yes, I will, but I'd trade that in a second for a cold ale and a warm stove, with Chowder tellin' one of his stories." Tom took a long pull at the cigar Byrnes had given him. "I'll kill him if I see him again. You know that."

Byrnes frowned and shook his head. "For the love o'Mike, don't tell me shit like that. I'm not supposed to know. If you've got to do it, make it look like a goddamn accident."

Tom figured Van Duzer never knew just how close to death he'd been.

But perhaps he did, for over the next few weeks Van Duzer became more and more frantic. Tom heard reports of his telegrams and visits to the powerbrokers of the city, of doors slammed in his face and wires left unanswered. He was even turned away at the Union League Club, his club of twenty years, asked to leave by the doorman.

Gradually, news of him shriveled and died, and he was rarely seen in the daylight. Van Duzer was no fool. He realized that if it was possible to ruin him, then it was equally possible to kill him, a thing he hadn't credited much in the safety of his office. In time, he became hermitlike, a condition Tom encouraged by occasionally spending long hours idling near the park within sight of his townhouse.

One evening, not quite six months later, while crossing Twenty-first

Street at the corner of Park Avenue, Van Duzer was run over by a beer wagon. It was on its way to the Players Club. The huge horses bowled him over, the broad, steel-shod wheels did the rest. Eyewitness reports were that he wasn't looking where he was going when he stepped off the curb. "He kept looking over his shoulder," the cop at the scene was told.

It's pretty here," Rebecca said. She and Mary, Tom and Mike were walking the dappled paths of Moravian Cemetery on Staten Island. Chowder always said that he'd like to be buried there, even though it was terribly far from the city.

"If it's good enough for Commodore Vanderbilt, its good enough for the likes of me," Chowder used to say. Vanderbilt's tomb there looked something like a Grecian temple set into the side of a hill, a long, curved drive and a huge cast-iron gate guarded it from curious eyes. They could see the gate as they walked to Chowder's grave.

The trees spread overhead in a cool, green canopy, shading the granite stones and spires, mausoleums and simple, faded markers. Squirrels skittered from tree to tree and a rabbit watched them pass from the base of a large rhododendron.

It was early September. A year had passed. It was the anniversary of the day Chowder died. His stone was set on the side of a gently sloping hill. The grass, Tom noticed as they approached, had grown in well. It didn't look new any more. No evidence remained of the ragged hole, the large pile of earth. Even the bright green of the fresh grass had darkened, so that Tom could not tell exactly where the grave had been.

He stopped before it and Mary's hand slipped into his. Mike stood to one side, looking at the writing on the stone. He read it all, the name, the date the inscription, but it said nothing to him. It said nothing of who Chowder Kelly really was, at least not to him. "Uncle Chowder," as Rebecca called him, had been an almost mythical figure. Legends followed like him like smoke followed fire.

He was a man of great wamth and humor, of flexible morality, yet unbending will, and if even half the stories Mike had heard of him were true, he'd been a breed apart from the cops he knew, except for Tom.

He watched Tom put a hand on the stone, and for just a second bow his head. He knew how much his father missed Chowder, knew how Tom had dreaded this day.

"Chowder would have liked it here," Mike said. It didn't sound right to him, but he felt the need to say something comforting. Tom and Mike exchanged a look. It was nothing more than a split second glance, a crinkle at the corner of the eye, a turn of the mouth, but they understood each other completely.

Tom nodded, and the ghost of a grin crept across his face. He shrugged and said, "I suppose. Chowder never was one for peaceful places, though he wanted to be here, sure enough. He liked the bars, the beer gardens, the dance halls. He should have been cremated and put up behind the bar at McSorley's in a big, silver urn. Now that would have suited him fine!" Tom said and grinned. Mike and Mary smiled, too.

Tom reached into his pocket and took out a rubber-rimmed porcelain stopper from a beer bottle. He laid it on the top of the stone. "Had one for you, old friend," Tom said. "Nice and cold, just like you liked it. Everybody at the bureau says hello."

Tom took a deep breath and looked around, seeming suddenly self-conscious. Rebecca, who'd been looking for rabbits, walked up and stood by Tom.

"He died on God's doorstep," she said, reading the inscription on the stone. "That must be very good. What does it mean, Daddy?"

Tom looked down at her and petted her curls. "Just something Mitchell said," Tom told her as he looked up at the trees.

Postscript

William West Durant did more to develop and popularize the Adirondacks than virtually any other man of the nineteenth century. More importantly, he set the standard for what development might be. The rustic architectural style of his four great camps, Pine Knot, Uncas, Sagamore, and Kill Kare established a vision of construction rooted in nature, an esthetic sharply at variance with the prevailing Victorian style. Describing Pine Knot in 1881, Seneca Ray Stoddard said, "Men took a circuitous route in order to gain a glimpse of it, and to have been a guest within its timbered walls and among its woodland fancies was to wear the hallmark of the envied."

But, for all his vision, Durant was no great businessman. He built on faith, on the self-assured conviction that others would share his vision, if only they could be exposed to it. Rarely, if ever, did he actually see a profit from any of his ventures. He invested heavily and entertained lavishly. He built a huge, 191-foot, steam-powered sailing yacht, in order to be better accepted by the class of society he wished to woo.

Princes of Europe and captains of industry took to the waves with William. In the end, it yielded him nothing and only hastened the end.

William's biggest mistake was to deny his sister her share of their father's estate. Taking over from Thomas Durant after his death,

William considered it his duty and prerogative to carry on and shepherd the family's business ventures as he saw fit. Unlike his views on architecture, these values were deeply rooted in his Victorian upbringing. He resented her demands and her questioning of his judgment.

Perhaps he intended to give her more when his investments paid off. But his investments never did pay, and Ella became increasingly demanding. She finally brought suit, but it was delayed until 1899. By then his properties were heavily mortgaged, his great camp Uncas sold to J. P. Morgan for far less than it cost to build. Ella Durant finally won her suit in 1901, when the court ordered William to pay her $753,931. Ella never saw a dime of it.

William West Durant died in 1934 at the age of eighty-three. After losing his empire in the Adirondacks, he tried his hand at a number of business ventures, including hotel manager, mushroom farming, and surveyor, and he often worked on lands he'd once owned. He never lost his aristocratic bearing or his taste for a well-cut suit.

On August 12, 1936, his widow unveiled a stone and bronze marker dedicated to him, opposite a newly formed lake created by the Civilian Conservation Corps. It was christened Lake Durant. The bronze plaque credits William with "developing the Adirondacks and making known their beauty." That marker stands just two miles from the hamlet of Blue Mountain Lake. William was interred in the family's mausoleum in Green Wood Cemetery. Ella was not to have a place there.

Mitchell Sabattis continued to guide sporadically for special clients over the following years. Tom and Mike would come sometimes in summer, sometimes in fall, spending days with the old man hunting and fishing. They were always sad to leave.

On April 17, 1906, Tom got a telegram from one of Mitchell's eight sons saying that Mitchell had died the day before.

A pure-blooded Abanaki Indian, Mitchell Sabattis was the son of Captain Peter Sabattis, who served in both the Revolutionary War and War of 1812. Mitchell was a founder of the Wesleyan Methodist Church in Long Lake, a builder of fine boats, and one of the greatest guides ever to walk the north woods. A recreational park in Long Lake bears his name.

• • •

The Prospect House went into a long, slow decline. Recurring deficits forced Frederick Durant to mortgage the property, and in 1898 his brother Howard foreclosed and took over the hotel. The short Adirondack tourist season made it nearly impossible to turn a profit on such a grand establishment, especially in light of less-expensive competitors across the lake and elsewhere.

In 1903 two guests came down with typhoid. In the fall of that year it closed its doors forever. It stood empty until 1915, a grand, ghostly presence, an echoing reflection of the gilded age of Adirondack development. It was finally dismantled, the lumber and furnishings sold.

The white buck, which was kept penned beside the lake since it was a fawn, survived for only four years. One winter, while corralled inside the barn, it got into a bin of oats and ate itself to death.